# SAVE THE VAMPIRE

## WILDE CONTRACTS
### BOOK 3

## MAZ MADDOX

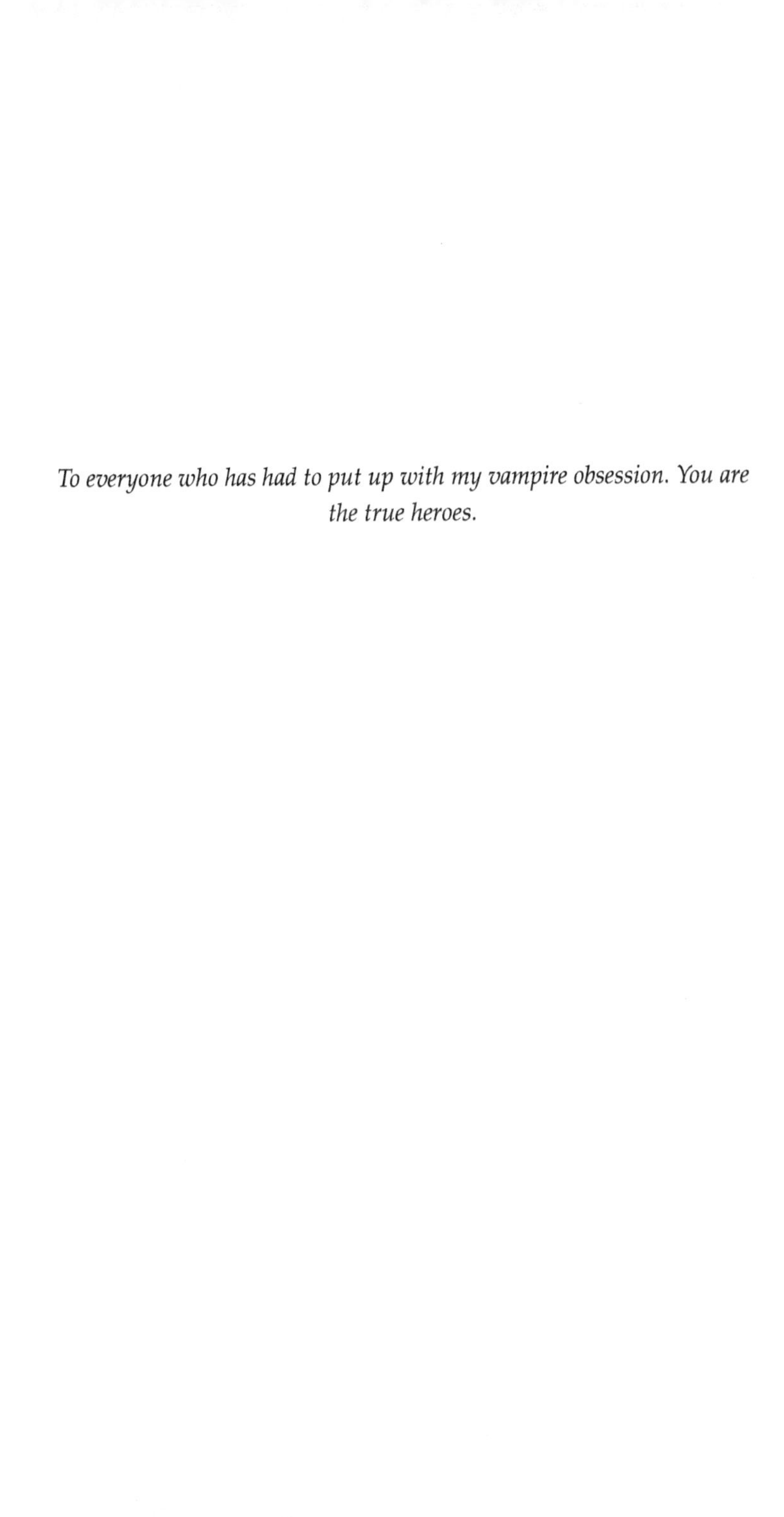

*To everyone who has had to put up with my vampire obsession. You are the true heroes.*

# CHAPTER
# ONE

"DALLAS WILDE, you better not have killed that poor little thing."

Barnaby stood over my death altar with his hands on his hips, dangerously close to brandishing a wagging finger.

"I asked you to bring the head, not your judgment," I reminded him. "Hey, Funus."

The skull in Barnaby's possession swiveled his glowing yellow eyes over to me.

"Good morning, acolyte."

"There are plenty of things you could murder that I wouldn't care about. What about a cockroach or a spider? Mice are intelligent creatures."

"I don't think cockroaches have souls, Barns." I wiggled my fingers in the air as a demonstration. "I needed something with little hands."

That finally got his finger wagging with gusto.

"A mouse is a perfect practice specimen for your training," Funus agreed until he heard Barnaby take in a pre-rant inhale. "But of course if you killed it, that's not nice. Horrible even. Shame on you."

"Oh, for the love of the Saint." I picked the thing up by its tail and held it upright like a mouse-sicle. "I bought it frozen from the pet store. It's snake food." I set the mammal flavored icy treat back onto my altar. "I'm not a monster."

Barnaby tossed me a dismissive sniff of satisfaction.

Adjusting Funus on his pillow, he said, "I'll come back and get you when you're done. I rented that new documentary we wanted to see."

"Oh, wonderful!" Funus's eyes brightened. "Thank you, dear."

I rolled my eyes as Barnaby's cheeks flushed.

"Oh my God, get out. Your affection offends me. I'm doing death magic shit and I need to get into the vibe."

Barnaby didn't acknowledge me now that he had no ammo to wield accusations of mouse murder, and walked past to leave Funus and me to my dark bidding.

"Shut the door behind you!" I called, grunting in agitation when I heard his footsteps leave the room without the accompanying door closing. I lifted off of the floor and stomped over, shutting the door with a bit more force than I should have. "How the hell do you stand that fussy little shit twenty-four seven?"

"You bring that out in him, not me." Funus scanned over my death altar carefully, humming through his teeth. It had taken me a few times to remember the placement of the candles, even longer to dedicate memory space for the runes that I'd written across the hardwood in chalk.

The glass jar containing Zane's ashes was placed beside me. He wasn't part of the ritual in the technical sense, but if I had to suffer through novice level bullshit to get his ass back to life, then his ashes had to endure it with me.

As a previously savant necromancer reduced to a fumbling novice, the biggest struggle was putting up with all the extra flair that went into pulling a soul back from the void. When I still had my powers, still held the Goddess's scythe in my chest, I could feel death magic like cold, slippery tendrils snaking up my arm as it crawled from the void. The power of death was at my fingertips, reluctantly obeying my command like an unruly octopus I'd wrestled into submission.

I had gotten pretty okay at it. It almost felt like second nature by the time we had gotten into the crypt and found Funus.

Now it took me hours to feel even the smallest blip of death magic as it passed by, even with the reanimated skull of one of the Death Goddess's chosen training me.

It was frustrating, insulting and fucking heartbreaking each damn night.

But I had to keep going.

I had to keep trying to find him, one little piece at a time.

"This will do," Funus told me, satisfied with my altar. "Do you remember the mantra I taught you to recite in your head?"

"Yeah." I flicked my lighter to life, the cheap plastic cool against my palm as I took my time lighting each candle. "I remember."

"Close your eyes and recite the mantra of the Goddess, hold the visions of the void close to your heart," he instructed me with the same docile tone he did each time. Funus had the patience of a skull that had been sitting dormant in a crypt for hundreds of years, unfazed by the snail's pace my training had been going thus far. He honestly didn't have anything better to be doing, other than watching history documentaries with Barnaby, which sounded like torture if you asked me.

I complied, exhaling out all the air in my lungs to try and settle my mind. Sitting still and reciting mantras wasn't easy for me, and fighting the war against my desperation to do literally anything else and my heart's ache to see Zane again was never ending. It was up to me to get this right—to take the time to learn necromancy from square one—even if it was incredibly, painfully, gruelingly boring.

The Goddess mantra was as dry and repetitive as the psalms I'd had to learn for the Saint's church as a kid. All human created religions were fucking terrible. Jinn got to have full feasts when they gathered for their services, onis got to go on a hunt. A hunt! Like with bows and shit. It was so cool.

And sex demons?

Well.

Orgies, of course. Which sounded way more fun than sitting on a pillow in my room chanting about how merciful and amazing death was. Yay, death is great, it's part of the cycle of life, all things balanced between, blah, blah, blah.

Oh, my God I would have killed for something to eat or to be brandishing a bow instead of talking to myself. I'd even take hearing about the orgy instead of going. Someone tell me a sexy story instead of whatever the hell this was.

Fuck.

I wasn't paying attention. How long had I been thinking about food and sexy stuff instead of doing the mantra thing?

I rubbed at my eyes and shook out my hands, reluctantly starting over.

Okay.

Death.

It's great.

*The void is all around us, part of the cycle of life that brings balance to the universe. The void is unbiased and eternal, an endless expanse that holds all that was and will be.*

But was it truly endless? That's impossible, right? Even the known universe in space had a beginning and an end. Wasn't the sun supposed to burn out and leave us in darkness, thus ending the living universe as we knew it? And at that point, if there's no intelligent life left to perceive the universe wouldn't that mean—

*Focus, hunter.*

I breathed in deep, holding his words in my mind. Focus. I needed to focus.

This wasn't just practice for the sake of it. I had a reason for trying to house this power again.

A grumpy, book obsessed, gothy reason.

I had to get my shit together.

I held the mantra in my mind. I remembered standing in the void with him.

The shadow with red eyes, the thumping of his beating heart encased in a skeletal hand. The ripple of the void danced away from me as I stood beside him, marveling at how close it had been with his blood on my tongue.

I remembered the Goddess's presence beside me.

I remembered how pleasant the cold was.

With my mind calm and visions of the void in my heart, I reached a hand out to let it hover over the body I meant to control.

"The void is close but won't listen to mortals easily," Funus reminded me. "You have to be persistent. Patient."

Those two attributes weren't high on the list of skills I'd mastered, but I wasn't about to let that stop me.

The chill of the thawing mouse breathed against my palm, and I used the sensation to draw in more memories of the death magic I used to control. I focused on the old feeling of ants dancing across my fingertips, the frigid grip of tendrils on my arms.

I wanted the void to hear me, to part and let me reach in.

This would be the time Zane would have placed his hand on my shoulder and squeezed, anchored me against the tide of darkness. The phantom touch made a chill dance up my spine, a tight breath escape my lips.

He could always find me.

*Find me now.*

*Find me now, Zane. Please. I'm here. I'm right here.*

*Please.*

*Please.*

I felt it.

A small thing, a fleeting kiss of cold spark against my fingertips. The void was there, teasing me, letting me know it could hear me knocking.

"Hold it," Funus whispered. "Lock that feeling into your mind and hold it still."

I twisted my hand and curled my fingers in, grabbing the

threads of magic that tangled themselves like spider silk. It felt like a whisper compared to the powerful arms I had felt before, but it was there. Fragile and fleeting.

I held on as tight as I could to something as wispy and intangible as a broken spider web, sweat prickling my hairline from the effort. I set my jaw and pulled tighter, the webbing slipping and resetting into thicker threads with each tug. I kept pulling, demanding more, wanting to feel the ants, the tendrils, *something* close to what I knew I needed.

"Don't force it," Funus was saying. "The connection is fragile, acolyte. You need to do this in steps. You need to develop a baseline."

The threads between my fingers hummed, not quite cold enough to be a true void connection, but much stronger than the frail webbing it had been before. I knew the void was close, because I had seen it before.

I had seen it with Zane on the island when I was dying, and again when I had healed my leg and needed to be reassembled.

I *knew* it was close. He was close.

I had to find him.

I took a breath and pulled hard, focusing on the darkness of the void I had met previously when my life as a necromancer was tied to a vampire. I was a powerful, death magic wielding badass once. I could be again.

I *was* going to be again.

Or I'd die trying.

I felt the cold chill race up the threads and tighten around my fingers, felt the hum of magic as the void opened a tiny window under the mouse.

"Slow and steady," Funus was telling me. "Hold the control. Don't fight it."

The cold bit into my skin, the feeling of death painful against my living flesh. I wasn't a necromancer yet, just an asshole who was dabbling in things beyond his mortal soul. The instinct to jerk my hand back and slam the doorway into the void shut screamed, but I locked it away next to the never-ending sadness I felt knowing I had let Zane die in my arms.

My vampire had died because of me.

It was my fault. I deserved to feel the cold. Deserved to feel whatever horrors that would grind me into pieces as I ripped his soul back from the void.

Starting with this stupid little frozen mouse.

I would bring this thing back to life to prove that I had mastery over both planes of existence, and nothing was going to stop me—not even the Goddess herself.

It took one loose thread to undo all of my hard work.

Before I had even placed my hand into the void, I felt one thread snap and coil away.

Then another.

And another.

"Fuck," I hissed, curling my hand into a fist as I tried to rein them in. The window started to shut, the presence of the void disappearing as quickly as it had appeared. My muscles strained as I held on, temples pounding and sweat trailed down my neck as I desperately tried to hold on to the magic.

"The connection is hard to maintain. Don't fight it. Narrow your focus," Funus was saying, but I couldn't listen to him. The control over the magic was slipping too fast, the threads melting away before truly forming.

The final bit of magic fell away, the chilly touch of death replaced by warm blood flowing back into my fingers.

The void closed. The threads just a fading memory. The frozen mouse on my altar thawed without ever budging an inch.

"It takes time, Dallas," Funus told me as I shoved to my feet, pacing the anger out of my body so I didn't kick him like a soccer ball.

It wasn't his fault I'd failed. I knew that. Hell, I wasn't even mad at him. I just really wanted to punt something across the room and he was the perfect size.

"I can't get the threads to stay solid! As soon as I feel the traces, they slip away," I raged, throwing a pillow instead of kicking the skull. "It never felt like this before. It was always so overwhelming and powerful, like arm wrestling a fucking kraken. Now it's like I'm slapping at passive aggressive cobwebs."

"You had the Goddess's scythe before," Funus reminded me. "That type of power normally comes from a lifetime or two of study, hard work and dedication to the magical craft, acolyte."

I rubbed at the pounding in my temples, scrubbing my eyes as they threatened to get glassy.

"I can't wait a lifetime to see him again, Funus."

The gentle skull sighed, heartbroken even without the torso to house a heart inside.

"I know. I wish I had a short cut I could teach you. I really do. You'll get there, Dallas. I know you can. We need to work on getting you grounded, finding you an anchor to help the magic from slipping."

"An anchor?" I dropped my hands away, blinking resolve back into my vision. "What do you mean?"

"Having an anchor keeps your mind from wandering, thus solidifying your grasp on the void's threads." His bright yellow eyes followed me as I paced. "Normally, that's a Thrall. They can help ground you to the void. But since you don't have one, we'll need to find you another source to keep you focused."

"Like what? Music? Weighted blanket? Guided meditation? I'll try anything, Funus. Name it."

"We can try all of those things," he said gently. "Whatever helps to maintain your concentration. You need to be patient. This is going to take time, but I'll do my best to keep it under a lifetime. I promise."

"Under a lifetime" wasn't the estimation I wanted, but it was better than "never."

It would have to do until I could find a solid short cut. Or I got my goddamn scythe back.

*Hang on a little longer, Zane. I'm coming for you.*

My despair and pity party was interrupted by the unmistakable beat of the police pounding on the front door. No one else knocks like they want your door to cave in like the cops, I'm certain it's part of the training process.

"Ballsy coming up to Sias's place with that energy." I blew out my candles and shoved the thawing mouse back into its plastic container. "You gonna get the door, Funus, or should I?"

"I would but it seems like my legs are asleep," Funus played along, which is why he was my favorite. "Unless you want to toss me at the doorknob and hope I can grab it with my teeth."

"Nah, Barns will get mad if we try that again." I picked Zane's jar up and placed it back onto the bed next to Twig's pillow. We had found a comfortable arrangement that allowed her to sleep next to his ashes without trying to knock them onto the floor. There was a brief scare when she couldn't reel in her feline instincts to shove objects off high places, which involved me diving across the room to catch Zane in a free fall.

From that point on, the jar slept between us on the bed. And Kevin judged us for it, because he's literally the best.

With Zane safe and sound, Funus was scooped up into my arms before I let Twig back into the room.

The moment I opened my bedroom door, she sprinted inside with a whiny, disappointed scream.

"I told you the mouse *isn't for you*!" I shuffled around her as she tried to trip me, hoping to see me crash to the ground so she could pluck the mouse-sicle off my body. Her stick tail shook like a rattlesnake as she followed me all the way down the hall, occasionally dancing on her hind legs to try and paw at the plastic coffin.

"This is my practice mouse, you fiend!" I lifted the container higher. "I need it for death stuff!"

This mattered not to the tiny beast. She demanded tribute, and I was the insufferable brute that was not giving in to her demands.

The pounding at the door had picked up in rhythm, which

signified whoever was playing the Cop Knock Solo was getting pissy.

"Barns!" I called, shuffling down the hallway to avoid stepping on a Twig. "Come get your head."

"Who in the *world* is at the door?" Barnaby materialized down the hallway, taking the cheerful skull as it was passed to him. "Who did you upset now?"

"Like, recently? Or within the past few months?"

"Should we be concerned?" Funus asked from Barnaby's arms. "They sound…persistent."

"If they were the bad guys, they wouldn't be knocking," I tossed over my shoulder as I made my way for the door. Sias's mansion wasn't gigantic, but it was large enough that it took me a leisurely stroll to make it to the foyer. You know a place is fancy when it has a room for the front door that was bigger than my whole damn apartment.

Twig was delighted when I picked her up so she could chew at the plastic mouse container, and I tucked her into the crook of my arm while I swung one of the double doors open.

"Hey, my favorite DHAP officers!" I greeted Preston and Seyyid. "You're looking haggard and underpaid today."

"You fucking deaf, Wilde?" Preston greeted me with his normal level of assholishness, which meant he was doing much better than the last time I saw him. "I've been knocking for ten minutes."

"I can go back in and let you round up to a solid twenty if you want."

"Can we come in?" Seyyid placed a hand on Preston's shoulder, calming the fire before it could lash out and burn me. "We need to talk to you about something."

Seyyid, who was the lesser of the two evils, still had bruising around his left eye from when he had been clobbered during a vampire attack. Normally, I'd chalk it up to inexperience with handling the undead jerks, but this time I had to admit his defeat wasn't exactly his fault. The vampire that had surprised him had been one of Florence's monsters: an undead vampire grunt that had still retained its bio-magic abilities after death.

Which should be impossible.

Seyyid had taken a nasty hit to the head and almost gotten to visit the void permanently, but he'd survived if only to keep Preston from going into freefall.

I shoved the door open and stepped aside, letting them shuffle in. The weather had started to turn from frozen and miserable to soggy and miserable with the changing season. Spring was threatening to warm us up and bring on the allergies, and I was trying to avoid it as much as possible.

I was already going through enough without adding itchy eyes and a dripping nose to the mix.

"As happy as I am to see you," I told them with the same dryness my sinuses currently had. "I am a very busy man."

Twig watched the two men with her ears back, little fangs puncturing through the lid of the container.

"Nice place," Preston mumbled with the bitter jealousy of an underpaid and overworked government employee. Demon and Human Alliance and Protection officers made more than regular beat cops, but that didn't mean they made nearly enough to handle the specific hells of navigating magic regulations. "How'd you score this level of sugar daddy?"

"Because I have a huge, well-endowed personality." I shifted Twig in my arm so her little rear paw knives stopped digging into my skin.

"There's something going on in the city," Seyyid jumped in. "We're not exactly sure what, but we're hoping maybe you could shed some light on it."

"More weird vampires?" I guessed as Seyyid fished his phone out of his pocket.

"Not exactly." Seyyid tapped on the screen before pivoting it in my direction, producing a fuzzy picture of a black cloud surrounded by DHAP officers. "This was taken in Midtown three days ago. Does it look familiar in any way?"

The grainy picture wasn't doing much in providing anything tangible, but the urgency in Seyyid's voice told me it was worth another look. Upon further scrutiny, the cloud in the hastily snapped picture wasn't as incorporeal as I thought. It wasn't so much a cloud as an ink smear, and my brain rattled around as I tried to make sense of it.

"The only thing I could think of is a Thrall. They can turn into mist, but...this is too dense." I offered the phone back to Seyyid. "Was there connected vampire activity? Drained bodies, grunts, anything like that?"

"I don't think this is a Thrall," Seyyid corrected, wisps of silver trailing up like smoke from his jinn eyes. "It was more like a hole. A rip."

"Officers located this after a citizen called it in. They said the air tore open and this was left behind," Preston stepped into the conversation. "Wilde, something came out of the fucking thing."

My stomach turned sour. "A tear?"

"A creature came out of it," Preston reasserted. "It took three officers to put it down."

"I don't know what this is," I confessed, the sour state of my stomach warming into resolve. "So, skip the guessing games and tell me everything you know."

"All we know right now is that the tear happened around three in the morning, and there was no vampire activity reported in the area," Seyyid took over again. "The tear was contained using concentrated life magic in an amplification device, but it took a heavy blast to get it to knit. As for the creature, we don't know."

"You don't know?" I echoed, mystified. "You don't know like you don't know how to describe it or you literally don't know?"

"It's classified," Preston growled. "We don't have clearance."

"Bullshit," I shot back before I caught Seyyid's wince. I hadn't noticed or truly cared that the two DHAP officers before me weren't in uniform until that moment. Preston sporting the scruffy beard of a man whose future was uncertain, and Seyyid looking exhausted around his magic, silver eyes.

I offered them Twig to pet as an apology.

"You're freelancing this case?" I asked.

"You could say that," Seyyid lamented. "We had to call in favors for this much info. The rest is locked up tight."

"They're calling it an 'unclassified magical anomaly,'" Preston growled, rubbing Twig between her ears. "We've been benched pending investigation after I went to them about the vampires still holding on to their bio-magic. They still don't believe us."

"Even after Seyyid was attacked?" I snorted. "What the fuck else do they need? One to walk over and give them a formal greeting?"

"One officer not following protocol and getting hurt on the job is not evidence," Seyyid explained. "We're on leave for a while, and are being watched carefully."

"Do you know if the creature that came out of the rift is still alive?" I asked and Preston shook his head.

"It's dead. We got that confirmed." He smoothed Twig's hair down and exhaled. "We think there are more, but we can't get confirmation. If there is a pattern or something setting these things off, we don't have that intel."

"But we do know that DHAP have ramped up patrols in lower east Midtown bordering the Swallows," Seyyid provided. "That seems like a good place to start."

"Saints, this is bad." I rubbed my face with my free hand. "Alright. I'll get out there today and start scouting the area. If you two are being monitored, maybe give me space. We don't need your buddies trailing me."

Preston had started piercing me with his cop stare, brows pinching the skin into a crease.

"What do you think this is?"

I glanced down at Twig, who was back to busy rabbit kicking the mouse container. "Without seeing this thing or what came out of it, I can't say. It sounds like dark magic, but I don't know of any necromancer that summons creatures beyond vampires."

Preston was going through his own shit, and I knew that. The man had almost lost his boyfriend in a brutal, bloody fashion, and in return he was thanked for his service by getting kicked to the curb. Under slept and haggard were a fucking understatement for the state this guy was in.

And I knew he didn't like me. Hell, I didn't like him. He was a prickly asshole on the best days, and I knew if it wasn't for Seyyid, he would have tried to punch me more than once.

He didn't know.

But that didn't keep me from going numb with rage the moment he spoke.

"Why don't you ask your vampire boyfriend about it?"

I put Twig down.

"What did you say to me?" I heard myself ask, but I wasn't driving anymore.

Seyyid had placed a hand on Preston's arm to get him to back down, but his bulldog wasn't listening to commands.

"You don't exactly have my unbridled trust, Wilde," Preston spoke around a scowl that aged him twenty years. "Last time I saw you, Seyyid was in a coma and you were palling around with that fucking Thrall—"

I punched him hard enough to break his nose, but Preston's face was a brick. Clearly it wasn't the first time he'd had his face punched with the attitude he had, so his nose was much more pliable to greeting a row of knuckles. Both of our training kicked in at the same time, two hurricanes of military infused aggression throwing each other around on a marble foyer.

Only I was cool with throwing knees into dicks and going for the eyes. Saint's Army trains to kill, not contain.

I was also really fucking mad.

Before I could cripple Preston or make him unable to sire mini-assholes, I felt my temper cool into a concrete, ironclad choice not to continue to pulverize him. It washed over me like a wave of clarity, like I had known all along that's what I wanted to do.

I let my fist drop to my side, the fingers curled in his collar relax. Preston blinked in a haze, his eyes the placating silver of manipulation magic, as he released his vise grip around my wrist.

"There we go," Seyyid was telling us, his jinn magic a blanket of reason around us. "Neither of you want to keep fighting. You're both ready to calm down."

"Ugh." I pushed off Preston and rubbed at the ebbing grip Seyyid had over my skull. "Yeah, alright. I'm done. Get your jinn magic out of my head."

Preston made a similar grunt of acceptance as Seyyid pulled him to his feet, his eyes easing back to their normal color.

"Are we done being apes?" Seyyid quizzed us both, dusting his boyfriend's shoulders off.

"Didn't realize that was going to hit a fucking nerve," Preston grumbled, wiping some blood off his lip. "Fuck's sake, Wilde. If your Thrall might know what this shit is—"

"Zane," I snapped, my temper threatening to give his face an encore. "His name..." I trailed off when the grief kicked in, freezing the anger into an icy dagger pressing into my belly.

"Do you think that the tech you went hunting for has anything to do with what's happening in the city?" Seyyid pressed. "Do you think it's connected?"

"Maybe." I rubbed at a spot on my jaw, annoyed that Preston had landed a solid hit during our scuffle. "Florence has some strong necromancy magic. I aim to get it and destroy it. Maybe it'll solve both of our problems."

Preston's cop gaze had lost some of its teeth after the fight, but the old dog wasn't down yet.

"Give us a reason to trust you. You're keeping something from us, and we've given you everything. How do we know this necromancy shit isn't something you're tied up in?"

"I am tied up in it," I shot back. "I'm fully fucking tangled, Cheslock."

"You have a Th— Zane," Preston corrected. "And you're going after some strong necromancy shit that might be causing monsters to spawn in the city. Look me in the eyes and tell me you're not going after this crap like our ancestors did, Wilde. We're human, we fall for this shit."

I ground my teeth so tight I thought my molars would disintegrate.

"I'm going to destroy that thing, not use it in some weird undead power fantasy. I'm a vampire hunter and necromancer assassin, it says it right on my fucking business card. I don't care if you help me, Cheslock, but don't stand here in my sugar daddy's foyer accusing me of being something I'm not. I'm not a goddamn monster."

Preston's jaw bunched as he ground out his frustration, the heat starting to fade from his eyes. A soul deep sigh escaped from his flared nostrils, and I saw his hackles drop.

"That's fair," he lamented. "I don't like you either, Wilde, but I can at least admit that you're not a monster. You," he paused to choke on his words a second. "You did help Seyyid. You kill vampires. I trust that you're not actually trying to do something evil, at least not with this."

"I'm not evil," I agreed. "I'm ambiguously aligned, but I'm not evil. You can trust me on that."

The solid, confident stride of Sias could be heard echoing down the hardwood hallway before he made his appearance in the foyer. He was dressed immaculately as always, a bespoke suit with the jacket left behind, a vest tailored to show his broad shoulders and narrow, belted waist covered by tailored slacks and designer shoes.

What really brought the whole look together, was the plastic apron covering his ensemble, smattered in what one would consider an alarming amount of blood.

"Ah, there you are, love," Sias purred. "I was finally able to get our guest to speak. Join me in the sunroom and we can discuss."

His eyes flicked to Preston and Seyyid, the blue hue darkening only a fraction. "See your guests out."

He turned and left without another word, the snap of a latex glove traveling with him as he peeled the bloody mess off his hands.

There was an awkward moment when the only noise was the fading sound of Sias stripping off his gloves and me clearing my throat, but I managed to scoot around the gobsmacked DHAP officers to open the front door.

"Drive safe, officers. Send me the address of where that tear was, and I'll check it out."

"You really think we're going to ignore that?" Preston turned his head to me.

"Sias is really into finger painting." I flashed a smile. "It's a fully immersive experience. Highly sexual. Nothing you wanna hear about."

"You gotta be kidding me, Wilde."

"You get your info your way, we get it ours." I placated Twig with some pets as she mewed at me, bored with the mouse coffin she couldn't break.

"Seyyid," Preston whined as his partner took him by the arm and gently guided him out.

Seyyid made a point to lock eyes with me, the silver wisps of his magic like fog. "I'll send you the address. Don't make me regret this." He tugged his partner along with him. "One battle at a time, Preston. First the tears, then we'll look into…whatever that was."

"Finger painting," I reminded them, hurrying them out before shutting the door behind them.

I waited until their arguing traveled further from the door before I let out my breath and rescued the mouse coffin, now sporting cat teething decorations. It was deposited in the freezer before I found Sias in the sunroom.

"I'm not sure if it was awesome and hot that you just dismissed two DHAP officers while wearing an apron of gore, or if I need to resign myself to shooting them at some point, which would be a bit of a bummer," I told the incubus who was reclining on a couch like he was posing for his tenth oil painting. The apron was gone and I had no clue what he did with it.

"They're not a threat." Sias motioned for me to sit. "Have you eaten?"

"No, but I have a feeling you're about to tell me something that's going to kill my appetite anyway." I landed on the couch with much less grace or poise as the slick sex demon.

"You need to eat," Sias scolded. "You can't keep skipping meals, darling. This is important."

"Is Reynolds still alive? That was a lot of blood on you."

It made my stomach churn just saying Reynolds's name out loud. The bastard had been my well paid, criminal doctor for years before he sold me out to Florence and took Zane from me.

Reynolds was the sniveling dog turd that had shot my Thrall with the healing nano tech, dissolving him from the inside out like the vampire had been made of cotton candy.

Sias's eyes swirled an aggressive shade of yellow before cooling into an ocean blue.

"He is. For now."

"Good." It took me a breath or two to unclench my jaw. "That asshole doesn't get to die yet. Not when Zane is still gone. Were you able to get anything useful out of him?"

"Through the groveling and mewling, he did mention that there had been discussion of testing the tech controlling the vampire grunts in some secret place in the city." Sias checked the status of his nails, no doubt checking for bits of Reynolds that had possibly bled through the plastic. "He didn't know where, unfortunately."

"Does he know anything about the tech? How it works?" I pressed.

"Not the specifics. He was able to explain that they are tethering them together with implants at the base of the skull, syncing them under one master control. The magic is necrotic in nature, but altered in some way using jinn influence frequencies. Perhaps Dex can build something to counter it."

"Yep. My appetite is shot." I rubbed at my poor, stressed stomach. Instead of it being an endless cavern for me to toss junk food into while gallivanting around the city, it was currently perpetually full of cottony anxiety. "A master control over grunts using manipulated death magic is just *so great*. Love that for us."

"Speaking of death magic." Sias tilted his head, gold catching the sunlight at the tips of his curled horns. "How did your lesson go this morning?"

"Shitty." I rubbed at my eyes, exhausted from my attempt at necromancy. "Not much progress to report. I'm really bad at this whole dead stuff business."

"You'll get there, darling. I know it's impossible for you, but try and be patient. The wait is always so rewarding."

"Yeah, when it's something fun like ordering a cake or edging. Then the pay-off to all the waiting is delicious. Trying to grab onto the void's magic to bend it to my will isn't at all like fighting an orgasm or eating icing."

Sias hummed. "What did the cops want?"

"We have a fun new problem. Apparently there's some mysterious rifts tearing open across the city."

"What do you mean 'rifts'?" Sias lifted a golden eyebrow.

"I don't know yet. They said a tear opened up in Midtown and something came out of it. They specifically used the word 'creature,' which I'm not thrilled by." I bounced my knee to keep from springing up. "I have a bad feeling that they are void tears."

Sias motioned for me to continue, a furrow settling onto his handsome face.

"When Zane and I were at the cemetery, the scythe kind of… fired out of my chest and hit a tree." My chest bloomed in warmth from the memory before wilting into dust. "The blade tore into the void like a rip. So, it is possible for strong enough death magic to cause tears. I don't know that this is Florence or if it's a very ambitious necromancer causing a separate issue."

"Lovely," he said wryly.

"My thoughts exactly." I lost the battle of containing my anxiety and got to my feet. "I'm going to go prowl around Midtown to look for more of these rips. I can't sit around here meditating to the Death Goddess any more today."

"I'll bring the car around." Sias stood, his suit refusing to hold a single crease.

"You're giving me a ride?" I asked stupidly, to which the beautiful incubus in front of me regarded with amusement.

"I'm coming with you. If there's something tearing holes into the city, I'd like to know why. I have a lot of real estate here, you know."

"Sias, this is death magic. You can't get close to it," I reminded him. "It'll consume you, or make you something undead and gross."

"Good thing life magic can be infused in weapons." He checked his watch. "If we leave now, we can miss traffic."

"You really want to prowl around the city with me to hunt forces of death that might be ripping holes between realities?" I clicked my tongue. "Might dirty your suit."

A silky landslide rumbled through his chest as he chuckled, and I felt a trail of heat climb through my fragile being. It made me shiver to feel something other than cold grief, and that bliss quickly splintered into sharp barbs of guilt.

"I'm not one to be sloppy, darling," he purred.

"My mistake," I managed, my cheeks erupting into flames as his long, elegant fingers curled around my chin.

"And Dallas?" He gave my chin a squeeze. "You're not missing breakfast. Get something on the way to the car. I'll know if you don't."

Sias left me standing there in his sunroom, a little dumbstruck.

And kind of hungry.

I HADN'T REALIZED how many holes were in Zane's jacket until I started wearing it.

With the winter winds being slowly suffocated by the spring humidity, I no longer needed my thick jacket to keep me safe from the cold. Zane's "cool guy" leather jacket was perfect to keep the chill away, even if it was a little too big around the shoulders.

I was never going to tell him that, because he'd give me endless shit for it.

That fucker had been stabbed, shot and bitten at so many times that his jacket was basically scraps of frayed leather by the time I decided to adopt it. Sias had been kind enough to have it patched for me whenever I needed it, without question.

The beaten-up jacket was Zane's, and I couldn't bear the idea of losing any more of him.

My patched up, secondhand vampire jacket somehow still looked badass, even when I was walking side by side with a super model sex god. We were quite the mismatch of chic elegance and frumpy, yet handsome, tangle of tattoos and sleep deprivation. My blond hair was in desperate need of a cut, my thorny roses tattooed around my neck really accented the dark bruising under my blue eyes. Sias always looked like a stack of gold stuck with an adorable bum sporting punny shirts and a ripped up jacket.

Sias strolled with the lazy stride of a panther on the hunt, but one that was bored with the offerings of the world. The blue in his eyes lifted into more alert shades of turquoise and lilac, but the range was limited these days. It was rare I saw him take on any other shades than the blue and violet of a bruise, sometimes with spikes of yellow if he was reflecting on what had happened to us.

At least he was bruised and not bleeding. I felt like I was on the verge of collapse most days, my heart punctured and draining slowly with each passing day.

The spring day bit hard enough to bring me out of my misery, though it soothed that sting with a little bit of sunshine. The ice was thawed and gone from the sidewalks of St. Athesall, which allowed more foot traffic for businesses. Midtown was bustling with late breakfast hustle, the scent of pastries and coffee still clinging to the cool air.

The area Seyyid had sent us to investigate was painfully normal, without a scrap of evidence tape or murmurings of nosy civilians. Midtown wasn't an area of the city that stayed awake that late into the night, so it wasn't outrageous to believe that there had been very limited exposure to whatever the hell had happened.

Everything seemed boring. Typical. Normal.

Which was kinda disappointing.

Not that I wanted a damn tear into the void to still be present around a bunch of innocent people or anything. That would make me kind of a bastard, and I was trying to keep myself at "lovable scoundrel" levels. I was just hoping to get a peek into whatever the hell was going on, and a normal, sunny spring morning in Midtown wasn't helping us get very far.

"Maybe we could ask some of the locals," Sias offered as we scanned over the spot Seyyid had sent us to. "Someone had to have seen something."

"No one is going to talk if DHAP slapped them with an

NDA," I explained. "It's not worth getting your life turned inside out legally. Midtown is generations of family businesses and regular people trying to keep their heads down. They're not going to spill to strangers." I kneeled and held my magic detector charm in my palm, hoping to get a little buzz of warning.

"You don't have connections out here? Informants?"

"I do." I stood, dusting grit off my jeans. "But even your money isn't going to get them to risk their dad's business. Ushen might talk if they've heard anything, but I don't have any human meat for trade."

"That does complicate things." Sias let his gaze float over the neighboring buildings and the ones across the street. "I'm assuming DHAP would have wiped any security cameras that may have caught anything."

"Wiped and burned," I agreed. "This is a dead end. Let's keep moving. Seyyid mentioned that there may have been more rips, hence why they've upped their patrol around here."

"We should be mindful to stay out of their way," Sias mumbled as he watched an "undercover" DHAP officer stroll across the street, the body language all wrong for a regular guy buying coffee. "They're going to notice us if we keep meandering around here."

"I'm guessing that if there were more in Midtown, they've already patched up any leaks," I explained as we abandoned the tear site and moved on. "But we're right on the edge of the Swallows, and we both know that place doesn't get the same type of attention. Maybe we can find looser lips there."

"One can hope." Sias fell into step beside me, colorful eyes on the lookout. "What sort of 'creature' lives in the void, exactly?"

"Other than vampires, I haven't a clue." I shivered at the creeping cold feeling slipping up my spine. "By definition, the void is nothingness. It's death. Nothing alive can come from the void, unless a necromancer pulls it out like they do with Thralls."

"So life can materialize from the void," Sias offered. "Maybe a soul somehow breached the vale in the same way Thralls do."

"Gods above, I fucking hope not. What the hell would that even look like?"

"I suppose we'll find out, won't we?"

"You said that way too calmly," I pointed out, failing to suppress a laugh. "I'm the trained dead thing hunter and this whole thing is giving me a stomachache. How are you so relaxed? Is it the suit? Do I need to get a suit?"

"We don't know what we're up against, so I refuse to give it an ounce of my concern until proven otherwise," the richer-than-sin sex demon explained in a tone of absolute coolness. "I'll let you know once I've changed my mind."

"Noted."

It didn't take long for the cozy yet well-loved antique buildings of Midtown to take an abandoned turn. So much of the Swallows had been built up and stripped away that the borders seemed to be holding up out of pure spite. With the sharp ebbs and flow of a harsh economy, the more fragile pieces of St. Athesall had been left to fall in on itself while skyscrapers shot up like rockets.

The Swallows was alive in the cracks between poverty and prosperity, hardened by resolve, and refusing to be squashed out completely. Corner stores might have bars over the windows to keep them from being smashed in, but the neighborhood was tight knit and protected by a stitched together family of proximity.

I liked it there. It was honest, even if it was punctuated at times by violence.

"Are we looking for some human meat to give to your chatty connection?" Sias offered as we drifted deeper into the Swallows. "This is a rough side of town."

"Not exactly." I shoved my hands into Zane's jacket pockets. "I have some connections who will know if anything has happened within the Swallows, but I'm not going to lie—I'm not on the best terms with this guy."

"You don't say," he said flatly.

"Not everyone finds me as charming and handsome as you do." I batted my lashes at him and he huffed a laugh.

"Darling, I hate to be the one to reveal this to you, but you can be a bit…" He weighed his options in his head before slapping me with velvet truth. "Hard to digest for those not accustomed to sharp personalities."

"That is the nicest way anyone has ever called me a 'pain in the ass.'"

"How much friction should we expect from these individuals you've pissed off?" Sias slipped his hands into his jacket, the wind moving some hair from his face as if he had commanded it to. "I only brought one extra clip with me, you know."

"Maybe Marthas has forgiven me after Florence paid him off? I did fuck his boyfriend though, so…" I tipped my hand from side to side. "We got a fifty-fifty on that one."

Sias tsked me. "Dallas."

"Not my best moment, okay? I can't believe I'm still dealing with the fallout over that." I shielded myself with Zane's jacket, my shoulders blocking the wind. "And I feel like an asshole about it."

"Well, asshole moment or no, he doesn't get to kill you over it." Sias adjusted his jacket, a flash of gold from his gun catching the light as it rested in the holster on his ribs. "I'm not in the mood to argue today."

"Let's hope he's not in an argumentative mood then."

Since it was so damn early in the morning, most people who thrive during the twilight hours were likely sound asleep. It didn't thrill me to be showing up in Marthas's territory to rouse him from his slumber, knowing full well he likely still wanted me skinned alive. Waiting until night to try and chat with the guy seemed like a stupid move since he'd have more goons around him, and the fact that the veil between our realities was fraying put a sense of urgency to my travels.

I hadn't been back to Biodome since the fateful night of my Big Ass Mistake, and the building was a slumbering giant in the sunlight. I was used to the place being alive with dancing bodies and pulsing neon lights, but it seemed almost sickly when it was closed up and resting. It was easier to see the cracks and stains, how dirty the neon lights were when they weren't distracting you with brilliance.

"I don't think anyone is here currently," Sias mused as we wandered around behind the club, stepping over the scattered cigarette butts and pieces of broken beer bottles. "It seems very empty."

"He has an apartment below," I tossed over my shoulder. "I think there's a back way in, but I have to remember where."

The door in question made itself known after we rounded a dumpster, a faded "employee only" sticker dying a slow death stuck above the knob.

"This seems like a risky move," Sias commented as I wiggled my lock pick around in the guts of the handle. "There's no alarms?"

"No one would be stupid enough to break into this place." I jiggled the pick around a bit more, scraping against the pins. "Marthas isn't known to be understanding."

Sias exhaled through his nose, checking his weapon casually as I jammed the last bit of defiance out of the knob.

The door released, and we stepped through into the dark, quiet hallway of a silent, criminal club. The iconic dome that gave the place its name was cloudy, muting the sunlight as it tried to sneak its way inside. The intrusive light was harsh against the scraped dance floor and scuffed bar counters, the smell of disinfectant and mold clung to the walls.

Being back unlocked some old memories, half buried behind a wall of haze brought on by my tendency to indulge in party drugs, yet clear enough to tap dance across my sore heart.

The last time I was inside this stupid place, I was sprinting away from a lot of emotions I didn't understand. It felt sobering to be back there in the silence and sunshine of daylight, when there had been so much darkness and deafening distractions prior.

I pulled Zane's jacket tighter around myself, noting the stitching where a knife had plunged through it. My body shivered from the memory of red eyes in a strobing light, the remembered smell of blood and spilled alcohol making my stomach twist.

There was something else haunting this place beyond my heartache and regrets though, something dark and rotten.

Something dead. Something that perhaps was never fully alive. A chill danced its fingers across my soul, like the Death Goddess was tapping me on the shoulder and I couldn't take a breath.

The black veins on the floor were swallowing the light, made of shadow and nothing, and I felt my blood turn cold.

"Fuck."

"This place feels like a tomb," Sias whispered. "Something is wrong."

"It is a tomb," Marthas's voice found us before I could locate him, my hand reaching for my weapon in vain.

The mountainous imp glowered at us from the bar, his gun trained on us lazily while he sipped coffee. If I thought the sunlight was harsh on the interior of the club, then it was brutal on the obviously exhausted gang leader parked at the bar. Marthas was a mess of sleep-deprived anger, the bags under his eyes as telling as the three-day old sweats he sat in.

"It's a goddamn cemetery," he finished after taking a long gulp of coffee. "And haunted at that."

"What the hell happened here, Marthas?" I asked, daring to take another glance at the black scars running across the floor. "What is that?"

"I was hoping you could tell me, being as you're the necromancy guy and all." He gestured to the ground with the barrel of his gun. "That's all that's left after that fucking tear ripped open during a Saturday night."

"Did your DHAP officers mention a club?" Sias asked me, and I shook my head. "How did you keep this from getting out?"

"Better question." Marthas pulled the hammer back on his gun. "Who the fuck are you?"

"Be nice," I warned. "We came here to ask you if you heard about tears happening in the Swallows. We got a heads up from some DHAP contacts that this shit was happening, but I had no idea one went off in your club."

"Seems like an awful coincidence that my life gets fucked sideways out of nowhere and then suddenly you show up, Wilde." Marthas tried to make my head pop with the hatred in his glare.

"I appreciate that you think I'm somehow a fucking wizard, but I assure you I'm just a regular badass, and very much ill-equipped to summon a tear into the void." I showed him my palms and tried my best to sound amicable. "Can we pretend to not hate each other for just a little bit?"

"I'm not that good of an actor. Plus, I really hate you." The barrel of his weapon flicked in a bored yet threatening gesture. "Toss your weapons to the ground and kick them over."

Sias made his stance on the request known immediately. "I'm not doing that."

"It'll be easier if we just humor him." I pulled my gun free from my waistband and placed it on the ground, kicking it toward the bar with a soccer style tap using the side of my foot.

"You too, handsome," Marthas drawled. "I know you have a piece under that jacket."

"I'm not putting my expensive, custom automatic with gold plating and ivory handle on the ground and scuffing it with a kick," Sias clarified. "You'll just have to shoot me."

This information was news to me, and I stared at my complicated, hot as hell and clearly a little nuts friends with benefits like the mad man he was.

"You brought a gold-plated gun on our recon mission?"

"Of course." He aimed his eyebrows at me like I was the one being ridiculous. "It matches my horns."

"Maybe bringing you was a mistake."

"Set it on the fucking stool and back away. Gods above,

fucking incubi." Marthas pointed to the stool in front of the bar. "You're more trouble than you're worth."

Sias exhaled like he was doing us all a favor by complying, and sauntered over to Marthas with about as much urgency as an annoyed house cat.

A gun-shaped slab of gold and ivory privilege was placed on the bar stool and Sias stepped backwards to meet me back at my side.

"We good now?" I asked Marthas. "My ugly gun and his monstrosity are now on your side."

"You didn't answer my question." Marthas aimed his ire and weapon back on Sias. "And you are?"

"Annoyed," Sias deadpanned, unfazed by Marthas's flex, his eyes remaining a cool blue. "You know who I am, we can stop with the power play. Your desperation to seem in control is boring."

The stubble on Marthas's jaw rippled as he clenched his teeth, gaze swiveling back to me.

"I'm not here to cause trouble, man," I repeated. "Truce. Cease fire. You can go back to hating me after we get this figured out. I'm sure void tears are bad for business."

"How do I know the moment I lower my gun that your guard dog vampire isn't going to swoop in and cause shit?" he spat. "You think I didn't notice he wasn't here?"

Sias's eyes swirled a sharp yellow as I felt the knife of grief twist in my side.

"He's dead," I replied, my lips numb.

"Bullshit."

"That's your one," Sias hissed, venom lacing his words. "Tread carefully."

Whether it was the exhaustion finally winning over, or the fact that Sias looked ready to rip him into pieces, Marthas finished his coffee as he eased the hammer down and set the gun on the bar.

"Alright, Wilde." He rubbed at his eyes. "Truce. I'm too

fucking tired to handle the mountain of bullshit you bring with you."

"Great. Now, tell me everything that happened that night. What did you see? Did anything happen leading up to the tear? Anything you remember."

"Nothing happened beforehand," he told me as I made my way cautiously to the black markings lacing the floor. "It was a regular night, maybe around one AM. One minute it was just a normal night, then the next the floor opened up like a mouth. I was on the balcony above when it happened."

"Do your bouncers have magic blockers and detectors?" Sias asked, and Marthas nodded. "Did they pick up a surge?"

"Yeah. Death magic." Marthas shivered, rubbing his big arms like the chill was too much. "It went out like a ripple, set off all alarms."

The darkness carved into the wood was matte and stained with death, spidering out from the healed gash curved up like a crooked smirk.

"Gods, don't touch it!" Marthas barked as I ran my finger across the gash, haunted by the unnatural cold that seeped up from the floor.

"This was the void," I confirmed. "Traces of it are knitted into this reality."

"We can't get it out," Marthas strained, swallowing back fear. "I tried to hire someone to rip the floorboards up, but no one will go near it. I don't blame them."

"People were dancing here when..." I asked, but Marthas was already nodding, eyes shut to shield himself from the memory.

"Yeah. Four people fell in before the crowd realized what was happening. It caused a panic, and we evacuated before it could take more people out. One of my guys threw a life magic infused overdose kit into it, and it choked it out before it could spread more. We got fucking lucky, Wilde. It was going to take this whole damn place down."

"How did you keep this quiet?" Sias kept his distance from the floor, but studied the markings with curious, purple eyes.

"Paid off the families affected and shut the place down. Told everyone it was an unfortunate accident with the floor caving in." Marthas smoothed his messy, short hair back over his stubby horns. "No one really saw much during the panic. Easier to believe the floor caved in over the goddamn void eating people."

"Not to freak you out more, but my DHAP connections mentioned a creature. Did you see anything like that when the floor opened up?" I tested the floor with a push of my fingers, relieved it didn't give.

"I heard that too, but no. Thank fucking God, no creature." Marthas leaned against the bar, forgetting to keep his steely features from sliding into humbling fear. "What the fuck is going on, Wilde? What could cause this?"

"I don't know. This has to be a new necromancer playing with forces they shouldn't, and I'm going to track their ass down." I pulled my knife free and carved a chunk of the void stained wood out. It felt like a piece of thawing ice in my hand, not cold enough to burn but still chilled me down to the bone.

My magic blocker hummed with warning as the piece was placed in my pocket, a dull pulse of death magic detection going off from the proximity.

"Do you know of any other tears in the Swallows?" I asked Marthas. "I'm hoping maybe these things have a pattern, or something that makes sense."

"No, but I have ears on the ground." Marthas hefted his large form from the bar and rolled his neck, but the tension in his shoulders didn't ease. "If any pop up on my side of town, I'll relay the info."

"Anything you get is useful. By the way, I moved, so you can't just swing by and knock my door in again. You'll need to call me." I pulled a card from my pocket and waved it.

"I know you moved, and I don't need your idiotic card." Marthas snatched his coffee mug off the counter. "And I'll stop kicking in your door when you stop stealing my shit, like that jacket you're wearing."

"You'll have to pull this off my corpse." I plucked at the collar of the jacket, the faint scent of grave flowers and rainwater still present enough to drive a needle into my heart. "Plus, you look like you've been wallowing in the same sweatpants for days. I don't want your sad stink all over it."

"I'm going to get that jacket back, Wilde," Marthas promised. "You're too stupid to stay out of my territory, and you won't always have a cheap shot vampire or a gold smuggling sugar daddy with you."

"You two act like you've never seen gold plating before," Sias grumbled. "It's not that uncommon."

"He's actively threatening me and you're mad he's making comments about your gun?"

"Oh, please." Sias rolled his teal eyes. "You're threatened daily, darling. I can't take them all seriously."

"Get this shit fixed, Wilde," Marthas cut back in. "I don't know how, but I feel like this is somehow your fault."

"What the fuck did I do?" I scoffed. "I'm just as dumbfounded about this crap as you are. I don't go around opening portals to the void for kicks, man."

"Call it a hunch," he spat. "Get out of my club. Take your ugly brick of gold with you."

The grizzled imp lumbered off to go feel sorry for himself and eat dirt, and I retrieved my gun from the ground. Sias's ugly gold brick was slipped back into a holster, and we left through the busted back door we came in from.

"Always lovely to catch up with Marthas."

"That's two instances we've heard about tears being sealed with life magic," Sias mused as we put Biodome behind us. "Which makes sense, but I imagine that won't solve the problem forever."

"With my necromancer powers being crap now, the one silver lining is that I can use life magic again without it turning me into a walking skeleton." My leg tingled with the memory of my leg sizzling away into a charred, bony nightmare during my last healing visit. "So we can at least bring some life magic with us in case we run into anything. In the meantime, we can bring this piece of the wood from the club to Dex, see if she can make use of it."

"Have you ever seen anything like that?" Sias's eyes turned a frosty blue as I examined the piece of void tainted wood in the sunlight. "Just looking at it makes me feel cold."

The warmth of the sun refused to seep into the material, the blackness void of any features or logical temperature.

"No," I admitted, a twinge of fear snaking up my spine. "Which means we have to find more."

"I was optimistic you'd say the opposite."

"We're not going to stop this unless we can follow the tears to the source. Whoever is doing this is unstable to say the least." I pocketed the piece and felt the cold nipping through the fabric of my pocket. The chill of death unsettled the most human part of myself, the ever-present knowledge that one day, inevitably, I would be joining the darkness as all dead things do. Hell, I'd been there and back so many times, I practically had a punch card. One more trip and I might be able to get vacation property.

There was a quiet place that festered near my broken heart, coated with madness and reckless loss, that was excited to feel the cold again.

It was closer to me now than it had been since the scythe was taken. Since my powers had been stripped away.

Since Zane died.

He was closer to me now than he had been in months.

It thrilled me. It made me dangerous. Selfish.

If those tears could be made, if there was a way to pop the window open to the void without having to dedicate a lifetime to learning necromancy, it was worth finding.

I'd stop whoever was responsible *after* I had the chance to get my vampire back.

# CHAPTER
# THREE

"THERE'S MY FAVORITE GUY."

Dex looked surprisingly friendly when she smiled. I had never seen that look on her before since she typically had the emotional range of an irritated boar with an affinity for chewing gum. Even her bubble blowing was passive aggressive on the best of days, so this was a huge departure from what I was used to. Her tusks fit her smile in shape and sharpness, her oni horns painted in black and white stripes like they were trying to hypnotize us with glee.

"Wow, Dex. I'm happy to see you too!"

My comment made her cheery attitude plunge back to the normal glower, and I was given a snort as she passed right on by as I opened my arms up for a hug.

"Not you, jackass. I mean the guy who pays me."

I stood with my pride in crumpled bits on the floor in Dex's new, shiny lab as *my* hired tech thug snubbed me to go chat with the guy *I* introduced her to. All I got was a bubble pop and the cold shoulder while Sias got the beaming smile of a well-paid oni nerd.

"Dex. Lovely as always." Sias's eyes lifted to a lilac, and I flipped off the back of Dex's head. Was I a little jealous she liked him more than me?

Yes.

Was I also simultaneously bitter that she got Sias to do the flower purple eyes even though I know I could easily get him to go full horny pink whenever I wanted?

Maybe.

Okay, yes.

But I never claimed to be an adult about my feelings, and Dex was a butthole.

"What can I do for you?" Dex continued to address Sias, ignoring me as I commented on the amount of neon she had slung all over the place. The lights kept beat with her thumping techno music, the smell of soldered metal and burnt magic assaulting my senses.

"Actually, I believe Dallas has a request," Sias explained like it was a novel concept.

"Yeah, hi." I waved as she rolled her eyes my way. "Remember me? Your previous favorite guy? The one who got you into this cyberpunk rave we're standing in?"

A purple bubble inflated in front of her face and popped with sass.

"What do you want, Wilde?"

Realizing I wasn't going to get any warm apologies or even false sincerity, I got down to business and dug the void-touched piece of wood from my pocket.

"There's been void tears happening in the city. This is a piece of wood that was touched by the tear after it was sealed up."

Dex's bored glare shifted into sleepy surprise as she held out her hand for the piece.

"Ew. It's cold." She cringed the moment it touched her skin, the contact sending a shiver up from her hand that then shook down her body. "Gods, it feels *creepy*."

"It's technically a piece of the void, so hell yeah, it's creepy. It's death."

"Metal." She moved to one of the tables stretched out in the technicolored lab Sias had set up for her. Wires, circuit boards, crystal fragments, metal bits, and plastic bobs littered the work-space in a chaos only Dex understood, waiting to be crafted into some genius piece of tech infused with magic.

"What are you wanting to do with this?" she asked over her shoulder as she wrapped some copper wire around the wood. "Harness it? Use it as a weapon? Channel the void into a beam?"

"Can you do that?" I asked the same time Sias was shutting down all of our fun.

"No," he was saying over my excitement. "We will not be harnessing death. Do your best not to go unhinged just yet, darling. We have a lot to do, and we don't need a literal Doomsday device at this juncture."

I booed him and I got a steely glare in return.

"Don't be a brat, Dallas."

My heart did the little pitter patter down to my dick because I knew damn well what that tone meant. I knew that tone so well, in every single position, all over his office, and sometimes in his nice car.

The sizzle of that promise cooled and died before it could go too far, my heart refusing to give the effort to feel much else beyond the ache. A coil of shame wrapped itself around my heart and tightened as the color in his eyes drifted back into blue.

I hadn't seen pink in his eyes in two months.

I didn't know if I'd be able to get them back to pink again with the giant, Zane-sized hole in my chest.

"We need a way of knowing where these tears are happening," I explained, shoving my feelings aside for them to rot elsewhere. "Can you make a location charm with this material? Or at least a magic detector tuned to the void?"

Dex grazed on her gum like a tusked cow, dark eyes narrowed over her tinkering.

"The magic in this thing is faint, yet still very strong, which isn't shocking. The void doesn't behave like naturally occurring magic, I guess because it lives outside of this living world. Figuring out the frequency of *death* is going to be kinda tricky, but I can give it a shot." She angled her head up to peer at Sias. "Are we sure this isn't going to cause another void? Or like… kill me?"

"If I give you a bonus, would that help ease your fear?" Sias offered casually. "Because this is critical, otherwise I wouldn't have brought this to you. I can't make promises, but I am confident in your abilities to not kill yourself."

"I don't know how stable it is," Dex explained. "Magic has specific properties, rules."

"So does death," I jumped in. "Treat it like you would life magic. They're two sides of the same coin, according to a very chatty head I hang out with."

"Says the human," Dex scoffed. "There's a reason only your lot fucks with life and death, man. The rest of us aren't that arrogant."

She had a point, and I shrugged in defeat.

"Yeah, well. We don't live as long, so we have to be extra stupid to make up for it."

Dex rubbed her hands together as her machines started to light up with the frequency bouncing off the void wood on her table. The dials whipped around like windshield wipers on full blast, the copper wire shaking the wood across the metal table.

"This little thing packs a punch," she mumbled, excitement dancing in her eyes. "This is going to take me a while."

"It seems like most of these tears are happening at night." Sias rotated his wrist to check his watch. "You have a few hours before we'll need it. We'll be back this evening."

"You want me to unlock the secrets of the void's frequency, harness it, then program a piece of unstable technology to home in and direct mortals to its very existence?" Dex's smile was back, ferocious in the promise of uncharted secrets being ripped apart and put back together again in a shiny, probably neon package. "I'll have it ready by eight."

"You are insane," I said. "Why don't we hang out more?"

Dex didn't bother to respond, the grip of discovery upon her and rendering her deaf to the realm of technology illiterate normies like me.

And probably because she didn't like me much, even though we should totally be friends.

"Are you ever worried she's going to sell the inventions she makes for you to other people?" I asked Sias as we left the building, stepping back into the sunlight. "I mean, she's cracking the code to track down the void. That can't be safe in just anyone's hands."

"She signed an NDA when she started to work for me." He strolled beside me, unbothered by the events of the day thus far. "Anything made in that lab is my property, so if she were to flip and sell it to someone else, I would take her father's business, and sue them into a pit. Plus, I pay her well and give her the means to pick apart the fabric of magic whenever she wants. She's not going to give that up."

"Fair. I take it you hire people like Dex a lot if you're used to speaking unhinged so fluently."

Sias hummed, giving me a knowing look.

"I've had some practice."

"Hey, I'm sexy chaotic, she's scary unhinged. They're similar, but different species of crazy." I fell into step as we took a turn different to what I was expecting, veering off course away from his home. "You have somewhere you need to be?

"I need to pick up some supplies since we're out and have time to burn." He lifted his chin in the direction we were heading. "It's not far."

"Doesn't Claudia pick up your stuff for you? She's often complained that my adorable tardiness has held her back from snagging your dry cleaning."

"Not everything," he admitted. "And I'm on leave from the office, so she's on paid vacation until I return."

"You? On leave?" I couldn't help my face from reflecting the blatant shock and open suspicion I had about that statement. "Are you dying? I've never seen you take a weekend off, not to mention a damn vacation."

"I'm taking time to help with Zane, darling." He lifted one golden brow, which sliced me down the middle. "I haven't been back to the office in months."

I felt a bit like a self-absorbed jackass for not realizing that Sias hadn't been back to the office. Scratch that, I felt like a massive, mountain-sized jackass for missing the extent of his presence around his own damn house.

Instead of saying something heartfelt and grateful, like a normal, not asshole would do, I asked, "Won't your stakeholders get anxious or something?"

"You have no idea about the structure of my business."

"I do not, no," I admitted immediately. "But I have heard those words orbiting business lingo before, so I went for it."

He hummed, steering us into the business district of the city. The humble, family-owned buildings made of bricks and history had been bulldozed over to pave the way for tiered parking lots and towering shrines to commerce. The bustle here was different now, the meandering, chatty crowds popping into delis to snag something to eat a thing of the past. Now the passing conversations were quick, snappy orders to buy and sell, heads angled down into phones to make sure they didn't miss a life-changing email.

It was Sias's realm; fast money, cutthroat politics, and an endless sea of backstabs and bankrolls. He swam through the guppies like a shark, the jittery crowd willing to step into traffic so as not to upset his pace. I was the sexy little sucker fish on Sias's underbelly as he guided us toward our destination.

My shark pivoted to a strip of cafes and restaurants that catered to the busy business fishies that now took up residence on this side of town, offering fast, trendy dishes like "organic, hand-fed salads with vegan lettuce tossed in a pretentious dressing of bullshit" or something like that. I'm pretty sure they could legally shoot you if you attempted to order anything that even shared a shelf with processed sugar, and they made sure the prices reflected that.

Needless to say, I rarely ate in the business district, except when it came to the hipster coffee places.

I'm going to be vulnerable and honest: your man likes the flavored lattes made by dudes named Brice with the cute foam art on top. It makes me feel good, and I'm only a little ashamed about it.

But if you tell a single soul, I'm going to sic Kevin on you.

I was passively admiring the smells of the nearby chain coffee place advertising a new mocha latte masterpiece when Sias held out a piece of plastic with a spending limit higher than my opinion of myself. The promise of reckless spending and a mocha latte curled away from me as I reached for it, and Sias pinned me with a steely lavender look.

"Order food," he commanded. "Something moderately healthy, not just coffee."

"I ate before we left," I protested. "And the sign says it's a limited-time flavor, Sias. Who knows when I'll have another chance."

The lavender threatened magenta as he repeated himself, "Food, Dallas. Don't be bratty with me unless you're willing to pay the price."

Our little cat and mouse game used to lead to so many sexy shenanigans, and it stung all over when I had to pop the flirty bubble by sighing in defeat.

"Yeah, I got it." I held out my hand for the credit card. "Food it is."

The plastic was pressed into my palm, and I warmed when the color of his eyes didn't change. Either Sias was more deprived than I thought, or it genuinely made him excited that I was going to be eating properly.

"Good boy," he purred, which did all sorts of gooey things to my chest. I might be wounded, broken into pieces and hated myself most days, but damn if that didn't glue some of my fragments back together.

Sias drifted off in a different direction, disappearing into a shop as I floated away to find something to eat.

As previously stated, most of the offerings around this section of town catered to crowds in much higher income brackets than myself, but I now had the power of a rich man's credit card in my hands. Unfortunately, my appetite was about as powerful as an anemic, elderly chihuahua, so I ended up with a cup of soup that I forced myself to down at least half of before Sias showed back up.

He gave a sharp look to the cup of coffee I was sipping and I wiggled my half empty soup canister to cool him off. The bag hanging from his arm held a fabric covered box, the logo of which I didn't recognize. Whatever it was, it looked breathtakingly expensive, and I was hesitant to relinquish his credit card back over when he held out his hand.

The travel time back to Sias's mansion was a breeze because he had called his driver to come pick us up. Apparently he had hit his walking limit for the day and didn't care to hoof it back to the house. The ride was short compared to the normal grind of using trains and buses to get around, but it gave me just long enough time to sink into a tornado of thoughts around the suddenness of the void tears.

It had been a long time since a necromancer of this caliber was this crazy or ambitious enough to cause this type of stir in St. Athesall. The last time we'd had a void related fiasco had been almost sixty years ago when there'd been a literal horde of vampires roaming the streets. St. Athesall had been closed down, people trapped within a city sized arena with undead creatures trying to rip them apart, the government having to send in waves of armed zealots to try and quell the madness.

It had been the height of the Saint's Army's power, and it had kicked off what my family lovingly referred to as "the good ol' days." They'd stormed into the city like tyrants, murdered the undead like only holier-than-thou humans could, and made sure everyone knew about it.

Technically, they did save the city.

But they also hadn't been excited to give up the power they had obtained—this was the part I'd had to learn outside of Magnus's schooling. I'd been taught that the Saint's Army being disbanded was because of "bureaucratic bullshit," not because they were a little laissez-faire with the non-human casualties.

The likelihood that my old family would catch wind of these tears was as certain as the sun rising the next morning. They *would* find out, and I wasn't thrilled at the idea of them crawling into my city in the hopes of getting involved.

Although, if I was being honest, having their skill set tracking this fucker would be amazing.

You know, if they didn't fucking hate me.

I was lost in the idea of having to face Magnus's scowling mug and Austin's piercing disappointment when the car rolled to a stop. Sias was almost all the way out of the car by the time I blinked back to reality, and I was a few steps behind as we headed back into the house.

"You alright?" he asked as we went into the kitchen, gaze flicking in my direction as he began unbagging his expensive, cloth-wrapped box. "You're quiet, which is rare for you."

"Ha. Ha. The incubus has jokes." I swung the freezer door open and snagged the frozen mouse. The tiny corpse rattled inside as I gave it a little shake. "I was thinking I need to step up my game with this whole necromancy shit."

"What's really on your mind?" he tried again, seeing past the deflection. "You were scowling way too much for it to have been 'necromancy shit,' love."

"You've gotten mighty insightful and I kinda hate it." Feeling exposed, I rattled the mouse a bit more to give myself time to untangle the unease coiling in my chest. "You're familiar with the Saint's Army, yeah?"

He gave me a nod, pausing from his task of untying what I realized was patterned silk from around a lacquered box.

"With these tears happening all over the city, there's a good chance they're going to be showing up like a bad odor." My teeth biting at my lip did nothing to distract me from the soup in my belly going sour with nerves. "I kinda grew up there. At their compound, I mean. They're family, and we don't get along."

I rarely got to see Sias surprised, and if I hadn't been admitting that I grew up in a military household of radical, human zealots trained to seek and destroy the undead blight, I would have been delighted by his forehead wrinkles.

"You did?"

"Yep." I watched the mouse roll to the side of the container absently. "I did."

"Ah." He drummed on the lid of the box with his fingers. "When you say you don't 'get along…'"

"They'll probably try and kill me, and by proxy, you." I winced. "Depending on if we're in their way with these tears. They kinda know about my former powers in a very bad way."

"I see."

"I didn't want to have to pile on." I exhaled, not feeling lighter after airing out some of the skeletons in my closet. "But you should probably know about *all* the factors trying to murder us, not just the void tears and gangs I've pissed off. Sorry, my family is…complicated, and you're roped into it since we're…uh…" I floundered, trying and failing to conjure the term for whatever the hell we were.

"I don't care what they think of me, love." Sias saved me from my torment, sliding the lid of the dark wooden box open. "And I hope you won't take it personally if I react in kind if they threaten either of us."

"I'm hoping it won't come to that, so we'll see." I gave up on trying to get the mouse to flip as I watched Sias extract a few small, diamond shaped glass vials from the velvet lined box. Each one was topped with a crystal, the contents inside churned like drops of vibrant pigment in floating water.

Sias left his station and came to stand in front of me, a wash of tobacco and sandalwood coated me as his eyes swirled into a rosy color that made my toes curl.

"Don't worry about them. One threat at a time," he whispered, easing my nerves from a wildfire into a much more manageable simmer. I felt my shoulders relax, his charm magic a warm hug coating my body. His hand found a familiar perch on my lower back, the touch gentle, almost sweet. For a few, fleeting seconds, I almost didn't feel like the world was crushing me with one crisis after another, and that my heart wasn't split into pieces.

Just for a few seconds. It was lovely.

The rosy color in Sias's eyes sharpened into an orange, the charm dispelling like a candle being blown out by a blown kiss. I missed his hand when he carefully removed it.

"While you work on speaking with the dead, I'm going to go have another chat with our *house guest*."

He meant Reynolds, of course, which made my upper lip snarl.

"Tell him 'hi' for me, yeah? Maybe a few well-placed ones around his dick with some knives."

"I absolutely will." Sias kissed me beside my mouth and placed the vials he was holding into my palm. "Be a dear and give these to Barnaby since you're heading that way."

I saluted him with my mouse container and accepted the vials, making my retreat out of the kitchen to go track down Barns and his skull.

Out of all the spare bedrooms in the mansion, Barnaby had chosen one very close to my own. He insisted he did so because he didn't want to have to "constantly run around" when delivering Funus to my room, but I suspected he simply wanted to be nearby. I didn't press him on it, because I also didn't want to acknowledge that him being a few doors away made me feel comforted.

He was an annoying little shit who constantly fought me on everything, but he was *my* annoying little shit that constantly fought me on everything. We had a charming, sibling relationship that meant we'd also have each other's back and we looked out for one another, but it also meant we had to try and kill one another at least once a week.

So it wasn't out of the ordinary for me to knock on his half open door and waltz in announcing, "I've come for some head."

"That's still not funny." Barnaby didn't bother to look up from his book, which was propped in his lap while he lounged in his bed. Beside him on the nightstand was the head I was looking for, placed on his fluffy pillow with the electronic book tablet he read from. Since Funus was missing limbs to turn pages and didn't have lips to use a jabbing device to push buttons, we had a device made he could bite with his teeth to click the digital pages along.

Funus's orange eyes moved my direction, and he let the controller drop from his teeth to speak with me.

"Another round?" he asked, always excited to teach. I appreciated that he never seemed to hate the idea of teaching me, even though I was fucking terrible at the craft he had dedicated his life and afterlife to.

"We have some time to kill before Dex has the void locator done. Now's as good a time as any to get some mouse-o-mancy lessons in. Barns." I dangled the vials as he looked over. "Delivery from Sias."

"Oh, wonderful. I was feeling peckish." Barnaby closed his book and set it aside on his pillow, sliding off the bed to accept the vials.

"What are these?" I asked as Barnaby considered the color options placed in his hand, opting on a glittery tangerine vial while the others were set aside in a drawer.

"Concentrated intimacy energy vials," he explained, priming the top of the crystal with two quick turns. "They're similar to the sex crystals you'd trap your encounters in for me, but much better. Those crystals could only hold one encounter, these vials have dozens. Just a small drop fills me for two days."

"Damn. They look and sound expensive as hell." I watched as Barnaby pulled a dropper similar to perfume bottles out from the top. A swirl of magic clung to the tip, dropping like heavy mist onto his tongue as he held it out. His eyes flared the same color as the vial for a moment and he sighed happily.

"Ah. Delicious." Barnaby capped the bottle and twisted it shut, burping a little. "And to answer your question; yes. They are breathtakingly expensive for this level of concentration and verity. I told Sias he didn't need to shop for my meals in the same place he gets his, but he was rather insistent."

"He's really pushy about food." My attempt at commiserating with him backfired, as the fussy incubus turned on me. I got the full assault, complete with finger wagging and the furrowed brow of a disappointed grandfather.

"He's pushy because you haven't been taking care of yourself, Dallas Wilde. You're not eating properly and you've been exerting yourself too hard."

"You can't be on my side for two second, can you? It's physically impossible." I turned from my assailant and looked down at the skull watching from the sidelines. "Ready to go do some terrible necromancy?"

"Nothing worthwhile is ever brilliant from the start, Dallas," Funus chimed in with his version of a smile, which was a pleasant tone and bright eyes. "Each time you practice, you continue farther along on your journey."

"You are so delightful, Funus." I scooped him up and tucked him under my arm like a football. It always made Barns bristle, so I did it constantly. The battle between scolding me on my eating habits and correcting my handling of Funus flushed Barnaby's face to a cherry red.

He glared for a full breath, too annoyed to find anything else to say besides, "You are *impossible*."

I blew a kiss his way as we flounced out of his room, and he didn't even bother to catch it. So rude.

"At the risk of you rolling me down some stairs, I do have to point out that he's right," Funus whispered to me once we made it safely down the hallway. "You're working very hard on channeling your magic, which will drain your energy very quickly. Proper nutrition is important to maintaining your strength."

"Yeah? You're a dead guy and you do great. I don't see you chomping down some trail mix." I placed Funus on his pillow near my alter, and set the sealed mouse container onto the floor. Twig was sound asleep against Zane's ashes, her cheek pressed against the glass while her tail wrapped around the jar. I decided to let her sleep, so I just touched the lid to let Zane know I was home.

"That's a perk of being dead," Funus was telling me from his pillow. "I don't need to eat. But you're still very much alive, I'm afraid, so you'll need to continue the tradition of burning calories."

"The downside of being alive," I explained to the head on the floor as I gave Kevin some bloodworms. Sias had been spoiling him with some top-grade bloodworms that had extra minerals or some shit like that. I had insisted that Kevin liked the store brand best, but was proven wrong as soon as he had his first taste. I was pretty sure Kevin loved Sias more than me because of the new treats. "Is that you tend to feel like shit when someone you love dies. Kind of fucks up your drive to eat."

Kevin snatched a freeze-dried worm from the surface and gobbled it down, flipping his tail my direction. He totally agreed with me, because he was a true friend.

"I'm sorry to say, that doesn't go away after you die," Funus said remorsefully. "Grief transcends that barrier. Us grieving dead get to skip the physical ailments, but the heartache sticks around."

"Well, that sucks." I flopped down onto my pillow opposite of Funus. "Who did you lose? Is it okay if I ask?"

"I've been undead for two centuries, child." His eyes flared in a weak Funus style smile. He always sounded like a sweet, old grandpa when he called me "child," but this time it sounded as heavy as a gravestone. "I've lost everyone I've ever known. My grief will continue on after I am dust, but my memories of them keep them alive in my afterlife. It is my bittersweet solace."

"That's beautiful, Funus."

"I have my moments." Another weak flare of a smile. "Let us begin."

# CHAPTER
# FOUR

YOU SAID *you can always find me.*

*Find me now.*

The chill of the death magic coiling up from my altar raised the hair along my arms. The fleeting kiss of cold at my fingertips felt fragile, a breath away from vanishing back into the void. Tangled spider silk draped over my fingers, the threads barely there at all.

"Patience," Funus reminded me gently. "Gentle but persistent. This is not your realm, so you need to be invited in."

I wished there was an easier way to knock at death's door and get the results I wanted. There was the direct approach, which was me getting as close to physically dying as possible without actually crossing over, but that left me too vulnerable to do much else. Going to the void through a crappy death alter was much safer and at least kept me in control, but goddamn was it ineffective.

But hey, I guess it's better than dying.

My fingers curled slower than last time, allowing the death magic to sit comfortably with me without getting tugged too quickly. I forced myself to be still, to pull in slow breaths and hold them before attempting to move the threads a little bit more.

Icy trails moved over my skin like scurrying spiders, jumping from my fingers to my wrist before crawling up my arm. I moved at a glacial pace, one knuckle bending at a time, before my fist finally closed around the bundle of silky threads.

"Good," Funus whispered. "Very good. Ground yourself, acolyte. Keep yourself present in this moment."

The threads had never felt so tangible, so solid, or as *real* as they did in that moment. They had gone from silky threads to brittle hair, the weight bowing them down toward the floor.

I exhaled, lifting my eyelids enough to peer down at the mouse lying in the center of my ritual altar. It was still frozen in death, unmoving and unresponsive to the magic flowing around it.

*Find me now. Find me now, Zane. I'm here.*

I began to caress the threads with my fingers, feeling them slide across my palm. Gentle. Careful. The magic was holding firm with my movement.

A spark of cold—sudden and sharp—swam up my arm like a ghostly tendril. It was nothing like the Kraken grip I used to feel when the scythe was with me, but it was the most progress I had ever felt thus far.

My heart began to hammer, a thunder of promise beating in my chest as I tightened my grip around the magic resting in my palm.

The tendril snaked up further.

I saw my breath fog.

The mouse's foot twitched.

Then the threads began to break, one by one, as the tendril fell away like someone had snapped the window shut.

My chest froze, heart crumpling in on itself as everything began to slip away, falling apart just as I'd had the smallest hint of hope.

Not this time. Not again. I wasn't going to limp away.

I shut my eyes tight and pulled the collar of Zane's jacket

closer, dipping my chin to take in a full breath of grave flowers and ozone, of grief, and love, and loss.

If grief transcends death, maybe it could put in a good word for me. Maybe it could cross the floor and hold the door a little longer.

It hurt to hold his scent in my lungs, to remember how he had felt in my arms, how he pressed his forehead to mine and swore to me—*swore to me*—that he'd find me before he died. He had been my vampire. Mine.

And they took him away from me.

I had let them take him away from me.

"Dallas," Funus sounded worried. "Ease back. You need to calm yourself."

Cold rushed me, coiling up my arm like a serpent dragging its belly across my skin. The threads in my palm had thinned, but didn't melt away completely, solidifying into wire that bit down with purpose.

I breathed in deep again.

Zane's hair had been between my fingers, his lips pressed to mine, fangs grazing my tongue.

He had saved my life. He had found me in the dark. He had held me close and kept me safe and *I killed him.*

"Dallas!" Funus was far away when the room went dark.

My palm was burning from the angry threads slicing into my skin. The snake coiled around my arm bit down at the joint of my shoulder and punctured bone deep.

It knocked the breath out of me, which came out as a black cloud.

Wet thrashing on the floor knocked out a candle, the flame licking up away from the floor. The mouse was screaming, its tail pinwheeling, eyes red and wide.

The floor was opening.

A sea of black rippled under the screaming, undead mouse.

Someone was telling me to stop, but there was no turning back now.

I pulled the threads with all I had, and reached for the void to rip the door open wide.

The slap of the magic releasing me was violent enough to knock me backwards, and I cracked my back against the bed frame as the door to the void slammed shut.

I felt everything at once: the shock of the threads being gone, the rush of warmth bringing me back from the grip of death, the brightness of the room I found myself in once again.

And the searing pain in my mutated arm.

I had seen my body transform when I had played with death magic, seen my flesh melt away to reveal the charred, black bone of a void infused skeleton. This was nothing like before, nothing like when I had the power of a deity's weapon on my side.

My skin cracked like I was made of cooling stone, a rolling black cloud leaking from the gaps like my bones had been replaced with vapor.

"Shit!" I announced to the room. "Oh, *shit!*"

"Dallas, to me!" Funus was yelling. "Quickly!"

I crawled over to Funus, pulling Zane's jacket off me to see the extent of the damage. My entire arm from fingertips to shoulder was smoldering smoke, skin flaking away like ash and reforming into inky scales.

"Place your corrupted hand on me," he ordered, eyes flaring as bright as the sun. "Do it now, child, before it is too late."

I placed my hand on his skull, splaying my fingers out to wrap my grip around him. His bright eyes danced with light, rolling in amber flames as he spoke a language only known by the dead. The smoke roiling under my cracked skin began to bleed out, swirling across the floor before seeping between his teeth.

Orange flames darkened into a black cloud, his jaw opened wide to accept the corruption from my arm in one long, seemingly endless inhale. My skin knitted together where it had solidified and broke, the gray replaced by my normal flesh tone. By the time the tips of my fingers had their natural form back, Funus's eyes were nothing but black fog.

His jaw snapped shut and the smoke in his eye sockets faded into nothing.

The empty skull sat silent in front of me, cold and still.

I was nailed to the floor in horror, staring at the lifeless skull that had been coaching me just seconds ago.

There was nothing.

Just bone and grief.

"Funus?" I felt my heart stop, a cold so deep in my marrow I thought it was going to freeze me solid.

I reached out to touch him, to try and undo what I had done, my mind an endless vacuum of horror as I tried to imagine telling Barnaby that I had taken Funus away from him.

From all of us.

Funus's gasp made me scream in an octave I didn't think I could achieve, and I had a full fucking heart attack as the skull's eyes flared back to their bright orange once again.

"Goodness, that was a tough spell to conjure," he said through a breath. "Got a bit of a headache from that one, if you can believe it."

"Fucking Saint, man!" I grasped at the pain in my chest. "You scared the soul out of my body! I thought you were gone!"

"Well, technically I was for a second. I had to put that void piece back in place." He swiveled his eyes up to me. "That was incredibly reckless, Dallas. You almost got yourself turned into something horrible. That was a careless, rookie blunder that should have killed you—what are you doing?"

"I'm hugging you. I'm hugging the crap out of you." I fell backwards against the bed with Funus pinned to my chest. "That just took years off my life. Barnaby would have murdered me with that stupid penis cup he smuggled out of the store before it closed. What a way to go."

"Please," Funus snorted. "He'd kill you with the ivory fertility comb, not the phallic chalice. More practical that way. And I was serious about the blunder, Dallas."

"What the hell was that, exactly?" I gave my healed hand a

flex and angled Funus so he could see my face. "I've used death magic before and I went toasty skeleton, not smoky ash monster."

Funus's lack of eyebrows made it difficult for me to tell when he was frowning, but the tone of his voice held the dubious tone of a wise, old wizard.

"There is a difference between channeling necromancy and reaching into the void. What you did was swing the door open wider than you were ready for and reached into the void to try and take a short cut. The void reached out in response."

"It wasn't a short cut," I argued. "I thought I was making progress. I thought Zane's jacket could help me stay grounded."

The skull was flummoxed by my answer, and sputtered in a way that showed his ancient age.

"*Grounded*? You thought that was grounded?!"

"Well, no. Not now," I mumbled. "In hindsight, it maybe did the opposite. But hey, I got the mouse to move!"

"Dallas," he scolded. "I promised you that I would guide you. I will uphold my word, but you cannot do that again." His fiery gaze cooled, orange smolder melting down into a patient flame. "Barnaby would kill me too, you know. If something were to happen to you."

"I'm pretty sure he likes you more than me," I teased, but let the joke go when he dropped his eyes at my response. "Yeah, okay. That's fair. I don't want him to murder you either."

"Promise me," Funus pleaded gently. "That you will never reach into the void like that again. Not until you are ready."

"Promise," I lied.

"Thank you," he said around a long breath of relief. "I think that's enough practice for today, wouldn't you say? I'd love to rest a while and get the taste of void out of my mouth."

"What does that taste like? Also, how can you taste, exactly?" I set him aside as I picked up the mouse from the floor, the body thawed and disgustingly soft.

"Like cigarette ashes and spoiled meat," Funus answered like he wanted to spit. "I don't recommend it."

Twig was watching us from beside Zane's ashes, ears angled back to clearly show that she did not find our antics amusing.

I gave the mouse a little jiggle in her direction.

"What, it comes to life from manipulating life and death and suddenly you don't want it anymore? Picky, picky."

She went back to napping, and I decided I should probably get a new mouse corpse.

"I could go for a drink. Maybe three." I scooped up the head while still holding the soggy mouse and escorted them out of the room. "I wonder what Sias has stashed in his bar."

"I'd love a glass of wine myself. Too bad I lack the anatomy to enjoy it." Funus sighed, mourning the loss of such refined things as skin and taste buds. "But I suppose that is a small price to pay for immortality in the service to the Goddess."

"If you say so."

I decided to toss the mouse before returning Funus to his roommate, and dropped the damp rodent into the trash near the garage. The sound of broadcasters chatting away about ReNew pulled me in like a curious hornet ready to sting, and soon I was standing in Sias's media room next to Barnaby.

"What is this?" I asked as we entered, passing Funus over to him.

"Apparently Florence Pierce just announced a new wave of exclusive products that are said to aid in reversing aging." Barnaby accepted Funus and cradled him facing the monitor so he could watch as well. "Her stock price has shot through the roof."

"Of course it has," I said, or rather growled. I was pissed. The talking heads on the show flapped their gums about Florence's "revolutionary" product, which had launched only for diamond members of ReNew. Each tiny vial of the coveted serum had a price tag that was so outlandish, it was only known to the people who were privileged enough to afford it. This, of course, came out at the same time ReNew was launching a slew of other products available for the rest of the cretins, promising similar though less potent results.

Seeing a "mineral infused blouse," which was just a fucking ugly shirt with sparkly threads, selling for almost two hundred dollars because she promised it would help your heart beat longer made my blood boil.

And don't even get me started on the scented candles she was peddling that somehow smelled like "Immortality." Give me a break.

"She's using the scythe." I wasn't finished growling. "She's somehow using it to make these stupid ass products and getting richer from it."

"This is just what she's willing to let be public," Barnaby pointed out. "Who knows what other schemes she has in the works behind closed doors. What damage she's already caused in the medical field."

"I have to find where she's keeping that damn thing. She doesn't get to wring out more money while I stand here with a soggy mouse and no vampire."

"A what?" Barnaby asked, but I was already storming out of the room. "Is that a euphemism?"

My heart might be fractured into a million pieces, but it still had the capacity to thunder with rage. How dare that evil witch exploit *my* fucking scythe to make more money as well as keep Zane from me. I had to find where she was keeping it stashed, had to hunt it down so I could rip everything away from her like she had done to me.

I just needed a lead. A thread to follow. *Something* tangible.

The annoying thing was that Florence Pierce was smart. She wasn't going to leave an easy path to follow.

She'd make a mistake. She'd forget a detail. She'd make the wrong person mad, someone who'd be willing to betray her.

I'd find it and when I did, I was going to kick her ass.

I went searching for Sias, wanting to know if he was able to "extract" more information from our old pal Reynolds. My first stop was his bedroom, which was a giant space that housed all the fun goodies you'd expect a rich, deadly sexy incubus to have.

The whole suite was bigger than my previous apartment, complete with an orgy ready bed equipped with hidden compartments for all the toys, straps, oils and other assorted bells and whistles.

And probably literal bells and whistles, if that's what you were into.

I had spent many a night in that room, but I'd never woken up there the next morning. The "no sleep over" policy was law in Sias's home, and I knew better than to ask twice.

Striking out of the sex palace bedroom, I traveled further into the house than I usually did, passing a few vacant guest rooms, an extra shower room I didn't know existed, what looked like a wine storage room with a tasting bar, and ended up at a set of double doors which had one swung open wide.

It had been two months since I moved into Sias's place, and a good year and some change of visiting before then, and I'd had no damn idea that the man had a game room.

Scratch that.

It was a whole fucking arcade.

Billard tables—yes, plural—sat under hooded lights with stained glass shades, comfortably sharing floor space with a few pinball machines lining the wall. I strolled past an air hockey table ready for action only to find Sias Llon'nai, head of the Llon'nai tower, and stoic sex daddy of his lair, throwing a bowling ball with expert precision.

The sound of pins cascading down after a masterful strike filled the air, and he stepped back to glance up at the score displayed over the stripe of polished wood.

He only noticed I was standing behind him when he turned to retrieve the ball spat out by the machine near his seat.

"You *bowl*?" I erupted before he could speak. "For real?"

"Seems like a silly question to ask given we are standing in my bowling alley."

"You never once mentioned you bowl. I never even knew about this room until today." I did another slow spin to take everything in. "You have pinball machines. Darts. What the fuck, Sias?"

Sias didn't defend himself, nor did he even attempt to explain further. He simply presented an extra ball waiting on a rack and said, "Join me."

"So you can stomp me?" I eyed the score, and even not knowing a damn thing about the game, the amount of Xs on the screen seemed like a good thing. "I've never played before."

"I'll teach you." Sias tapped at the computer screen controlling the display, and the impressive score was wiped away. After a few more taps, our names were assigned some rows with a clear scoreboard.

"You knock the white things down, right?" I snorted, yanking the extra ball off the rack. "I think I can handle that."

"There's an art to it, like all things. Come." He waved me forward, instructing me to stand near the strip.

"If I had a dollar for how many times you've said that to me."

"And like those previous times, I promise you'll have the time of your life if you follow my instruction," the incubus purred, placing one hand on my lower back and the other along the fingers I was using to cradle the ball. "Will you be a good boy for me?"

"You know I won't," I teased back. "But you can teach me to throw some balls."

Sias hummed, a smirk tugging at his lips, his eyes a rosy shade.

"Take two steps, swing back and let the ball slide free of your grip. Don't throw it, slide it."

My hand was brought back as I moved, Sias guiding my underhanded toss in a mime before I tried it myself. The ball bounced from my first attempt, barreled down the strip like a drunk hedgehog before landing in the gutter.

"Yikes." I winced. "That one doesn't count. It was my first throw."

"Is that the rule?" he asked with mock surprise.

"Of course that's the rule. C'mon, man. That's like bowling 101. The first throw doesn't count if it sucks."

Sias slid his fingers into his ball and hefted it up, waiting as the pins reset.

I watched with interest the way his shirt stayed tucked into his slacks, even when he was throwing around the weighted ball down a wooden runway. There had to be some sort of charisma-based charm he had on that belt to keep everything in place, because it was unnatural how his strong shoulders and back could flex the way they did without his shirt popping loose.

The ease in his strength brought ghosts to my skin, faded memories of his touch. A wave of goose bumps lifted across my arms when he stood back to watch the pins fall, eyeing them with the same passive, pleased look he often had when he watched me obeying a command.

I hated the stranglehold sorrow had over my libido.

I hated how grief kept me distant, kept me from feeling anything other than a phantom of what my desires once were.

I hated how it was keeping me cold.

It also wasn't lost on me that there were two empty crystal vials sitting on the table next to Sias's jacket, meaning he had been starving all day.

And I had done nothing to help him.

I was momentarily consumed in feeling like an asshole when Sias's voice slapped me out of my depression daydream.

"How did the lesson go?"

"Fine." I busied myself with putting my fingers over the vent, the cool air calming my nerves. I wasn't quite ready to admit that I *might* have almost killed myself and Funus because I had lost control, so I piloted the conversation away from my less than satisfactory necromancy lesson. "I saw on the news that Florence has announced some new products aimed to help restore youth and some other bullshit."

"Oh?" He sounded bored, his attention on his throw. While my first throw was a meandering example of mediocrity, his was a lightning strike that knocked all the pins down in one swift movement.

"I think she's using the scythe to make this shit," I clarified. "The serum she made headlines with shot her stocks up. She's doing exactly what she said she would, which means she's going to be moving into the health field next. Did Reynolds give you anything else? Any clue where she might be hiding my scythe?"

Sias's brows creased in thought, eyes clouding with ocean waves periodically sliced by traces of yellow anger.

"Apparently Florence mentioned a 'new facility' to Hei while Reynolds was present, but they never elaborated on the details when he was around. It was implied that this place wasn't exactly known to her investors, and that its existence might ruffle some feathers."

"Yeah, I would imagine screwing around with ancient necromancy magic to make products would raise some eyebrows." I grabbed my ball once the machine spit it out and went back to the starting position. "I wonder if she's stupid enough to have this mysterious 'facility' within the city."

"She's too smart for that." Sias moved behind me, sliding his fingers over mine. The touch sent an electric trace over my skin, arcing from my hand over my shoulder and zigzagged down my spine. "Let the ball slip free, don't throw. One smooth motion. It will keep it from bouncing."

"I know she is, but damn that would make things convenient." I exhaled through the sparks dancing over me. "How do you keep it from sliding into the gutter?"

"Practice." Sias slowly pulled my arm back and guided me through a throw. Once he was satisfied I was moving correctly, he hummed deliciously and gave my arm a blissful squeeze. "Well done. Now you try."

He stepped back and let me try my first official throw, empowered and a little dizzy.

I knocked down a total of two pins.

"I'm going to be a master bowler in no time."

"Kegler," Sias said, grabbing his ball.

"Isn't that when you clench your—"

"No. It's not." He motioned for me to scoot aside. "Since we know Florence is likely holding the scythe in a recently built or acquired building, it will help us narrow our search. I can have public records pulled, and maybe your DHAP friends can do some investigating."

"My DHAP *connections* currently aren't working, so I don't know what they can provide in a professional capacity. It's still worth looping them in though." I watched Sias swing and slide the ball in one fluid motion, another bright X for his scorecard. "You're not even trying to go easy on me."

"You don't like me going easy on you." Sias strolled back to me. "You've made that very clear in the past."

"Touché. But for the record, I'm a real sore loser when it comes to things outside of fucking." I grabbed my ball. "I will pout."

"Noted. I'm still not going to hold back, darling. Now I just get to beat you and see you pout. I'm having a great night." He rotated his wrist to peer at his watch. "I'll help you get a strike, then we should head out to Dex. She'll be ready for us by then."

"You are mighty confident that I'm going to ace this within an hour." I held up my fingers to indicate my current score. "I have two down thus far."

"And you're about to get ten."

"So you say," I hedged. "You're going to feel really goofy when I flub this after sounding so cocky."

"And you are going to make an ass of yourself when it works." He moved me to the starting line, hands on my shoulders so he could center me.

"What got you into bowling?" I asked over my shoulder. "I can't imagine you hung out in bowling alleys a ton as a kid."

"I wasn't allowed outside of the boarding school until I was seventeen." Sias angled my shoulders. "Place your foot forward."

"Boarding school?" I complied with his instructions as I continued my questions. "Is that pretty common for incubi?"

"From my station, yes. I was a product of a breeding agree-ment between two established houses, and it was expected that I attend the academy during my formative years. Back straight." He pressed on my lower back. "You want the ball to go right down the middle."

"So, no skipping school and hanging out in arcades, huh?" I smirked back at him and he pushed my head back center. "No rebellious years? Smoking in the bathroom, cutting class, going against Mommy and Daddy's plan?"

"No. I kept my head down, graduated top of my class, used my wealth and influence to obtain an empire, and killed anyone who got in my way." My chin was lifted with his fingers, his chest brushing my shoulder. "Aim for the center pin. Keep your gaze straight."

"All of that tracks." I moved as he instructed, and inhaled when he told me to. "So, then how did you end up a master Kegel?"

"Kegler." Sias moved my elbow back. "Take two steps, inhale, and slide. Don't hesitate, and don't let the ball bounce." His breath slid over my cheek as he spoke, a wash of tobacco and amber kissed me as his hair moved. "Understood?"

I nodded, and he stepped back.

My feet moved, taking two full steps as my arm swung back, my grip releasing just as Sias sucker punched me from behind.

"My ex-wife got me into bowling."

"Your *what*?" I spun around, almost crashing to the floor as my foot slipped on the slick wood. Somewhere behind me, a collec-tion of pins exploded.

"You got a strike." Sias pointed to the board. "As I promised."

"You have a wife?" I almost slipped again as I stormed over. "Since fucking when?"

"Ex-wife," he repeated, way too calm. "I divorced her, and my other spouses when I left my harem ten years ago."

My entire world spun clockwise as my brain tried to unpack this info.

"You told me you hated harems."

"I do." His gaze was back on me, dark blue and trending teal. "I was in one for five years, and I was miserable."

"What happened?" I asked before I could filter it properly. "Shit. That's rude. It's none of my business."

Sias looked amused, a smirk teasing on his lips.

"One of the things that attracted me to you was your reluctance to talk about the past. I don't like revisiting my failures. I sure as hell don't want to share them." His teal eyes were clouding over with somber waves of aqua and soft gray. "Considering how much we've been through, and likely will go through, it seems a little juvenile that I keep sidestepping this conversation."

Obviously, Sias had a past before me. I knew better than to think for a second that the guy didn't have a trail of hearts behind him given he was at least a decade older than me, but I was always shit with guessing demon ages. I never in a million years would have guessed he was married, or part of a damn harem.

Mr. Nothing Complicated wouldn't even let me sleep over after a stretch of fucking like rabbits. Imagining him in domestic bliss sounded like a fan fiction I'd crafted after getting drunk on wine coolers while binging romantic comedies.

Sias was a stoic, stoney businessman with an insatiable appetite and a small collection of favorites he sometimes shared at parties. He was absolutely not a husband.

"You don't owe me your past," I said. "Even with all the shit we've been through, and will go through. I mean, we've got literal portals to death opening up around us and a crazed woman making trinkets out of ancient magic. We have plenty going on, but I'm never going to shake you down for your history, Sias."

"It's not a debt, it's a gift," he corrected. "Given freely."

My poor, fractured heart thumped around in my chest, bruised but thrilled to have a sting of happiness creep in.

"Okay," I hedged. "Then why did you leave? Why keep it a secret?"

"I expected too much." Sias watched the pins being reset, lost in a memory for a few blinks. Aqua clouded with gray grew dark with sapphire regret. "From myself and them. I wasn't enough to keep us strong and together, which was an impossible burden. When the cracks started to form early in the marriage, we didn't stand a chance. It was a house built on sand, and I limped away with pieces missing."

"I'm sorry." I felt uneasy standing in the silence that followed his confession, my hands itching to try and reach for him. "One person can't keep a family together. That's not really fair."

"No. But one is enough to shatter it," he whispered, and I felt those words like arrows in my chest. "We mortals are fickle, fragile creatures."

"Yeah." I rubbed at my aching arrow wounds. "Sorry I don't have cool powers to make you feel better like you do for me. But…" I trailed off, almost losing the steam to continue before I forced myself to push through the discomfort. "…thank you. For letting me know you a little more. For trusting me."

Sias's eyes washed into a lavender field, and I stood in the middle of it.

"Trust," he said softly. "I think we've earned a little of that."

It felt nice to take a full breath without feeling the pinch of loss, even for just a second.

"Yeah," I agreed. "I think so."

Sias had given me a piece of his trust. It was rare, precious and fragile, and it was placed in my grubby hands.

I wish I could say I held it with the care it deserved.

# CHAPTER
# FIVE

"HELL NO," I told Dex, refusing to budge. "No fucking way."

Dex rolled her eyes like *I* was being the unreasonable one.

"What do you think is going to happen, Wilde? It's going to give your phone a virus?"

"Best case scenario it gives my phone a virus," I argued, like a reasonable, not crazy person. "Worst case, I drop my phone and it causes a void tear to open up and eat me!"

Beside the grumpy oni popping bubble gum in my direction, sat a confused jinn woman wearing a beanie pulled over her long hair. The light from her silver eyes made her nose ring shine.

"Does he not know how apps work?" she whispered to Dex, not quiet enough to hide what she was saying.

"I know how apps work," I barked, lying through my teeth. "But Dex said she'd need to install a chip into my phone to go with it."

"It's no less safe than any of the other shit I've made for you in the past, dumbass." Dex snapped another bubble. "If you want to be able to find the tears in real time, you need the app and the chip."

"Fine." I whipped my phone from my pocket and slapped it

down into Dex's palm. "But if your app rips open a void tear, I'm coming back here to throw you into it."

"If my app causes a void tear, I'm going to be rich," the jinn woman said. "So, please let me know if that happens. I'll give you a cut for your beta testing."

I side-eyed Dex as she pried open the back of my phone and started stabbing around in its sensitive parts.

"Who are you again?" I asked the stranger while I watched my phone get mutilated.

"Kimi." She tucked her legs up into the office chair she was perched in and wrapped her arms around them. "You're the weird necromancer guy who like, makes fish dance or something, right?"

"I train them."

"To dance?"

"No," I shot back, then had to admit, "Yeah, sometimes, but that's not *all* I can teach them to do."

Kimi gave me a slow nod. "Cool."

"He's really sensitive about the fish stuff," Dex said while she continued to violate my phone.

"You're damn right I am. I take pride in my work."

Kimi tilted her head. "In fish aerobics?"

"Fish dancing! I mean training!"

Dex snorted a laugh and Kimi grinned with all of her teeth. I was being tag teamed by two nerds.

"Alright." I narrowed my eyes at Kimi. "I like you."

"Gross," Dex chimed in, holding my phone out. "I put a shortcut to Kimi's app on your phone. If you open it up, the app uses the tech I installed to ping for tears."

"No shit?" I took the phone back, angling the screen so I could see the new, non-negotiable app. The layout was very similar to a popular GPS app most people used to navigate around the city, with the exception of a drop-down menu, which allowed the user to check for open noodle places nearby. A little dot radiated a little wave every few seconds, and some digital numbers stagnated a reading of zeros above it.

"When it catches something, it'll give you a coordinate and a direction." Dex pointed at the numbers. "Pay attention to those. It should also give you a path to get there. Kimi has it programed to pull from WayMaps data for real time traffic and stuff."

"What's the range?" Sias asked, peering over my shoulder. "How close do we need to be for it to pick up a signal?"

"In theory, it should pick up anything within ten to fifteen miles."

"What do you mean 'In theory'?" I lifted my gaze from the app. "You don't know if this works?"

"This is the first time we've ever made anything like this, Wilde. We can't exactly beta test it safely," Dex parried. "Did you expect us to try and find a void tear?"

"I mean…yeah."

"This is fine, Dex. Thank you," Sias stepped in as Dex's oni magic started making her look a little threatening. Her fear magic made it seem like her tusks were curving out to stab me, her eyes fogging over with inky swirls of anger.

Her pissed off aura faded as Sias sent her payment through his non-death-magic-altered phone, and she tossed him a smile.

"Always a pleasure doing business with you. If you don't get any readings tonight but you hear back that there were tears, bring it back and we'll try and run some calibrations."

"Noted."

"I'm still coming back here if this eats my hand or something," I warned, but Dex had already swiveled her chair back to the tangle of tech she had been working on.

"Yeah, okay, bye," she said without looking up.

"Bye, fish guy." Kimi waved. "Have fun jazzercising your clients."

I thought about flipping her off, but decided to wave instead. I liked Kimi, even if her officemate was a grumpy bucket of butts.

And I was totally going to teach Kevin to jazzercise.

"Where should we start?" I mused as we walked out of the cyber-topia that was Dex's lab. The sun had been set for about an hour, the air cooling into a crisp reminder of spring's reluctance to let go of winter's hand. I pulled Zane's jacket closed and zipped it up while Sias buttoned his long coat beside me.

"I think the most logical step would be to case the areas we know tears have occurred." Sias nodded ahead. "Midtown will be swarming with DHAP officers. The Swallows would be better."

"Yeah, let's not run into cops while I have a phone loaded with illegal magic. They get especially snippy when it's death magic." I pocketed my phone and fell into step with him, trying to mentally tell the wind to stop biting at my ears. "You have those life magic blessed bullets for your ridiculous gun, right?"

"They're already loaded." He cut his eyes my direction. "It's killing you that you're not mocking it right now, isn't it?"

"It's so ugly, Sias! Why a gold gun? Are you an eccentric prince from an action movie? Are you color blind to gold specifically? Like, do you think the gun is gray somehow?"

Fog bellowed from Sias's lips as he chuckled, a velvety sound I very rarely had the pleasure to enjoy.

"I'm just saying," I continued, my own laugh shaking free to join the fun. "You have money to have really nice pieces and you got bamboozled into a slab of melted jewelry that fires bullets."

"It was a gift," he relented, eyes dancing into a minty color I'd never seen before.

"Someone gifted you a golden gun?" I jabbed, grinning so wide my cheeks were starting to hurt. "Who?"

"An old flame."

"Was he a war lord? A tomb raider? Did he find a lost sarcophagus and fashion a gun from it?"

Minty green turned into a stunning sea foam and the most magical thing happened. So magical, so unexpected, so unbelievable, that I stopped in my tracks to stare with unbridled amazement.

Sias fucking *blushed*.

"Oh my God," I exhaled.

"I am not loving how you're handling this."

"You're blushing. Are you…are you *embarrassed*?" When his eyes started to trend into an acid color, tinting angry, I surrendered. "Okay, okay! Not embarrassed. It's not that big a deal that you're *fucking blushing* right now."

"Are you done?"

"Yes. I'm done. I'm done." I chewed my lip to keep from grinning. "It was a war lord, wasn't it?"

Sias inhaled deeply and turned away from me, continuing the march toward the Swallows.

"Mob boss," he admitted when I trotted back over to his side.

"Like the *mob* mob? Like whack a guy and throw him over the bridge with bricks tied to his feet?"

"I was freshly divorced," he defended himself. "He was a rebound and a lack of better judgment." The acid splash to his vision cooled back to a hazel. "When we ended things, he gave me this gun because he said it reminded him of my horns. Sharp, beautiful and deadly."

"Aw. What kept you from being Mr. Mob Boss? Not into organized crime?"

"It was never meant to be serious," he reminded me. "When the passion started to wane, we parted ways. Simple as that."

I tucked my hands into Zane's jacket and curled it around myself, the cold especially biting with my heart caving in.

"Speaking of passion," I segued terribly. "I haven't seen Vix around."

I tried not to notice when his eyes shifted from his fun shades of embarrassed mint to somber blues.

"Vix left to join an exclusive harem about a month ago."

This took me by surprise, not because any harem wouldn't be blessed to have her, but because I didn't think she was scouting for one. She was a staple at all of Sias's parties, both the sexy kind and the casual ones. While she and I had never engaged in any bedroom antics together, I did adore her.

It broke my heart a little that she wasn't coming back.

"Seriously?" The wind was able to sneak under my collar and gave me a pinch. "Damn. I should have sent a gift or something. I didn't know."

"She sends her love." He gave a weak smile. "That's how these things go, darling. I'm very happy for her."

"Me too, but still…" I balled my hands in the pockets of the jacket and held on to my resolve, my chest doing nothing to warm me even though my heart was starting to pound. "I noticed the vials. In the arcade."

"What about them?"

My hands started to sweat, so I had to air them out in the biting cold.

"I know you're not eating well with Vix gone and me being uh…*distracted*."

"I eat fine," he answered cooly, but the icy current present just beneath the words made me shiver. "You don't need to fret about my sexual energy intake, Dallas."

I could feel he was annoyed, but my curiosity was too strong to change topics just yet.

"Are they as good as the real thing? Or is it like comparing ice cream to the freeze-dried crap?"

Sias's eyes flared into a shock of pink, a lightning strike of hunger before fading into calm seas.

"Nothing beats absorbing energy from your companion in real time as they writhe in pleasure, darling. The vials are a good stop-gap, and I pay for the purest essence available, but they do pale in comparison to the exquisite taste of the real, raw thing."

The combination of my anxieties and his colorful explanation had caused me to start fidgeting, and I about wore out the cuff of Zane's jacket.

"Do you have a favorite flavor? They come in flavors, right? I saw the colors," I rambled, like a nervous idiot.

Sias exhaled through his nose, a bull lazily announcing his frustration.

"No. They're all…fine. Bland. There's a reason I call you, Vix and Bastian my favorites. I'm rather picky."

I'm a fucking dumbass.

"Right. That makes sense. Can you live off those? I mean, I know Barnaby does, but he doesn't like sex. He just needs a drop and he's set for days."

I knew better than to have asked, but I was the reigning champ of asking stupid questions I didn't want the honest answer to.

"I can make do for a while, but I'll need something more tangible soon."

Guilt was a sharp, evil thing when it wedged itself under the ribs like his words did.

I didn't know if I had it in me to carry the burden of letting both of the men I had feelings for down so spectacularly.

Zane's death had been so sudden and shattering, I hadn't realized the small, quiet one happening between Sias and me. How long would it be before I was handing over a trinket so he didn't forget me?

"I'm sorry," I finally admitted, chest on fire from the acidic slashes to my heart. "You've been helping us so much and I've been such an asshole about everything."

"What?" More annoyance, a touch of anger.

I was somehow making it worse.

"I'm just—fuck. I'm so bad at this. I'm sorry, Sias, for not being available. The least I could do is fuck you for helping us like you have, and I've shut all that down."

My elbow was caught in Sias's grip, our progress into the Swallows halted. The sting of my anxieties transformed into an itchy scrape along my hairline and down my neck, and I rubbed at my old scars to keep the sensation from spidering out into something painful. I was busy glaring at a crack in the cement, envious of the stony surface and its resolve against the assault it was able to bare.

"Dallas."

I forced my eyes up. Yellow, I thought. Yellow and orange

would be nice to see. Goddamn him if they're blue, because his pity would hurt more than anything in that moment.

I wasn't sure what to do with his emerald gaze.

"I need you listen to me very carefully." He was speaking with a calm firmness I would have melted for in bed. I held my breath in anticipation, my heart thundered, and my mind started falling into the static numbness that I reserved for when I needed to get ready to file it away into my "this is too fucked up to remember for a while" vault.

That vault sucked, by the way. It often got leaky and made for shitty nightmares.

Emerald peered into my eyes, gold flecks rimmed the center, framed by brows falling into a creased furrow.

"You don't owe me sex," he told me quietly, fingers warm against Zane's leather. "Not now. Not ever. I'm helping you because I want to, not because I expect anything in return."

The static around my brain was getting slippery, the input not what I was expecting. I was starting to see little dots floating around the edges of my vision, and I quickly exhaled the first thing I could think of.

"Are you sure?"

"Yes." His brows deepened their crease. "I'm sure."

"What about the…something tangible?"

When did I forget how to speak?

I continued, unable to stop my rambling.

"I don't want you to starve, and I like sex with you. A lot. It's one of my favorite things. It's just hard for me to get in the mood because of how shitty I feel, and I can't even really get my own engine going, if you know what I mean. Why am I telling you this? I'm just kidding about that last part. That was a lie. Everything works great! Haha! Oh my fucking God, can you just toss me into traffic, please?"

Sias inhaled slowly and put a finger to my lips, commanding me to stop talking, bless him.

"I want you at your best," he told me. "I won't accept anything less than perfection. You're mourning. You're hurting. That won't do. Until we can remedy this, I won't take even a sip. Do you understand me?"

The lumpy mess that had once been heart shaped had been thrown around in my ribs like a rattling marble, but now it settled into a little nest of hesitant comfort. The static fog had cleared, and in its place, I felt a horrible feeling of vulnerability I didn't care for. Sias had peeled away layers of callous armor and given my soul a little squeeze.

"Sounds like a lot of trouble for something to eat." I had been going for teasing, but my throat was a little too tight.

"Like I said," he said with a grin and a blooming rose in an emerald field. "I'm very picky."

I was right in the middle of swooning when my phone interrupted everything.

The buzz in my pocket hummed in a pattern I wasn't familiar with and I fished it out to check the notification screen. A little bubble had surfaced to the top, announcing that the app had located a tear nearby.

"We got one." I unlocked the screen and tapped on the notification, summoning the app to life. An unnecessarily cartoonish grim reaper was pointing ahead in the direction the tear was being pinged, a soft ripple floating out to indicate how strong of a presence it was radiating.

"I hope this means it's small," I mumbled, showing Sias the screen.

"Let's hope so." He followed me as I pursued the animated grim reaper in the direction of the void tear. "What's the plan when we find it?"

"I want to see it before we seal it." I tossed him a quick glance, hoping he couldn't read my excitement. "I want to see if I can learn anything about what's causing it before we shut it down."

Sias gave a nod, his eyes washing over with lilacs touched by orange flame. He was ready for a fight, steeling himself for something awful.

I was practically giddy.

A real tear, a peek into the void that wasn't reliant on me holding it open, was a damn good shot at trying to yank a dead vampire back into existence.

Or at least to try and see if he could hear me.

He should be able to find me. He promised he could.

*You better be listening for me, asshole.*

The ping from the app intensified as we drew closer, the happy reaper dancing near a stretch of apartments.

"Fuck," I hissed, worry seeping its way into my good time. Why the hell did this tear have to pick a populated area to make its appearance? A damn apartment complex? With grandmas and kids?

Diabolical. And really inconvenient for me.

We followed the ping around the aged brick building, windowsills spilling over with potted plants and wind chimes. A bike with pink tassels was dropped near a front door with a faded number, the tire looked a little flat. Their neighbor had a doormat that said, "wipe your paws." Through a cracked window, we could hear someone yelling that dinner was ready, and commanding everyone to wash their hands.

The tear was a blight hovering near a small sandpit in the shape of a turtle, black veins growing out to touch the discarded sandcastle buckets.

It looked like a nightmare had punched through into the waking world, scarring reality with a gash of emptiness. The darkness within the rip made me dizzy as I stared at it, a bone deep fear stopping me from inching too close. Even the weeds peeking out from under the concrete seemed to lean away from its presence.

It was only about six inches long: a slanted, vertical strike oozing black vapor like evil dry ice with veins crawling in multiple directions like a fungus.

"Whatever you want to learn from this thing, do it quickly," Sias warned, glancing at the apartment building that was too close for comfort. "I don't want anyone getting swallowed by this thing like they did at Marthas's club."

I had to force myself to travel closer, my feet practically glued down from the primal fear I had of the floating doorway to death. Knots of hesitation formed in my gut, my heart crawling its way through my throat. The life essence in my pocket warmed my thigh as I drew closer, reacting strongly to the pulsing death. The only silver lining to losing my necromancy powers was that I could hold the thing without bursting into cinders, and I was damn thankful to have it with me then.

In hindsight, I should have known better than to have felt relieved.

And I should have brought way more fucking weapons.

I inched over to the monstrous affront to the realm of the living, the scars on my neck itching from the presence of the Goddess, and stared into the abyss.

Cold recognition split me down the middle as I peered into the void, or more importantly, the way the void was peeking through. I had seen a tear like that before.

I had *caused* a tear like that before.

This was caused by my scythe.

I remembered the way the tree had split when the blade had crashed into it, the way the void looked staring back at me through the hole. The slash was the same, but somehow much, much angrier than before.

How was this happening and why?

But more importantly, at least to me, if this was made with my scythe, was it just a window or a true door into the void?

I had no choice. I had to knock and see.

I forced myself to exhale, my lungs shaking from how hard my heart was beating. My vision blurred as I stared down the darkness.

*You said you could always find me.*

My fingers were trembling as I lifted my hand.

"Dallas," Sias warned from behind me as I stepped closer to the tear. "It looks like it's growing."

*You* promised *you'd always find me.*

"Dallas!"

I whispered to him, through the gateway between realms, into death and darkness and nothingness:

"Find me now."

The invitation was sent. Signed and sealed with intent and loss.

I just wished it had landed in the correct vampire's hands.

# CHAPTER
# SIX

I MAY HAVE FUCKED UP.

My attempt to get a message to Zane through the void tear wasn't my best idea, but it wasn't the worst by far. Did it knock on the door to otherworldly evils and invite them in?

Sure.

Was it likely going to kill me?

Maybe.

Peeking into the void and trying to pass a note was at least romantic.

After I whispered into the void, I got an answer back.

The tear pulsed like an angry wound, the gash crawling up and out like a spiderweb of darkness. Cold, unforgiving death magic frosted the air, freezing my breath into plumes of black fog as I scrambled backwards. Everything living near the void that wasn't able to crawl away withered into dust, weeds fell in on themselves and little ants evaporated into smoke. The sand in the plastic turtle sizzled and blackened into glass and splintered out in awful directions.

The terrible pull of the void was too uncomfortable to ignore, and terrified occupants had started leaning out of windows and doors to see what the hell was happening.

"What is that?" a human dad demanded from the "wipe your paws" door, a little girl peeking out from behind his leg.

"Inside! All of you inside!" I screamed. "It's death magic!"

"I believe I was to tell you when I changed my mind about my concern levels," Sias hissed through his teeth, the fear in his voice snapping my attention back to the tear. "I've officially changed my mind. I'm very concerned."

I saw the form stepping through, a humanoid shape made of black smoke, dipping down to duck through the widening tear marring the surroundings.

My heart stopped.

For a few, fleeting, beautiful moments, I felt like I was floating in a daydream come true.

Red eyes opened, glowing orbs of blood magic, aiming right at me.

"Zane?" I pleaded, desperate.

"Darling, that's not Zane," Sias answered in a rush, curling his fist into my jacket to yank me back into place beside him.

I wasn't ready to believe him. I was ready to run headfirst into that smoky body and hug him with everything I had.

Imagine my heartbreak when another set of red eyes opened below the first pair.

Then another.

And another.

They floated and rearranged as the body expanded, its back splintering into spider legs with webbing between them. What had been human-like hands sharpened into brutal claws, solidifying into obsidian razers. The thing straightened its spine and opened its mouth, which ran the length of its torso with endless teeth and hunger.

It wasn't Zane. It was something I'd never seen before—a void creature unlike any vampire I'd ever faced.

And worse yet—yeah, worse than the vertical mouth, spider wings and too many eyes—was the magic tangled up inside of it.

Death magic was a given, the cold, ever present aura of the

void haloed around it like a living nightmare. It was the crippling fear magic swirling with the luring charm attraction that threw me for a fucking loop.

Beyond the halo of black magic surrounding the creature, thin threads of glittering malice draped out and attached themselves to the occupants standing outside, almost invisible but just present enough to catch the shine of fear in their eyes.

"This is bad," I breathed in a rush, my magic blocker struggling against the complicated tapestry of conflicting magic pouring off the damn thing.

"It's manifesting heart strings," Sias growled, slipping his jacket off and tossing it over the kid's bike for safe keeping. We were right in the middle of a crisis, but I was momentarily distracted by how he rolled up his sleeves. "That's charm magic, Dallas. Physical embodiment of charm magic corrupted with fear."

"This is *real* bad," I corrected.

I hadn't even seen the little girl running toward the creature, pulled in by the charm magic like flies to a spider.

Sias scooped her up and caught her father as he tried meandering past, giving the man a quick, sobering slap to break the spell. I saw the thread melt away the moment he snapped back to reality.

"Get inside," Sias told him, passing the daughter over. "Now. Don't look back."

I saw others either buckling from the weight of their fear, or drifting over to offer themselves up for slaughter. The creature spread its leathery, webbed wings and howled into the night, a horrible, ear-splitting sound that made my knees weak for a heartbeat.

My neck scars itched.

The teeth in the creature's belly brought back horrible memories of the dark, of blood, of pain and agony.

It was a vampire. It was twisted and mutated into a new form, but a vampire nonetheless.

And I was a pro at killing those fuckers.

"Run interference with the locals," I yelled back at Sias, pulling out the sword I had strapped to my back under Zane's jacket. "Keep them away from it!"

Sias was already in motion, grabbing people and ripping them away from the vampire as they tried to crawl their way toward it. The magic essence in my pocket shone with brilliant light as I ran it over the blade of my sword, blessing it with the power to do some real damage to the undead.

I ignored the sting I felt from my pathetic necromancy powers trying to grow from my practice sessions with Funus, the darkness in me so fragile and benign that I was likely going to have to start all the way back over after handling this much life magic.

I didn't care.

I couldn't let this thing live, even if it meant setting my chances of seeing Zane again back a few months. This was my fault, and I was prepared to pay the price.

The vampire was eager to gobble up its prey, and was very frustrated when an incubus kept getting in its way. It charged, wings flapping to make it airborne for a few feet of movement. I flanked to the side as it drew closer, dodging an outstretched claw to clip one of its clawed, back limbs.

The life enchanted blade cut through it with a smoky hiss, lobbing off a spiked tip. An awful screech ripped from the beast as it turned its attention in my direction, all sets of red eyes on me. Pulses of icy silver rippled through the strings draped over the innocent bystanders, compelling them to draw in closer. A long, dexterous tongue lolled from the thing's vertical mouth, slashing at me with a starving fury, the scales lining it slicing a new hole in Zane's jacket sleeve.

"Easy, fuck face!" I tugged on the sleeve to see the damage, anger lining my vision. "This is borrowed!"

Fuck Face responded by anchoring itself backward on its creepy, spider wing things and opened its nightmare mouth wider, its black heart visible behind its lashing tongue. It reached out one of its clawed hands, wrapping its spindly fingers around a thread and pulled tight, summoning a helpless person too afraid to do much more than scream in terror.

A series of golden bullets pierced through its hand in a tight cluster, the life magic punching through its palm with the same smoky sizzle as my blade. The monster roared and flexed its wounded hand, and Sias kept his ridiculous gun trained on the beast as he shoved a wailing victim behind him.

"Cut the threads!" he commanded me. "Get them loose!"

I guess I couldn't make fun of his stupid gun anymore. It worked great, and he was a surprisingly good shot. The guy could bowl *and* shoot?

My, my, I was learning a lot about Sias today.

The threads tying the victims to the beast fell away with a few slices of my sword, the spell crippling them broken, but the panic kept a few of them from moving too fast.

I didn't have time to shake them free of their fear because the vampire decided that Sias was his next target. It spun with the agility of a spider, wielding its spiked legs with terrifying precision. Its legs plucked at the ground, shards of concentrated death magic spiking out from each impact as it lapped the air with its scaly tongue.

Sias fired a few more shots at the thing, nailing it across the chest and neck, and even though his enchanted bullets punched deep, they didn't slow it down. It hissed and widened its mouth, bones cracking to shove the ribs from its torso out of the way.

It made a horrible sound, a warbled echo of stolen screams torn from the void, and Sias snarled his lip in challenge. The flare of the vampire's eyes reflected in Sias's horns, soaking them in crimson.

Sias answered the flare with his own, his gaze fire laced fury as he discharged his clip and reloaded.

He wasn't afraid.

He was pissed.

He was going to go out fighting, shooting his stupid, golden gun instead of running for safety.

I swooned a little bit. Just a little.

Like a totally normal amount.

I moved before I could think better of it, throwing myself into a controlled slide between the spider-wing tips to slash my sword upward. The blade connected in the joint of one of its wings, knocking it sideways with the sudden drop of balance.

Sias took the opening and fired a few more rounds into the vampire's side, striking where kidneys would be and causing a howl to rip from the thing.

My maneuver worked great, and was totally badass, but I misjudged how fast it could use its other hand, the one not riddled with bullets.

The collision was brutal and fast, and I was met with the knuckles of a nightmare vampire's backhand before bouncing off the apartment building's wall. My vision splintered in a spiral, ears whining with the effort my brain made trying to stay conscious.

I heard Sias scream before my body was knocked back into the brick, caged in by claws as the vampire loomed over me. My sword clattered to the ground from the impact to my arm, the back of my head screaming in pain as it was knocked back into the building.

A blast of hot rot swallowed me as the creature opened its mouth, tongue slashing out to whip at my head. It caught me on the temple, grinding needle sharp scales across my skin. Blood trailed down my cheek, and I saw the vampire's eyes glow with hunger.

Sias's gunshots bit into the vampire's neck and cheek, life magic ripping away at its form but not doing enough damage to slow it down. The vampire was too focused on murdering me to feel its injuries, which I admit I was flattered by.

It's not every day a spawn of the void takes an interest, am I right, fellas?

Through the impossible number of teeth lining its mouth, I saw the swell of its beating heart tucked into the throat, the endless tongue swallowing down into the depths, and the emptiness beyond.

It was *not* how I wanted to go. It looked really icky in there.

But with my body pinned, my arm fractured, my head swimming, and no way for me to wiggle free, I was pretty sure it was out of my hands.

I wasn't even going to leave a pretty corpse for Sias to bury.

"Alright, ugly," I sneered at the vampire. "I'm going to give you heartburn from hell."

Its smoky lips peeled back from its teeth, bones shifting and cracking as it opened up wide to take a chomp out of its Dallas flavored snack.

Then hell froze over.

Gunshots rang out from my left, three piercing blows hit the vampire through its eyes causing it to rear back and throw me in pain. It wasn't my finest exit from a situation, the landing was rough, but I was able to scramble away before it could slam its massive claw back down where I had been.

Sias pulled me up from where I had landed, getting me to my feet.

"You saved my ass," I told him, breathless. "I thought I was vampire food for sure."

"I wish I could say that was me." Sias was panting like he had run a marathon. "It was them."

Our foe was flanked by three people in protective gear, firing semi-auto weapons loaded with blessed bullets punching holes through its torso. The Saint's Army logo reflected the streetlights in silver, and I felt my stomach go cold. Born from the necessity of fighting the undead and handling insane necromancers centuries ago, the Saint's Army was made up of exclusively human zealots who worshiped the Goddess's opposite, the Saint of Life. The Saint's Army used to be revered as saviors, swords of light used to banish evil. These days they're made up of misfits and orphans scooped up to serve as vampire fodder by homegrown militia ready to prove something.

"Immobilize it!" Austin was commanding the team, his voice rising over the chaos. "Paris, Worth, get the grounding charms around it now! Get it away from the tear! Beaumont, Haslet, get these civilians out of here!"

"I need to get to the tear," I told Sias quickly. "I need to get this life magic into it to seal it before it gets wider. Do you still have bullets?" I paused while he checked his clip, nodding that he was fine. "Go get more people out. Let them focus on the vampire."

Sias gave me a nod of understanding, but caught me with a clenched fist around Zane's jacket.

"Don't do anything stupid, Dallas," he told me, eyes flaring with emeralds rimmed in fire. "I will be very pissed off if you get yourself killed."

"Aw. You're cute when you're threatening me to stay alive." That wasn't enough to convince him to release me, so I added, "I won't do anything stupid. Promise."

His fingers uncurled. "You lie so easily."

I didn't confirm nor deny that I had been lying. I figured my actions would speak for themselves.

My former family had taken some nice chunks out of the feral vampire, but nothing seemed to be strong enough to take the fucker down completely. Both of its clawed hands were ripped through the middle, yet somehow functioned enough to slash out with purpose. Paris got a nasty graze across her back, her armor coming off in ribbons. Haslet got a slap with the scaly tongue, his leg bloody and torn.

The damn thing was using its body to block the tear, always retreating back after attacking so we couldn't simply toss something damaging inside of it. Each attempt one of the soldiers made to lob a piece of life magic into it was thwarted by the monster simply knocking it away or taking the hit itself.

It was buying time, but for what?

I snatched up my sword, my arm screaming in pain as I made my way over to the man in charge.

"Tell me you brought a life blessed grenade or something." I slashed through some threads as they tried to snake their way up my leg. "Something tells me that tear is about to get really nasty."

Austin glanced over his shoulder to snarl before snapping his attention back on the charms being placed around the vampire.

"Fuck off, Wilde. Stay out of the way."

"I can get around this thing if you get those charges set." I wiped blood from my temple. "But I just have a sliver of raw essence."

"I'm not giving you my bomb." He shouldered his rifle and took a few more shots to give Worth time to slide some charges in place. "You want to be useful? Help get the area clear."

"Your team is in pieces, Austin." I caught his arm and tugged him backward. "Stop being an idiot and let me help!"

Austin wheeled on me, nostrils flaring and sweat slicking his brow. He grabbed my collar and wrung it tight, bringing us close enough that had he not been like a brother to me, I thought we were gonna kiss.

"For all I know, this is one of *your* vampires," he spat, both figuratively and literally a little on my cheek.

"I like them with less teeth." I wiped my cheek. "Also, you saw it try to kill me. It's not one of mine."

"I don't trust you." He shoved me backwards so hard I almost fell on my ass. "Now get out of my way, or I'll put you down."

I showed my palms in surrender, and he went back to commanding his team I was clearly not part of.

I had been expecting something to that effect, but it still stung like a son of a bitch.

Alright.

Plan B: Wait until the monster was grounded, then throw the life magic grenade I stole off Austin while he was being a Grumpy Gus into the tear.

Easy peasy.

Austin set off a line of grounding charms under the vampire's spider legs, freezing it in place and forcing it down onto its belly. While the beast wasn't able to chase after anyone, it still had a tongue with insane reach, and the baffling ability to throw out corrupted heart strings like spider silk.

With its legs pinned and body starting to look a lot like Swiss cheese, the vampire got desperate.

Black veins had grown from the tear like a cancer, ignoring the natural laws to branch out in directions that didn't make sense. Some of them ran along the ground like gravity had pulled them down, others shot for the sky, attached to nothing but air and negative space. The void inside churned like a hurricane, and the threads spilling from the vampire thickened into rope.

Whatever fleeting hold they had on their victims solidified, and one unlucky bastard was too close to be saved.

The vampire froze its prey with charm so powerful, the man was cheering with glee as he was tossed into the gaping maw of the void creature, gobbled up like an after-dinner mint. Not one drop of the man was wasted, and the monster was rewarded with a renewed wave of energy from the fresh blood.

It rose up, crashing the hold the grounding charms had over it, and decided it was going to take out its frustration on everyone involved.

Great.

The ugly bastard was extremely pissed off at the scurrying humans trying to upset its dinner, which gave me a chance to rush its home base. The tear was festering when I finally closed the gap, the black fungus spreading from it starting to take a life of its own. Death magic spilled from all directions, the nothingness inside churning with a tornado of mutated bio-magic.

A wave of emotion trickled through my blocker, a tug of doubt whispering that I was making a mistake. I knew it was artificial, a trick of the magic cocktail fermenting inside of the void, but it made me pause for just a heartbeat.

Only a breath.

And its claws were in me.

*Hunter.*

His voice was so quiet, so gentle over the chaos surrounding me, that I almost thought I'd imagined it.

My fingers had started to pull the pin at the top of the grenade, hooked and ready to yank and toss right into the center of the madness. Behind me, a vampire was hissing and bellowing noises of nightmares and horror. In front of me, a different vampire was whispering in the dark.

My vampire.

*Hunter.*

"Zane." I wrung my eyes shut and steadied my grip, trying to shake his voice from my head.

*Hunter.*

Icy fingers grabbed at my chest, twisting my heart into pieces. I knew it was fake.

Of course it was fake.

Zane wasn't there. I knew he wasn't there.

"Zane?" I called out, hating myself for it.

The silence that followed crushed me, drowning me in a wave of sorrow so profound I thought I was going to fall into myself like a dying star.

I could reach him. I could get him. I just needed to get closer, to call for him, reach my hand into the void and—

"Fall back!"

The panic in Austin's voice was a beacon through the fog, and I snapped back to reality just as my hand neared the icy grip of the tear. His scream pulled me around, hot stones lining my gut as I witnessed the vampire get the upper hand.

The heart strings had grown barbs, wrapping themselves around the legs of Paris and Worth, and was dragging them screaming to the hungry maw of teeth.

Gunfire was coming in shorter bursts, life magic peppering the beast but doing little to quell its efforts. They were running out of ammo, their blades unable to cut through the sharp threads biting into their comrades' limbs.

I saw a flash of gold from two beautiful horns, a flurry of long hair, and Sias fired a few rounds directly into the vampire's mouth. His slick, polished shoe clamped down on the thread holding on to Paris, and he tried to stop the momentum of the pull by grinding down as he fired.

He was bleeding from his hairline, a streak of crimson painted the left side of his face. A bloom of red was over his chest, the fabric torn from where a claw or scaly lick had caught him.

His eyes were molten rubies of defiance as one of the threads wrapped around his neck. They didn't waver when he was brought to his knees.

Sias was going to die.

I was watching him die.

"No!"

I tried to spin away from the tear, but my arm was tangled in a mess of black veins growing from the void tear. The fabric of Zane's jacket melted into the touch, adhering to the sharp grip of malignant death magic. The void wouldn't budge as I shook my arm with everything I had, leaning my weight against its hold. The fabric stretched, the hem popped from my abuse.

"Let go of my fucking jacket, you ugly shit!"

I chanced a glance back, my heart wedged between ribs as Austin whipped his sword free and rammed it into the vampire's side.

A feral roar sounded from the beast, backhanding Austin with such force that his body landed limp across the hood of a nearby car. The threads attached to its victims tugged, bodies thrashing like fish on the line.

The creature turned, its mouth wide and starving, and I watched helpless as Sias got dragged inside.

Gold and defiant red.

Disappearing into the mouth of a vampire.

# CHAPTER SEVEN

I LET the void keep the jacket.

The fabric peeled away from my body as I slipped my arms free, abandoning the last piece I had of grave roses and rain. I couldn't think about that.

My body stormed over the pavement; limbs numb with white hot anger as I charged for the beast. All thought had left me, all reason and caution had been swallowed up when I lost sight of Sias.

All I knew in that moment was that I was going to kill that thing. I was going to strap myself to it and we were going to ride to the void together. I'd bring its ass directly to the Goddess and hand deliver its smoldering corpse to her feet.

Worth and Beaumont were doing all they could to drive the beast backwards, to slow its consumption of their friends, or at least wound the fucker in some way. Haslet and Paris were just a foot away from its mouth, grasping at anything they could to keep their limbs from touching the vampire's teeth. The corrupted heart strings were wearing down their resolve, bleeding through to charm them enough to give in to their fate.

Austin's sword was still sticking out of it like a meat thermometer, squishing around in its ghastly flesh. Since my sword had been slapped out of my grip a while back, I helped myself to his. I figured since he was very unconscious and I was probably about to die, he wouldn't mind.

The vampire wheeled on me when I ripped it free, its mouth cracking bone to open wide. The stench of death and blood hit me like an open oven, teeth lined with the torn fabric and skin of the victims it had swallowed.

Its thumping heart mocked me from its throat, a scaly tongue lined with razers thrashed out to meet me.

And I saw a flash of gold.

My heart stopped when I saw that stupid gun.

Sias had tied a barbed thread around the vampire's pounding heart, anchoring himself against the muscles trying to swallow him. Wild hues of burning amber and ivory flashed in his eyes as he pressed his golden pistol to the vampire's heart and fired twice.

The vampire jerked violently, a wet scream erupting from within. Black ichor flooded its maw, the tongue curling back in on itself to try and fish Sias out.

That was my cue.

I dove into the vampire's mouth and shoved my blade through the tongue, pinning it down against the bottom of the vertical jaw. Pain grazed my calf as teeth caught me, but I pushed my weight down into the blade to make sure it successfully kabobbed the damn thing.

The body thrashed, almost knocking me sideways into more teeth.

"Sias!" I reached for him, using the hilt of the sword to keep me stable. "I don't want to be in here in case this fucker has a sensitive gag reflex!"

"Has anyone ever told you," Sias huffed as he flung himself forward, grasping my outstretched hand. "That you crack jokes at very inappropriate times?"

"It's cute, right?" I pulled Sias free from the vampire's gullet, catching him before another thrash could throw him into its teeth. "Jump clear. I've got an idea."

His eyes widened, the arm hooked around my shoulders was covered in the mess oozing from the wounded heart. My fingers were starting to slip from the sword hilt, too wet with gore.

"This sounds like the type of very stupid ideas I warned you against, Dallas."

"Be mad at me afterward." I shoved him toward the front of the mouth as the creature's tongue bucked against my blade. The threads spreading out from inside its core began to melt away, releasing Paris and Haslet just as their feet crossed the threshold. Haslet's leg was cut bad, and he was screaming as the thread finally dropped its hold. Sias staggered out of the mouth and hefted Paris up onto her feet, Worth and Beaumont rushing to Haslet's side.

The two holes in the vampire's heart were starting to heal from the blood Haslet left behind on its teeth, the flesh stitching back together over the wounds.

This thing was never going to die unless we hit it with everything we had.

I hissed as my leg met a wall of fangs, ripping my jeans and biting into my flesh. My hand shook from the effort of holding the sword still, and I used my teeth to pull the pin from the life magic grenade.

Turns out the vampire didn't have a gag reflex, because the bomb flew down its throat without so much as a flinch.

I absently wondered if that was true of *all* vampires as I leaped from the mouth of madness and ran for my life.

"Grenade!" I announced as I fled, trying to put as much distance between me and the exploding monster as possible. The soldiers hit the deck, covering their heads like we'd been trained to do. Sias grabbed me by the ruined shirt and pulled me down behind a car with him as the eruption ballooned behind us.

The noise was a hollow thump that vibrated through the

ground, followed by a snowstorm of ashes as the damned void vampire melted away into sizzling dust.

I allowed myself a moment of relief, my head falling back against the car Sias and I were hiding behind.

The thing was dead and we weren't. We were banged up, bloody, and covered in vampire spit, but we weren't dead.

Truly the best-case scenario, even though I could have gone without feeling as sticky as I did.

Our moment of bliss was short lived, as screams sounded from the terrified bystanders watching the nightmare continuing to unfold.

Sias and I stood up from our hiding place to see the state of the tear had intensified into an infected wound of death magic. The veins had grown thicker and had started to creep up the side of the apartment building. People were fleeing in a panic from the fire exits, nearly trampling each other to escape.

Austin was back on his feet, dazed and bleeding from a cut on his brow, and was scowling at me.

"You used the damn grenade?" he demanded.

"Yeah, I used the damn grenade!" I shook vampire ashes off my arms. "It was the only way to kill it."

"That was how we were going to close the tear!" Austin's anger was losing against his panic. "What the fuck do we do now?"

I didn't have an answer. Cold dread sank marrow deep as I watched the tear churn and consume, an endless disease spreading over reality.

"You need to close it," Sias announced beside me, the idea so ridiculous I laughed.

"I can't close that! Are you insane?"

"You're the only one here with necromancy powers." Sias eyed the tear with open concern before aiming his attention back to me. "You have to try, love. It's all we have."

"Sias, I can't even bring a mouse back to life. I can't control something like that." I presented the tear to him with both hands, like maybe he didn't see how *bad* it was. "I couldn't do something like that when I still had the scythe!"

"Dallas." Austin held his side, wincing in pain from what was likely a cracked rib. "If you can at least stabilize it, maybe we can get some life magic inside and get it to seal. It sucks, but at least it's a plan."

"Fuuuuck," I groaned. "Why didn't you pack two grenades?!"

"Now that I know you'll steal one, I'll pack extra," Austin snapped. "You seeing this through or not?"

"Fuck you, Austin. I'm going to haunt your ass when this fails." I tried to swagger away, but it was hard to do with a limp. My leg ached from where the vampire's teeth had grazed me and my joints felt like I had been thrown into a damn wall or something.

OH WAIT.

I had.

"Fuck this day," I mumbled, limping with an equally banged up, bloody and gore covered Sias. "We should have just kept bowling."

Sias put my arm around his shoulders so I could lean on him. "You were going to lose anyway."

"I'd take losing at bowling over this, believe it or not."

It was nice to hear him chuckle, even if the circumstances were dire.

"I'll give you this," Sias lamented. "You do know how to make my evenings interesting."

We approached the tear like two cowboys riding into the sunset, knowing it was the final ride but still doing our best to look cool. I was limping, Sias was gross, and we had nothing else to lose. Either by some wild miracle this was going to work, or we'd get swallowed up into the endless nothingness waiting for us on the other side.

Pretty shitty night.

"You should stand back," I told him as we drew close to the

tear. "For when this inevitably fails, you can get a head start on running."

"I don't believe I ever gave you permission to give me orders." He eased my arm off his shoulders so I could stand on my own two feet while facing our demise. "You can do this, Dallas. Remember what Funus has taught you, and don't back down."

"Funus told me I'm too emotional and unpredictable for my magic channeling skills to stick," I confessed. "I keep pushing too far and botching the lesson. Last time I nearly opened the door too wide and almost turned into an ash monster, Funus had to save me."

"If you can open a door, maybe you can shut one as well," Sias countered.

I inhaled deeply as I stared down the tear.

This was beyond an "open door." This was a storm blowing away the whole damn house.

My confidence wasn't exactly through the roof as I took in a few deep, calming breaths, and fell back into the practiced mantra Funus had taught me.

My fingertips shook as I lifted my hands to hover over the icy tear humming with power. There was no mistaking the tug of death this time, no fleeting, silky spiderwebs teasing their presence. It thrummed through my body at full volume, ignoring any calm mantra I tried to put in place. The wily kraken I had once been able to wrestle was beyond my control, beyond my capability to sense it properly.

It wasn't tendrils and threads; it was a sonic boom of energy that almost knocked me on my ass.

"There's no fucking way," I managed through a gasp. My chest was filled with the chaotic drumbeat of panic, my temples pounding along with the symphony. The death magic was so strong, so overpowering, and I felt like my breath was being stolen each moment I tried to draw it in.

Through the fog of despair, a sharp, golden light pierced through and cloaked my reality in amber and tobacco.

A calmness settled over me, a wash of warmth that trailed up my neck like fingers and laced themselves into my hair. I felt them curl, squeeze just enough to let their presence be known.

"Relax," Sias purred into my ear. "Breathe, pet. Settle yourself."

The fear I had felt dropped away, the panic fading into a muted scream at the back of my subconscious. My heart began to thunder for touch, for release. For a moment I tried to turn into his lips, to feel them against mine, to feel anything beyond the cold assaulting me from the tear.

Sias squeezed my hairline, stilling me. I obeyed.

"You know this game, darling. You do as I ask, and I'll be happy. Are you going to be good for me?"

A chill ran up my spine at the unspoken promise, and I licked the dryness away from my lips.

"This doesn't seem like the right time for—" I tried but had to bite back a moan as he tsked.

"You answer, 'Yes, Sias.' You know the rules."

"Yes, Sias," I echoed, my heart hammering so hard it shook my voice.

The warmth of his breath trailed down my ear and kissed my neck, sending shockwaves of terrifying pleasure through me.

"Good, pet. Now. Lift your hands back up and focus on the magic in front of you. Do you feel it?"

There was no way in hell I was going to disobey him at this point. Every word he whispered was like a bolt of heat through my body, and I was starving for the attention.

I lifted my hands and felt the unforgiving, harsh death magic before me. It blasted through my hands like an artic storm, and I flinched from the sensation.

"The tear," I remembered. "It's too strong...I can't—"

"Yes, you can," Sias stepped over my words before I could finish. "You can handle this, pet. I've seen you take much more than this."

"I don't think death magic equates to the amount of di—" I

tried to quip but was stilled with another bone melting squeeze by his fingers. A wave of agonizing pleasure ripped through me as his magic tightened, and I felt my knees wobble.

"Yes, Sias," he reminded me through his teeth.

I had to catch my breath before I could respond.

"Yes, Sias."

"Then do as I ask," he commanded. "Reach out to the void and take control. Don't you dare disappoint me."

How could I argue with that?

The magic swirling around me thrashed, wild and unpredictable as I began to navigate through it. Funus had told me each night that all magic had a set of rules governing it, even something as endless and infinite as the void. If I played by those tenents, if I reached out in a way that it understood, I could control the ebb and flow of death.

I could understand what it was to be a necromancer.

I let my eyes fall shut, the charm magic around me a shield against the terror trying to flood my mind. My fingers waded through the waves of chaotic, corrupted magic, pinpricks of frostbite numbing them. Angry spirals from the void curled around my wrists, creeping up my arms as I searched for something I understood from my lessons with Funus.

The moment a spike of panic would begin to bloom, a squeeze at the back of my neck would stamp it back down.

"Breathe through it, pet," Sias whispered, lips trailing the cusp of my ear. "That's it."

Sias was going to make me develop a kink around controlling death magic, and I wasn't mad about it.

Whipping, thrashing threads spun around me, biting into my skin and freezing my fingers, wrapping my arms in a vise grip of unrelenting force until I finally hit bedrock.

The void.

The *true* void, buried deep within the wilds of the corrupted magic surrounding the tear.

I never thought I'd be so happy to feel death at my fingertips again, to feel those stupid, fleeting threads just barely graze my fingertips.

"There," I breathed. "The void. I can feel it through the tear."

"Good boy," Sias praised me, fluttering my heart with the need for more. "I need you to keep it open for me. Can you do that, pet?"

I hissed as he squeezed and I quickly corrected. "Yes, Sias."

I focused on the soft threads teasing my touch and curled my fingers, concentrating on the fragile hold I had. Tiny cuts of fear, false charm and snapping persuasion magic began to bite at my calm, but I closed it out of my mind.

A pressure began to form around my temples as I continued to concentrate, my fingers wrapping gently around the fleeting kisses of the void.

"Breathe," Sias reminded me. "A bit more."

Pain spread from where the pressure had begun, my breath catching from the sudden sting. I choked out a stuttered exhale as Sias spread his fingers out over the back of my skull and ran his nails over my scalp, soothing me.

The threads in my palm solidified, and I nearly sobbed when I felt the familiar, icy tendrils of death magic trail up my arm.

I had it. I had the void with me.

My head started to pound, the ache from maintaining control against the onslaught of outside forces crept down my jaw and threaded through my ribcage.

"Good, Dallas. Yes. Like that."

"Hurry," I pleaded. "I think my heart is going to stop."

"Almost there, pet. Almost," he promised.

The pressure was intense. Blinding. Just a little bit more. I could do it. I wanted to do it.

"Sias," I thought I whispered, but my lips didn't move. The cold bite of magic grew suspiciously numb.

My legs folded under me as I stopped breathing.

Death and I got to know each other again.

Ripples of the void were beautiful, shadows playing against themselves in an endless dance to eternity.

Somewhere deep in that forever, I had someone trying to find me.

It was hard to keep my thoughts straight, hard to keep them anchored to my conscious. That tends to happen when one travels into the abyss because typically when you're floating around in the void, you're…well…. very dead. Your physical you, the flesh and blood you, detaches from the more complicated, abstract you. That nebulous bit that lives between your favorite movie quotes and your first kiss starts leaking out into the void, taking all your daydreams with it.

It was nearly impossible to keep track of myself. I couldn't tell what I was thinking, what was possibly happening around me, and what was spilling out from my undefinable memories.

Grief. Pain. Fear. Panic.

Flashes of my life half-remembered floated in misshaped blobs in my hazy mind: holding my knees in the darkness of a vampire den, having a push up contest with Austin when we were preteens. I could smell the blood-soaked concrete, feel the grass of the training yard under my palms, the blurry edges of the two memories almost melting together.

There were others that didn't fit, that I couldn't place as my own in my dissociative state of dying.

A woman with hazel eyes was watching me with so much hurt I felt myself crumble inside. She had given so much of herself to me, to us, and I couldn't find it in myself to budge.

We were supposed to love each other. It was supposed to be so simple.

I felt terror as a new memory swam over me. I walked through sand, my legs disobeying me. The void was out there in the ocean waves, I knew it. I was going to meet it, but I was so afraid of it— that wasn't me. I wasn't afraid of the void. The salty taste of sea water choked me, and I fought, I had fought so hard…

This wasn't my memory. Something was wrong.

Everything started to fall away. The memories drifted from me like I was sinking into a deeper sleep, somewhere the false memories couldn't follow. The golden threads around me were breaking.

You said you could always find me.

*Don't take him.*

Find me now.

*I'll go into the void myself to pull him back.*

Find me now.

*Dallas. Can you hear me, pet?*

Find me now.

*Please. Dallas. Don't leave me.*

Find me now.

Find me now.

Find me—

*Hunter.*

I never thought I'd see those red eyes again.

In the darkness, in the forever, I saw the smoky figure of my vampire. He was a wisp, a trick of shadow and memory, moving like a fleeting flash out of the corner of my eye. He wasn't material, not in any true sense, but there was no mistaking those glowing red eyes.

I'd know those eyes anywhere. I saw them each night when I fell asleep. They lived in the best parts of me, sharing space with my deepest regrets.

Zane.

If I had the ability to reach for him, I would have. Standing in the void, losing all sense of myself, I was happy to let go of the threads keeping me from falling forward. I had finally found him. It had worked.

Twig would be so happy to see him. Maybe she'd stop being such a damn bed hog now that he would be back. I knew Barnaby would be thrilled to see him, because he had a mountain of crossword puzzles he'd been saving from their morning routine. He'd have a real chance to know Sias. I wouldn't stand in the way anymore.

We could pick up where we left off. We could figure this out together.

I was so tired.

I could finally rest.

Everything was going to be okay.

Red eyes filled my world, a shadow of my vampire floating before me.

*You're the damn master at hide and seek,* I tried to tell him, but my mouth wasn't working anymore. I hoped he could hear my thoughts. *I thought I'd never find you.*

The shadow shifted, his eyes settled over me. I couldn't understand why he looked so sad.

*Don't be too hard on yourself,* I thought at him. *Two months is a long time to hide. Pretty sure that's a record.*

Zane's ghost placed the outline of a hand to my chest.

I was dizzy with the sensation of crisscrossing patterns around my wrists, tangling up my arms before strapping over my chest. They tightened in bands of warmth, the void around us started to fade.

Zane started to fade.

*No.*

*No!*

Red eyes met mine, and I swear to God he somehow managed to smile. I couldn't see it. I felt it.

*You have to stay alive to bring me back, hunter. Don't fuck it up.*

Then, just when we were having a moment, a true reunion after months apart, after he had died in my goddamn arms—

He shoved me back.

I INHALED SO HARD I choked, my sight coming back to me in dappled blurs.

Someone was holding me up, but I was tangled in gold threads as a shadow retreated. I reached for it, but it was smoke and memory, disappearing as strong arms kept me from falling.

"I have you," Sias was saying, voice muddy as death was falling away from me. My heart thundered back to life. "Breathe, Dallas. Breathe."

"No," I whispered. "No. He was there. He was there. Zane—"

"I know." Sias kissed my temple and whispered another heart-breaking, "I know."

My vision came back in waves of nauseating clarity, the gold threads fading as the last traces of the void released me. The tips of my fingers burned as the tips regrew flesh over black bone.

Sias was rubbing my chest, warming me back up to a living temperature. Both of his arms were around me, easing me to the ground since my legs were too shaky to keep me upright.

I curled into the warmth offered, too weak and rattled for pride to take over as Sias cradled me against him. He rubbed my arms, occasionally checking my pulse with gentle fingers under my jaw.

"You did so good, pet," he whispered to me in his aftercare tone. "So good."

"We didn't get him," I reminded him. "He was there...he found me. But we didn't..."

I didn't think it was possible for Sias to sound like anything other than controlled, stern and focused.

I had never heard him sound so shaken.

"He sent you back to me," he whispered, lips against my temple. "I saw him in the dark. The shadow, right as the tear stabilized and the life magic started to seal it."

I had forgotten about the damn tear.

Honestly, I didn't fucking care in that moment that the whole world almost got swallowed up by a rip in reality, which probably makes me a complete asshole. I was too heartbroken to really give a shit as I sat there in Sias's arms, feeling very sorry for myself.

Sias's long, tired exhale was an unspoken novel of relief and exhaustion. The way he stroked my hair helped me realize that I was being a bit of a prick.

"Are you okay?" I opened my eyes and faced him, scanning him for injuries. "You didn't get too close to the void, right? Did anything touch you?"

Sias shook his head, eyes tired and bruised.

"I'm fine."

I had to rub my eyes to get my focus back, my brain stuffed with cotton and my energy drained like I hadn't slept in a week. Where the tear had been, only empty air and a cloudless sky greeted me as I swept my gaze upward. The danger was gone, sealed away by life magic's dominance over death in this realm, but the evidence of the event had left deep scars all over.

The cement was cracked and stained with ashen pockmarks and slashes; the sandbox shaped like a turtle had shards of obsidian spiking from it in jagged blades. Bricks had been marred with black branches trailing all the way up to the roof. Distant sirens blared, growing closer as the traumatized residents milled around in a state of shock.

"It worked?" I asked, truly dumbfounded. "We got it stable?"

"Yeah." Austin looked forty years older from the stress, still clutching his side from his battle wound. "You got it stable and we dumped all the life magic we had to get it sealed. I gotta say, Wilde, it was impressive, even if how you two managed it was... really fucking unnecessary."

His discomfort made me snort, and I remembered how sore I was from the effort. It was worth it.

"Ha. Prude."

Pain lanced up my leg as I tried to stand, and I inhaled through my teeth out of reflex.

"Did you dump *all* the life magic you had? Even the good healing stuff?" I managed through a wince.

"All of it," he mumbled, holding his side. "Unfortunately. Maybe we can get you—shit." His posture corrected, back straightening with his shoulders falling into position.

I didn't need to look to know who had arrived with the sirens.

"Easy," Sias warned as I started climbing to my feet. "You've just been through hell and back."

"You remember me telling you about my shitty family?" I groaned as Sias helped get me to my feet, my body begging to go back to the ground. "King asshole just showed up. I can't face him sitting down."

"I wasn't expecting him to show up with a fleet of DHAP officers." Sias kept his fingers around my upper arm to keep me from wavering.

"This day keeps getting better." I shivered from the cold breeze making itself known, and again from the memory of losing Zane's jacket to the corruption. I hugged my chest to keep from shaking as my past waltzed over, ready to fight.

"Knew I'd find you at the center of this shit storm, Wilde." Magnus leaned on his good leg, hand perched on top of his revolver. "The moment these things popped up, I knew they'd lead me right to you."

"I thought I told you to stay out of my city? Give me a wide berth, remember?" I set my teeth to keep my jaw from clattering.

"We got called in. Special assignment." He eyed Sias, annoyed by his presence. "We're working with the Demon and Human Alliance and Protection until the source of these tears are stopped."

I whistled. "They are desperate to call in crazy ass zealots."

"Professional death magic containment and creature elimination. Trained soldiers." Magnus took a quick look around. "You trade in your throat ripper for a sex demon?"

Sias's inhale was a lit fuse, and I motioned for him to stand down.

"Fuck you," I spat at the asshole human trying to start a fight. "We're not doing that. You say one more word about Zane or Sias, and I will assault an old man. I've had a really, really shitty day aiding *your* soldiers in this fight, Magnus."

"He's right, sir," Austin chimed in, begrudgingly, but still taking my side. "We wouldn't have been able to contain the threat had he not stepped in."

Magnus failed to look impressed, his stony, ancient face permanently carved in a look of wrinkled annoyance.

"Right. Lucky you were here," Magnus responded with such dry sarcasm that it mummified him another fifty years. "Funny how the last time we saw you was in a necromancy tomb, and now you just *happen* to be here to assist when vampires start ripping holes into the living world."

"You think I did this?" My laugh came out as a cough because my body was too achy to remember what humor sounded like.

"Sir," Austin edged back into the conversation. "I don't have a reason to believe that Wilde was behind the tear. He helped us get it under control and saved Paris and Haslet from getting eaten by the creature. He could have easily run and left us to die. But he didn't."

"Exactly!" I was excited someone was jumping to my defense. "Austin gets it. He trusts me."

"I wouldn't go that far," Austin was quick to keep my ego deflated, and finalized it with a sharp look that kicked me right in the heart. "But I will stand by my opinion that you didn't open the tear."

"Yeah?" Magnus placed a toothpick in his mouth, an old habit maintained after he gave up smoking. "Then who did?"

"I told you back at the crypt that Florence Pierce was going to cause trouble, and she is," I explained. "I know these tears are linked to her. She's fucking around with an ancient, powerful artifact she has no business owning. If we want this shit stopped, we need to take her down."

Magnus rolled the toothpick in his teeth as he glared me down, the flurry of movement behind him making his presence that much more solid. Medics and officers were rushing to help the injured and contain the area, yellow tape roping off the entire building and surrounding area. People in white biohazard gear were beginning to chip away at the magic residue left behind from the fight.

"You're working with DHAP, you can tell them to investigate Florence," I pleaded. "Magnus, she's behind this. She's not going to stop. We have reason to believe she's working out of a building she purchased recently—"

"An ancient artifact," Magnus repeated my words slowly, like I had misspoken. "Which one are you referring to, Dallas? The same one she hired you to find?"

"I told you in the fucking tomb that I wasn't going to give it to her—" I tried but he barreled over me.

"How'd she get it then?" Magnus tilted his head, aiming his better ear in my direction. "Hm? I thought you said you didn't have it back in the Silent Steps. You told all of us that you were still looking for it but, somehow, she obtained it anyway. Mind filling in the gaps for me, son?"

My high ground was slipping. I felt the conversation giving way underfoot like I was arguing on sand. Austin's jaw started to tick, his fists curling as I sorted through how I wanted to respond.

To try and regain my stance, I stupidly tried for honesty.

"I didn't know I had it."

"Sinners and Saint, son." Magnus barked out a humorless laugh. "That the best you can do?"

"It was in my chest!" I turned to Austin, hoping he'd somehow believe me. "It was sealed in there. It came out after I left the tomb and Florence—"

"You are something remarkable, Dallas, you know that?" Magnus tossed out the mocking praise, the venom behind it so potent it made me flinch. "You almost had your brothers and sisters fooled. Almost had them believing you were some kind of white knight swooping in to aid the fight."

"I'm telling the fucking *truth*, Magnus! I was going to destroy it, keep it out of her hands, but I just…"

"You *fucked up* is what you did." All mocking humor dropped from the old man as he wheeled on me, his voice honed to cut all the hidden little places only he knew about. "You tried to play both sides, and you fucked up. You unleashed something evil, again, but this time it's not going to be just a few family members who die. It's going to be hundreds. Thousands."

"Florence is the key to this," I tried to push ahead, but I was mortally wounded by his words and was bleeding out fast. "You have to tell DHAP to get to her."

"You're the one who caused this bullshit, Wilde. You brought the devil the key and paid with your soul. Saint have mercy on you, child. You know what they do to necromancers who cause this much mayhem. You saw firsthand what happens to them." Magnus cracked a knuckle. "I can't save you from what you brought upon yourself."

"We need him." Austin's voice was a whip crack, his words filtered between his clenched jaw. "He was able to calm the void tear and keep it stabilized. We can use him as a tool if nothing else."

My body shook, my arms frozen as I tried to rub feeling back into them.

"I don't think I could do that again and survive—"

"Your death will be a small penance for what you've aided," Magnus hissed, saddling up closer so he could glare down his nose at me. I was older now, able to see eye to eye with the man I had once considered my father. He'd pulled me from the darkness and gave me a means to fight against it. My home, my skills, my ability to kill the evils of the world and live to tell the tale was all because of him.

That was a long time ago.

And somehow, he still seemed taller than me.

"You know why I named my kids after old human cities, boy?" I could see the ruined toothpick in his teeth as clearly as the heartache creasing his brows. "Because when the demons came through into the human world, they tried to destroy everything we had been. Incubi, oni, jinn…they flooded into our realm and undid centuries. Your name carries part of what we were, and you disgrace it with what you've become."

I thought the cold was going to stop my heart. A shiver racked me, exhaustion ran icy claws down my back as I reached for a leather jacket I had thrown into the void.

Instead of swiping at the absence of comfort, my fingers met with the heavy fabric of a custom-tailored suit jacket.

It draped over my shoulders, blocking out the chill that was trying to tear me apart, and surrounded me in amber and tobacco. Sias smoothed the jacket over my shoulders, plucking at the garment where he had tossed it aside before the battle had begun.

He gave my arms a grounding squeeze, before he shielded me from the unforgiving glare of a man I had once thought was the tallest in the world.

"I've had enough of you," Sias said, in a quiet fury that lit a fire in my chest, his eyes crackling flames. "You disrespectful, ghoul of a man."

"The whore speaks." Magnus curled his fingers over the gun, his unease stoking the fire starting to warm me. "You can join him in prison for aiding if you want, pretty boy."

"I would absolutely love to see you challenge my fleet of legal counsel just to watch you get decimated for all you have." Sias chuckled, dark velvet curling into a noose.

"Big talk." Magnus spit his toothpick onto Sias's shoe. "We give the orders. And if I order them to throw you and that traitor you're trying to impress into jail, they'll happily comply to make sure their means to salvation is happy."

"Sure." Sias scanned the flurry of officers with a fiery gaze. "Which would you like to speak to? Lieutenant Brooker? I believe his mother is recovering in the St. Athesall general hospital, in the wing I paid for. Or maybe you'd like to try your luck with Captain Yama? Her wife's thriving culinary business just had a new restaurant open in one of my strip centers. I'm sure they'd love to have a chat." Sias clicked his tongue. "Best of luck with that."

Magnus's face was as impassive as ever, the vein in his temple pulsing.

Sias practically yawned as he added, "Never have a dick measuring contest with an incubus, Magnus. It's embarrassing."

I snorted a laugh, tugging Sias's jacket around me to keep me from shaking.

Magnus wasn't a fan of my reaction.

"This isn't over," he promised with icy ferocity. "Not by a fucking mile. He'll pay for his involvement in this, incubus, and you'll burn with him."

Sias's bored stare still held seething embers, but his voice was as cold and sharp as an ice pick.

"You threaten him in front of me again and I'll take you apart. Slowly."

If I wasn't so bruised and beaten, both mentally and physically, I would have fully swooned in front of everyone.

Sias pulled me closer and turned us away from the seething ghost lingering from my past, his arm wrapped around me to hold me steady.

"You alright?" he asked once we had a few footsteps away

from Magnus. "Can you make it down the street while I call someone to pick us up?"

"Is this someone going to take us to get healed?" I leaned against him to keep the weight off my injured leg. "Because I feel like a vampire chewed me up and spit me out."

"I have an on-call doctor who's meeting us at home. We'll get healed and take the longest showers." Sias pulled at his ruined shirt. "I might be in there for days."

I laughed, ducking under some caution tape with him as we made our slow escape from the calamity. My body was thrumming with a tangle of contrasting emotions and physical ailments; the sharp pain of shame and deep wounds spiking against soft scents of amber and tobacco.

The streets were closed off from traffic as police and DHAP officers contained the scene behind us, leaving the surrounding area tense with speculation and curious people peering from the curb. We had to hobble for a while to get away from the crowds and to find a stretch of street that wasn't swarming with bodies trickling out from surrounding neighborhoods.

The air was filled with distant wailing sirens and chatter, the cold spring breeze failing to cut through the fabric of Sias's jacket. His side was warm where I leaned against it, arm iron as it kept me pulled close.

"Hey." I stopped us from traveling further, my leg aching but my heart demanding more attention. Sias's eyes had eased into his ocean blue, hinting at a dark teal as he looked at me. "Can I ask you something important?"

"Of course."

"It's really important, so I need you to be honest with me," I pressed, holding his gaze so I could watch his eyes change color. "Do you promise me?"

His brows bunched, worry changing his eyes into a smoky blue touched around the edges in gray.

"I promise, Dallas."

"Okay." I inhaled slowly. "Do I have any gross vampire stuff on my face?"

Sias blinked, the gray starting to fade into a lovely shade of annoyed green.

"Do you…have gross vampire stuff on your face?" he repeated slowly, frowning.

"Yeah. Be honest. It's really important."

Sias stared at me for a few beats, fighting a frown.

"No, love. You're fine."

"Promise?"

"Yes." His frown won out, his eyes a bruised green and yellow. "Is that really what you wanted to ask me?"

"Yep."

I wasn't sure what color his eyes turned when I reached up and pulled him close for a kiss. I let my eyes fall shut as I captured his lips with mine, the kiss a slow, soft connection I'd never dreamed of attempting before.

It wasn't a tug of passion, a wrestling match of lust and desire leading to us tumbling into bed together. This was something much more complicated.

I wanted it to be complicated.

To drive the point home, I reached up and cupped his cheek, holding the moment like the fragile, precious thing it was. I wanted Sias to know this was meant to be a confession without ever having to say a word.

My heart was exhausted. My body a walking bruise piloted by a soul that had been half swallowed by the void. I couldn't be bothered to overthink what it meant when Sias placed his palms on my cheeks and held our kiss longer than I expected.

All I had the energy for was a cautious bloom of happiness.

When the kiss was released, Sias pulled me close into a protective hug, his eye color a mystery to me. I found a perch for my chin on his shoulder and allowed myself the chance to close my eyes and undercut the moment with humor.

"I take back all the shit I gave you for your ugly gun."

Sias breathed out quietly. "Apology accepted."

I was contemplating the scandalous idea of burying my face into his shoulder like the affection starved mess I was, when I felt him bristle under my touch.

"You better have a damn good reason for being here right now," he growled, the rage rattling up from his chest. For a few horrible seconds, I thought he had somehow read my thoughts and was rejecting my shoulder nuzzling desires.

It wasn't until I leaned away from him did I noticed Austin standing a few feet away, hands empty to show he wasn't there for a fight.

"I'm not here to cause trouble," he was explaining, but Sias wasn't in the mood for any more Saint's Army bullshit that night.

"You're about to find it if you don't *leave*," Sias continued to growl. "I still have bullets left, human."

"He's not here to fight," I told Sias, easing from his arms to stand on my good leg. "Let's hear him out."

"Three minutes." Sias checked his watch, which had somehow survived everything, even if it was sticky and gross. "Say your piece, then go."

Austin eyed Sias dubiously, eyebrow arched.

"You always let him boss you around, Wilde?"

"You really want to waste your minutes talking about the dynamics of our relationship?" I tapped the imaginary watch on my wrist. "Tick-tock, man."

"Alright, look." Austin exhaled, shifting gears. "I'm not going to ignore all the shit between us, and I'm not ready to say I trust you wholeheartedly. But I'm also not going to deny that this fight is going to be profoundly more difficult without your abilities. These rifts are dangerous, and while Magnus isn't ready to admit this yet, they're beyond what we're able to control."

"What are you proposing?" I asked. "You know damn well Magnus isn't going to be on board with us joining forces on this."

"No, he won't." Austin shrugged, wincing from the pull of

pain in his side. "But what he doesn't know won't hurt him. I lead my own task force. I get to make that call."

"You want to team up?" I eased weight onto my injured leg to keep my balance, the pain sharp but not enough for me to waver.

"Officially, I'm to bring you in if I see you again. Unofficially, it would be stupid to fight this alone." Austin pulled out a folded piece of paper from one of his many vest pockets and carefully closed the gap between us. He held the paper out for me to take, which I did.

Inside the fold was a phone number, hastily scribbled down.

Austin continued, eyes pinning me in place.

"I believe you about Pierce. If you find out something, I'm asking you to call me."

"How do I know you won't turn me over to Magnus?" I held the paper in my hand, ready to throw it back in his face. "How do I know this isn't a trap, Austin?"

The yellow streetlight over his head made the lines under his eyes sharp, the wariness weighing down his shoulders making him seem to stoop like an old man. We were only a few years apart, yet it felt like I was watching him age in real time, graying from years of grief.

"You saved Paris and Haslet today," he said quietly. "The part of you that refused to surrender them to that vampire is worth trusting again. I'm asking you to do the same. Please."

My leg didn't throb as badly as I shifted my weight, taking a moment to put the paper safely in my pocket. It only took a few tries to swallow the knot in my throat.

I was thankful there weren't more words between us as he turned and left, because I wasn't sure if I had the strength to handle much more.

Austin disappeared back into the chaos of the scene we had left behind, just as the sound of tires rolled up behind me. The sleek, black car of one of Sias's hired drivers parked at the curb, a capped chauffeur rounding the back to hold the door for us. He was paid well never to ask questions, and didn't bat an eye at the state we were in.

Considering we were bloody and covered in sticky, black, vampire goo, the guy was a fucking pro.

The journey between getting into the back of the car and arriving back at Sias's home was a blur, as I'd quickly passed out once my ass hit the leather. My leg was on fire from my injury, bones aching for a hot shower and three days' worth of rest. I had to be shaken awake and practically shoved from the car to leave.

Waiting for us by the front door was a human woman with short, graying hair and a noticeable lack of laugh lines. She held a leather bag in her hand and a professional apathy across her face, greeting Sias with a head nod as we shambled up the steps. The stress of the fight was starting to show in Sias's stiff movement and the winces he failed to hide, but I knew better than to try and insist that I could move around on my own.

Just like with all of Sias's handsomely paid freelance specialists, Dr. Stoic didn't care that we were stained with mystery stuff and had literal bite marks in our skin. She gently poked and prodded our wounds, asking about any broken bones before she began to clean and heal.

I was voted to get healed first, and I fought to keep my eyes open as I wavered at the edge of the posh couch. My body felt like a discarded piece of abused gum, so I didn't feel like doing the gentlemanly thing of insisting Sias go first.

"Before I get you healed, I need to get the object out of your wound," the doctor said casually, cutting the jeans away from my leg so she had better access to the rows of jagged, torn skin.

"The what?" I balked, hissing a sharp inhale of pain as she gave me a shot of pain killers right into the damn wound. "Ow, fuck. Did you say *object*? What object?"

She tapped something solid in my leg with her tweezers, and I felt bile bubble in my stomach. Whatever she drummed on was lodged deep enough to carry the vibration through the meat of my leg, and I made a series of very unflattering noises in front of the guy I had kissed earlier in the evening.

"Oh my God," I moaned. "If I throw up, will you still think I'm cute?"

"Don't throw up on my couch," he said dryly. "And I'll consider it."

"You're such a dick," I complained, trying to sound like I was joking, but my tone was far too whiny to be funny.

"Stay still please," Dr. Stoic said aiming her tweezers for the thing in my leg. In order to keep myself from flopping around and prolonging the process, I covered my face with my arms and complained the entire time she went fishing. I would've felt bad about being a total brat about the situation, but there was a goddamn thing in my leg and I had *died* earlier, so I felt pretty entitled to a meltdown.

To her credit, she didn't seem bothered. Or if she was, she kept it to herself like a professional.

After what felt like a lifetime of yelling about all the injustices my life was facing, the offending object was ripped free of my muscle and held up for examination.

"Looks like glass. Obsidian," she said, squinting. "The shape is strange though. It seems like the tip of a spear, or something like…"

"A fang," I managed to say while swallowing down a gag. "It's that damn void vampire's tooth. Ugh, that's so gross."

"Do you want me to dispose of it?" she offered, blinking in surprise when I held my hand out for it.

I grimaced as the bloody piece of vampire mouth fell into my palm. Since my clothing was likely going to be thrown out anyway due to the amount of nasty vampire crap all over it, I used a cleaner part of my shirt to wipe away the blood from the surface.

It wasn't a true obsidian color, but a red so deep and dark it gave the impression of black. The tooth was glassy to the touch and just as sharp, formed like it had grown out of a lightning strike instead of bone.

"Huh," I mused as I held it up to the light, which was swallowed instead of reflected. "It looks like the shit that was growing from the sand pit when the tear opened."

"Is it dangerous?" Sias asked, leaning over to peer at it. "Should we be worried it was in your body?"

"I don't know," I said honestly. "I fucking hope not."

Sias was not impressed with my answer.

"You're the vampire hunter here, Dallas. You have to have something more substantial than 'I fucking hope not.'"

"That thing wasn't like anything I've seen before," I pointed out. "I don't know what rules a corrupted void vampire plays by. I would imagine it's not made to turn people, just eat them, otherwise it wouldn't have been trying to pull everyone into its belly."

"What is your educated guess then?" Sias pressed.

"We're lucky to be alive and got some kick ass scars from it," I said. "And if that thing wanted to turn us into vampires, it wouldn't have swallowed that guy. It would have been a catch and release situation."

Sias exhaled and fell back against the couch, his eyes melting back to a calm blue.

"Alright."

"Are we fine to proceed?" the doctor asked, glancing between us. "With the object out, I can use healing magic to finish."

"Yeah." I pocketed the tooth and leaned back. "Let's get this over with so I can bathe and sleep for a week."

One gloved hand was pressed against my knee, warmth radiating out from her touch in a familiar tickle of life magic ants crawling over me. Normally that meant relief was just a few minutes away, the magic would heal the ripped skin of my leg, ease the fatigue in my bones and give me some energy back.

The sudden shift to a cold sting made me hiss, just as she ripped her hand away and shut the whole process down.

All my pain remained. My leg was a bloody mess, my joints

stiff, bruises continued to form where I had bounced off a brick wall.

My heart started to thunder.

"I'm sorry, sir," she said, shaking her head like I was terminal.

"What?" Sias creased his brow, his pained body giving his voice a frustrated edge. "He needs to be healed. He has gashes in his legs, not to mention he was thrown into a wall and might have a concussion—"

"Sir." She pinned him with a severe look, showing her palms. "I'll patch him up, clean his wounds and prescribe some pain killers, but I cannot heal this man."

Then she sadly said the words I had been longing to hear for months.

"There's too much death magic in him."

I DON'T KNOW how I got into Sias's bed or how long I'd been there.

From the amount of drool on his satin pillowcase, I'd have guessed I'd been asleep for a solid day and a half. I'd never had the pleasure of waking up in his bed, and it was as comfortable and luxurious as I'd hoped. Unfortunately, the lovely silk sheets and heavy down comforter didn't dull the throbbing in my leg nor the stiffness in my limbs.

I felt like shit wrapped in silk. It was quite the experience.

Every single deity I could think of was cursed as I forced myself upright, my skeleton having been replaced with termite infested wood that creaked when I moved. My vision was blurry for the first few blinks, slowly coming into focus as I knocked away the grogginess with the heels of my palms. Through my sheer unconscious need to be the center of attention, I had managed to travel to the middle of Sias's orgy sized mattress and made a little burrow for myself.

The place to my left had a dent where someone had been sleeping, the pillow cool and a few hours abandoned. I wondered if it was too much to hope that I hadn't made that dent myself, since there wasn't any drool on it.

To my left, a tiny bundle of fur napped a pillow away, curled up like a cinnamon roll.

Beside her was Zane's ashes, placed carefully between two pillows to keep it upright. The glass said nothing as I wished it good morning.

Because I moved at the same speed as a dying animal, traveling the expanse of the mattress felt like an eternity. By the time I reached the edge, I was contemplating falling back asleep to either waste a few more days in a comatose state or simply die to forgo the effort of standing. I decided it was best to try and soldier on, because I was starving and needed the bathroom enough to urge me to continue to live.

Once I got on my feet and took a few steps, living seemed less terrible. My body hurt, but my mind was starting to find the lighthouse of clarity through the drowsy fog.

I was no longer covered in vampire blood and grime, my skin smelling of soap and Sias's sheets. I was in my boxers, leg freshly bandaged, my bruises angry splotches of purple and green. My reflection showed two days of stubble, wild hair and the swollen eyes of a man who hadn't seen the sun for a while.

Needless to say, I was *very* sexy.

Due to the sheer achiness of every part of my existence, it took longer than usual, but I managed to wash my face, shave and get dressed in under a decade. Some of my clothing was waiting for me, clean and neatly folded, which was a novel idea. When I emerged from Sias's room, I looked almost presentable, even if I was moving like a beaten old man.

The smell of coffee was heavenly as I padded to the kitchen, where Barnaby and Funus occupied places at the breakfast counter while Sias poured more boiling water over grounds.

Unlike me, Sias was fully healed and had no evidence left of the fight with the void vampire. He was unblemished, beautiful and well rested.

Lucky bastard.

"You're awake." Sias motioned to his brew. "Coffee?"

"Dear God, yes." I saddled up to a stool by Funus and sat. "I'm guessing from the coffee and Barnaby's puzzle face that it's morning?"

"I don't have a 'puzzle face.'" Barnaby said, maintaining the face. "But no. It's late. Nearly eight at night."

Funus's eyes were angled up and away like he was listening to something for a heartbeat, then swiveled the yellow orbs my direction.

"Good evening, Dallas."

"How long was I out?" I took the cup offered to me with both hands and breathed in the rich vapor.

"Two days, off and on," Sias answered, passing me cream and sugar. "You'd wake up for short spells, but you were very drained. How do you feel?"

"Like shit." I shoved the proper amount of sugar into the black liquid before smothering it with cream. "But after some coffee and food, I'll be fine."

"The doctor said you should maintain bedrest for a few more days," Sias pitched, not sounding hopeful I'd comply.

"We've lost two days," I argued after a swallow of coffee. "Plus, you think this is the first time some otherworldly monster has tossed me around? Please. Normal Saturday night for me."

Sias hummed, not convinced but also not arguing.

"Do we know how many tears happened while I was down?" I asked.

"One small incident that was squashed quickly by the Saint's Army," Barnaby chimed in, taking a break from his puzzle. "Believe it or not, they're back in the media in a positive light for the first time in decades."

It was too early to be getting a headache, but one started regardless. I rubbed at my temple to ease it back, grumbling, "Great."

"I was able to obtain Florence's real estate records over the past five years," Sias swooped in to help ease the growing pain in my skull. "There's been a few properties around the city and just outside St. Athesall's limits that she's snatched up. She's been very busy it seems."

Thank the Gods for small miracles. "You think any of them would be worth searching? Any that seem like a facility she could fuck around with death magic and not get noticed?"

"Two come to mind," he said. "They're just outside the city limits, about an hour away in opposite directions."

I tapped on the lip of the mug, the rhythmic chime of ceramic under my nail a metronome as I let my brain churn.

"We could bring some magic detectors to each one and see if we can read anything out of the ordinary, but there's a good chance she installed dampeners to keep the signals low. Our best bet would to be somehow manage to get inside—"

"Do you hear that?" Funus interrupted.

I paused my tapping and listened, hearing only the calm hum of the fridge and Barnaby chewing on a pencil.

I gave Funus a shrug. "No?"

"Strange," he whispered, eyes bouncing around. "It was so clear."

"I can meet with Dex about making something to punch through any dampeners," Sias pitched. "Maybe she has something we can use."

"Worth a shot. If we each take a location, we can cover more ground and waste less time if these are dead ends."

Sias's scowl was telling me that he didn't love my idea.

"You want us to split up?"

"Dual recon," I corrected. "It's a sound strategy."

"Absolutely not."

"Why?" I snorted.

"Why? Dallas, you're beaten to hell. You can barely walk much less fight if the need arises." Sias shook his head when I opened my mouth. "We go together."

"I'm gonna burst your bubble here, Sias," I said with a wince, in mock concern for his ego. "This isn't the first time I've gotten my ass kicked and went limping after trouble. I don't need an incubus in white armor to come keep me safe."

"You're mistaken, pet." His eyes flashed a brilliant lemon lime swirl before cooling into a sweet lavender. "I'm not a knight in this scenario, I'm the *king*. And by my fucking decree, you will not put yourself in unnecessary danger while you are recovering. Are we crystal clear?"

I slurped some coffee and watched him bristle, the urge to see if I could get his eyes to change into a new combination of annoyed anger almost outweighing the delight I had at him being so royally protective. On one hand, the thought of Sias caring about me in a way no one else besides Zane had was giving me so many butterflies hatching in my belly that I was going to start levitating off the stool. On the other, maybe I could name the new color something funny, like lemon-lime-haterade.

I was still weighing my options when Funus yelled, "There! There it is again!"

"There's no need to yell!" Barnaby snapped, having dropped his pencil during the skull's outburst.

"You can't hear it?"

The kitchen fell silent as all three living creatures listened to silence, straining to pick up what the dead guy was hearing.

The hum of the fridge continued to moan, a bird outside sang merrily, the faucet beside me dripped once into the sink. There was nothing worth shouting about, nothing that sounded interesting or revolutionary in any way. Barnaby lifted a brow at me in a silent question, and I shrugged back in answer.

"I can't tell...where it's coming from..." Funus said, moving his eyes since he couldn't do much else. "It's so quiet, but it's there. Faint and quiet, but it's there."

"Funus, I think maybe you need a nap, man," I suggested when Sias lifted his hand to pause our conversation. His golden brows furrowed, head tilted as he tuned into something.

"You hear it?" I asked and he put a finger to his lips, hushing me. The kitchen fell silent again as Sias shut his eyes and frowned while Funus angled his eyes up and around. Barnaby and I shrugged at each other, completely dumbfounded.

Sias stood in meditation for a few beats, a hard crease forming on his brow from the effort of trying to locate the unknown noise. His eyes shot open in surprise as he moved to the freezer and swung the door open, unmuting the noise from within.

A scratching sound punctuated the calmness of the kitchen, tiny nails scraping down plastic in a slow, deliberate pattern.

"…whaaat the fuck," I muttered, lifting off my stool in shock. Barnaby gasped and covered his mouth, understandably horrified.

Sias reached into the cold of his freezer and pulled the source of the noise out, the little plastic container fogged over from frost. His fingers shook as he placed it onto the counter, the color in his face draining.

"I, um," His Majesty Sias floundered, eyes turning a shade I decided to name terror-gray. "I think it's for you, Dallas."

"Like a fucking phone call?" I hissed.

Sias nodded. "Yes."

"You can't feel her, acolyte?" Funus breathed. "She's present. Right now."

He was right.

I could feel her.

It was subtle; a barely perceived breath across the back of my neck, a whisper so soft I wasn't sure if I actually heard or imagined it.

But she was there, as real and terrifying as only death could be. My practice mouse tap, tap, tapped—waiting for me to answer.

Barnaby took a few steps to bolt from the kitchen, his body language screaming with how uncomfortable the entire scene was making him. Instead of running away, which I wouldn't have blamed him for, he turned Funus around to face the container and kept his shaking hands resting on top of the skull.

"No need to be afraid," Funus consoled him. "You're safe."

"If you say so," Barnaby whined. "But I'm going to be very angry if she kills the lot of us for something Dallas inevitably says or does."

"How am I already in trouble and I haven't even answered the mouse-phone yet?"

"Dallas," Sias said, voice low and uneasy.

"Yeah, okay. Okay." I took a long inhale and shook out my hands, exhaling slowly as I eased the top of the container open. The dead mouse crawled up and over the lip of the container like it hadn't been dead for weeks and frozen solid. It was piloted with false life, eyes glowing a haunting shade of black-green I simply dubbed "nightmare."

The tiny body crawled to the center of the countertop and stood back on its haunches, long tail curled around its back feet, mouth open wide to expose its rodent incisors. The receiver was unhooked, the phone call answered.

How exactly do you start a conversation with a Goddess when she literally cold calls you?

"Uh," I said. "Wilde Assassinations and Fish Training. Can I help you?"

Sias rubbed his eyes with his fingers. Barnaby slapped my arm and mouthed, "What the fuck is wrong with you?"

"We need to meditate," Funus explained quietly. "Open yourself to the void. She's telling you the door is open."

My stomach felt like a clenched fist when I remembered how horrible my last run in with the void had been. Tingles of ache spread out from where the vampire's teeth had ripped open my leg, my body cold from the brush with death.

"I dunno if I can, Funus," I admitted, sour and hurt. "I went too deep last time. I felt myself slip away...I heard Zane in there..."

"You can do this, acolyte," he insisted. "You peered into the void and made it back once; you can do it again. The Goddess of Death does not make herself known to just anyone." His yellow eyes pierced me, desperate. "We must know why she's here."

"Why me?" I rubbed at my arms, a chill shaking me. "You're the ultra fanboy. You talk to her."

"If she wanted to speak to me, she can anytime. I'm dead." Funus gave me a shine with his eyes, something of a tired smile. "You are her champion."

"I'm *tired*, is what I am." I held my arms. "I'm tired, and beaten up, and I just want my vampire. I don't want a world ending responsibility or some prophecy bestowed on me. I just want Zane. And more coffee. Is that so much to ask?"

Sias's hands were warm on my shoulders as he squeezed, the fist in my gut slowly uncurling as I felt his charm magic wrap around me in a cocoon.

"I know you're tired," he whispered, breath soft on my ear. "And you deserve a rest. But if you want Zane back, you can't keep a Death Goddess waiting on hold."

"She could have at least waited for me to finish my coffee," I complained, no longer tangled in knots but still disgruntled.

"I'll make you all the coffee you want after." He moved his hands to my arms, easing the chill from around me. "Follow your training and step into the void. I'll be here to keep you tethered."

I felt a swell of nerves start to form in my chest, but they unraveled as Sias slipped his fingers through my hair.

"Keep me from falling in this time?"

"I've got you," he promised.

"Like we've practiced," Funus coached. "Repeat your mantra, keep yourself centered, and answer her call."

I let my eyes fall shut as Sias squeezed the nape of my neck, tension releasing from my shoulders. His touch traveled down my spine, easing and grounding me like a solid anchor to the chilly floor beneath my feet.

The mantra slipped into my mind, the charm spell wrapping a thread over my chest to keep my heart from going off the beaten path. I wouldn't be chasing ghosts.

Not yet.

My hand lifted, and the cold spider web threads touched my

fingers faster than ever before. The void was much closer to the surface when the Goddess herself was waiting at the door. Sias purred into my ear, and I curled my fingers over the delicate strings that weaved across my palm.

With a tug, the void swung open with startling ease, and I was plunged into darkness.

Ripples over dark waters, shadows dancing along the edges, the void was calm and contained. Little slips of my conscious dribbled over the sides, and I caught a fleeting view of my first kiss, all awkward hands and panting promises. I'd forgotten his name, but I remembered his smile.

I also saw a woman laughing, tangled in sheets with arms around her. She was cuddling with a beautiful man, both with flushed cheeks and soft kisses, and I knew in my heart how much they had meant to me. And how devastated I was to see them again.

Who were they?

The moment the memories started, they floated away again, golden threads tugging me back before I could fall too deep.

I had almost died again, but not quite. It was much easier to stay at the edge during the visit when other magic and chaos wasn't slamming into you from all sides.

This visit was much more cordial, downright pleasant compared to the last one.

And just as my soul tugged back and I began to feel less like I was dying, the Goddess made herself known.

How I was able to feel a chill while I was in the realm of the dead was something only a Death Goddess could achieve, and her grip over me was soul deep and vicious. Bony fingers touched me, turning my head to see through eyes that weren't mine.

I saw the scythe in a stark white room, its crimson blade smoking from the industrial machines cutting pieces of it free. Vapor pulled at the edges of reality, threadbare windows into the void splitting like fabric. Obsidian crystals shot up from around the split, jagged and terrifying, taking the shape of teeth biting at the air. A mechanical arm dropped down and plucked them from the fissures like apples from a tree, dropping them into containers.

The scythe blade was being chipped away by machines, each new assault bringing more obsidian to harvest, and hungrier tears.

As each tear got pulled further apart, becoming even more unstable and wild with magic churning and lashing out from each wound, another robotic arm would seal it with a few careful shots of a high-powered laser, a crystal shard glinting from within. Across the robot's arm was stamped "Essence Mechanics" in bright, bold lettering.

A person dressed in a plastic biohazard suit stood beside the machine and pulled the infused crystal loose from the robotic arm, which was now smoking from the effort of channeling the magic, and placed it gently aside. The grunt whose eyes I was peering from lumbered forward to present a new one, its dead hand unaffected by coming in contact with the raw power of the chipped blade of the scythe.

My vision blurred as we jumped to another set of eyes, which was holding the shards in the dead hands of a vampire. We crushed the shards into dust with the help of machines, compelled to follow the orders of our Mistress. The dust was liquified, processed, and churned with charms and magic it had no business sharing space with.

I saw the bubbles of bio-magic being infused with death, creating something foul, horrible and unnatural. I saw how it transformed test animals into monsters with too many teeth, snapping them in half to shape themselves into new nightmares. I also saw a different test subject being brought back to life after a particularly well-maintained batch was injected into their veins.

This was a miracle drug just as easily as it was a method of creating undead creatures.

Great.

A shift, a flash—eyes closing and opening again in a new space.

The lab was gone, replaced instead by a cool, dark room with thin wisps of incense smoke trailing on either side of a death altar. The eyes I was peering from felt different, blurry, like I was trying to see through lenses covered in fog. A hand with thin, elegant fingers was holding an obsidian shard from a corrupted tear, blood trailing from a cut on their palm.

Through the fog, I could see the death altar was set up in the way Funus coached; the candles set east and west, ancient runes placed between them flanking the section meant for the offering. The vision was swimming, whether it was clinging to consciousness or death, I wasn't sure.

In the center where I normally had my mouse to practice on, a mound of ash was placed in a neat pyramid.

"Focus, madam," a familiar voice whispered, causing a flurry of acid to bubble in my gut. Hei had her hand on the shoulder of the person I was watching through, keeping them from tipping forward.

The obsidian was slick with crimson as the thin fingers of Florence's hand curled inward. The vision cleared more, the cradled shard humming with power as the mound of ashes began to smolder. Florence's eyes fell in and out of focus as she summoned a connection to the void, her grip on the blade shaking.

"Focus," Hei hissed. "Don't let it slip. Hold on to it."

I felt Florence's heart slowing as the void grabbed her, the power of the shard crawling up her arm in icy tendrils.

The smoldering ashes in front of her began to solidify, taking the shape of a screaming skull with sharp, blue eyes.

I knew that skull.

The last time I had seen them, Magnus was putting a life magic infused blade to their temple. They had been turned to ash defending the secrets of the Goddess in a forgotten tomb under the Silent Steps.

Florence was resurrecting one of the dead Necromancy Council members.

From their *ashes.*

The flames in the altar suffocated from the cold, a pure void tear opening in front of them like a curtain being pulled aside. The ash skull screamed in silence, eyes flickering in and out as Florence's vision began to waver again.

"Don't let it shut!" Hei was demanding, one of her arms outstretched for the void. "Hold it, damnit! Hold it!"

The ashes crumbled, Florence's heart surged back to a thundering tempo, and I was sent back to the present.

I was left shaking in Sias's kitchen, my heart matching Florence's panicked pace as I caught my breath.

Sias had me by the shoulders to keep me steady, but I felt more alive and decidedly warmer than the last time I had jumped into the void. I was able to blink my vision back to normal easily, and noticed that the mouse conduit had fallen back into its state of regular dead.

"Breathe," Sias was coaching me, soothing my post-void visit shakes with some gentle charm magic. A warm washcloth was placed behind my neck, and I almost asked him to marry me right on the spot.

The guy knew aftercare, I'll give him that.

"I don't know if I'll ever get used to that," I admitted, winded.

"What did she show you?" Funus asked, yellow eyes somehow wider, despite not having skin.

"Florence is ripping the scythe apart in order to make tears. They're taking the shards grown from the tainted magic and infusing them with bio-magic to make products in a lab," I explained, swallowing down some water before tacking on, "But that's somehow not the worst part of it."

"How is that not the worst part?" Barnaby demanded. "What is worse than purposefully ripping holes between realms?"

"She has one of the council member's ashes." I tilted my head to let Sias dab my chest with the rag. "She's using one of the shards to bring them back so she can open a doorway to the void."

"That's…*impossible*," Funus huffed. "I think you must have been confused, Dallas."

"I know what I saw. She brought Pereo back from her ashes and channeled that power to rip the void open."

"Goddess save me," Funus whispered. "To bring back one of the council for such a purpose…it's diabolical. Unfathomable."

"Necromancers can resurrect ashes?" Sias asked as he continued warming me up.

"No, child," Funus corrected. "Necromancers cannot. Only the Goddess's blessed can. They need her blessing and her blade in order to achieve that feat. Dallas is right: this is very, very bad. If they have the ability to open a doorway to the void, there's no telling what they could do."

"They're already opening up doorways to the void by fucking with the blade. Why bother with bringing back a member of the council?" I asked. "What am I missing here?"

"You saw for yourself how hard it is to navigate the corrupted tears. They're unstable, violent, prone to sending out monsters. What they were attempting was a direct pathway into the realm, something mortals are forbidden from achieving. To what end, I don't know—it's a pathway to madness. A door directly to the Goddess."

"A pathway directly to a Goddess," I mused. "You've been dead too long, Funus. Mortals trying to get to the divine is a very old story. Florence is trying to be immortal, all-powerful, or both. She can't just be satisfied with being rich."

"That's madness," Funus whispered.

"Nah, it's the most relatable thing about her. Show of hands, who would go after the power of a God?" I lifted my hand and swept my gaze around the room.

Barnaby glared at me, openly annoyed.

Sias had his hand up.

I pointed to Sias. "See? He gets it." Then aimed an accusatory jab at Barnaby. "You're just being difficult to impress the skull."

"We need to stop her," Funus pulled us back on track. "How do we get to her?"

"I have a plan, but I gotta make some phone calls." I eased off the stool and was painfully reminded that I had a bite taken out of my leg. "Fucking hell I hate vampires. All of them. Zane too. This is all his fault."

"Are you going to tell us this plan before you start setting things into action?" Barnaby buzzed like a fussy bee.

"Grab that backpack you use to lug Funus to museums. It's already late and we don't have a lot of time to get going. Be ready in thirty."

"I hate it when he does that," Barnaby was complaining to his skeletal husband. His tone switched just as I was limping out of the kitchen, and he very sweetly told Funus, "Don't fret. He's an idiot, but he'll help you get this sorted. It'll be alright."

Aw. I was going to give him shit for that later.

Barns wasn't wrong; I was going to help Funus get things sorted out. The Goddess had shown me what was causing the rifts, but she also showed me something much more important.

How I was going to bring Florence down.

And how I was going to get my vampire back.

"I need the clothes I was wearing the night of the attack," I told Sias as I hobbled toward his bedroom. "Or at least all the shit that was in my pockets, including my phone."

Sias's fingers caught my elbow and paused my attempt at speed walking.

"Dallas. You're still recovering from the last time we tangled with the void. Let's take a moment."

"We don't have time to—"

I blinked at the shadows playing across Sias's handsome features, his high cheekbones looked slashed on either side with horizontal lines that faded under my scrutiny.

"You feeling okay?" I watched his face, sure I had seen something.

"I'm fine." His brows lowered, finally caving under my stare by asking, "Do I have something on my face?"

"I thought you did." I reached up to touch his cheek but then thought better of it.

"You need to rest," he was back on that again. "You're better suited to fight the undead horde when you're not limping around and stiff."

"I'm fine." I rotated his elbow to manipulate the hand attached to it, his watch face catching the light. "We don't have much longer before it's prime void time. We need to get a head start this time if this is going to work."

"You're not *fine*, pet. You just woke up after two days of solid sleep. You need food, medicine, water." He tightened his jaw as I wrenched my arm free to continue down the hallway.

"We can get those on the way. Damn, I could go for a burger or twelve." I rubbed at my stomach and made my way into his bedroom, scanning it for any hampers. "Where did you put my old clothing?"

"They're gone, but your items are on the dresser."

"Gone??" I wheeled. "Like 'gone to the cleaners'?"

"No, love. Burned. They were covered in vampire spit and blood. There was no recovering from that."

"Ugh, I loved those jeans. Damnit." I reached for my phone when he caught my hand and turned me toward him.

"Dallas, listen to me."

If I wasn't on a mission, wasn't focused on what I needed to do to make my insane plan come together, the concern in his voice wouldn't have hit my ear wrong. I should have been moved that he cared, loved that Sias was showing more affection for me.

Instead, it pissed me off. Which he didn't deserve.

And I wasn't ready for the backlash.

"You're getting cold feet now?" I spat at him, angry and sore. "We go through all this, and *now* you're worried? If you want to hang back, be my fucking guest. But I'm not about to slow down because you suddenly give a shit."

There was no swirl of color in his eyes, no fade from one hue to another as emotions tangled together. The change was fast, a flash fire of bright yellow. Rage tinted his gaze into a firestorm ready to burn me alive.

"Suddenly give a shit?" he echoed, impossibly calm.

And because I never learn my lesson and had the "poke the bear" gene, I didn't back down.

A lot of unresolved things were coming out tonight, for better or worse, because neither one of us had ever prioritized therapy.

"You never gave a *shit* about sending me to kill people for you. You sent me after Omar, almost got me killed more than once, but now that you're being pulled along for the ride you suddenly care that I'm a little bruised. Are you worried about me, Sias, or are you worried about yourself?"

He let go of my hand, his gaze trying to burn me alive. He didn't move, his body a pillar of golden, molten rage.

"I didn't give a shit about you." His words were a cold slap that made me wince. "You were a fun ride. A momentary distraction. When I learned how proficient you were at causing chaos, I reveled in being able to aim you where I wanted and setting you loose. You were consistently, profoundly unmanageable and completely unpredictable. Dangerous. An asset. A fantastic weapon and a convenient, fun fuck."

I felt my fists curling, lungs burning as I held in the fire I wanted to unleash on him. My eyes were stinging, and I didn't want him to see the tears building, but I was frozen in place as my heart threatened to break.

All of my fears were true. He finally admitted what I had known all along. I didn't think it was possible for my heart to break any more after Zane died, but Sias had been holding it together so well until this moment. He let it all fall into dust.

And then.

He continued.

"When I died," he said, voice still unyielding and firm. "Drowned. I wasn't afraid. I thought I would be, but I wasn't. It was like drifting off into a dream of home. I was losing everything I was and welcomed joining the infinite stream of nothingness. My fear, Dallas Wilde, didn't start until I woke up in your arms. I snapped awake and you were there. You. The asset. The unmanageable chaos. You reached into the void and ripped me out, dove into the waters after me without a second thought."

My lungs shook as I inhaled, my vision clearing when the tears finally broke over the threshold. I didn't dare speak. I couldn't. I was too fragile to do anything but stand very, very still.

"From that moment," Sias whispered, yellow turning acidic green and then forest leaves. "I have been terrified of you. Terrified of you knowing me. Terrified of losing you. Terrified of how you make me feel."

Everything I wanted to say had turned into a solid knot in my throat, and I struggled against it as it calcified into an ache of hope.

"I am not a good man," he confessed, all yellow gone from his vision now. His irises were now emeralds flecked with gold, and they were all mine. "I'm selfish and cruel. I left my harem and family behind and cut ties. I have ghosts, mistakes, and so many enemies. But I will go to hell and back with you. I will help you rip the void open to get Zane back in order to make you happy. I will spit in the face of gods and would topple an empire for you."

He touched my chin with his fingers, lifting my lips toward his. They didn't touch, giving a breath of space to allow for his words to linger between us.

"Don't ever question my love for you again, pet."

If he had more to say, I didn't give him a chance to finish. Sias was pulled into my kiss, my hands holding his face to mine. I was practically clawing at him to bring him closer to me, for our bodies to touch, starved for his attention and affection more than I'd realized. My heart was still fractured and wounded, but able to swell with his words repeating in my mind.

I would hold on to those for as long as he'd let me. For as long as he'd allow me to love him back.

I had loved him for so long that it felt like seeing the sunlight after a decade of storms, new shades of warmth I had never felt finally unveiled. I wanted to stay in that sunshine, to hold him to me and breathe in the feeling of his affections.

His fingers threaded through my hair, thumbs brushing the tears off my cheeks as he swiped his tongue over my lips. I groaned against the sensation, parting my lips to taste him for the first time in months. Gods, he tasted like wine and sex, his skill set shining through as our tongues danced.

"I want nothing more than to taste you," Sias whispered, nipping at my bottom lip. "But you're not perfect yet. Not yet. Not until you get your vampire back."

"Are you serious?" My breath was coming out in freight train huffs from how extraordinarily turned on I was, my body wound up tight and ready to spring into action. "Saints, Sias, I'm ready for a marathon fuck and you're shutting this down? *Now*??"

"Yes." His eyes were just the most delightful shade of lusty magenta and emerald green. "I meant what I said about being a very picky eater."

"Oh my God, you're so *mean*." I was bowed from how badly my body was being ignored. "You tell me how you feel, get me so happy and horny, and then blame it on the dead guy? God, I am *so* into you."

"Go make your phone calls and whatever else you need to handle." He gave me a knowing once over. "Then you're going to tell me every single aspect of your plan while you eat some dinner before we leave. Understood?"

"You're an evil bastard, you know that?" I sighed as he lifted an impatient brow. "Fine. But I want pancakes. And extra bacon for leaving me with homework." I pointed at my dick and he rolled his eyes.

"Get to work then, pet. We have death to defy and pancakes to get."

"I'VE NEVER SEEN this part of the city," Funus mused from inside the backpack Barnaby was sporting. The small, mostly canvas bag was meant for people to haul around their miniature chihuahuas or less feral cats in, complete with a domed window for said animals to peer out of. Barnaby had it strapped to his front to allow Funus to sightsee from a better vantage point.

The skull looked hilarious draped in fake fur. It was a terrible disguise if given more than a quick glance, but most people in the city were so used to seeing people lugging their darlings in the damn things they didn't care what Barnaby's "pet" looked like.

"That's because this part of the city is not ideal for casual strolling," Barnaby mumbled, clutching the backpack like someone was going to try and snatch it from him. "The Swallows aren't exactly the safest part of town during daytime hours, so I'm not in love with being here so late."

"Relax. It's actually not that bad unless you stand out." I smirked at his bow tie. "You blend right in."

"You're not funny or charming." Barnaby hugged his bag tighter.

"Oooh, look at the art on the bricks! So colorful!" the centuries old skull cooed from inside his dog purse. "Barnaby darling, can you decipher that language for me?"

"It's graffiti, Funus. I don't know what it says."

"Oh! Look! A penis! You love those!"

Barnaby flushed bright pink. "I don't *love* them, for the love of the gods. I appreciate their cultural significance in fertility rituals. Dallas, shut *up*."

"Never," I managed through my wheezing. "I love everything that's happening right now."

"Gentlemen," Sias scolded. "Can we collect ourselves? We're supposed to be keeping a low profile."

"This was such a mistake," Barnaby continued to complain, but did it quieter. "I should have never agreed to this."

I wiped the joyful tears from my eyes and checked my app, the ping of void activity growing closer. The signal was weak, which was a hell of a blessing, and I shot off two text messages noting the approaching cross streets. I also paired my second cup of coffee with some pain meds, because the pancakes didn't do anything for the pain in my leg.

"I don't see anything. Why are we stopping?" Barnaby turned in two circles, eyes bouncing all around for signs of danger. "Where is it?"

"Relax, Barns. We're close. We gotta wait here a second." I offered him some coffee. "We're not going to let anything happen to you. Once I give the signal, you pass me Funus and go. You're not sticking around."

He took the cup and swallowed down half of the contents.

"Gods, this is such a bad idea."

"For what it's worth, I don't think it's terrible. Just slightly unhinged," Funus unhelpfully offered.

"Better than insane," I pitched, leaning on a light post to ease the burden off my leg.

"I'm already hating the sound of this," Preston Cheslock announced his presence, his scowl along for the ride. His silver-eyed companion gave me a friendlier nod as a greeting.

"What's this about, Wilde?" Seyyid asked. "Technically we're not supposed to get involved in the void disruptions, and neither are you."

"Technically alcohol is poison, but it's still fun to drink. It's all about how you handle it." I showed them my app, with the pinging signal of a baby void tear starting to emerge. "We're going to handle the shit out of this tear, and you're going to walk away with the evidence that Florence Pierce is directly involved."

"Gods above." Preston aimed his scowl at my phone, then brandished that look at me with the full intent to kill with it. "You're tracking them? How?"

"That info is classified." I leaned away as he swiped at it. "You want in on this or not? Cause I'm trying to be nice and not kick you in the balls right now."

"How are the tears linked to Florence?" Seyyid pulled Preston back by the elbow. "And how is going to one anything other than suicide?"

"She's causing them and you'll see." I pocketed my phone and gave Preston a skeptical glance. Once he huffed and fell into place beside Seyyid, I relaxed. "All you need to do is hang back, stay away from the void, and run interference if DHAP shows up early."

"We don't have jurisdiction over what DHAP officials do." Seyyid shrugged. "We're suspended."

"Do what you can."

"You're going to get us into deeper shit than we already are," Preston accused. "We're on thin ice as it is."

"If this goes as intended, you'll be brought back with glowing reviews. You're gonna have to trust me." I flipped Preston off when he barked a laugh.

"You're full of shit."

"Normally, yeah. This time I'm being honest." It was my turn to shrug. "I can't make you stay. Go if you want. But this is your shot to show your superiors that you were right all this time. That's gotta be tempting."

"Or we get kicked off the force and disgraced for partnering with you," Preston countered. "Not as tempting."

"We'll do it." Seyyid met Preston's gaze when his partner wheeled on him. "We're helping."

"You gotta be kidding me."

Seyyid was a handsome guy; fit, capable, smart, and had the biggest, magical puppy dog eyes I'd ever seen. I wasn't even dating the guy and I honestly would've done whatever he wanted in that moment. He wielded them with deadly precision, without needing to deploy his jinn persuasion magic.

"This is bigger than our careers, Preston. Win or lose, we have to try." Seyyid went in for the kill and gave Preston a small, playful smirk. "Not like you to back down from a fight."

Preston didn't stand a chance. He folded like paper under those silver eyes.

"Fine." Preston exhaled. "We'll back you up, Wilde. But I swear to God, if this is some bullshit runaround, I'm going to hang your corpse on my front lawn."

"Who are you pissing off now?" Austin gave Seyyid and Preston a quick assessment, his Saint's Army insignia tossing light back in their faces. "You didn't mention additional people being here."

"Saint's Army? Fuck's sake, Wilde," Preston growled. "You're partnering with them?"

"Before you both start spitting insults at each other, I can assure you that you'll bond over your equal disdain for me," I refereed. "Let's just skip to the part where we partner up and get this shit done. We need to strike while this void tear is still weak."

"Any interaction with this tear is going to give it a chance to grow," Austin cut in. "As soon as you start, DHAP and the Saint's will know about it. We'll have minutes before they're here."

"I just need a few. Funus is going to help stabilize the tear, and Sias is going to keep me tethered while I go diving. Austin, you get ready to attack anything that comes knocking. Preston and

Seyyid will manage unwanted DHAP or police," I explained, watching for any confusion. "We good?"

"How is he going to keep the void stable?" Preston asked, giving Barnaby a skeptical glare. "He have a secret necromancy power we don't know about?"

"Not me," Barnaby scoffed, unzipping the backpack, folding down the front to reveal the dome window. "This is Funus."

Funus twinkled his yellow eyes from under his fake dog pelt.

"Good to meet you all. I look forward to working with you."

There was an uncomfortable pause while the three stared at Funus in a mixture of appalled horror and morbid curiosity.

"That's a talking skull," Preston finally said.

"You *kidnapped* a member of the necromancy council?" Austin baulked.

"No, *I* did," Barnaby shot back defensively. "Because your lot were murdering all of them. Now, because of my heroic actions, we have someone to help us. Maybe think about that the next time you go about destroying animated history all willy-nilly, you overstuffed trout."

"You just got shut down by a dandy with a talking skull," Preston explained to Austin, like maybe he didn't know what had just happened.

"I will fucking *shoot* you," Austin said to Preston, like maybe he didn't know what would happen.

"Enough!" Sias used his mean voice, which was similar to his hot Dom voice so it did funny things to my insides, and probably all of theirs, too. "Let's go."

There was a noticeable lack of arguing as we moved as a unit toward the tear.

The Swallows had already seen its share of calamity with the last tear, which was only a few blocks west of us. This new one had the grace to appear further away from a residential area, opting for the privacy of a closed down high school instead. From the state of the building, it had been shut down for a good decade and left to rot. Where the hell the unfortunate teenagers of the Swallows went to further their education was beyond me.

The tear was hanging out near the abandoned gym like a delinquent student, sparking with just enough energy to ping my phone but not set off any alarms. It moved like an angry ghost, fazing in and out of view with wisps of black smoke and crystalized agitation.

"It's small, but it still gives me the creeps," Preston shivered. "I saw the damage those things can cause."

"It won't stay small long." I motioned for them to stay back, suggesting where they should stand. "Keep your distance and be on watch. We can handle this part."

"How sure are you that this is going to work?" Seyyid eyed the tear, wariness growing. "What if we unleash something worse because you meddled with it?"

"I've done this before, but this time we have Funus. He can manage the void better than I can."

"Centuries of experience," Funus assisted. "I have confidence we'll do just fine. But I would keep your distance, just in case I'm supremely wrong."

"Thanks, man." My sarcasm went right over the skull, and he twinkled his eyes.

"Take these." Austin handed Seyyid a round of life infused bullets. "If something gets close, aim for the head or eyes. If it doesn't go down, run."

"Saint bless us," Preston mumbled.

"The Saint watches and protects," Austin finished for him. "Don't miss."

Seyyid and Preston took my advice and moved a short distance away from us, posting themselves near the edge of the gym to watch for any unwanted police reinforcements.

Austin readied his own weapon, glaring at the tear as it jerked and hissed.

"This had better work, Wilde."

"Yeah, no kidding. You'll be a real prick if it doesn't." I held my hand out for Funus's bag. "Barns, you get far away from here. No reason for you to stay in the crossfire."

"I'd like to stay." Barnaby tightened his grip on the bag's straps. "If it's all the same."

"It's not," I corrected. "You're not staying here."

"I've joined you on dangerous missions before, Dallas. I went all the way through the Silence Steps with you. I saved Funus, helped you navigate the tomb, helped you escape—"

"There weren't any void vampires and shit last time, Barns. We're not about to solve some puzzles, we're about to rip open a door to hell." I moved to take the bag from him but he stepped back, his hand moving to rest on Funus.

"Barnaby, what's gotten into you?" Funus asked from his case. "This is no place to be defiant. It's dangerous."

Barnaby shucked the backpack gently, placing it on the ground so he could extract Funus and speak to him face to skull.

"Of course it's dangerous," Barnaby said to him. "That's precisely why I want to stay. You are being placed in the middle of things and you have no way of escaping if something goes wrong."

"I choose to be here," Funus argued. "It is my purpose to guide acolytes through the way of the Goddess—"

"I'm not leaving you!" Barnaby announced, eyes growing glassy with frustration. "You stubborn old man, I'm staying right here. You are just going to have to deal with it. You're stuck with me, for better or worse, and I would argue this is a prime example of 'worse.'"

Funus had lost the ability to look humbled or moved when his eyebrows had decayed off his face years ago. He didn't have lips or cheeks, no laugh lines or freckles. There was nothing human about his facial nuances after centuries of being just bone and personality.

Somehow, through magic or maybe just love, the way Funus's eyes danced did the job just fine.

"Well, then." Funus watched Barnaby with the big, bright

yellow eyes of a dead guy who, at least in a metaphorical sense, was feeling his heart flutter. "I suppose you'll just need to stay."

"Good." Barnaby sniffed, satisfied. "I'm glad we got that settled."

I knew better than to try and convince him of how stupid he was being. I probably would have done the same thing. Funus was a pretty charismatic dead guy. I wasn't one to judge. I had been chasing my own dead dude for a while now.

"You good, Barns?"

"Yes." Barnaby angled Funus forward, holding him securely under his jaw. "Please be careful, Dallas. I will be very mad at you if you get us killed."

"Noted." I moved to the tear, pulling in the steadying breath I needed to keep my guts from turning to liquid. Sias was at my side, his hand resting between my shoulder blades.

"Tell me I'm not making a mistake," I said to Sias quietly, looking to him for the confidence I was starting to lose. "That I'm not going to get us all murdered. You heard Barns. I'll be in trouble."

"We aren't backing down now. And if it comes to that, I'll handle Barnaby." Sias moved his hand up to squeeze the nape of my neck. "Ready?"

"No, but we're doing it anyway." I wiggled my fingers to get the blood flowing, then tucked the obsidian vampire tooth against my right palm.

The void tear before me sputtered at my presence like an angry hornet, small and vicious. I knew that the moment I reached for it, called upon my weak connection to the death magic within, all hell was going to break loose.

My heart started to thunder at the anticipation of danger, fear nipping at the tender spots just beneath the adrenaline high.

Sias's fingers threaded through my hair, giving just the perfect amount of pressure.

"You know the rules, pet," he breathed into my ear, charm

cooling the sharp stab of fear threatening. "You don't stop until I say. I'll tell you when you've had enough."

I swallowed. "Yes, Sias."

"Don't keep me waiting." His free hand slithered down my arm, lifting my wrist up to the tear. "Show me what you can do."

My temples pounded for a moment before easing, my chest a steady beat of terror mixed with a little bit of excitement.

Here we go.

I shut my eyes, fell into the bliss Sias cloaked me in, and reached for the void. Cold sparks danced over the tips of my fingers, little bites of warning from the corruption swirling through the magic. There was fear, compulsion, whispering for me to run, flee, fighting with the orders to give in to the darkness and let it swallow me whole.

It was faint at first, whispers in the dark, waiting just outside my thoughts as I curled my fingers around the familiar threads of death magic. The tear before us crackled with energy, swelling out and exhaling an arctic gust.

The threads across my fingers began to solidify from spider silk to strings, dancing around the piece of artificial scythe resting on my palm.

I curled my fingers around the strings and pulled the rip line, chaos roaring out from the other side.

The tear burst open, corruption splintering out like needles in all directions. Fear plunged a knife through my chest for a scaring moment, smothered quickly by Sias as he felt me recoil.

"Breathe," he commanded, squeezing my hairline. "Good, pet. We've just started. You can't fall now."

"It's powerful," I managed through gasps of air. "Really fucking powerful."

"Push through, slow and steady." He hissed a lovely sound of satisfaction as I adjusted my grip on the threads and held fast. "That's my pet. Good boy."

A bewildered, "My God," punctured through, which I knew was Barnaby. I heard Austin grunt in agreement.

"Hold on tight!" Funus cheered from the sidelines. "I'm going to wrangle this mess as best I can!"

The corrupted magic pulsed and pushed, the energy nails raking down my skin. Cold threads wrapped around my wrist as my ability to hold death magic grew stronger, reinforced by the obsidian and Funus's guidance. The pressure of conflicting magic started to feel less noisy as Funus forged a pathway and through the growing chaos, I saw the void ripple, pure and open.

I had to bide my time.

My chance would come soon enough.

But the monsters inside saw us first.

I barely had time to duck as the horde took flight, pouring from the tear in a swarm of teeth and terror. Leathery wings made of bone and blades piloted the bat-like mass of creatures, a good twenty or more swirling hungrily above our heads like vultures.

"What the hell are those?!" Barnaby screeched, hugging Funus to his chest. He screamed again when Austin started picking them out of the sky using his gun. The creatures he managed to hit fell to ashes, but the mass was not pleased with the attack. The tiny bundles of evil began swooping down, screams so shrill and horrible they sent a sharp shiver through my eardrums.

Austin hissed as one bladed wing caught his arm as another slashed his cheek. The scent of fresh blood made the swarm scurry in the sky, eager to get a taste of him.

"Barnaby." Sias caught his attention, revealing his ugly as hell, but efficient, gun from the holster at his ribs. He pulled it free and presented it to him. "Can you shoot?"

"Is that a gun?" Barnaby looked amazed, because of course he did. "It's beautiful!"

"Take it." Sias pushed it into his hand. "Shoot at the bats."

"I...I'm not exactly..." Barnaby floundered.

"Barns, it's not hard," I told him, trying to keep my focus on the tear. "Point the deadly end at the sky and pull the trigger. Hold on tight or it'll jump out of your hand. Don't shoot us."

Barnaby ducked and yelled in alarm as a bat swooped at his

head. As commanded, he aimed a shaking hand toward the sky and fired once, somehow sending a creature into a ball of dust.

"I hit it! I did it!"

"Great! Do it eleven more times!" I yelled, jerking as his next shot whizzed past my head. "I said *don't shoot us*, Barns!"

"I'm doing my best!" he screamed at me, like I was somehow the asshole in this situation.

Funus joined in on the "yelling at Dallas" game. "Keep your focus on the tear, acolyte!"

"Tell your boyfriend to stop trying to kill me!"

"He's doing fine!" Funus defended. "Focus on your task!"

"Ah-ha!" I grinned at them. "You didn't say he wasn't your boyfriend! I knew it!"

"Will you shut the fuck up, Wilde!" Austin yelled the same time Barnaby called me a bloated pig fart.

Sias gripped my hair and sent a wave of threatening pleasure through me that nearly buckled my knees.

"You focus on *me* now, pet," he said through his teeth. "Don't disobey me again. We're not done, and you've left me unsatisfied."

"O-okay. Fair." I swallowed. "But in my defense, Barns was trying to kill us."

"Yes, Sias," Sias growled the reminder, my body vibrating from the grip he had over me. My head was manipulated back to the tear, fingers gripping my hair while the other snaked around my waist. "Don't make me tell you again."

My heart hammered, the threads in my grip tightening as I regained control.

"Yes, Sias."

With my sights back on the pathway, I curled my fingers to hold it steady, waiting for the moment to strike. Corruption scraped at me, driving needles of panic and unwanted impulses through my temples.

Not yet.

Not *yet*.

"I hear sirens!" Preston called over to us. "They're coming this way!"

"Breathe," Sias coached as worry started to mount in my chest. I felt the arm around my waist pull me closer. "Don't stray from this moment. Stay right here."

We needed more time. We had to wait.

If we didn't time it just right, it was all going to fall apart. We weren't going to get another chance.

Not yet.

Almost.

Almost.

Gunfire and the piercing screams of the void creatures swirled around us, punctuated by Austin's orders and Barnaby's yelling. The tear grew bigger, spikes of obsidian stabbing through the air as glassy blades of death. I felt a shard pierce sideways, almost grazing my hip. Sias held me too tight to react.

It was getting too wild, too close, but whatever panic or self-preservation I needed in order to care was smothered by Sias's overwhelming charm magic. All I could feel were the calm bindings cocooning me in a golden embrace, even while death wrapped its tendrils around my fingers.

Through the darkness, through the veil of churning corruption and growing calamity, I saw it.

My opening—small, a blink, I had moments before it would shut forever.

I also saw a muzzle lined with teeth and eyeless sockets powered by malice charging with a body of powerful muscle and claws coming right for us.

Nothing could ever go as planned, could it?

It was easy to decide how to handle this extra helping of bull-shit in an already stressful situation. Whether it was because I was being soothed by daddy Sias's fingers, or because a talking skull was helping to pave the way into the void, I'll never know. Either way, I saw the solution plain as day.

The window of opportunity was closing, a vicious beast of

undead evil was charging, and I had to act. I turned in Sias's arms and kissed him, the jolt of surprise in his eyes and from his lips wonderful.

Before he could do much else, I placed both hands on his firm chest and shoved him backwards as hard as I could. He flailed, Barnaby dodged the sudden appearance of a staggering Sias, and I turned back just as the big bad beastie attempted to rip through the void.

The maw snapping through was bleached bone and acid-stained teeth, scaled tongue lashing as it tried to rip at the seams of the tear.

I heard Sias scream my name as I charged, wrapping my arms around the muzzle of the feral death hound, and shoved it back into the void.

The beast slashed but couldn't keep its grip, tumbling backward into the tear.

Taking me with it.

# CHAPTER
# ELEVEN



HERE'S THE THING.

The living aren't meant to be in the void.

That's kind of the whole point, isn't it? The nothingness, the absence of any life, light or presence. It's supposed to be an endless expanse of blank space, an anomaly of logic that doesn't play by any rule of physics or reality. To us living idiots, we know from our scientific laws that energy cannot be created nor destroyed, thus contributing to the wonderful entropy of the perceived universe.

But the void is all the little bits in between reality and nonsense. It's fragments of dreams you can't remember, the thoughts slipping away from your conscious when you try and hold on to them too tight.

It's nothing.

And despite my self-deprecating humor and what others might want to chime in with, I am *not* nothing. I was a big, handsome slab of *something* tumbling around like a rock in the void's dryer. I wasn't supposed to be there. I was fucking things up for all the nothings just trying to do their thing.

Not a great place to be.

My conscious had visited the void a few times, slipping out of

the flesh vehicle I piloted around and wielded with reckless abandon, but my body had never gone all the way inside. I wasn't sure
what the hell was going to happen to me.

I also couldn't wrap my mind around how I wasn't instantly
dead.

I didn't have a ton of time to grapple with my impending
death or my questionable mortality because the beast I had
tackled was very pissed off. We sank like heavy rocks in the
endless darkness, all while the damn thing was trying to take a
chunk out of me. Flashes of teeth snapped, claws swiped, and a
hole was ripped through my new jeans.

I couldn't get through a week without ruining a pair, I swear
to the gods.

Pain seared into my ribs as one of its blows landed, lacerating
my skin just deep enough to hurt like a son of a bitch. I couldn't
wield life essence anymore due to my upgraded necromancy
status, but I did have a regular knife I could stab into the damn
thing's paw as pay back.

It made a howl that rattled like breaking bones, which was
arguably worse than getting slashed, but I felt a little vindicated
regardless.

It didn't take long after that for my mind to start to slip, little
spills happening as we plummeted through a realm I had no business being in. I was dying, fading, as all living things do in the
presence of the void. Cold was grabbing at my limbs, thoughts
drifting off before springing back in a snap of panic.

I had to focus.

I had to make it out. Had to grab what I had come for.

I had to fucking *try*.

The terror of failing coiled in my stomach like a snake, but I
shut my eyes against the nothingness and breathed.

Could I breathe in the void? I didn't know. Maybe I was
psychologically breathing. My lungs moved, or at least I believed
they did, and I tried to center myself away from the overwhelming urge to submit.

To float away and die.

I focused, I held on to my thoughts and centered myself, repeating Funus's stupid mantra because why not go for broke and see if the Death Goddess could hear me. I was basically in her damn house, if she couldn't hear me then it wasn't going to happen.

Give me strength. Give me guidance. Give me peace in your embrace.

I am a child of death.

I am yours to love.

I am yours to command.

I am yours to…

Damn, I couldn't remember anymore. To obey? To submit? It was something that made me feel icky because I don't like being commanded or submitting. Responding negatively to authority was kind of my jam. Unless it was for sex stuff, then it was fun.

*That's some deep psychological shit right there. Maybe it had some-thing to do with my relationship with the only father figure I had in my life. Ew. Does that mean Magnus contributed to my kink?*

*Alright, that made me gag. I'm gagging. Gross.*

*Shit, am I losing myself? Am I dying or do I have ADD?*

*I'm dying, aren't I?*

*Son of a bitch.*

More little spills. Maybe one big one.

I saw a fragment of a memory. Austin was letting me crawl into his bunk because I was scared of the dark. I was so scared back then. He never made me feel bad for it. Even when we were little kids, he was always so much bigger than me.

*"Just this one time,"* he'd tell me, even if it had been the tenth time already. *"You gotta learn to stop being afraid."*

I felt safe with him, right up until the end. Right until the moment I saw the protective part of him die in the fire I had caused. I missed him so much.

Things got a little muddy after that.

My memories were a slushie of mistakes and cherished moments I never wanted to forget.

Old birthdays. Running in the forest.

Panting in ecstasy while Sias leaned over me, eyes a rainbow of delight.

Zane standing under the moonlight in a cemetery.

Kevin blowing a bubble at me for the first time, his color just starting to come back after a lifetime of neglect.

I felt my chest warm, strings wrapping me in a vibrant glow that brought me back into a soft awareness.

My head swam, memories that weren't mine filtered through like they had broken through a dam.

The same beautiful woman and man I had seen tangled in the sheets before, their smiles gone, suitcases packed by the front door. My heart was breaking. Never again. I'd never let someone close again.

*"You're a monster."*

I had loved them so much.

No.

Sias had. He had loved them. They were his biggest regret.

Why the hell was I seeing his memories here?

A wave of comfort washed over me, my mind flushing back to life as I let my eyes flutter open. The void was still around me, I was still falling, still lost in the void. Golden strings fell with me, but I wasn't alone.

A shadow.

Red eyes.

It was him.

My vampire.

*I need to find the window,* I thought. *Before it closes.*

A cold grip took me by the shirt, throwing me into a new direction of sideways freefall. I could always count on Zane to be efficient, but he was never one to prioritize comfort. I spun, my poor body and brain barely intact after being in the void longer than I should, and landed with a hard kick to the ribs.

The window was still open, if only barely. The laser had been deployed, and the magic was already at work.

It was now or literally never.

I forced myself to the tear and felt the threads of the void tighten in my grip, the strings tight and icy as I pulled them with everything I had.

The window swelled open, and I reached out.

My lungs filled with air the moment I leaned out of it, and I nearly choked trying to take as many breaths as I could. The poor bastard who had been jotting down notes in the lab nearly had a heart attack, grabbing at their chest in complete shock.

"Sorry," I managed, snatching the discharged vial containing the infused crystal from the robotic arm. "Gotta borrow this. Uh. This was a nightmare. Go back to sleep."

The person did just that and hit the ground. It wasn't because I commanded them to do it so much as they had fainted, but I'd take my wins where I could.

I kicked off back into the void, vial clutched in my hand.

*Give a guy a ride back?* I thought out to the pair of red eyes staring at me. *Maybe a little nicer this time?*

The way my shirt was grabbed was a decided "no," and I was once again hauled in a direction that didn't quite make sense. I spun, flying through the nothingness, my lungs burning as I held on to the air from the lab. My heart was a thunderstorm, brain a little gooey from the trauma, but I was somehow still alive.

I just had to not die for a little while longer.

Zane's throw helped me get most of the way back to the tear I had fallen from, and I began to claw and scramble my way toward it. I couldn't breathe, and my head began to swim.

I didn't know where he went. His smoky form had vanished back into the darkness before I could give him a proper "fuck you" for not aiming better.

Not yet.

Almost.

In the light of the tear, I saw a golden lifeline, an outstretched hand, eyes churning with a rainbow of terror, affection and hope. I slapped my palm against Sias's and grabbed on, and was heaved from the void in one strong pull.

"Dallas," he breathed, holding me so tight I thought I was going to turn to dust. "Gods damn you."

Seyyid and Preston had joined the fight against the flying nightmares, bigger ones had manifested since I'd disappeared. Most of the little ones were gone, but there were a few eagle-sized bastards trying to dive bomb their heads, intent on doing damage with talons of wicked obsidian.

"Where the *fuck* did you go, Wilde?" Preston screamed at me, storming over. "We gotta get that shit sealed NOW!"

"Move out of the way," Austin yelled, bloody and coated in the dust of the winged creatures he was still fighting. "I have to seal the tear."

"Not yet." I caught Preston's arm and shoved the vial into his palm. "As promised. This is what you need."

"What the hell is this?" Preston's eyes darted to his hand then me, and I was too preoccupied to notice how far away from Sias he was standing.

"That's from the lab creating the tears. Check the patent associated with the tech, it'll lead you right back to Florence."

"Patent?" He snarled. "Are you *serious*? We went through this for a piece of busted magic tech you think Florence is associated with?"

"She is. She's too much of an egomaniac not to patent that tech." I rolled my neck to coax some pops from my spine, and shook out my hands. "Now get out of my fucking way. Austin, don't touch the tear until I'm done."

"Wilde, we don't have time. Magnus and the DHAP are almost here, and more creatures are pouring out of—"

He bared his teeth at me when I grabbed his shoulder, only easing the snarl when he saw the intent in my eyes.

"I have to do this, Austin. I have to make it right. Please." I swallowed. "Just this one time."

There was a little piece of him that I never thought I'd see again, a spark for just a moment.

It was there and gone in a blink, but I saw it.

"You're insane," he spat, but didn't make a move as I released him. "Go. Fast."

"One more round," I told Sias, only then noticing the slashes on his cheeks were bleeding. They sat just below his eyes, resting on his cheekbones.

The blood looked a little too dark.

He wiped away the blood with one hand while the other slipped back into my hair.

"I'm fine, pet," he told me before I could comment. "One more round."

I should have noticed how pale he was. Or how his horns were curling the wrong way. Or how dark the ring of his iris was. I should have noticed a lot of things in that moment. But I was too close to making things right, too close to bringing it all home.

"I'll never ask you for anything ever again," I promised him. "For at least a week."

"Please," he teased, tone dry. "No need to lie to me."

We approached the tear, and I glanced at Funus, who was still tucked against Barnaby's chest.

"I'd hurry, acolyte. Whatever you plan on doing, we don't have much time."

"I'd like to go home, Dallas, preferably in one piece," Barnaby commented. "Do wrap up."

"One last thing, then we'll go." I leaned my head back into Sias's grip. "Ready?"

"Always." Sias pulled at my scalp, his charm magic slithering over me like snakes wrapping up their prey. It felt…dangerous. Deadly. A flutter of delicious panic trailed through me before easing into a sense of calm understanding.

He had me now.

There was no use fighting it. I wasn't *safe* per se, but he would allow me to live. For now.

I shivered, and Sias's breath was sweet as he cooed.

"You know this game, pet. You're not leaving this time. You do as I say, and I'll be happy."

"Yes, Sias," I whispered.

"Good. Now." My hand was lifted to the tear. Sias's fingers looked like they had been dipped in ink up to the first knuckle. "Let's go get your vampire."

I felt the threads in my hand. I wasn't sure if they had ever left. The obsidian vampire tooth in my palm pierced the skin as I squeezed my hand shut, my blood pooling before dripping over the edge.

The void welcomed my hand like a hungry cavern of ice, a chill bone deep and sharp trailed up my arm.

"I offer my blood," I spoke to the void and the Goddess within. "I hold a piece of your blade. I am an acolyte of the council, and follower of your guidance. I will vanquish your enemies, wield your magic, and surrender my soul to your void. I want my Thrall. *My* vampire."

The cold in my bones hardened, gripping tight and freezing the marrow within. The pain was sharp and unforgiving, splintering in all directions. I screamed through my teeth but held strong, using everything I had in me to keep my fist closed over the tooth.

"Breathe, pet. Breathe," Sias whispered, easing the horrible pain with a squeeze of his warm magic.

I managed a few quick breaths, my fingers numb as the cold locked my elbow painfully in place.

"You said you could always find me," I pleaded to the tear, the corrupted magic starting to stab out and strike my skin. A blade hit my hip, my thigh, razers biting into me.

"We need to go! Now!" Austin was screaming.

"Fuck, if DHAP show up they're going to shoot us for being this close," Preston was pleading. "Seyyid, we have to go."

"We can't leave them, Preston!"

"Put me down and run, darling. Please. It's not safe!" Funus was yelling.

"I told you no! I'm not going without you and that's final!"

"Bring him home, Dallas," Sias cut through the noise. "Be perfect again."

"You said you could always find me," I begged. "Find me now, Zane."

Sirens were blaring. Creatures were screaming above our heads.

"Keep your heads down! More creatures are coming!"

"Saint! They're bigger than the last swarm!"

"I sell antiques! I'm not cut out for this!"

"Goddess protect us!"

"Find me now."

Find me now.

*Find me now. FIND ME NOW.*

Thump.

Thump.

A heartbeat.

Subtle at first. A soft flutter against my palm.

Thump.

Thump. Thump. Thump. THUMP.

The pulse chased up my arm, my fingers gripping the sensation through the cold, through the overwhelming anguish of the void's grip.

My heartbeat was in time with the pulse, chest tight, breath stuck as I marveled in the sensation.

When I finally was able to breathe again, I choked out one command: "Pull."

Sias wrapped his arms around my chest and heaved backwards, leveraging his weight to help me rip the beating heart from the void. My arm didn't budge, the glacial grip both horrible and agonizing. I screamed every single foul word I could think of as the void fought me, Sias digging his heels into the ground to pry us backwards.

I felt the heart pounding in my hand, felt the sting of the corrupted magic stabbing at my skin, felt the ice freezing my blood and twisting my bones.

I wasn't going to let go.

Not for anything.

Zane was coming back to me, or I was going to die trying.

I felt something give, a sudden release of the force holding me, and my world flipped backwards as we went crashing to the ground. Sias was under me, groaning from the pain of having someone land on top of him during a fight with gravity. I scrambled up, staring in heartbreaking horror as the tear began to slowly close like a healing wound.

"No!" I screamed so violently my throat was raw. "No, don't let it shut! I'm not done! Not yet!"

"We're out of time, Dallas, we have to go!" Austin was pleading, trying to get me to my feet. "Please. Listen to me!"

"I can't go without him! I'm not leaving without Zane!" I struggled against his grip, trying to get back to the tear as it shrank, the corruption still crackling around it.

"Are you trying to get yourself killed?!" Austin shook me. "Is that what you want? For all of us to die?"

In a moment of anger, of heartache and despair, I swung at him with intent to knock him on his ass for getting in my way.

The blow would have connected, if half of my arm wasn't missing.

Austin's eyes went wide as I took stock of the missing section of my right arm. Just below the elbow, the skin was healing over black bone that had been snapped clean like something had bitten it off. My arm and hand were gone, the skin scarring over a stump where they used to be.

As I marveled at how much my missing arm didn't hurt. There was no blood, no shock. The magic had cauterized it in a flash, perinatally reshaping me.

The tear began to move.

The borders of it hissed with the corrupted magic, smoky

fingers reaching through to shove the opening wider. A shadow ducked through, one foot and then the other, holding the void open for its massive frame. At its center, resting in the broad chest, a heart was beating, flanked on either side by black, skeletal fingers.

My fingers.

The sight of my hand protectively cradling the heart vanished as the shadow began to materialize, the vapor turning to solid flesh and blood. Pale skin wrapped over bone and muscle, red orbs forming eyes that blinked as it came to life. The same clothes he had died in were somehow back on his body, unmarred by the tragedy that had taken him away from me.

Zane smoothed his shirt down, blinked in confusion, then reached back into the void to grab his jacket.

He gave it a good shake before looking at me.

"I think you dropped this."

Until that moment, I knew exactly how I was going to handle seeing him again. He would say something dry and unamused; I'd clap back with something hilarious and charming, just decimating him with how clever I was. Maybe I'd admit I missed him if I was feeling generous or particularly moody that day, but for the most part I was so *sure* I was going to play it cool.

I did not play it cool.

Nor was I cutting and witty. I did not verbally spar with him and give him a cheeky, subtle acknowledgement that I had missed him in some small way.

Zane caught me in his arms as I flew into him like an airborne missile, and I'd started crying about midway there. I was audibly sobbing into his shoulder, practically climbing him like a tree because I didn't want anyone to try and snatch him away again. I think I tried talking, but it came out as wailing gibberish pitched high enough for bats to hear it.

So much for being nonchalant.

"Easy, hunter," he rumbled, warm and solid around me. "I've got you."

"I thought I'd never see you again," I confessed, figuring the whole sobbing like an idiot kinda ruined the facade anyway.

"I don't want to step on the moment," Austin said, stepping on the moment. "But we kinda have flying creatures trying to dive bomb us, cops inbound and a fucking tear still open!"

Oh.

Right.

All the other shit happening.

"He's right, I'm afraid," Sias's voice floated into the conversation. "Zane, lovely to see you, darling, but could you help us fight off the swarm while I get us an escape route?"

Zane unwrapped his arms from around me, and had to pry me loose from the vise grip I had around his ribs.

"Just a few more minutes!" I argued.

"I need to be able to move to fight." Zane scowled at me.

"*Fine*," I growled, reluctantly releasing him so we could not die or whatever. "But I'm going to cuddle you so damn hard later."

"Let's focus on the problem in front of us," Zane said, snapping back into his serious Thrall nature. I almost missed that his cheeks were flushed just a shade darker.

"Dallas!" Barnaby yelled as he shielded Funus from an inbound attack from above, one of the creatures screeching as it ripped into his shoulder. Preston and Seyyid did their best to take out more of them, but they were impossibly fast and craving blood.

"Get the void closed," I told Austin. "We'll handle the flying things."

"Thank the Saint." Austin passed me his gun. I tried to take it with my right hand and had to change tactics the moment my stump was presented.

"That's going to take a minute," I mumbled, taking the gun with my left.

"It's loaded with life essence bullets already," Austin said. "I hope you can still aim worth a shit."

"I can shoot lefty in a pinch. Zane, get to Barns and Funus. Keep them safe. Sias, you said you can get us a way out?"

"Yes, but we need to—" Sias's attention snapped to the tear, just as it started to crackle and spread out in agitation. "Something's wrong."

"No shit," Austin growled as the sirens of the inbound DHAP forces came into view. "We're out of time. They're here."

It was hard to count exactly how many vehicles were roaring toward us, their dazzling lights blinking with authority. The wail of the sirens and the screech of the void creatures created a horrible symphony of agony. Their noises seemed to piss each other off, causing the voidlings to attack with more force as the world around us crowded in with guns drawn.

At least they fired on the creatures first, which was nice of them. Gunfire sounded off, dust from the flying creatures above us floated like ashen snowfall.

The screeching had stopped when the final monster was blown away, giving us exactly three seconds of peace before we became the center of attention.

The void tear crackled. It didn't like being ignored.

"Get on the ground! Hands behind your head!" a voice amplified over speakers ordered us from behind dancing lights.

"We're the ones fighting this thing, you twits!" Barnaby yelled from the ground, holding Funus.

Seyyid and Preston were quiet, palms raised. Blood trailed down their wounds, expressions stuck between pain from injuries and concern for their precarious careers.

"I'm with Saint's Army!" Austin called out. "I have to get this tear handled! You need to *stay back!*"

"We know who you are," Magnus's voice cut through like a hot knife, his familiar stride silhouetted by the unforgiving lights. "Who do you think gave these officers life bullets and told them to fire?"

"Sir, the tear is still unstable—" Austin tried but Magnus wasn't having it.

"You're not in command here anymore, boy. Step aside." Magnus's gaze bounced from the tear to me, to Sias, then snapped to Zane. If he had been chewing a toothpick, the thing would have been ground to dust. "You."

"I remember you." Zane snarled. "Showing up late to fuck things up again. At least you're consistent."

"I had hoped my boy killed you off. That's disappointing." Magnus clicked his tongue. "Too bad. That's alright, I'll have a good time pulling you apart for information."

"Sir, the tear," Austin pleaded. "It's shrinking but it's still dangerous."

"I'll handle the tear." Magnus tossed a set of handcuffs to Austin. "Cuff the traitor and shoot the incubus. He's been compromised. We'll take the vampire alive."

"What did I say about threatening my people in front of me?" I warned, my stride forward interrupted by Zane who grabbed my shoulder. "You so much as touch *any* of them, and I'll kill you myself."

"Your little demon there doesn't count as a person anymore," Magnus explained, his stormy eyes flicking over me, pausing at my arm. A hint of pain lanced his face upon seeing it. "God-damnit, Dallas."

"Sir, let's just take care of the tear first and we can talk—" Austin hesitated, which was enough to be a slight in Magnus's eyes.

"You will follow my orders, soldier. You are already on thin ice, and I will not repeat myself." Magnus set his jaw, eyes piercing and unyielding. "He's not your brother anymore, son. He's a necromancer. He's lost to us. Do not follow in his footsteps. I can't lose you too, Austin."

I saw Austin flinch. I saw how deep those words cut him.

I also saw the impossible weight on his shoulders from a task he shouldn't have been given. He was exhausted. Beaten. Tired.

Torn.

It broke my heart.

Both of them broke my heart.

"Hey," I called out to my brother. "You gotta learn to stop being afraid."

When Austin looked at me, I could have sworn I saw the same kid I knew from years ago. Just for a second.

We didn't have time to think, to sit in the moment and take it for what it was worth, because the void tear had enough of our mortal prattling.

It expanded its mouth wide, and spat out a wave of hell we were not prepared for.

# TWELVE

THE SILVER LINING about being surrounded by cops is when the void decided to barf out a tornado of nightmares, we had some extra firepower.

We had gone from an uncomfortable family altercation involving the police, to an all-out fight for our lives in a blink of an eye. The void tear Austin kept trying to warn everyone about decided it was time to prove his point and opened up wide enough for a new swarm of winged bastards with razor talons to make a dramatic entrance.

They burst onto a scene in a long scream, circling all the living bodies ready to be snacked upon. They didn't wait to attack, and to our collective horror, they had a new game plan. Instead of dive bombing a few at a time to take chunks of our skin bit by bit, they moved as a unified swarm of death. The collective group of nightmares—what do you call a group of nightmares? A night terror maybe?—swooped down as one cloud of evil, grabbing a helpless officer off the ground. It took a few agonizing minutes of screaming and panicked firing into the terror to get the body to drop, only to realize that the blood had been drained and he was a dried husk already.

"Nope," I announced, grabbing Barnaby from the ground and heaving him to his feet. "Barns, time to run."

"Dallas," Barnaby's hands shook as he zipped up Funus's carry case and strapped it to his chest. "You're not about to say something incredibly stupid like you're staying behind, are you?"

"I gotta help take these things out. Go. Meet us back at Sias's place."

Barnaby's trembling fingers grabbed my arm and squeezed, a set look of determination almost masking his terror.

"You don't owe them anything," Barnaby told me. "Don't you dare get yourself hurt for a group of people who don't deserve you. Kevin will never forgive you."

"Tell Kevin that I promise I'll be home soon." I gave my fussy, fretting, obnoxious landlord-turned-friend-now-brother a quick hug before pushing him in the direction of safety. "Go."

I was proud that he didn't look back as he ran for his life, hugging Funus's case to his chest with all he had.

Magnus was barking orders at the cops to take cover and retreat, his voice standing out in all the screaming and gunfire. Dust from the few winged nightmares they had been able to hit danced in the breeze, but there was still way too many for us to feel safe.

Preston and Seyyid disappeared into the fray, diving after the wounded to help them escape. I lost track of them quickly after that, Seyyid's silver eyes a fading lighthouse overtaken by the chaos.

I hoped like hell they made it, but I didn't have a chance to dwell on it.

"I have to help Austin get that damn tear closed." I passed Zane my gun. "Zane, Sias, keep us covered. Stay away from Magnus, I think he's trigger happy."

"Work fast," Sias said as he cocked his ridiculous gun. "The corrupted magic around it is starting to splinter, and I desperately need a shower."

"Keep your distance from the tear, hunter," Zane warned. "It's too volatile." He lifted his chin in a silent command to go before turning his attention on the swarm.

Austin was bleeding from a fresh cut to his shoulder when I slid to a stop beside him, the swarm of danger above us starting to bank into a sharp U-turn.

"Please tell me you have something strong to seal this thing," I asked him. "Like maybe a goddamn life essence nuke."

"I wasn't expecting it to be this wild," he admitted, fear pinching his features. "We're going to have to pray the Saint is with us today."

"Maybe with you. We haven't spoken in a while, and I think I technically belong to the Goddess now. Tell me how to help."

Austin ground his worry between his back teeth.

"You can get closer than I can." He pulled a plastic cylinder covered in duct tape, rigged with a few wires and a trigger. "We need to make sure this goes *in* the tear for it to have any chance."

"Austin." I took a measuring breath. "Why the hell do you have a home-made life bomb and not a professional grenade?"

"Because you *stole* my last fucking grenade, Dallas," he shot back. "And this trip wasn't sanctioned. I couldn't steal supplies without Magnus knowing, for all the good that did me. I'm not supposed to be here, so I had to make my own bomb."

He shoved the thing into my hand and hooked my finger into the trigger. I felt the thing click.

It was already primed.

"You'll have five seconds before it explodes after you release the trigger," my insane brother told me. "So, hold tight until you're ready to throw."

"You asshole," I whispered, holding the trigger down. At best the thing would blow off my last remaining arm. At worst I'd be flaming Dallas chunks. Needless to say, I was a little pissed off Austin didn't walk me through his plan before I was volunteered into it.

"I'll keep you covered. Don't miss."

"Yeah, thanks," I snapped. "Remind me to kick you in the ass after this."

The swarm above us swooped down and yanked another person off the ground, spinning into a funnel of screaming, black bodies as the poor human in the middle was bled dry. They were moving faster, gaining strength with each victim they snagged. The swarm moved like liquid terror as it dropped the drained body and busted through the windows of one of the cars.

Magnus, the remaining DHAP officers and anyone else with a gun was trying to pick off what they could, but the swarm was getting increasingly harder to hit.

If anything else came out of that tear, we'd be done for.

The tear was having a great time as I approached, spitting and crackling with the growing madness spreading from its seams. Sharp obsidian created a barrier of jagged blades across the ground, which was tricky to navigate through without adding more damage to my jeans. These were already ruined from my wounds, so I barely snorted in annoyance when I felt more of my pant leg get ripped away.

I guessed it was time for me to get fitted for a suit of armor, because it really was getting ridiculous.

The void churning from within the tear was angry and vicious, nothingness clouded by a tangle of magic that shouldn't be there. The corruption reached for the sky like sharp branches, and I inched closer to give myself the best shot at getting the bomb where it needed to go.

The tear hissed and groaned, a fresh wave of screaming behind me was partnered with the sound of peeling tires.

I dared a glance behind me, horrified but not surprised that the DHAP forces had decided to retreat. A few bodies littered the ground, skin like jerky from all the blood being ripped from them by thousands of starving little mouths. I couldn't find Preston and Seyyid, and I quietly hoped that they weren't among the dead.

One of the vehicles trying to reverse had the windshield smashed through before they could escape, the bodies ripped into the air while the car still rolled backward. The air began to smell like burning rubber and ash.

I winced in pain as a shard bit my calf, but I trudged ahead to get the goddamn tear under control.

The tear pulsed, the sounds of crystalizing magic crackled around my feet as I held my breath.

I prayed like hell Austin could build a decent bomb.

I prayed again that I could throw decently left-handed.

And I absently wondered which deity I was actually asking, and which one would answer.

I didn't have to wait long for that answer, and I had a feeling that the Death Goddess wasn't done testing me. Not sure why she thought it would be funny to toss more fuel onto the fire, but I was starting to think this shit was personal.

My throw was fine, albeit a little crooked. Austin's trigger did have a delay, so my arm wasn't blown off.

And, most importantly, the bomb contents were just the right firepower to rip the void tear into pieces and slam the door shut with a hissing, vicious thunderclap of finality.

But not until one last monster came out to play.

I recognized the sound of the grisly bone-breaking roar instantly, and had the natural panic reaction to duck as the huge body of the void beast came barreling out of the tear just as the bomb exploded inside of it.

The creature's dark fur bristled as it landed, claws digging into the earth as its eyeless sockets stared blankly ahead. Its teeth parted as it rumbled a growl, the sound like bone fraying before a clean snap.

The tear sealed shut like a knitting wound, the corrupted magic around it crystalizing into shards that shattered across the pavement. It was a win, but hardly the final nail in the coffin. The beasts above us swirled like a hungry storm, rallying around their fellow nightmare as it bared its sharp teeth our way.

The void hound turned its massive head toward me, the fur stopping just shy of the black bone of its powerful jaws, and lashed its scaly tongue out like a coiled viper. It looked like a bear and a dire wolf had an unholy nightmare baby and had come back from the dead ready to eat faces and cause mayhem. Its fur was midnight with hues of raven blue, its sockets flashing gold for just a second before it snorted out a rush of angry air from its nose hole.

And then it charged.

I snapped off an obsidian blade and rolled to the side, ready to stab the damn thing and hoped to hell it could bleed. A black mist formed around the beast as it stormed toward me, its massive head yanking back as Zane materialized around it and trapped it in a choke hold.

Zane's massive arms flexed with effort as he fell backwards with the beast trapped in his grip, both of them thrashing as he tried to snap its neck. The hound's claws raked over Zane's arms as its teeth snapped in fury, blood lost in the black fur.

"Hold it still!" Sias ordered, voice strained.

I rushed to help, to try and stab the thing or injure it in any way I could, but the rain of gunfire bouncing off the hound's jaw sent me staggering backward.

"You'll hit them!" Austin was yelling at Magnus as he fired. "Stop!"

"I'm not letting that thing get away. Damn the rest," Magnus spat, landing a few bullets dangerously close to Zane's head.

Zane yelled through his teeth as he strained to rein the hound in, his arm bleeding horribly, bullets dancing around his head. I was torn between rushing to tackle Magnus, place myself as a shield somehow, or use all my effort to try and kill the damn hound.

The swarm above us let out a unified screech, spinning in a tornado of claws and teeth as it chose that moment to descend. A hailstorm of little bodies funneled down, spinning around Magnus and Austin like they meant to sweep them up and swallow them whole.

The mass was so thick I could barely see through the storm,

black fur and razer teeth flashing between glimpses of Magnus and Austin trying to figure out how to escape.

"No!" I cried out, panic ripping me in half.

I couldn't let them die. I didn't want them to die.

The sounds of Zane screaming, the hound's jaws snapping, and the screaming promise of my former family's demise was almost too much.

Who do I save?

How do I save them?

What the hell was I supposed to do?

A wave of calm began to settle over me like fog, dense and heavy, and for a heartbeat I thought I was about to fall into a blissful high. My limbs grew heavy, muscles relaxing, and the shard of obsidian in my hand fell to the ground as my fingers simply gave up on holding it.

I blinked hard, battling my senses. I needed to fight, needed to keep the hound from ripping Zane into pieces and killing us all.

I knew this. I *knew* I had to snap out of it but…

Gods, did I feel so…nice. Relaxed. Almost satisfied in some way.

The struggling bodies beside me fell still. Zane's grip on the hound eased, his eyes almost fluttering shut as he grunted in agitation.

"Hunter, something is wrong…" he was saying, fighting to stay angry.

"Yeah," I agreed, watching in quiet fascination as the big ass void hound that had been trying to kill us grew still, newly formed orbs in his eye sockets churning with gold. "Something is definitely wrong right now."

It took me a moment to realize what the feeling was, because I had never felt it quite as dark, as primal and wicked. It was the shivering sensation of nails across my scalp, lips on my skin, leather tightening around my wrists.

"What's…happening?" Zane blinked his red eyes as gold danced around the rim. "I feel…uh."

"Comfortable and a little aroused?" I prompted. "It's charm magic. Really strong…kinda scary charm magic."

"Relax," Sias told us, his voice black velvet stitched with golden threads. "I think I have it under control now."

"What?" I asked in a daze. "You have what under control?"

"All of it," he whispered, the magic around me coiling into something dark, sensual and threatening.

Sias was different.

Very fucking different, bordering on terrifying.

He stood like a regal demigod, cracked gold and black wounds. His long hair was caked in the black ichor that now dripped from the cuts on his cheekbones. The blood ran down his chest and ruined his expensive shirt, discoloring the buttons. The gold at the tips of his horns had cracked where they'd failed to keep shape, the tips curling in harsher than they used to.

His skin was too pale. His fingers ink-stained and sharp.

A black rim held his eyes hostage, the color swirling from vicious hues of emerald and ruby, stormed over with foggy grays.

Something was desperately wrong.

But even with all the black weirdness leaking from his face, or the horns doing funky things…he was hot.

Deadly.

Changed.

Maybe evil. Well. Eviler, let's be fair. He did torture a guy for information earlier, remember? We're all a little complicated.

But goddamn. Sias was sex dipped in black magic.

His horns had twisted a bit more, the gold bent around the new harsher coils and the ink stains on his fingers had grown sharp at the tips. The black ichor that had been falling from the cuts on his face, however, had finally stopped weeping.

I stared at the haunting beauty of the cuts opening for the first time, sleek golden eyes revealed from within. All four of Sias's eyes blinked, the new ones fixed in gold while his normal set churned in vibrant hues of rose.

"That's enough attitude for today." Sias snapped his fingers and pointed to his side. "Come."

The pull to follow his order was almost overwhelming, and it took me a second to realize he was talking to the fucking hound.

The massive beast birthed from the void—the hound, not Zane —rose to its feet and followed the command. It padded over to Sias like a well-trained pet, sitting on its haunches at his feet and looking up to him expectantly.

"What the fuck is happening?" I asked Zane and whatever deity felt like answering me.

Zane shook his head, rubbing his eyes with his fingers.

"Goddess. Sias, what have you done?" The vampire blinked, the gold fading from his vision. "You followed Dallas into the void, didn't you?"

My stomach twisted, fear lancing through me like a knife.

"Please tell me you didn't, Sias," I begged. "Tell me you weren't that stupid."

"Stupid?" Sias lifted his gaze to me, all four eyes hardening. The hound growled, sensing its master's agitation, but Sias settled it with a pat to its bony head. "Let's discuss 'stupid,' Dallas Wilde. Which one of us tackled this thing into the void in the first place?"

"It was coming right for you, Barns and Funus! What the hell was I supposed to do? Yeah, okay. Maybe it wasn't the best thing to do in hindsight, but it worked! And that didn't mean you needed to follow me in."

The second set of eyes cooled as the others swirled into a calmer purple, dancing toward blue.

"I felt you getting lost," he whispered, like the admission was cutting him. "I felt you slipping away. You couldn't feel me from outside but I felt you spilling out, fading. I took my chances. I paid my price."

"What the hell do you mean 'paid your price'?" I fought against the ache forming in my chest. Zane had gone quiet, which made the panic etching a cavern through my ribs sting that much harder. "What the fuck does that mean, Sias?"

"Later," Sias promised, his eyes flicking to the swarm surrounding Magnus and Austin. "I have control over the flying creatures for now, but it's slipping. Too many little minds in a flurry, it's like trying to herd feral cats."

"We don't have enough bullets to take these things out." I glanced around at the carnage they had already afflicted. "They're too fast. We might just need to make a run for it."

"If you can get them to fly high enough, an impact with the ground should handle them," Zane said. "Straight up, then down hard."

"Can you do that?" I asked.

Sias set his jaw and focused his eyes on the swarm, his fists curling in concentration. I felt his magic slither by us like an icy python, crawling out and around to choke the mass of flying voidlings spiraling around their meals. The control Sias wielded was choppy, the tiny bodies not completely obeying as he sent them in a careening arc skyward.

Black dripped from Sias's eyes, breath beginning to saw from his chest. Pain pinched his features as he fought against their will, his magic pulling golden threads cracked with black veins.

Magnus and Austin kept firing at the swarm as it lifted around them, some ash falling from a few successful hits. They had been too focused on staying alive to notice the swarm was being piloted away from them. They didn't stop shooting until the little bastards were almost beyond the clouds in a scattered mass of twitching, screaming dots.

Sias exhaled through his teeth in a grunt of pain as he extended his tainted charm magic to its limit before snapping it back.

They fell like screaming rain, diving headfirst into the ground, charmed into ending their undead lives by a sex demon touched by the very void they had been birthed from. Ash erupted all around us as the mass of voidlings met its end.

It was haunting, awful.

And totally badass.

Sias raked his long, messy hair back from his face as the last bits of ash blew past his polished shoes, pale and exhausted from the effort.

"Gods, I need a drink," he said. "And a very hot shower."

I was upon him before I thought better of it, forgetting for a second that there was still a big ass void hound at his side. Sias smelled of ash and blood, with just a trace of amber and tobacco. I held on to that scent as tightly as I held on to his body, my heart and mind a storm of relief and regret.

Where his hair wasn't caked in black blood, it was soft against my skin.

"I never wanted you to go into the void," I whispered to him. "I'm sorry. I'm so fucking sorry, Sias."

"I couldn't let you drown, Dallas," he whispered, lips finding my cheek. "You would, and have, done the same for me."

"Not like this," I argued, heart splintering into sharp, unforgiving barbs. "Goddamn you, Sias. What the fuck are we going to do now? Maybe Funus knows of a way to reverse this, to change you back. Maybe—"

Sias pulled back to look at me, study me like I was something he couldn't wait to devour.

"It's done. There is no walking it back now, Dallas. You gave a piece of yourself for your vampire, and I gave a piece of myself for you. Win, lose, life or death; we are all tangled together now. There is no untying the threads."

"Perfect word for them," Zane said softly, somehow materializing beside me. His red eyes pinging between us, watching something I couldn't see. "Threads. I saw them in the void like a beacon. Felt the pulse when you called out to me."

"What does that mean?" I watched Zane tracing the invisible bindings.

"I don't know," the vampire confessed. "But there's something here. It hums like dormant power lines. It would be worth exploring."

"Exploring how, I wonder," Sias mused softly, one set of eyes flaring rosy pink for a moment.

"One thread at a time," Zane said, his eyes dark.

Fear danced at the edges of my blooming elation, the feeling as acidic as it was fragile and wonderful.

Was I stupid enough to believe, even for a heartbeat of time, that this would somehow all work out in my favor? That I could be lucky enough to be helplessly tied together with the only two people I'd ever wanted?

A damn incubus and a vampire of all things?

That's not how it works. No one gets to live happily ever after, especially not someone like me. I had known since I was a lonely teenager staring at the dying betta fish in a cup that I would die alone, because I had already set that destiny in motion.

It was supposed to just be me and Kevin until the end. I remembered vividly having that conversation with him the day he got his color back, the first time he blew a little bubble at me.

*Just me and you, little guy. Because who the hell else would have us?*

Wouldn't it be so nice if it somehow worked out that I had something wonderful?

That would be a great ending to a very fucked up story.

"Dallas," Magnus's voice was always such a fantastic mood killer. The hound at Sias's side growled, reminding me it was there.

"Oh, shit. I forgot about you," I said to the thing, inching away from it. "It's uh…still good, right? Got a leash on it?"

"He won't hurt you," Sias confirmed. "He's mine now."

Zane grunted. "I don't love that you can have that sort of control over void creatures, Sias."

"Don't worry, love. I don't put leashes on people unless they ask."

Magnus was staring daggers at me as I turned away from whatever the hell was happening between Zane and Sias, which admittedly my brain was trying to sizzle about. It took me a few hard blinks to get back into character, shaking off any lingering distractions.

The void hound's growl was like a splintered bone, and it lifted to all four feet as Magnus took a few measured steps our direction.

"We're kinda having a moment, Magnus." I gestured between the three of us. "Can you come back later with whatever bullshit you're about to start?"

"Your incubus is corrupted, kid." The gun in Magnus's hand stayed at his side, but his fingers were twitchy. "Void touched. He's a ticking time bomb, and when it goes off, he'll turn and kill you."

"Pretty sure he's already turned. He's got four eyes." I pointed to Sias's face, which the incubus didn't enjoy. My hand was slapped down and I mumbled an apology.

"You're dealing with shit you know nothing about," Magnus continued. "Step aside. Let me handle this."

"Or I could rip you in half," Zane offered with a shrug.

"I like that option," Sias agreed, patting his snarling void hound on the head. "Optimal for me, if I'm being honest."

"Relax," I told the bloodthirsty duo before turning my attention back to my twitchy father. "No one is 'handling' anything. We're on the same side. We want these tears stopped, same as you. We leave here in a weird but acceptable truce. That's what's going to happen."

Magnus's jaw clenched, head shaking as he tightened the grip around his weapon.

"Dallas, you need to listen to me. You've strayed down a path that will only lead to darkness and damnation."

"I'm fine, thanks," I tossed back, his sincerity like sandpaper. It was starting to rub me raw. "Mind your own damnation and I'll do the same. Are we good? I want to go home and I'm really sick of you today."

Magnus's eyes hardened, posture stiffening. I saw the change in him like a door locking, whatever love he had for me sealed up tight and buried. My heart responded in kind, letting my compassion for him fall away into the dark part of myself I never wanted to recognize.

Zane relaxed at my side, his form starting to turn misty.

It had gone from a bargaining session to a showdown, each of us with our weapons ready. Only one would be left standing, and I knew it would be me.

Austin did too.

So he reacted first.

Magnus crumpled as Austin knocked the butt of his gun against his temple, the old man folding into a heap from the well-placed blow.

Magnus never saw it coming. None of us did.

I don't think Austin did either, if I'm being honest. The open horror on his face once Magnus's unconscious body was on the ground was proof enough that he had acted on instinct instead of logic.

I stomped down my shock and glanced at the amazed faces at my side.

"Go on ahead. I'll be right behind you."

"You're sure?" Zane glanced between me and Austin, his hesitation clear. When I gave him a nod, I was thankful he didn't press. My head was spinning, my heart in a constant state of flux, and I wasn't sure how well I could explain myself. "Hurry," Zane warned. "We shouldn't stay in the area long. We've wasted enough time as it is."

I agreed, and asked, "Sias, can you still get us an exit out of here?"

"Of course. Zane and I will meet you at the rendezvous point." Sias snapped his fingers and the hound turned its attention back to him. "Don't linger, pet."

"Me or the hound?" I asked, but Sias just smirked. Zane rolled his eyes and followed Sias, leaving me alone to deal with my family drama.

Austin wouldn't look at me as I went to him, his eyes locked on Magnus as he kneeled beside him.

I swallowed before I could speak. "You know what I'm going to say."

Austin inhaled, trying to hide a sniffle.

"He's not going be very happy when he wakes up," I continued. "He'll know it was you."

"I know." He wiped the tip of his nose with his wrist. "But I gotta do this. I can't run."

"Austin, you could come with us—" I tried, but he shook his head, eyes seething and rimmed with tears.

"I don't run. I'm not you."

"No, you're not," I lamented, the verbal stab deep and brutal. "You're a stubborn asshole and I love you. You have my number. Use it if you need it."

He said nothing in response. I was grateful for that.

I left my brother behind to face our adoptive father and his judgment, and tried my hand at one last sincere prayer to the Saint. Maybe it would still filter through, even if I technically belonged to the Goddess now. Magnus had always told us the Saint could hear us if we spoke from the heart.

My heart was begging for Austin to figure out what he needed to be happy. And for Magnus to not be a bastard for once.

I wasn't going to hold my breath on that second part. Some things even a deity can't change.

GETTING a void hound into a car was fun.

There was no way in hell we were going to try and take the train or a bus back to Sias's side of town with the new puppy in tow. Even the stoic, uncaring masses of St. Athesall would notice a terrifying, undead hound following us around, what with its skeletal head and razor sharp teeth. People had their limits.

Instead, Sias had one of his driver's case the area for DHAP officers and any lingering Saint's Army people before scooping us up in a speedy get away. The most shocking part of my night, besides ripping Zane from the void, Sias's new set of eyes and abilities, *and* seeing my brother knock Magnus out, was witnessing a crack in the veneer of one of Sias's driver's professional demeanor.

The guy looked a little uncomfortable with the hellhound. There was a tiny flinch.

My guy had seen literal dead bodies being dumped into the trunk in multiple trash bags and had put up with Sias and me fucking very loudly in the back seat, but he finally looked a touch uncomfortable with the undead beast hound.

I loved that dude.

I almost thought he was going to say something. There was a little hesitation right as he started opening the back door for us.

It was a little tricky to fit us all inside considering how monstrous the damn beast was. I ended up squished against the window to try and avoid touching its fur, while the bulk of its body ended up mostly in Zane's lap. The vampire wasn't particularly amused by this, but Sias was exhausted and I think Zane felt bad.

I didn't argue because I didn't want Zane to shove the damn thing into my lap. It looked heavy and it was kinda funny that he got stuck with it.

The driver held the door for us as we piled out onto Sias's driveway, the night air thick with a threatening thunderstorm. I inhaled the smell of brewing rain, thankful to smell something other than dried blood and ash.

"C'mon," Zane was saying to Sias as he helped him out of the car, their hands clasped together so Sias could be heaved to his feet. The calm drive had given us all permission to let our guard drop, and Sias had gone from tired to bone deep exhausted, and was looking understandably sick.

"You still feeling bad?" I asked him, returning to his side to offer support. Sias allowed me to loop one of his arms around my shoulders, not protesting as Zane did the same.

"Tired. A little weak."

His second set of eyes had shut fully and were starting to blend back into his skin, which was clammy and sticky from the black goo that had leaked out earlier.

"How do we help him?" I asked Zane as we practically dragged Sias inside. "If he went into the void does that mean he's..."

"I don't know," Zane said. "I've never heard of someone without death magic going into the void and coming back. This is beyond me, hunter."

"You can help me by taking me to the shower," Sias mumbled. "I'm disgusting. I want a hot shower and my bed."

"You can barely stand, Sias. I think if we dump you into a shower you'll drown." I worked with Zane to heft our incubus up the steps to his front door. Forgetting I no longer had a right hand, I tried to adjust Sias's weight to open it and nearly dropped him in the process.

We managed to get Sias inside without him crashing to the floor somehow, and were greeted by an armed antiques dealer ready for battle. Barnaby wielded a bat shaped suspiciously like a penis cocked above his head and yelped when he saw us. The weapon flew from his grip, missing us by a hilarious margin, and clattered across the marble flooring.

This, of course, was a horrible method of attack, but was the epitome of fun for the hellish canine, who thought Barns was playing with it.

The beast birthed from the void gathered the wooden cock into its mouth with obvious glee, butt wagging in anticipation for more.

The dog, not Zane.

"Hi, Barns," I greeted my terrified, former landlord. "Can you stop hurling genitalia at us for a second and get Funus, please?"

"It...what...there's..." Barnaby floundered, jumping up onto a couch as the dog returned the phallic weaponry. "What is happening!"

"Sias trained an undead hound to love him because he went into the void and now has crazy powers that none of us understand. So, could you pretty please go get Funus before I lose my shit?!"

Barnaby stared at me with wide eyes, his gaze pinging from the hound, to the barely conscious Sias, back to me, then to Zane, looking for answers.

"Good to see you, Barnaby. He's not full of shit, we do need Funus."

"O-of course. Right." Barnaby descended the couch one tentative foot at a time, skirting around the hound like he was sure the thing was going to take a bite out of him.

"Thanks!" I shouted at him sarcastically as he ran away to do Zane's bidding, since apparently, I was full of bullshit.

With the couch now vacated, we placed Sias down onto the soft cushions to rest. I propped his head up with a throw pillow and smoothed away some of the hair tangled around his horns.

"Can you go get him a wet towel?" I asked Zane. "Kitchen is down the hall, to the right."

Zane followed my directions and disappeared, and Sias scowled as I moved some hair from his face.

"Are you in pain?"

"No." Sias adjusted his head and blinked his normal set of eyes. They were the same hot shade of green I knew from when he told me the story about his stupid golden gun. "I don't like people fussing over me."

"Yeah, well. Getting tossed around the void a few times qualifies for a bit of fussing, I think."

"I'm just tired," he defended. "Pushed myself a bit too hard with these new powers."

"Understatement of the year." I sat on the ground beside the couch as Zane returned, warm washcloth and a glass of water in hand as well as an extra, dry towel draped over his arm.

"Are you hungry?" Zane asked as he parked himself on the couch, sharing a cushion with Sias's hip.

"No." He reached for the cloth Zane was holding. "Give me that. I can take care of myself."

"We know you can. But it's kinda nice, isn't it?" I asked. "Having people around who don't mind wiping weird blood off your face?" I brushed a strand of hair away that had been stuck to his cheek. The void hound beside the couch rested its giant head across Sias's legs and sighed through its nose hole. It whistled a bit.

Sias's eyes cooled to an emerald around the edges, embarrassment and pride still lingering in the centers.

"I don't hate it," he confessed after a few heartbeats.

"When you say you're not hungry, do you mean you don't

crave anything at all, or you feel a pull for something else?" Zane wiped some of the crusted blood from Sias's cheeks and neck, his movements careful.

"Are you asking if I want blood?" Sias lifted his brows. "Do you think I'm going to turn into a vampire?"

"I don't know." Zane frowned as he smoothed the cloth over Sias's jaw. "I don't know what any of this means. I'm trying to cover all bases."

We heard Barnaby and Funus bickering long before they made an appearance, their hushed squabbles not as quiet as they thought. They came into the room and Barnaby stood a few feet back, his fear of the hellhound still firmly in place.

"By the Goddess! It really is!" Funus's eyes lit up when he saw the beast, who was now trying to climb up onto the couch. The creature was far too big to have any room on the narrow furniture, and compromised it by just hefting its chest and head up to sprawl over Sias's legs. Its golden eyes dimmed a little, and we collectively leaned away from it.

"Is it…sleepy or are we about to die?" I asked warily.

"We're both very tired," Sias explained. "No need to be alarmed."

"That is truly amazing," Funus said from across the room. "Influence over creatures of the void is rare, even for the savants of necromancy. Though, I suppose we'll learn more as your powers manifest."

"You don't sound surprised that Sias has *any* powers, Funus," I probed, a sharp suspicion clawing at my stomach. "Do you know something about this?"

"Ah." Funus cleared his throat out of nervous habit, since he didn't have a throat to clear. "I do, yes."

"What the hell, Funus?" I stood, pausing when Sias grabbed my hand and tugged.

"Relax."

"Relax? Are you serious? I thought you fell into the void by accident. Was this shit planned?" I looked between the two parties. "Barnaby, stop being a worm and get over here. The dog isn't going to hurt you."

"I'm fine here, thank you." Barnaby squared his shoulders. "You can hear Funus just fine." He squeaked as I took a step to snatch the head away.

"Knock it off," Zane barked, passing me the rag as he stood. "You're a pain in the ass like this. Sit. Barnaby, I'll take Funus if the dog is making you uncomfortable."

"I'm just not sure how it responds to outsiders," Barnaby admitted, cradling Funus against his chest. "I'm the only one here not part of the void club now, you know. I have a right to be cautious."

"It's not going to hurt you," Sias told his fellow incubus. "I promise. Please." He gestured to the matching chair beside the couch, inviting Barnaby to sit with us.

Barnaby took a long, measured breath and inched his way over, sitting right on the edge of the chair in case he needed to make a speedy retreat. Funus was placed on the armrest so he could chat with us.

I knelt back down on the floor, still angry but tasked with cleaning Sias's cheeks. I dabbed some dried blood away and allowed the process to calm me down a little bit.

"Tell me what happened," I told Funus. "And what all of this means for Sias."

"This wasn't planned, not in the way you think," Funus explained, yellow eyes darkening with sincerity. "I was 'holding the door,' if you will; keeping the void stable for you. After you tackled the hound in, Sias went tumbling in after you. You sank like a rock, connected to the void through our lessons and your... well. Prior visits. Sias didn't."

"I was trying to find you," Sias whispered. "But you fell so fast. I could sense you deep down in the void, but I didn't know how to get to you."

"I felt him starting to drift. I took it upon myself to offer guidance, as is my nature." Funus's 'smile' was weak, his eyes brightening just a shade too pale. "If he were to find you, he'd need to ask the Goddess. With him not being human and having no training, I brokered the meeting. Helped explain the terms."

"What terms?" Zane asked for me, since my throat had gone dry.

"Sias is part of the void now. Not a true child like you, Zane. Not a vampire. Sias is one of her converted; soul bound and under her charge. His soul will join her when he dies, not allowed to roam free in the void with his passing."

I was able to find my voice after a few tries, but the only thing I could think to say was, "Goddamnit, Sias."

A fistful of sadness curled in my chest, an impossible weight of expectations I knew I could never fulfill. I wasn't worth such a high price. Sias had been a damn fool to cash in his ticket for someone like me, and I felt that bitterness like a twisting knife.

"Can it be undone?" I looked to Funus. "If I go to the Goddess, if I tell her I'd take his place—"

Sias forced himself upright, eyes burning like emeralds dipped in gold. The anger was plain on his face, his handsome features dark as he aimed his fury my way.

"You don't get to make that call, Dallas."

"You gave up your soul, Sias! What the fuck!" I felt like my chest was trying to cave in on itself from how helpless and horrible I felt. "I'm already heading down that path with being a necromancer. You shouldn't have to give up a blissful eternity because I jumped into the tear like an idiot."

"You haven't been paying attention," Sias hissed. "That's not what happened."

"The Death Goddess saw an opportunity and jumped on it, is what happened," I corrected. "Snatched a non-human soul to join her harem. That's gotta be a rare treat for her. Like a taste of gourmet after being surrounded by fast food hamburgers for centuries."

"I wouldn't call us *hamburgers*. Bit rude," Funus mumbled, and Barnaby gave him a pat.

"The Goddess doesn't trick people, hunter," Zane added, deathly calm. "You're panicking because you're scared."

"Fuck you, Zane. I'm really annoyed at you right now, but I kinda missed saying that."

"Scared?" Sias looked to Zane. "Is that what you're feeling from him?"

"Hey! That's necromancer-vampire privilege," I cut in quickly. "Zane, shut up."

Zane crossed his arms and shut up, but the seed had already been planted in Sias's brain. Fucking vampire.

"Dallas," Sias whispered, the sound a snake hiss but without the threat of a bite. The golden anger in his gaze had softened, not quite gone. "Do you truly think anyone would be able to trick me? Do you think I'm that naive? Stupid?"

"I think even very powerful, dangerous people can be desperate. Getting lost in the void doesn't give you the upper hand," I said diplomatically. "And I don't want you to pay too high of a price for...this." I gestured at myself. "I don't even have two hands anymore, I'm damaged goods."

Sias watched me, emerald eyes flecked with gold, skin pale and bruised. My heart was hammering as he took a deep breath, seeming like he was about to unleash a fury on me I wasn't prepared for.

Imagine my surprise when he caught my chin and kissed me beside my mouth, pinning me with twin jade daggers that felt like they would pierce through my soul.

"You and I have some things to discuss, Dallas Wilde. But tonight, I'm going to bed, alone, so I can rest, and you are going to catch up with your well-earned vampire." Sias motioned to Zane's arm, which was still slashed to pieces from his wrestling match with the hound. "I believe some feeding is in order."

Guilt lanced me at having forgotten about his wounds, followed by a deep, warm excitement that bloomed at the remedy.

Zane needed to heal. He needed my blood. I was a bit of a bastard for being excited about that, but I couldn't find it in myself to care. The last memory I had of him before his horrible death was feeding him drops of blood from my tongue, my back pressed against the cold marble of a mausoleum.

God, that felt like a lifetime ago. I had been craving to revisit that moment like it was etched onto my soul.

A grin curled Sias's lips when I felt my face growing hot, a velvet chuckle tumbling from him.

"That's what I thought. I won't dare get in the way of that. For now."

A spark ignited in me over that comment, and I had to breathe through the thrumming desire to let my imagination cartwheel into Smutville.

My face was on fire as I glanced at Zane, the hammer of realization that he could peer into all my dirty little emotions hit hard enough to make me wheeze.

The cheeky vampire had his features schooled, giving nothing away at Sias's comment or the horny thoughts bouncing around like pinballs in my head. Zane offered his hand to Sias to help him to his feet, steadying him with a firm grip around his elbow.

"Take good care of him, Zane," Sias told him, tone growing serious. "He has shut himself off from care since you left. Make sure he gets a full release, hm?"

"My *God*, Sias!" I sputtered, flustered. I was actually flustered. He *flustered* me. "I know you're an incubus, but c'mon, man."

"I think that's my cue," Barnaby mumbled, getting to his feet.

"You sure you're okay?" Zane asked Sias, choosing to ignore the blatant sex talk. "I don't like how pale you are right now."

"I'm fine, love. I just need some time alone to recover." He placed a sweet kiss to Zane's cheek. It made me feel things. Sias clicked his tongue, summoning the loyal hellhound to his side. The massive, undead beast wiggled its backside as Sias leaned on it for support, happily assisting his master.

"I'll check on him later," Barnaby offered as I stood there like an idiot, feeling helpless and a little bit like I had inadvertently triggered a ticking time bomb. "I have some spare intimacy magic vials he can have to help him recover his strength."

"Thanks, Barns."

"Of course." Barnaby positioned Funus to his side and gave my shoulder a squeeze, then turned to give Zane a quick, chaste hug and an awkward pat on the arm. "Good to have you back, Zane. I've saved your books for you and have some new ones I've picked up while you were gone. If that's alright."

"I've missed you too, Barnaby," Zane replied with an amused grin. "Thank you."

Barnaby allowed himself to smile, reminding everyone in the room how handsome he was when he wasn't glowering like a cantankerous grandpa.

"Right. Well. Off we go." Barns gave the hallway a nervous glance, like he was expecting the hound to be waiting to pounce, then scuttled off like a nervous spider clutching a skull.

I watched Barnaby disappear down the hallway, Sias and his hell beast gone from view as well. My head was threatening to burst from all the thoughts rolling through me, fear tripping over confusion and butting heads with the lingering guilt. I wasn't sure which direction I wanted to go as I stood in Sias's foyer, beaten and bruised, having liberated my vampire but cashing in Sias's soul to achieve it.

I shouldn't have been so distracted by Zane's presence.

I felt like a supreme asshole for letting my mind drift to the one thing I had wanted for months.

Yet there I was, being an asshole and staring at the big vampire watching me with a look not dissimilar to a starving monster, ready to eat me alive.

The gap between us was closed with two steps, Zane moving to stand before me so I had to tilt my gaze up. A few months ago, I would have called him a prick for lording his height superiority over me. In that moment, it wasn't just pushing my buttons, it was rewiring my circuits.

If it had been anyone else, I would have just jumped him there and then, pulled him down onto the couch and demanded all manner of filthy things, not giving a screaming shit who saw us.

But with Zane I was…awkward.

Nervous.

Hilarious, right? Zane. The big, gothy jerk with his flowy hair and oh-so-cool leather jacket, the vampire who had befriended a *kitten* and read murder mysteries. The same jackass who failed constantly at being my bodyguard, complained about my brilliant ideas and undermined me in front of my fish daily for months.

I wasn't supposed to be nervous around that guy.

I was Dallas fucking Wilde. I didn't get nervous.

This was new for me. I hadn't been nervous around a boy since I was a lanky teenager trying to unfasten a belt buckle in the back seat of a car.

To be fair, Zane wasn't a boy. He was a big, thick slab of undead bastard who wanted my blood and could do amazing things with his tongue. Not to mention he had *fangs*, which I was still grappling with, but was too excited to care about.

He was everything I hated. Everything I had dedicated my life to eradicating. A creature of malice and evil, birthed to serve death and be a blight on human and demonkind alike.

He was *forbidden* in every sense of the word.

The weight of that was making my palms very clammy. It wasn't a great start.

His voice was as calm and deadly as the rumbling before a volcanic eruption.

"Does your leg still hurt?"

I forgot how to form words for a second so I tested my weight on it and gave him a so-so gesture.

"S'fine," I managed, wiping my palms on my tattered jeans.

"Good," he said simply, then turned my world upside down in a very literal sense. One second, I was standing there feeling sweaty and tense, the next thing I knew I was being tossed over Zane's huge shoulder like I was a sack of flour.

It happened so suddenly and with such fluid force that I yelped in alarm.

"The fuck!" I balked, flailing like an honest-to-God fish.

Zane growled, "Where's your room?" in a way that shot right to all my fun parts.

"Are you whisking me? Am I being whisked?"

"Room, hunter," he snapped. "Otherwise, I'm tossing you outside."

"What else are you offering to toss? Because if you're going to be tossing—ah, okay, okay!" I pleaded as he started marching toward the front door. "Hallway to the right with the big mirror. Head that way."

Zane spun and walked with quick determination, and I got a prime view of his ass as I was whisked away like a very handsome princess. I would have preferred to have been carried like a damsel in distress instead of a burlap sack but, luckily, we didn't have far to go.

"How many fucking rooms does this place have?" Zane mumbled as I copiloted from behind him. When we finally made it to the room I had claimed, Zane kicked the door shut with his heel before literally throwing me onto the bed.

# CHAPTER
# FOURTEEN

THE THOUGHT of poor Kevin having to witness my debauchery entered and vanished from my mind as I flew through the air. Had I not been airborne, I would have at least tossed a towel over Kevin's tank for privacy's sake because I knew I was going to get judgmental bubbles later.

Twig was blissfully absent, no doubt perched on one of the many windows throughout the house looking longingly out at the birds she wasn't allowed to kill. It saved us the embarrassment of having to pause the momentum to escort the kitten out of the room. Kevin might give me judgmental bubbles, but at least he stayed out of the way.

I've had my fair share of trysts over the years and been manhandled in some fantastic ways. Being hurled onto a mattress by a snarling, determined Thrall wasn't so much as being manhandled as it was a religious experience. Zane moved with a divine purpose that had me mumbling a prayer as he tossed his jacket aside and practically ripped off his shirt.

I was pushed backward onto the mattress by a tidal wave of man, and he made it very clear there was no chance in hell I was going to escape. Not that I wanted to—I was happy to drown inhaling the scent of rain, old paper novels and grave roses.

I would drown forever if he wanted me to.

If our first kiss was a storm, our second one was a goddamn tsunami; an endless onslaught of roaring emotions and hunger. His lips tasted like cool water and traces of the void, his fingers demanding any scrap of clothing on my body be removed.

I was too busy running my fingers through his silky, stupid hair to obey his orders. I moaned at how it felt in my grip, the sensation better than I had ever imagined.

And Gods, had I imagined it. In the long nights caught between bitter heartache and shattering guilt, when I could muster the will to daydream of having him again, I'd dreamed of gripping his hair in my fist and kissing him with everything I had.

For the first time in months, I felt something beyond anguish, hurt and despair. I wasn't about to let go now.

It was painfully annoying that I only had one hand, because I was torn between touching his hair or the rest of him. Having to choose caressing *or* fondling was incredibly frustrating.

Being as it was the first time I got to get up close and personal with Zane's ample chest and the hairs that occupied it, I dropped his long locks so I could grab a palmful of skin. The delicious contrast of hard muscle and soft hairs tickled all the way down my arm, squeezing a rush of breath from my lungs.

"I'm going to rip this fucking shirt off you if you don't cooperate," Zane hissed, lips barely parting from mine long enough to get the threat out. "I need these clothes off of you, hunter."

I had become so distracted with wanting to touch his nipple that I tossed out a placating agreement without hearing him, and decided to focus my efforts on other things. The delicious pink nipple stood up when I ran the pad of my thumb over it, and I'm fairly sure I purred like a house cat over the reaction.

Due to ignoring the vampire's prior warning, my poor shirt did not survive his attack.

The fabric was torn in half because of my failure to follow orders but, in my defense, Zane had pink nipples and I wanted to touch them. I'm pretty sure a jury of my peers wouldn't convict me of secondhand shirt murder over these circumstances.

Zane's very talented tongue left its dance with mine and traveled with his lips across my chest, repaying my nipple assault in kind. Where he got a quick tease with my thumb, my nipple got a heavenly trace and a swirl for good measure. Since his chest wasn't up for grabs anymore, I replaced my hold back into his locks and ran my nails across his scalp.

A burst of fireflies flooded my belly as he traveled south, an overwhelming fluttering of growing excitement and hazy fear as he popped the button to my jeans.

Zane lifted his gaze after planting a kiss under my navel, eyes hooded and seeming to glow under his dark brows. My fly was opened, his gaze never leaving mine.

"Do you trust me, hunter?"

"That heavily depends on what you're about to pitch."

He hummed, fingers hooking under the waistband of my jeans and sliding them down slowly, my briefs doing a horrible job of shielding just how excited I was at the events so far. I was practically bursting out of the fabric, and the way his pupils flared just made things way worse.

The vampire watched as my body responded to his hungry stare, and he ran a tongue over one of his fangs.

"I want to use teeth."

"*Where?*" I pressed, my hesitation teetering on the edge of terror.

Zane ran a palm over my thigh, gripping it to nudge my leg open more before he ran a thumb under the leg of my boxer briefs. He stopped at the sensitive skin of my inner thigh and pressed down.

"Right here."

"You want to...to bite me?" I clarified, an electric shock shooting through my core. It was like a concentrated bolt of emotions splicing through me, fear burning white hot with the searing fantasy of feeling Zane's teeth in my skin.

"I want to feed on you while I touch you," Zane whispered, running a knuckle up the outline of my cock.

"Oh damn," I said in a rush. "That might actually kill me."

"You'd survive," the cheeky vampire promised. "Barely."

My poor heart couldn't decide if it wanted to body slam out of my ribs and make a run for it, or if it wanted to just burst in place and be done with life. My hand left Zane's hair so I could shake out the nervous tingling in my fingers, my body thrumming like an electric wire.

"What if it's too much?" I asked, my cheeks burning. "What if I can't take it?"

Zane slithered over me, caging me under his weight and furrowed brow.

"You know I'd never hurt you, Dallas," he said.

His words and presence tap danced all over my chest, and I felt like melting into the mattress and embracing the gooey feelings I was having.

It's hard to maintain a poker face when the guy you're crushing on with your whole damn heart could read your hand.

"I know," I confessed. "I'm…" I chewed on my lip and finished with, "You know. You can feel it."

"I can feel a lot from you right now, but it's hard to untangle. You need to talk to me. Tell me how you're feeling."

That was sweet enough as it was but then the asshole disarmed me completely.

It was uncalled for.

Unfair.

Fucking brutally unfair.

Zane took my hand and pressed it to his heart, the thumping under his skin strong, steady, and beautiful. I felt my fingers twitch, felt his heart beating in my palm.

I was ruined. I was not a man anymore. I was a gooey pile of nothing in a very expensive bed with a vampire marinating in it.

"I'm nervous," I admitted. "Nervous and a little scared. This is a lot. How I feel about you… I don't want to mess it up."

"You won't," he pledged in a whisper, finding my lips to sink me into a calming mantra of deep, slow, bone melting kisses. I pulled him as close as I could, desperate to have his skin pressed into mine, shivering at his thick ridge which stabbed into my hip. Our gentle, passionate kisses turned feral as I rolled my hips up into his, his snarl returning as I nipped at his bottom lip.

"Don't play this game, hunter."

"You're the one who wants to use teeth, vampire." I grinned against his lips. "Let's use some teeth."

I swiped my tongue up and ran it across his fang, piercing it just enough to draw a sweet line of blood. Zane's breath caught, the red in his eyes turning vicious.

I leaned back to watch his pupils blow wide as I licked my lips to coat them in a little bit of crimson.

"You can't kiss me until I give permission, right?"

"Dallas," he said through his teeth. "Don't tease me right now."

"You don't have the power right now." I licked my thumb and ran it over his lips, hissing in delight as his skin broke out in fine goose bumps. "Oh my God, you get goose bumps!"

"Goddess help me," Zane prayed. "Give me the strength not to snap."

"Too much for you, oh great vampire Thrall? Can't handle it?" I used my thumb to add a few more bloody points of interest on my body, starting to light the fuse to Zane's dynamite.

I was either going to overstep and the vampire was actually going to kill me, or *I* was going to be the one blowing up all over the place. I decided to roll the dice.

Why not go out with a bang?

Zane's eyes flared like brake lights as I pulled the waistband of my briefs down enough to reach my cock, and drew a line of blood from root to tip. As an extra little tease and a merry little fuck you, I mixed a bit of blood in with the bead of precum shining like a cherry on top.

The final line was placed on the inside of my thigh.

An invitation.

One I thought I'd never give.

"Say it," he growled, fists curled in the sheets, breathing like he was about to combust. "Give me permission. Now."

"Say please."

"Dallas, I swear to the Goddess—" he snarled, and I waggled my finger.

"Ah-ah. Say, 'Pretty please.'"

"Pretty." He spat out the words like they burned him. "Fuck-ing. Please."

"This is the best day of my life."

"*Dallas.*"

I grinned, having no clue the hell I was about to unleash. "Alright, goth boy. You have my permission. Don't let me down."

The vampire Thrall did not like being teased.

The jeans that had been resting peacefully around my calves were thrown across the room, and my briefs?

Gone.

Destroyed.

Torn into little pieces.

Zane didn't undress me, he mauled me. Then, like the starving vampire he was, he attacked me like I was a buffet to devour. My tongue was the first thing he sampled, the zing of our necromancer-vampire bond igniting in a way neither of us were prepared for. Our tongues met, blood was transferred with only a few quick swipes, and my body lit up like the city at dusk.

I made a very embarrassing mewling noise the same time Zane moaned in the most delicious way I'd ever heard. The combination of blood magic and his voice nearly pushed me too far, and I almost shoved him away to catch my breath.

"Zane," I warned, voice shaky.

"Yes, hunter," he panted, flicking his tongue across my lips. "Yes."

"I think...I might," I tried, but my words were swallowed as he dove back in for another taste, slamming the gas pedal down to full speed.

My body coiled so tight I thought I was going to choke, breath catching in my throat as I came undone with just a few strokes of his tongue against mine. I groaned into his mouth, my fingers tangled in his hair, lips quivering as the ecstasy rocked me.

It was my turn to pray, but not to any deity. I was praying to the goddamn Thrall that just made me come with a kiss.

"Oh my God," I managed between gasps. "That was...fucking intense."

"Was?" Zane licked his lips, eyes flaring bright. "I'm not done with my dinner, hunter."

"I don't know if I can—*holy shit!*" I lifted up off the bed when Zane licked the blood from where I had placed it on my chest, my body igniting again like the mind-bending orgasm I'd just experienced was a mere appetizer. My muscles quaked under his touch, his lapping tongue racing through me like shockwaves.

By the time he licked his way down to my hips, I had fallen backwards on the bed and was nearing another peak, my cock as hard as it had been when all of this started. Evidence of my previous combustion was all over my belly with some even on my chest, and I had a feeling it wasn't going to stop there.

The vampire was going to drain me.

And he hadn't even touched me below the waist yet.

"Oh my God," I whispered again, nerves setting off like fireworks down my legs, curling my toes.

"I told you," he growled, showing too much teeth. "This was a game you didn't want to play, hunter. I'm going to lick every single spot you left blood for me, and I'm not going to stop until I'm full. Then I'm going to fuck you into this mattress until you scream my name."

Alright, yeah.

I wasn't going to live through the night. I should have written a will, bequeathing all of my belongings to Kevin. Maybe written Barnaby and Funus a farewell letter. Sias was going to live the rest of his days wondering what dying via vampire sex tasted like. It had been a hard life, but at least I got to go out the way I wanted: getting brutally railed by a hot guy until my heart gave out.

Not a bad way to go, if I say so myself.

I blinked up at the vampire I'd maybe teased just a touch too much and swallowed.

"Too late to call a truce?"

Zane chuckled deep in his chest, the sound a rolling thunder under dark clouds. It was the kickoff to the raging storm of a very sexually starved Thrall.

I'll give him one thing, Zane was not a liar.

When he said he was going to taste every piece of skin I had placed drops of blood, he meant it. His mouth found each spot where there was even a trace of blood, and used his tongue to clean the skin completely. Each bloody discovery sent a new wave of ecstasy up my spine, sinking into the marrow of my bones and permanently changing me. There was no way in hell regular sex was ever going to satisfy me after experiencing the erotic firestorm of our bond.

This guy was ruining me.

Rewiring me.

And I fucking loved it.

More than once he'd had to pin me back to the mattress because of my squirming, my hips lifting off the bed involuntarily as he licked up each new drop. His skin was warming from the micro feeding, taking a livelier flush each time he imbibed off of me. The grip he had around my thighs made me sob with happiness, but my hand was knocked away as I reached for my ignored cock.

"Don't. You'll rub the blood away."

"Please, for the love of your Goddess." The irony of my begging was not lost on me. "Fucking touch me, Zane. I can't stand it."

"Hold still," he commanded, voice boiling with barely

restrained lust. "If you wiggle too much, I can't promise there won't be teeth involved."

"How the hell have you not erupted into flames from all of this edging?" It was hard for me to string together a full sentence with how hard my heart was pounding. "I've already unloaded once and I feel like I haven't felt release in *years.*"

"I have more control than you do."

"Bullshit," I said around my heavy panting. "It's because you haven't had any blood so you're not able to pop like me. Don't act like you have this locked down."

"Whatever you need to tell yourself."

He ran his palm over my hip with one hand while the other pinned my thigh to the sheets. He dipped his head, long hair tickling my skin, breath kissing my straining cock.

Zane ran his tongue over his lips. "Hold still, hunter."

The flat of his tongue traveled from my base to the very tip in one long, languid motion, and I failed at my one task of holding still. My body jerked as I wrung the sheets in my fist, back arched at the hot pleasure curling my spine. The tension pulsing through my hips made the vampire have to put effort into restraining me as he continued to lick through my convulsions.

The bond between us, the power that tied our souls together, amplified each time his tongue touched my skin. I felt my heart pounding in time with his, felt the ebb and flow of mutual pleasure rolling between us.

Mine was white fire, bright and explosive; Zane's a continuous smolder, threatening to become wildfire.

By the time he had slowed down enough to let me catch my breath, I was seeing stars, though I was determined to see what type of wildfire Zane was capable of.

Zane lifted his head into my touch as I took his locks into my fingers, watching me as I gave his scalp a squeeze.

My voice didn't skip, didn't hesitate; there was no fear present as I gave my Thrall the command I never dreamed I'd give.

"I want you to bite me."

Zane's throat bobbed, color flaring in his eyes.

"Bite me, Zane," I repeated, firmer in my decision. "Inner thigh. Drink just enough to fuck me properly."

I felt the coals of desire in him flash with heat, saw the way his pupils blew wide at my command.

"Yes, master," my Thrall said, a vapor of black smoke curling from his skin. The grip he had around my thigh shifted to my knee, angling my leg so he could reach the tender flesh he hungered for.

I kept my grip on his hair, but loosened it so I didn't tear it from the roots. My pulse drummed up my throat and into my ears, body vibrating from anticipation and the aftershock of two massive orgasms. Excitement bloomed like roses in my stomach, the thorns sharp along the sides but too beautiful to care.

Zane kissed my skin lovingly, reverently, like he was worshipping before taking a holy offering.

His eyes fluttered shut as he bared his fangs, and I marveled at how breathtakingly gorgeous he was.

This man, this vampire that I had tried to kill in earnest not that long ago, the thrall who had stalked into my life like a black fog, this being who had me at the tips of his fangs. He had pulled me from the darkness, hugged me when I was heartbroken, helped tear down the walls I had built to keep people from hurting me.

When his fangs pierced my skin, I knew I'd never be the same again.

Pain bloomed from the bite, icy panic hitting my veins in a rush. I jerked and sucked in a breath through my teeth, forcing myself to breathe through the initial shock of feeling fangs enter my skin again. Zane's low hum of satisfaction was a balm, soothing my discomfort and giving me permission to relax. The icy pinpricks of pain warmed into a pleasant euphoria, our bond forming a cocoon around us.

Zane's palm traveled from my knee to the other side of my thigh, holding me in place with gentle caresses as he pulled my blood into his mouth. Color flushed his cheeks, darkened his lips, and gave a new heat to his skin. My body melted into the sheets, relaxing enough that I could feel the waves of pleasure pouring from him.

His ecstasy pooled around me in gentle tides, each pull he took from me made the sensations stronger. My head started to get fuzzy just as he pulled back, teeth stained in crimson, tongue catching the drops that escaped his bite. He pricked his thumb with his fang and guided his healing blood over the wound to seal it shut, and I saw the ripple of the void dance around us from the contact.

Zane's smoldering embers burned into a growing flame as he rose up to his knees, the heart I'd held within his chest beating with new life. Our pulses matched in intensity as he worked his jeans open, shoving them down enough to let his cock spring free. My blood in his system had given him a glow, skin flushed and radiant. It was the first time I got to see him in his full glory, to see how very blessed he was.

My body, which should have been beyond exhausted as well as dehydrated, went rigid at the sight of what was in store for me.

Zane's eyes were the brightest I'd ever seen them, neon and vicious, the vapor from his skin melting into a cool mist that fell away as he popped open the lube in his hand.

"When did you get that?" I asked in a haze.

The vampire ignored me, palming a nice supply of lube across his monstrous cock with just a few languid strokes. The bottle was thrown over his shoulder before he grabbed my hips and dragged me closer in a show of strength that made me groan. Watching his muscles flex under his newly flushed skin made my mouth water. Knowing I was the reason he was not only hot to the touch, but also incredibly hard, was setting fires in me I never knew I had. I wanted to see Zane ablaze with lust, watch him turn into a roaring fire and let him consume me completely.

I felt the moment that fire finally ignited into an unstoppable inferno, the connection between us searing.

I crooned in a sob of fantastic agony as Zane drove into me hard, the burn as shocking as it was irresistible. The stab of pleasure that hit me took my breath away, my lungs filling with the scent of rain soaked pages and funeral flowers. The denim of his jeans was rough on my skin as he fucked into me, adding to the biting contrast of hot skin and silk sheets.

I had never felt Zane so warm before, never felt sweat form across his brow, seen it drip from his handsome features. My palm was planted on his chest as he bucked, thick arms caging me in as he took out all of his frustrations on me. Of all the things I found erotic as hell while my vampire was fucking me, his hair getting stuck to his neck was the single hottest thing I'd ever seen.

The undead vampire was running so hot from wanting me, he'd momentarily defied death and had a living body temperature.

I pushed up from the mattress and looped my arms around his neck, burying my fingers in his hair as I kissed him. Zane rolled back and brought me with him, refusing to break our connection as we shifted to a different position. His grip on my hips held me steady as I rode him, our breaths clashing between frantic, hungry kisses.

I took in a long inhale as I let my head fall to the side, inviting him to kiss my neck. Zane moaned like the sensation of his lips on my neck was heaven, the kisses gentle and sweet compared to the intensity of our fucking.

A barrage of butterflies had taken flight in my chest, wings of fragile hopes and desires I had never spoken into existence. They made me gasp, made me moan and hold on to him tighter, wanting him to feel every tiny wing beating for him.

Zane's nose brushed mine, hand cupping my cheek to hold me as he pressed his brow into mine.

"Say it," he pleaded in a whisper.

"You can feel it," I breathed. "Tell me you feel it."

"I feel it." He stroked his thumb over my jaw, bright eyes boring into me. "I want to hear you say it. Please."

I swallowed, the butterflies lifting away the last threads of doubt and fear that had corroded me for so long.

"I love you," I told my vampire. "I love you, Zane."

He exhaled in a rush, eyes falling shut like the words had reached in and kissed his soul.

"I love you, Dallas. So much."

The butterflies consumed me, fanning the roaring flames that already burned molten hot within me.

I was desperate to feel him unravel, wanting to seal the confession with a moment of ecstasy. I rolled my hips with his, drunk on the thrumming connection between us, with how my name sounded on his lips. Zane's nails bit into my skin as he drove up into me, breath hot against my neck, sweat trailing down his temples.

Rain soaked pages and grave roses smelled different with heat, like cool summer storms and petals blooming in the shade.

I felt my mounting release trigger in response to him, to his scent, to the sharp bite of his grip on my skin and the way his lips held the stain of my blood. Zane slipped his hand between us so he could stroke me and used his other to keep me from getting bucked off his hips.

Zane's eyes shifted as he chased after our release, the dark circles rimming his red irises going smoky, clouding the whites in his eyes like a fog. His fangs grew longer, his bottom teeth sprouting a new set that hadn't been there before. His flushed, human-like skin changed to be almost transparent, taking on a translucent deathly black vapor, his heart within a glowing beacon of pounding, red light.

Zane roared, his eyes flaring, his void form solidifying as he finally found release, taking me along for the ride.

True to his damn word, Zane made me scream his name.

My body was trembling as I slid off his lap, watching in morbid fascination as his body returned to his regular vampire shade, in both color and density. I fell back onto the pillows, sweat slick and exhausted, my body coated in three orgasms and vampire spit, wondering how my life got to be so awesome.

"Uh," I said after a beat, watching him grow solid and normal again. "You always turn into a cloud when you come?"

"No," he admitted around his sawing breath. "That was a first."

"Really?" I grinned, feeling oddly proud. "I was the first boy that made you go cloud?"

"I'd call you an idiot, but I'm too tired." He slid off the bed and raked his hair back, the sweat keeping it slicked back more than usual. I felt a little like a lovesick puppy watching him pad around my room for a bit, exhaustion tugging at my vision.

"Don't go to sleep," he warned as he drifted back over to the bed. He offered his hand to me and gestured for me to sit up. "Let's go rinse off. Then you can sleep."

I took his hand and let him haul me to my feet, following in a daze as we migrated to the shower in my bathroom. Unlike Sias's personal bathroom, my shower wasn't a multi-headed hydra of waterfalls big enough to bathe a football team. My private shower was just big enough for us to wedge in and get in each other's way, elbows knocking into ribs a few times and Zane's temple knocking into the shower head twice.

It wasn't the best way to cap off the overwhelmingly wonderful night we'd had together, but we escaped the tiny shower only a little annoyed and finally clean enough for sleep.

Zane was sitting on the bed holding his jar of ashes as I floated out of the bathroom in some fresh pajamas. He studied the contents inside, an expression on his face I couldn't quite read.

"I thought those would be gone," I told him, sitting beside him. "But I guess technically you're in a new body? I'm not sure how that works."

"I don't either."

"Do you want to get rid of them?" I asked, and Zane shook his head, rolling the jar to the side to watch the ashes build into a mountain before crumbling again.

"I don't think so. I'm not sure what to do with something like this." He set the jar aside. "It's not something I'm going to try and unpack tonight."

"Yeah. One emotionally impactful thing at a time." I rubbed at my eyes, exhaustion making them as dry and gritty as the ashes. "Would it be clingy and a little stupid if I asked you to stay with me? Just until I fall asleep?"

"I was going to stay anyway," he said with a tired smile. "I'll go grab a book after you're asleep."

I couldn't suppress a dumb smile as I crawled into bed, my heart fluttering as he crawled in after me. He lounged back and hooked his arm around me, inviting me to curl up with him.

"Don't tell anyone I like to cuddle," I said around a yawn. "I gotta keep my street cred."

"Sure."

I burrowed into his side, slipping my hand under his shirt to place my remaining hand over his heart, and fell asleep listening to it beat.

# CHAPTER
# FIFTEEN

I DREAMED about living ashes and angry fish.

The angry fish part of the dream no doubt came from my betta putting a curse on me for having to witness my sexual gymnastics with a vampire. I never taught Kevin voodoo, but I wouldn't put it past him to sneak out to the library for some light, occult reading, especially if he was feeling vindictive. That fish had all the time in the world and enough spite to curse me a hundred times over.

The dream with the living ashes was easy enough to unpack. It's not every day you see someone examine their own combusted body in a jar. In my dream, the jar had shattered and reformed into a ghostly vapor of Zane, red eyed and angry.

I was scared of it. It felt…powerful. Wrong. Seeing it made my chest freeze and my missing hand itch.

The feelings lingered as I woke up, a pinch where my ribs still felt stoney. My missing hand felt like it had fallen asleep somehow and I wondered if Zane could feel it around his heart, like physical white noise wrapped around it.

He was gone when I woke up, which I expected. I didn't think the guy was going to haunt my tiny room for hours while I was comatose, especially when I knew for a fact Sias had a massive library somewhere in the mansion as well as a game room to go enjoy. Zane would have plenty to keep him occupied while the rest of us slept.

I found some clothing and tugged everything in place, only grumbling a little bit at the slower pace I was forced to endure with one hand now missing. I was going to have to shake Sias down for a new, fancy robot hand soon because doing everything single-handed sucked.

After dressing and begging my spiteful, voodoo fish for forgiveness, I left my room to go check on Sias. I didn't like the state he was in last night after our trip to the void, nor was I thrilled that the big, scary death hound seemed to be attached to him. Sure, the thing seemed docile, but if it had a sudden change of heart, Sias was going to get ground up and spat out before we could leash the damn thing.

Morning sun slid over the marble flooring of the foyer as I passed by, the cool blues and golds alive within the amber light. The fading scent of coffee warmed the air near the kitchen, paired with the sweet smell of pastries resting on the counter. The box had been gently closed, the contents inside picked through by the other living members of the household. I knew for a fact Barnaby was a monster for donuts with sprinkles, even if he acted like they were beneath him. The sprinkles left behind in the frosting ring was damning evidence of his feast.

I snagged one on my way to Sias's room, devouring the thing before I reached his doorway. His bedroom, which was basically a whole damn apartment within the mansion, was vacant when I leaned through the open door. The sheets on his football field bed had been made for the day, all evidence of sleep or sex smoothed away into a perfect circle of satin and silk.

I drifted further into the house, following the lure of music that hummed from the open arcade door. The melodic sounds of brass horns danced with the singing chime of piano keys, playing low enough to allow the sweet sound of laughter to slide through. I didn't recognize the laugh at first, the delight in his voice elusive and hypnotizing. I'd never heard him sound so light.

I parked myself at the threshold of Sias's game room, leaning on the dark, wooden doorframe to marvel at the scene before me. Zane stood with a billiard cue in his hand, eyeing the table as Sias lined up his shot. Sias was still smiling from whatever had summoned his laugh, the creases around his mouth catching the light from the ornate, glass lamp hanging overhead.

"You talk a big game, Zane," Sias was teasing, his gaze fixed on the game. "You sure you want to make that bet?"

"Just hit the balls, Goldilocks."

Sias tsked, tossing a glance to the vampire as he searched for his angle.

"You can do better than that, Zane. You call Dallas 'hunter,' so you're not terrible at pet names."

"I call him 'hunter' because he is a vampire hunter. It's not a pet name, technically." Zane leaned on his cue. "You're stalling."

"Not stalling," Sias corrected boredly. "I'm working out how to beat you in three moves." He didn't respond as Zane snorted. "So, you give pet names based on job titles then?"

"Not a pet name," Zane insisted dryly. "But sure. Do you want me to call you 'CEO'?"

"That's not very cute."

"Boss?" Zane cracked a smirk when Sias cut him with a scathing look. "I could always go with 'demon.'"

"About as creative as calling a hunter 'hunter,' I suppose."

"You could always go with 'Daddy,'" I pitched as I headed into the fray. "That's what a lot of us call him."

"I'm not calling him that," Zane said, glancing my way as I strolled over to the table. "You found the donuts, I see."

"Yep. Barns ate all the sprinkle ones if you were looking forward to those." I licked some icing from my fingers and leaned over to try and make sense of who was in the lead. Sias's cue landed gently across my chest, his eyes flashing a serious shade of mustard.

"This table costs more than your entire apartment, pet. Don't get crumbs near it."

"Hey, now. I am pristine, thank you very much. I'm not a sloppy eater." I showed him my palm and backed away. "Maybe go with 'Grumpy' as a pet name."

"You have icing on your face," my bodyguard added, unhelpfully.

"Just for that, I won't let you lick it off." I swiped the corners of my mouth. "Who's winning, anyway?"

"It's tied." Sias tilted his head and added some chalk to the tip of his cue. "This is your chance to change your wager before I decimate you, darling."

"Maybe I should go with 'cocky' for you," Zane parried. "Works on a few levels."

"Cocky implies that I'm overly confident and a liar." Sias slid his eyes to Zane, flaring a strawberry hue. "I have no reason to lie about my abilities, just like I have no reason to be overly generous with this game."

Sias had rounded the table to come within a breath of Zane, his rainbow eyes studying the undead vampire, who kept his features remarkably unreadable.

"I don't shirk on a bet." Zane nodded to the table. "Play, or I'll win by default."

"Alright, vampire. You had your chance."

The gold in his horns flashed as he leaned over, his chest hovering just above the dark red felt, fingers a sightline for the cue to rest. His lithe torso stretched the fabric of his button-down, as did the slacks over the curve of his perfect ass. Sias slid over the pool table like he was begging to be fucked over it, yet somehow poised enough to crack a ball across the table and knock it into a pocket.

He moved to the opposite side of the table and leaned over, the angle something wonderful to behold, and I suppressed a shiver as Sias arched his back and leaned down, tapping another ball into place with a well-placed hit.

"Not bad," Zane admitted.

"How the fuck are you paying attention to the game?" I whispered to him, and he tossed me a knowing look.

"You always lose at pool, don't you?"

I presented the scene before him as Sias slowly straightened himself out, smoothing his clothing back into place.

"Obviously!"

Sias had either been ignoring our whispering or was so caught up in being a sexy pool shark he hadn't heard us because he strolled over, unbothered by how flustered I was.

"Should we call it now, dear?" Sias asked Zane coolly. "I could have this arrangement set up within the next thirty minutes."

Zane's deep, red eyes stalked the table, one finger drumming on the side of his pool cue as he untangled his options.

"Sleep well, pet?" Sias curled his lips in a smug smirk, eyes swirling into a playful pink, the warm light of the overhead lamp brilliant on his gold-tipped horns and bronze skin. The cuts on his cheek where his freaky, extra set of eyes lived were hidden, his fingers no longer dipped in ink.

It was a strange sensation to feel my cheeks warm from the question, as if the incubus in the house hadn't picked up on the intense sexual energy from last night. I had no doubt Barns had felt it too, and was avoiding us to keep the awkwardness down to a minimum. Only one of the sex demons living in the mansion enjoyed the aerobics that went into feeding, and that man was watching my face heat up in real time.

My new sense of modesty turned Sias's eyes into a flash of bubblegum pink, his pupils flaring.

"Dallas Wilde," Sias purred, salivating. "Are you *blushing*?"

"What? No! It's hot in here. I haven't had enough to eat. The lighting in here is weird." I tugged at my collar and tried to control the warring stings of embarrassment and flutters of affection.

Sias leaned his cue beside the table and slithered closer, charm magic teasing from him but not strong enough to put me under his spell. Pink flared before melting into hues of purple, lime and olive, landing somewhere between rich emerald and peridot.

"I've never seen you shy," Sias whispered in awe. "I could get very addicted to that."

It occurred to me in a slap of sharp clarity that my eruption of nerves and newfound anxiety wasn't just because I was still unpacking my night with Zane—fucking with a love confession and all—but because we never talked about Sias. We dove right into bed, changed our relationship overnight, and I never bothered to hit pause and ask about my attachment to the guy whose house we were currently occupying.

It was sobering to realize I had perhaps fucked up two of the most important relationships of my life in one night. A classic Dallas move, if I'm being honest, but not one I was proud of.

Horny disaster when stressed strikes again.

"Shit," I said out loud as everything sank into the marrow of my bones and chilled me to my core.

"I've changed my mind."

Zane's voice cut through me like a hot knife, cutting my chill and striking all the sensitive emotions crawling to the surface.

"What?" I said, horrified that he was responding to the confusion he felt tumbling around inside of me.

"On the bet," Zane clarified calmly, and I nearly melted into a hot puddle across Sias's nice pool table.

"So much for shirking on a bet," Sias teased with a chuckle, but Zane shook his head.

"The original bet still stands. I want to add something when I win."

"Oh?" Sias leaned his hip on the edge of the table as Zane scanned over his options. "When you win, hm? Dallas goes shy and you get arrogant. What a morning. Alright, Zane. What do you want to add *when* you win?"

"Repayment for the first game." Zane lifted his eyes to Sias. "With interest."

"Now that *is* interesting." Sias glanced over at the table, then tossed a dismissive shrug to him. "Alright, vampire. I'm happy to keep taking you for all you have."

"Mmhm." Zane placed himself near Sias and leaned down over the felt, the plain black shirt he wore flashing a little skin near the waist of his jeans as he stretched his arm out over the table. The cue was lined up and snaked forward with one quick, decisive strike, sending the ball into a geometric pattern of trick shots.

In a matter of moments the game was over, and Sias was left openly impressed.

Zane could play pool. Apparently pretty goddamn well.

Sias lifted his eyebrows as Zane raked his hair back. "I suppose I owe you an apology. That was masterful, Zane."

Zane set the cue down on the table and faced him. "You set that shot up for me to win if I was smart enough to see it, and if I was skilled enough to make it. You wanted me to win."

For the second time that morning, I got to hear Sias laugh. It sang out over the calm of the room: a rich, velvety sound that ran down my back and knocked the breath out of me.

My heart tightened like it was caught in a trap, rapid beating boarding on panic. I knew Zane could feel my emotions spiking, knew he had to feel the hornets in my stomach. It made it so much worse knowing he could feel my pull toward Sias, and how deep the guilt and worry was splitting me.

How the fuck was I going to untangle this mess?

How the hell was I going to tell the vampire I love that I couldn't just walk away from the incubus I had tethered myself to for so long?

I'd never hear Sias laugh again. He'd go cold again, and Zane would go back to being a resentful shadow.

I swallowed the knot in my throat and opened my mouth to speak, but couldn't get the words out.

Sias was oblivious to my panic, and Zane chose to ignore it. I almost turned to leave, but Sias's playful banter kept drawing me back in like a golden light to a heartsick moth.

"I'm still not convinced you downplayed your abilities to get your way," Sias was jabbing, smirk stuck to his face. "But fair is fair."

"I didn't take you for a sore loser, Sias."

Another snicker, Sias's eyes darkened into a rich red, dancing in sharp magenta around the center.

"You're starting to truly impress me," he purred, ever the flirt. "How do you want your payment?"

I had no clue how much money Sias had taken from Zane at that point, or where the hell a dead guy got any money. Zane had been alive…what? A few hours? What type of black-market bullshit did a vampire do to have money to throw around at a pool table with Sias Llon'nai?

Those questions would never be answered, because I could not have been more incorrect about what currency they had been using.

Fundamentally, completely, *mind fuckingly* wrong.

"I'll take the first part now."

Sias was pulled off the table he leaned against by the collar of his shirt, his gasp swallowed by Zane's mouth as their lips crashed together. Sias grunted as he was pushed back into the wood, his ass connecting with the edge of the table as Zane tangled his fingers into Sias's blond hair. Their kiss was fierce, tongues flashing and fangs bared, the familiar slither of Sias's dark-tinted charm magic coiling around them as the lines in his cheeks opened just a fraction.

Sias sucked air through his teeth as Zane angled the incubus's head back with a tug of his hair, the kiss broken as Sias nipped at Zane's bottom lip.

"Interest," Sias panted, his second set of eyes flaring before sealing again.

Zane huffed, his red eyes bright from excitement, swirling with the fading charm magic. His hand dropped from Sias's hair and Sias hooked his fingers into Zane's waistband to straighten himself.

"I look forward to the rest of the payment, Zane." Sias smoothed Zane's shirt down for him, scanning his face with eyes the same deep red as the vampire's. "And bonding a little more."

"Likewise." Zane allowed Sias to brush his hair back from his face, only moving back as Sias pulled his phone from his pocket.

"Duty calls. Could you be a dear and make sure our pet doesn't hit his head when he faints?" Sias gestured toward me as he strolled away, the spots in my vision darkening.

"Breathe, hunter. If you pass out, I'm leaving you here."

I inhaled at the command, blood rushing back into my brain from where it had been pooling much further south. I couldn't remember words or what order they should go in from the brain damage incurred while in a state of erotic shock, so I just pointed at Sias and made a squeaking noise.

"There you are!" Barnaby announced as he came racing into the arcade, oblivious to my state of mind. "I've been looking all over. You need to see what's on TV right now!"

"What's going on?" Zane asked like a logical person. I, however, was still reeling and refused to focus on anything else.

"Not now, Barns! Things are happening! Things!"

"Your inability to communicate properly is why I insist you do crossword puzzles with me, Dallas. Your vocabulary is abhorrent," Barnaby scolded.

"Things!" I pleaded, embittered.

"What's going on, Barnaby?" Zane came back as the voice of reason.

"Florence Pierce's compound was just raided," he said quickly. "It's all over the news. Her board just removed her from her company and DHAP is seizing her assets."

"Holy shit," I said, remembering my extensive vocabulary again. "Has she been arrested? Did they mention the scythe?"

"I'm not sure. I ran to find you as soon as they mentioned the raid," Barnaby explained as we followed him out of the arcade and into Sias's entertainment room, not to be confused with his movie room which was a literal theatre he'd had built for screening films. Funus was waiting beside the remote on a large couch, parked in front of a massive TV screen that stretched the length of the wall.

Sias's big death hound was napping across the rug, snoring through its open nose hole, with Twig curled up as a loaf in the strip of sunlight beside it. The cat blinked lazily upon noticing Zane, and rose up onto her feet with a stretch before trotting over for some demanding pets. She made a noise that was mostly vocal purring when Zane scooped her up into his massive hand and lifted her to his chest, smothering the little rat-tailed feline with affection.

I was just a *little* jealous of how much attention the cat was getting. Considering I had hogged him for the entire night, I decided not to demand the same treatment. For now.

Barnaby picked Funus up to hold in his lap as he sat down, Zane and I sitting on either side of them as the broadcast continued. Twig nestled against Zane's stomach and happily mewed while she got the base of her tail massaged.

The talking heads on the screen painted the picture of Florence being a troubled business tycoon, with whispers of shady practices involving the deeply illegal tampering of magical tech. ReNew was quick to make a public announcement essentially throwing her to the wolves, disassociating themselves from her "disappointing actions." Her massive estate was seized, the factories raided, including the one tucked away just outside of St. Athesall that had been gutted the previous night.

I recognized the robotic arm used to slice into the scythe in the still shots of the abandoned factory, most of the contents inside burned from the massive fire they had started before they fled. They had covered the truly damning evidence by way of complete destruction, but the patent tied to the company was enough to drive the final nail into the coffin.

Any traces of the necromancy she was involved with was either gone, missing, or shielded from the public. The pretty news anchors didn't drop the scary "dark magic" term once, even when they mournfully announced that she had most likely been involved with bio-magic tampering on a level that would get her thrown in prison for decades. It was no shock at all that she had fled without a trace.

Florence Pierce was a ghost, as was her right-hand woman, Hei, and the empire they had built. I would have been thrilled, if the ghosts hadn't likely disappeared with the goddamn scythe.

"Why do you look so sour? This is a good thing, isn't it?" Barnaby quizzed as I got to my feet to pace. "This means the tears will stop. The place she was using to rip apart the scythe was burned down."

"She still has the scythe, Barns. She's not going to stop, funding be damned. I don't think someone like Florence is going to just toss her hands up in defeat when she has the literal key to the Death Goddess in her hands." I rubbed at my aching temple, trying to summon a plan. "We have to find her, but I have no clue where to start looking."

"She's got connections all over the world," Zane pointed out. "She could be anywhere."

"She won't be able to go far with her face plastered all over the news. She'll go into deep hiding. Did they mention if her stupid wellness island got raided?" I asked Barns, who nodded.

"That was the first place they looked, actually. Apparently the rich customers there did not take kindly to being disrupted during their mud bath."

"I wouldn't either, that was legit. Don't make a face, it was nice. You're close-minded," I told the vampire as he scowled.

"Maybe Sias has some connections we can leverage. People in high places that might be mutual acquaintances," he pitched. "Someone has to know something."

"Worth a shot." I moved to go find said influential incubus when the sound of the front door being assaulted by a fist caught my attention. There was only one guy I knew who knocked with the same frantic authority of a cop with a search warrant, so I got ready for Preston Cheslock to come bearing late news of

Florence's fall. I rolled my eyes and changed course, heading to the front door as the pounding continued.

"Relax! I'm coming, Saint be damned," I called out to placate the annoyed officer before jerking the door open. "I know about Florence," I greeted, but was surprised that Preston wasn't alone.

Seyyid was at his side, as usual, both of them bandaged up from the harrowing battle with both their coworkers and the swarm of ugly little bat voidlings. How the hell they ducked out of getting tossed in jail for their involvement was an honest-to-God mystery, but that wasn't what threw me.

It was the extra guy standing with them that was screwing with my head.

"You need to go. Now," Austin said from beside them, a fresh black eye marring his face and a bloody split on his lower lip. His light brown eyes bore into mine, determination creasing his brows.

"What are you talking about?" I asked, and moved as they barreled inside. "What the fuck is going on?"

"They're on their way, Wilde," Preston told me quickly. "DHAP has put out an arrest warrant for you."

"For what?" I snapped, fury storming through my veins. "On what grounds? I've been assisting on repairing and stopping the damn tears!"

"After the insanity of last night, Magnus has sway over DHAP right now," Austin explained. "He told them you're involved with Florence."

"A lot of officers saw you go into the tear," Seyyid cut in. "Magnus has them convinced you're the necromancer Florence hired to either cover the tears up or to cause them. Preston and I did what we could, Wilde, but they're not listening to us."

"You gave them the evidence, right?" I looked between the two officers. "That has to count for something. Why the hell would I give you a critical piece of intel if I'm involved with her?"

The shame covering Preston's features told me the answer before he said a damn word. My vision grew bright around the edges, and I stormed toward him, ready to knock his damn teeth in.

"You son of a bitch," I hissed, my arm caught by Seyyid as he stepped in the way of my wrath. "You took the credit, didn't you? You sold me out!"

Preston at least had the decency to look ashamed, but he spit out his words like venom.

"It was either that or we'd be in prison right now, Wilde. Our whole careers have been upended because of your bullshit, remember? The goddamn tech vampires, the intel we handed to you on a silver platter. You think that shit didn't have consequences?"

"I saved your goddamn boyfriend!" I shook free of Seyyid's grip as he shoved me back a few steps. "If it wasn't for me, Seyyid would be a mindless, grunt vampire trying to rip you apart. And this is how you repay me?"

"I repaid you by throwing my career into the toilet, Wilde, and by coming here to give you a chance to escape. We're even."

"Not by a fucking long shot, Cheslock." I balled my fist, convincing myself it was worth burning some time in order to get a few good swings in. My commitment to cracking his teeth was paused midstep as Seyyid threw one more bomb my way.

"They're not just coming for you, Dallas. Magnus named Sias as one of your associates. They're going to come after him too."

"Bullshit," I spat. "You're trying to keep me from beating your boyfriend's ass, Seyyid. Move, or you're going down too."

"I'm serious," he pressed, silver eyes meeting mine and holding true. "You have thirty minutes to get out of the city."

"He's telling the truth, Dallas." Austin caught my shoulder and pulled me back, turning me to face him. "We gotta go. Right now."

I felt like smashing everything in sight, including both of the betraying cops and some of Sias's stupid, oversized vases for the hell of it. The way Seyyid spoke, and the fact that my estranged brother seemed to be both telling the truth *and* trying to save my ass, had me reevaluate my priorities.

"Fuck you both," I said to the cops I used to somewhat like. "Get out before I sic my fish on you."

Preston tugged Seyyid back to his side right about the time Zane rounded the corner, no doubt feeling my unbridled rage threatening to spill over the top. His blood-colored eyes sized up the two retreating cops, but lingered longest on Austin.

My vampire was all business when he asked, "What's going on?"

"DHAP is on their way. Magnus has convinced them I'm in bed with Florence. We gotta—wait." My brain took a beat, rewinding to the last thing Austin had said to me just moments ago. "What did you mean 'we' have to go? You're not tagging along to bring Magnus right to us, Austin."

Austin's jaw bunched as he failed to keep the tension from his shoulders. He had the posture and attitude of a kicked, junkyard dog; his bite ready, but the fight had already been beaten out of him.

"I'm on the run now, same as you." He shoved his hands into his jacket pockets, the bruising around his eye tender and swollen. "You want my help or not?"

"Magnus do that to you?" My outrage was apparent, hitching a ride with the anger from the previous betrayal.

"We don't have time for this chat right now, Wilde. Twenty-five minutes left." Austin turned his attention to Zane. "The incubus has cars, right? We need to load up what we can and head south. It's the fastest way out of the city."

"We *need* to find Florence and the scythe," I hissed. "Do you know where she is? Any leads on her whereabouts?"

"I have some theories, but I'll tell you in the car. Get your shit." Austin lifted his chin for me to hurry, posting himself by the front door to be on lookout for inbound DHAP patrol.

Zane followed me as I turned and rushed back to the entertainment room, my mind splintering into several thoughts at once. There was no way we were going to make it out of the city with everyone on alert. We needed a place to cool down and hide, and I needed to get my hands on some guns, intel, burner phones and a low profile, stolen car to escape in.

"Get Barns and Funus to the garage. I need to grab Sias and my duffel of killing toys for the road. Bring any cash we have, no cards."

"What the hell is going on now?" Barnaby began his complaining, but got to his feet so I didn't snap at him. "What did you do?"

"Trust the wrong people. You don't have time to pack a bag, so don't ask." I scooped Twig up and cringed back a little as the big hellhound lifted its head. "Hey. Big uh…doggie. Can you be a good boy and go guard the garage?"

The beast tilted its head at hearing it had the chance to be a "good boy," the backend of its massive body wiggling. It didn't immediately comply, so I tried a different angle.

"Go get Sias, boy. Go on. Go get Daddy!" I watched with newfound interest as the spawn of the void scrambled to its feet like a drunk Great Dane and bolted off to do as it was told. "Huh. Do all things from the void respond to praise like that? Should I start calling you 'good boy,' Zane? Shit, don't hit me, I'm holding your cat!"

"I have a bug-out bag stashed in my room," Barnaby announced before Zane could kill me. "It has a week's worth of supplies. Grab it on your way, Dallas. We'll meet you in the garage."

I raced down the hallway, impressed with Barnaby's foresight and a little mad at myself for not doing the same, and rushed to my room. I placed Twig on the bed and gave her some treats to keep her busy, then grabbed my duffel of fun time murder accessories from under the bed.

"Kevin, we got a Hide and Seek situation, my man." I shoved some extra supplies into the bag as I moved to his tank to give him some bloodworms. "We're taking the hellhound with us, but you need to look after Twig."

Kevin peered at me from his coconut hut, an irritated bubble popped from his mouth.

"I know. I'm sorry. Be good and I love you. Don't answer the door for strangers."

I kissed my fingers and pressed them to the glass, and I got a tail flick in return. It was going to take a mountain of blood worms, and probably a new pirate ship, to make him love me again, but I'd figure that out later.

Barnaby's bug-out bag was easy enough to find, since he had it labeled beside his bed with a note in cursive tied to it with ribbon. I snagged it, and Funus's little dog bag, before sprinting down to the arcade to find Sias.

"Hey," I slid into the dim arcade, double fisting bags and starting to break into a sweat. "We gotta go. DHAP is on the way and—" He held up his hand for me to pause, pulling in the last drag of a thin cigarette.

"I know." Sias exhaled a long puff of smoke, the cloying scent of tobacco hanging like morning fog over the abandoned pool game. "DHAP froze the bank accounts they know of, but that's not important. We have friends within the city that will help keep eyes diverted as we plan our next move. They're also buying us some time with a few traffic jams so we can escape."

Sias pushed off the pool table and slid his fingers along the corner pocket, a deep, wooden sound sliding into place. The velvet top popped up on one side, the balls rolling and sliding into the pockets as he lifted the hinged, false top. Inside the billiard table where I had watched him and Zane make out like horny teenagers earlier that morning contained a suitcase, some ammo, a spare handgun and a pack of the same, thin cigarettes.

I guess those were crisis smokes.

Sias hefted the suitcase out and handed me the spare gun and ammo. The false table was sealed again with a simple push, and pocketed the crisis smokes for later.

"We have a few thousand in here, some gold, passports and

burner phones. Trying to flee the city now would be stupid, so we'll need to lay low for a while."

"You are so sexy right now."

"I know." He nodded toward the exit. "Let's move, pet. We'll take the SUV."

I passed him Barnaby's bag and we got moving, the big hellhound following close to his side. There was a small, vindictive part of me that almost didn't whistle for Austin before we escaped for the garage, but I couldn't bring myself to be that much of an asshole. I wasn't ready to say we had started repairing bridges at that point, but I knew he was walking away from a newly burned one.

Like it or not, and I definitely did *not,* he was family. And I think I was all he had left.

Sias's eyes flared a new shade of murder orange as he saw Austin, but I put my hand on his chest before he had a chance to rip my brother's head from his shoulders.

"He's the one that gave us a heads up. He's coming with us," I said with an authority I faked well. "He has information we need."

"If I had more time, I'd *take* that information instead." Sias adjusted his gun holster he had just strapped on and pierced Austin with topaz severity. "Misstep, child, and I'll feed bits of you to my hound."

The beast growled as if on command, the sound like shattering bone under a grinding boulder.

"Maybe you should sit in the very back," I told Austin, pointing to the back row.

"Just keep that thing away from me," Austin mumbled as he tossed the hellhound a wary glance, crawling into the back seat to sit in solitude.

"I don't trust him, Dallas," Sias told me as Austin made his way into the car. "He's under the thumb of your father and his loyalty is questionable at best."

"I have a feeling that's not a problem anymore." I threw my

bag into the SUV. "But if I'm wrong, I'll handle it myself. I love it when you're in scary mode, Sias, I really do. It makes me a little afraid and it's incredibly hot, but I need you to dial it down to simmering, threatening Daddy. Not murder Daddy."

"I will not tolerate you getting hurt, pet. And I am in no mood for leniency today." Sias's horns curled just a little bit, the lines on his cheeks almost opening.

"Pretty sure if he was going to make a move, he would have done it before I got the vampire and scary, death incubus." I opened the passenger side door for him and offered him the seat.

"For his sake, I hope you're right." Sias angled his head toward the SUV and snapped his fingers. "Malphaslanexus."

The big hellhound leaped into the car and padded over to the window, its green tongue lulling out to one side.

"Did you just speak in tongues?" I watched the beast pant excitedly about the car ride to come, its big, clawed paws pricking the leather as it shifted its weight.

"That's his name."

"His *name*? That's a horrible name." I looked to my body-guard, who I had momentarily forgotten never had my back. "You agree, right? That's way too long for a name."

"That's the name of the incubus knight who guarded his queen's family from invasion during the demon uprising. Goddess, hunter. Read a book." Zane took the keys from Sias as a final insult and began making his way to the driver's seat.

"Stop smiling, he's not cute," I told Sias as I followed the asshole vampire around the car. "I'm driving. You don't get to insult me and drive the car."

"Shut up and get in or I'll throw you in." Zane lifted the keys above his head so I couldn't reach them. "I'm serious, hunter."

"So am I. I'm getting us the hell out of here because you drive like a grandpa." I tried to hook my stump over his bicep to jerk his arm down, reaching for the keys with my only hand. Zane snorted out like an annoyed bull and glanced over the driver's seat to the simmering murder Daddy.

"Little help, Sias?" Zane asked.

A cool slither wrapped itself around me like a languid snake, relaxing my muscles and gently squeezing the fight out of me.

"Relax, pet," Sias tossed over to me, eyes a vibrant purple with a sharp, black edge.

"I'm starting to regret a lot of things," I mumbled as the back door to the SUV was opened on Zane's side of the car. I tried to knock Zane's grip off me but I was shoved ass over head into the back seat next to Malpha-whatever.

I was reduced to squeezing into the middle seat beside Barnaby and the huge ass hellhound, only one of which was happy about my presence. Austin kept to the shadows in the row of seats behind us while Funus happily watched out the window from Barnaby's lap.

Sias's charm magic eased as we rolled out of the garage and onto the street, which helped me snap back into planning mode.

"We can't try and get out of the city yet," I told them from the back seat, leaning forward to insert myself into the command center. If I wasn't able to drive, I was at least going to be the annoying copilot calling the shots. "We're going to need to head somewhere we can hide out and swap cars. Sias has some money on him, which will make the swap a little easier."

"Do you have an idea of where we can go?" Barnaby asked from the back seat.

"Yeah." I rubbed at my eyes, the headache blooming and starting to press at my frontal lobe. "I know where we can go. It's going to suck but it's all we have."

"I already hate whatever you're about to say," Zane said through an exhale.

"Yeah. You should. He's not going to be happy to see you either."

# CHAPTER
# SIXTEEN

"I KNOW what you're going to say, but hear me out," I said before Marthas could slam the door in our faces.

We must have been quite the sight, if I'm being fair. Standing on the asphalt of his vacant club's parking lot was the guy he hated most (me, obviously), the vampire wearing the jacket he'd stolen from him after punching him in the face, the incubus who'd insulted him last time he was there, a beaten and bruised Saint's Army asshole, and Barnaby, who had never mastered the art of suppressing judgment from his face.

Funus and Malphie—which is what I was calling the hellhound—waited in the car so we could surprise Marthas later.

"You have some balls, Wilde. I'll give you that." Marthas scanned over us like we were a pack of raccoons going through his garbage. The midmorning sun was highlighting how little sleep the man was getting, and reflected on the bits of silver in his growing stubble. Stress had aged the mountainous imp by a few years, and was in the process of carving lines beside his eyes and caverns along his mouth. Stress had given his hair some silver streaks, which made his hazel eyes bright despite the bruising under them. His hair had gotten shaggy enough to almost hide his short, stout, imp horns resting on top of his skull.

"Those tears that ripped your club open? We know what caused them and we're trying to make sure they don't happen again. We need a place to lay low while we regroup," I pleaded. "This is the last place DHAP and Saint's Army would look for us."

Marthas continued to lean on the door, tired and unimpressed, his eyes landing on Zane as I explained our dire circumstances.

"I thought you died."

"I came back," Zane answered back in the same icy tone.

"Huh." Marthas's brows twitched upward, his mouth settling into a contemplative frown. "What's the void like?"

Zane thought for a beat then answered with an honest but curt, "Quiet."

"Thank the Gods for that." Marthas shoved a brick against the bottom of the door to hold it open and moved inside, the invitation to follow apparent.

A budding sense of relief filled my chest as I followed, my strange posse at my heels. It didn't feel like a trap, but the lack of arguing, pleading, bargaining or begging had me very uncomfortable. There was no such thing as free favors or acts of altruism in the Swallows, especially not with the leader of the Broken Horns.

The club was the same hollow, haunted place it had been when Sias and I had last paid a visit, though the dance floor had now been ripped away to remove all the black scarring from the tear. Dust from the destruction covered the bar tables and countertops, the smell of old carpet and broken wood drifted through the air like falling leaves.

"Fixing the place up, huh?" I stepped around some busted wood paneling as he meandered further into the club, bypassing the demolished dance floor and creeping into the more private section of the building.

"There's no fixing this place. It's cursed," Marthas explained as he escorted us past the VIP section and down some winding steps. "It's getting demolished next month."

"You could always flip it. The building is still structurally sound, and the big open windows on top would lend itself to a lovely garden space," Barnaby waxed poetically, doing his best to be helpful.

"I doubt anything would grow in this place, sweetheart. Too much death." Marthas navigated us through a section of the building I had never been allowed in before. I had seen his office, the private game room where his thugs relaxed in while awaiting orders, and had even gotten a peek into the "stock room," which was mostly illegal guns, ammo, some very raw magic tech and expensive hexes and charms. The door to that room was locked behind a heavy door riddled with wards and bolts, and I knew better than to ask what was left of its contents.

I had never seen the guts of Biodome empty of Marthas's soldiers, a horde of young imps ready to crawl through the streets armed with guns and vicious loyalty. It was eerie not to hear the muted thump of club music and the buzz of crime within Marthas's little kingdom, even more so when the big man himself moved with a shroud of gloom.

Past what I was familiar with was what I could only really describe as a barracks built into a basement, some private rooms with simple beds tucked along a common living space with an old couch, a medical cot with basic supplies, a fridge and TV. It was shockingly comfortable and looked more like a family basement for game night than a belly of a gang front. It even had the standard basement musk of threatening mildew clinging to the worn carpet.

Marthas pointed out each room as he spoke.

"Some of you are going to have to share beds. There's only two rooms and a couch. Bathroom is there, just one shower. Water pressure sucks and it's not very hot, so don't fucking complain."

"Oh, this is…surprisingly not awful," Barnaby gave the couch a testing poke and wiped his hand on his slacks afterward. "I expected much worse. A fresh coat of paint and some basic cleaning and this might even be pleasant."

"The maid is off today," Marthas said dryly. "I'll make sure to relay your concerns to HR."

"Sorry, he's not used to talking to people," I told Marthas and Barnaby stabbed me with his frown. "So, what's the catch, Marthas? What do I need to do for us to stay down here?"

"I don't need or want shit from you, Wilde." Marthas swung a cabinet by the medical cot open and pulled a rattling bottle of pills from inside. He set them on the counter near the kitchenette, which was comprised of a microwave, sink, rack of dishes and abandoned box of cereal.

"I know you better than to think you're giving this to us for nothing." I watched him carefully as he dug through the freezer and tossed a cold compress onto the counter next to the bottle of pills.

"One of the girls that was swallowed up on the dance floor was named Fiona." Marthas popped open the bottle and swallowed down two pills, then capped it and slid it back next to the compress. "Her grandmother came knocking a week ago. She threw the money I gave her for her discretion back into my face, and repeated her granddaughter's name the whole time she told me what a piece of shit I was. She used the word 'devil' and hoped my soul rotted in hell instead of finding peace in the void. You. Saint's Army boy."

Austin lifted his gaze to Marthas, assuming correctly he was being summoned.

"Your Saint believes in redemption, right?" Marthas asked. "How does that work?"

"Depends." Austin shrugged. "What did you do?"

"I watched the floor open up and swallow people alive. Watched them die in my club and paid the police and their families to stay quiet." Marthas rubbed at his stubble, the pull of exhaustion tugging at his eyes. "What would your Saint think of that?"

Austin weighed Marthas's words behind equally tired eyes,

one of which was mottled a painful green and angry purple from a brutal right hook.

"Fear is just as poisonous as violence. You didn't kill them, but you responded out of self-interest and fear, which to the Saint is worse than shoving them into the tear. The only redemption is sacrifice, otherwise there is no salvation for a cowardly soul."

Marthas huffed a humorless laugh, a ghost of a smile almost flickered to the surface.

"There's your answer, Wilde. I have a penance to uphold if I have any shot at a nice, quiet afterlife. If you really are stopping these tears, keeping other little Fiona's safe, then I'll play nice for now."

"That's the plan," I told him, being honest to him for probably the first time in our entire, rocky relationship. "We know Florence Pierce is the one ripping open holes by meddling in some nonsense she has no right to be messing with. We just need some time to formulate a plan, and maybe some supplies if you're feeling generous."

"That's a big fucking maybe, Wilde. Don't push it," Marthas warned, shoving the cold compress and pills Austin's way across the counter. "For the shiner, handsome."

Austin scowled, but moved to grab the supplies quietly.

"It just occurred to me that we didn't grab Twig and Kevin before we left," Barnaby erupted in a fit of fretting. "If the DHAP raid the house—"

"Kevin's on it. He'll look after Twig too," I explained, annoyed when Barnaby gave me a scathing look. "My fish is very capable of handling a kitten, Barns. Do I look worried?"

"No pets," Marthas added, assuming the conversation was trending in that direction. "I'm going back upstairs. Listening to you all is giving me more of a headache."

I slashed at my throat in a miming gesture to silence Barnaby as he opened his mouth, his urge to tattle about Malphie almost overpowering. Marthas lumbered back up the stairs and we waited until his big footsteps disappeared before collectively exhaling.

"I need to grab the skull and the dog, then ditch the car," I told the room. "Zane, can you do your mist thing and make sure Marthas isn't turning us over to DHAP?"

"I don't think he's lying," Austin said, cold compress easing the swelling in his face.

"You don't know him like I do. We're not exactly friends."

"Yeah, I could pick up on that," Austin snorted. "But he strikes me as a guy who isn't in a hurry to involve himself with cops. Nor does he seem like someone who would invite us down into his private living quarters as a ploy. He wants redemption. We're his shot at that."

"God, it must be exhausting being the white knight all the time." I rubbed at my eyes. "Zane, just come with me. You can carry the skull."

"What should I be doing then?" Barnaby refused to sit anywhere in the basement, opting to stand on a piece of carpet that didn't seem as ragged.

"Hang out. Don't leave the basement. Same goes for you, Sias. With an active warrant out for you, we need to keep you hidden for the time being."

Sias was ready to argue but thought better of it, instead he took the bills from his wallet and pressed them into my palm.

"Be safe and bring me back something sugary. I either need candy in my body or a power fuck session to ease this anxiety."

My brain went into overdrive for a moment, smoke no doubt bellowing from my ears as I tried to tweak the plans I was in the middle of executing.

"Maybe we could stick around for just a bit longer, I mean the car's parked in a good spot..." I began, body warming as Sias's eyes took on a teasing shade of strawberry.

"There are other people in the room," Austin reminded us. "People who don't want to hear this."

"Focus," Zane reminded us, not sounding nearly as annoyed

as he normally did. "Sias, don't distract him right now. He's fickle enough without your help."

"Fine," Sias drawled. "But only because I like you taking charge. It's…attractive."

"Did anyone hear me say I don't want to hear this?" Austin repeated himself, but we all ignored him.

"I'm perfectly capable of assisting in the mission at hand—not the sex part obviously," Barnaby interjected. "This isn't the first time we've been in danger, you know." He smoothed his shirt down and then snapped his fingers with a sense of glee. "Ah! I can make an agenda for formulating plans! Surely Mr. Marthas has some stationery and maybe some highlighters. You can fetch them on your way out."

"I'll get right on that." I was clearly sarcastic in my tone, but Barnaby's excitement about making a pointless itinerary shielded him from my annoyance.

Despite thinking that Sias's idea of staying behind to help him *relax* sounded like much more fun, we went with my stupid plan of ditching the car and fetching the undead things we were attached to. Zane and I made our way through the guts of Biodome and out through the back where Sias's car was parked along the side alleyway. Since Malphie wasn't technically alive and Funus was a talking skull, we didn't have to worry about leaving them in the parked car with the windows up, which came in handy for tricking Marthas into agreeing to let us stay.

Malphie lifted his giant head when we popped the side door open, his backside wiggling against the seat when he realized it was us. I was thankful that no one had tried to steal the car while we were inside, but I kinda wished someone had tried.

Imagine boosting a nice ride only to be face-to-face with an undead void hound instead of a car alarm?

That would be a great reality TV show, if you ask me.

"Did it work?" Funus asked from Barnaby's seat, eyes swiveling to me. "Do we have somewhere to hide out?"

"Shockingly, yeah." I tugged over his dog carrier backpack

and unzipped it. "I didn't exactly tell him about you and Malphie though, so we're going to try and keep you both a secret for as long as we can. He's a normie—not someone used to seeing a lot of living dead things."

"Ah. Well. I hope he's a reasonable man then."

"He is not." I picked him up gently and placed him into the dog carrier. "But we have some rooms to stay in. You'll have to bunk with Barnaby again, hope you don't mind."

It was meant as a tease, but I caught the way the skull managed to express a wince by flickering his glowing eyes.

"Funus, I was joking," I explained, instantly feeling horrible for hurting the undead man's feelings. "I'm sorry."

"No, no. Please, there's no need." He attempted to brighten his demeanor but it fell short. "I was lamenting before you returned to get us that poor Barnaby is caught up in all of this and it doesn't seem very fair. He is also a...what did you say? A 'normie'? I sometimes wonder if perhaps I wasn't around, that he would have moved on to much safer endeavors."

"Barns is a stubborn brat, Funus. He'd be here regardless, I promise." I took him back out to speak with him at equal height. It was always a little awkward to talk to one of the brightest minds while he was staring up at me from a dog case. "Plus, he's not exactly going to walk away from it now. I saw how he yelled at you when we were dealing with the tear, my man. Pretty sure he's smitten."

Funus hummed a laugh, eyes momentarily flaring with joy before dimming again.

"I have been dead for centuries, acolyte. I have served my Goddess faithfully as a vessel of knowledge and guidance. But for the first time in all these years, I have regret." Funus's gentle admission knocked a hole in my heart, his whispered tone one of lifetimes of loneliness. "What cruel fate is it, to finally live long enough to find someone to care for, only to be unable to hold their hand? Share their favorite foods? Experience the warmth of the sun together? How is it that my heart breaks even when I don't possess one anymore?"

"I'm sorry, Funus," I told my friend, my own heart aching for him. "I can't imagine how that must feel. But I know, without a shadow of a doubt, that Barnaby adores you. You make him happier than I've ever seen him, and I've known that fussy mess for years. You two will figure out your own normal, which I'm sure will be weird anyway, even if you weren't a talking skull."

Funus laughed again, eyes regaining some of their shimmer.

"He loves you, you know. Very much," he said simply. "Remember that when you rush into trouble down the road, Dallas Wilde. We must take care of his heart, you and I. Barnaby needs both of us."

"Don't get sappy on me, skull," I teased so I didn't get teary eyed in front of a member of the council. "You gonna be okay? We're going to need your help figuring out where Florence is hiding and in getting the scythe back."

"I'll be fine," he assured me, sounding bright again. "Just a moment of melancholy is all. I will assist in every way I can."

"You're a good guy, Funus, and I respect you a lot." I set him back into the dog carrier and zipped it up. "Please don't think less of me for this next part."

"Oh, boy," Funus said around an exhale, not even attempting to argue.

"Malphie," I sang to the hellhound, earning more butt wiggles and excited claw taps. "Do you know where Daddy is?"

The big, dopey creature with glowing eye sockets sniffed the air with its nose hole, the sound similar to a vacuum cleaner inhaling dust from a tube. He tilted his head, the fur along his spine lifting before he bounced out of the car. He stood beside me and sniffed again, his gaze snapping to the open back door of Biodome.

"Good boy," I praised, looping Funus's dog carrier around the hellhound's shoulders so the case rested on his back.

"Goddess, let this creature have balance," Funus whined. "If it falls, I'll crack my head."

"He won't fall. Or at least…I'm pretty sure he won't." I gave Malphie a pat on his skinless head before saying the magic words. "Go get Daddy!"

Malphie fired off like a bat—or maybe dog?—out of hell, clamoring across the parking lot before leaping through the open door.

"God speed, Malphie." I gave the hound a salute and turned to climb into the car when I ran into Zane. Before I could hurl an insult about him being a fleshy brick wall in my way, I was pulled into a sweet, painfully romantic, slow kiss.

It was as surprising as it was disarming, and I fell into the hypnotic rhythm of it before my brain could catch up.

I was dumbstruck when he pulled back, lips tingling and breath lost.

"What was that for?" I managed after knocking the knot from my throat with a cough.

Zane nodded to the building. "That was kind. What you said to Funus."

"It's true." I shrugged. "They've gotten really close since you've been gone. It's obnoxiously adorable. I didn't know one of your turn-ons was being nice to sweet, old skulls."

"A few months ago, there was no way you would have been that vulnerable to an undead." Zane ran his thumb over my cheek, his skin alive and still flushed from last night. "My turn on is seeing your emotional growth."

"And my nice ass, right? Where are you going?" I tossed my hands up in exasperation as Zane rolled his eyes and walked away. "I'm being vulnerable to an undead right now!"

"Get in the car, hunter."

# SEVENTEEN

DITCHING the car was tricker than I thought it would be, but we were able to get it into a chop shop with a decent payout and obtain a pack of candy for Sias. It was late in the evening by the time we made our way back to Biodome and rain had begun to pour in earnest by the time we ducked inside.

The drumming of raindrops on the club's signature glass ceiling was deafening without the thump of music, the flashes of lightning giving the creepy atmosphere of the dark building an even more ominous tone. Biodome was more like a haunted house than a place for revelry and party drugs in the state it was in, so I was pleasantly surprised to hear music drifting up from the lower levels.

Light from Marthas's lounge area was the only life seen within the building from the upper floor, bleeding up in thin hues of amber and carrying the scent of pizza. Zane and I descended the stairs, escaping the sorrow of the haunted club and into the relaxed scene of low rock music, a few boxes of pizza that had been picked through, and two men who hated my guts commiserating over beer and darts.

"I thought they trained you lot to aim," Marthas heckled

Austin as he landed a miserable shot on the dartboard. "You need me to tack pictures of vampires on it for you to hit anything?"

"You normally talk this much shit over a friendly game?" Austin asked as he lined up his next throw.

"Only when my opponent sucks this bad." Marthas glanced my way as we stepped into the room. "Wilde, put your vampire in front of the board. Maybe your brother can hit something then."

"Zane doesn't like getting poked by just anyone you know." I cackled as the picky poker slapped my shoulder. "I'm learning your love language is assault."

"My hate language is assault," Zane corrected. "I'm going to go check on Barnaby and Sias."

"I'll play you for my jacket back," Marthas tossed out to Zane. "We'll trade the darts for knives."

"Buy a new one with the money you win off him," Zane fired back, gesturing to Austin. "Otherwise, I'll happily remind you how the last fight went."

Marthas chuckled, palms up. "Easy, vampire. I was fucking with you. By the way, the golden incubus is upstairs in the atrium. The professor is in the basement."

Zane hummed that he wasn't amused and changed course, heading back the way we came to go find Sias. Marthas watched him until his figure disappeared.

"He always that pissed off, or do you bring that out in him?" Marthas asked me.

"It's a side effect of being dead. No sense of humor. You got money on this game?" I snagged a slice of pizza from the box and shoved some in my mouth.

"Hundred bucks," Marthas answered. "I'm about to double it."

"Uh-huh." I finished my bite and stole Austin's beer off the table. "Heads up, Austin. He's a sore loser."

"So, what's the plan exactly?" Austin asked, focused on the

game. "How are we going to find this Florence Pierce now that she's gone into hiding?"

"That is a damn fine question." I hadn't realized that the beer I stole was unopened and sealed with a twist off cap, and I weighed my options of how to tackle the situation that would have been a breeze with two hands. "How does one find a self-righteous health nut who has thus far been not only cheating death, but manipulating it in unforeseen ways?"

"Before someone else does," Marthas added, cracking open a fresh beer for himself. Show off. "She's got a bounty on her for fleeing DHAP. A hefty one too."

"Do you have any leads?" Austin paused his game to give his attention to the imp. "Have you heard anything? You can keep the reward money. We just want the scythe."

"Well, hold on now," my business side entered the negotiations, now sitting with a beer pinched between my knees. "I think a 60/40 split sounds reasonable if he has a solid tip."

"If I had anything, I sure as hell wouldn't give it to you for 60/40, Wilde. I'd pay someone the entire total just to kick you in the ass."

"How hard?" Austin jumped in before I could fire off a well-timed "fuck you."

Marthas chuckled, taking a pull from his beer.

"We're going to get along just fine, army boy."

"Yeah, ha-ha." I took a break from my beer opening attempt to flip them off. "I'm flipping you off too, Austin, but I'm using my ghost hand."

"I'm assuming your lack of a real answer means you have no idea how we're going to find her." Austin took aim and threw, grumbling at the bad result. "So, we're just what? Waiting around?"

"Yeah, right now we are," I confirmed, ignoring his eye roll. "We have no leads, and DHAP is breathing down our necks. I'll use what we have to try and cash in some favors or get some intel.

Someone has to know something. It's just a matter of finding who."

"Whatever you say." Austin threw another bad shot and sighed. "My depth is off."

I gave up on holding the beer with my knees and twisting, since the slippering thing just kept rotating with my twist.

"Getting knocked in the head will do that," I said.

Austin stabbed me with a sharp side eye as I studied his profile. The bruising was still bright on his tan skin, though the swelling had gone down considerably. I hadn't had a chance to take in the full state he was in during our panicked flight from Sias's home, and my chest tightened at seeing the full extent of the damage.

It wasn't just the black eye that marred him. His lip was split from a second or third blow to the face, jaw peppered with a few, lighter bruises. The Saint's Army patch that should have been on his shoulder was notably absent, thin threads and torn fabric hung in ripped disgrace, the force of the removal scarring it beyond repair.

"Stop staring at me. I'm trying to concentrate," he mumbled.

"What happened, Austin?" I asked after he threw, the dart bouncing off the wall and clattering to the floor.

"Pretty stupid question." Austin gathered up his darts and passed them to Marthas. "You know what happened. You were there."

"What happened when you presented your case?" I stood and tried to line up the bottle's cap with the edge of the table and knock it loose, but it just gouged the wood.

"You really think the old man was going to let me present a case?" Austin scoffed, offended that I assumed he'd play fair. "After what I pulled?"

"Presented a case?" Marthas asked as he tossed his first dart, which landed near the middle. "What does that mean?"

"Saint's Army rule," I explained. "If a soldier disobeys a command from our leader, we have a chance to argue why in front of the community. It would be up to them to decide if our action was just or not. It's supposed to be non-negotiable."

"Unless it's a time of war." Austin fell into a seat at one of the tall tables around the room. "Which this is. My actions were clear, so he responded in kind."

"That's bullshit," I snapped, the injustice of it causing my anger to boil to the surface. "If we can get you in front of everyone, especially Paris and Worth, they can vouch—"

I had expected anger from him. Outrage fueled tenacity for the justice he deserved. Austin was the best of us, a true soldier through and through. He bled devotion to the Saint, to the Army's cause, vowed to me when we were way too young to understand the gravity of his words that he'd die fighting the undead scourge.

There was not a scrap of that left in him when he interrupted my misplaced rage.

He was quiet.

Tired.

Changed.

"Dallas, you're not getting it. I don't want to go back. I'm done."

Standing felt way too hard when I heard how devastated he sounded, and I found myself falling into a seat beside him because I couldn't fight gravity anymore.

A hot stab of guilt split me open as I sat there, staring at the beer I had failed to open.

"This is my fault," I admitted. "I shouldn't have pulled you into this shit."

Austin took my beer and opened it for me.

"It is your fault," he whispered. "If you had stayed as a traitor, a coward fallen from the sight of the Saint, I think I would have been able to shoot you when he told me to. And I hate myself for that. Hate you for being better than I thought you'd be."

We sat in silence as his words hung like well-aimed darts in my chest, and I scrubbed my eyes to keep the sting of tears at bay.

The beer was delicious, and a little foamy from being shaken from my botched attempts.

"You're mad at me for *not* being a coward?" I clarified.

"It would have been easier if you were," he agreed.

"I'm…sorry?" I coughed a laugh, the fragile grip on my shield starting to slip. His barrage of honesty was cutting through my sarcastic armor, hitting the weak spots only he had access to. "I can try to be more of a coward in the future if that helps."

"I don't think you can," Austin said. "Despite everything, you've managed to be a decent man. I'm not ready to say I forgive you, Dallas, but I can admit you're worth standing beside."

My eyesight had gone completely soggy, reality a warbled mess of blurry colors as I swallowed past the knot in my throat.

"Man," I managed, voice embarrassingly strained as I dashed at the betraying tears from my checks. "Fuck you for making me cry in front of Marthas."

Austin huffed a noise that sounded almost like a laugh, but I couldn't see him through the damn tears. By the time I was able to scrub my vision clear, Austin had fallen back to his normal, contemplative glower.

Marthas set the darts and a fresh beer on the table for Austin, which he took as a great excuse to stand. He moved away to take his position to throw a few more shots at the board, his aim improving but still horrible in comparison to his opponent.

"Since I got to see you cry like a baby," Marthas said, still lingering by the table. "I'll let it slide that I specifically said no pets and not throw you on your ass."

"You mean the skull or the hound?" I sniffed back some of the stray moisture still trying to escape my eyes.

"I mean the big ass beast that ran through my bathroom looking for the incubus. While I was in it," he leveled his glare at me. "The skull at least apologized."

Laughing helped ease the tightness in my chest, even if it likely deducted points from Marthas.

"Oh my God. This day got a little better because of that."

"Thin ice, Wilde. Thin fucking ice."

I decided to finish off Austin's beer since it was almost gone and the grumpy imp had brought him a new one anyway.

My goal had been to shamble down into the basement and face plant onto bed since I was feeling particularly emotionally raw from my brief but impactful chat with my brother, but I realized with a groan that I still had Sias's coveted pack of cigarettes in my pocket. Had it been for literally anyone else, I would have thrown it out the door and hoped he found them on his own, but that wasn't going to fly with Mr. Gold Plated Guns.

Pretty sure he would have ordered me out to get him a fresh pack if I let it hit the ground. Not to mention I wasn't about to be passive aggressive to a guy who owned a hellhound.

It was humbling to realize I was on a shorter leash than that damn dog.

Even in the dark, I knew how to navigate the halls of Biodome. The place had been my second home since I was a homeless teenager. I'd been ready to dive headfirst into danger, drugs and sex, and a nightclub owned by a notorious imp gang leader had been the perfect place to pitch my growing assassination business. I'd been young, armed and hadn't given a shit; Biodome was like heaven.

The rainfall had eased a bit when I wandered out from Marthas's VIP area, the thunderous pounding calming into a steady drum line. Memories of past nights played out in the shadows as I trailed up the serpentine stairwells that connected the floors, the building quiet enough for me to hear them creak.

The atrium section of Biodome was themed with flora in mind, but there was nothing alive inside the club other than us (Zane excluded, obviously.) An intimate dance floor of polished jade lived under the massive glass ceiling fogged over from time and the elements, flanked on all sides by a few narrow tabletops and a smattering of long couches tucked into dark corners for more *private* conversations.

I'd rarely had the money to afford the atrium section of the club, but when I did, I had plenty of fantastic *conversations* there. And a few harrowing nights of being dangled over the edge after being caught conversing with the wrong people.

The storm pressed against the glass above as I ascended, tapping out its own thunderous soundtrack and accompanying light show. A bright flash hit the jade floor in a piercing shock of silver, illuminating the dark corner of the bar where the monsters were lurking.

A vampire with red eyes watched me from where he sat beside a demon whose horns captured the light of the storm and held it captive. I could see Zane's gaze as the lightning faded, the glow sharp as it slid over me. Sias's horns seemed to twist in the dark, his voice a velvet snake coiling around its prey.

"Come here, pet."

I obeyed, traveling across the atrium to where the vampire and demon lay waiting. Sias lounged beside Zane on the forest green couch, one arm draped over the back with his fingers dangerously close to Zane's shoulder. The vampire at his side indicated for me to sit between them with a jerk of his chin. My heart began to drum as quickly as the rain above us, the rolling thunder shaking the butterflies loose in my stomach.

I knew Zane could feel the flutter, knew Sias could taste my excitement by the way his eyes flared into a dazzling magenta. I eased onto the cushion between them, my nerves wound tight and fingers twitching, unsure of where to focus first.

"It's come to my attention that we have some unfinished business." Sias's fingers slid across my nape, feather soft and teasing. "Some debts to be repaid and bets to cash in."

"Debts?" I lifted a brow at him. "What debts? Every cent you've ever given me I've earned in one way or another."

"Not monetary debts, little pet." His fingers trailed up into my hair, nails dragging deliciously across my scalp. "I believe I told you I would help you get your vampire back so that I could taste you at your best."

"Ah, right," I mused, my heart beating like a war drum. As if I'd ever forget that.

"I was able to taste just a tease last night." Sias inhaled slowly, his fingers slowly curling in my hair. "Even from across the house it was…invigorating. Your energy together is a storm of shadow with bursts of bright, raw, carnal pulses. I felt my threads hum when he fed on you, felt the thrall of your intimacy like a plucked harp string."

I swallowed as my mouth started to water at the idea of Sias feeling us together, drinking in the energy of Zane biting and fucking me.

"You felt the void sing to you," Zane told him, a warm palm sliding over my thigh. "Threads bind you to us, my feeding and his pleasure vibrated through the strings."

"More than that, my dear vampire. It wasn't just a ripple through our bond." Sias ran his hand over his throat, his second set of eyes starting to crack open. "I felt the moment your teeth went into his skin. I've never felt something so powerful, so erotic. The sensation made me lift off my mattress and writhe. I almost sprinted down the hallway to demand I fuck you both right then and there, but I forced myself to be patient. Give you time to find yourselves."

"And now that you have?" Zane placed his hand on my thigh, the touch electric. Sias inhaled like he was walking through a pleasure garden, eyes alive with colorful excitement.

"I'd like to join you," the incubus purred. "Taste you. *Enjoy* you. I want to join something as beautiful as the two of you, but only if my presence will add and not disrupt."

My chest felt like it was full of rubber balls ricocheting off my ribs as I warmed, Zane's hand on my thigh and Sias's confession igniting a fire inside me. Sias's fingers trailed down my cheek and across my jaw, finally grasping my chin and rotating my face in his direction. Blooming fields of pinks, emeralds and violets greeted me, a wave of amber and tobacco surrounded me.

"I think we should give him the night he deserves, Zane," Sias whispered to him, eyes still fixed on me. "He's gone through hell and back for us both. I want to spoil him. Worship him. Maybe see if we can get him to squirm a little bit."

Zane's chuckle rumbled like an engine, his hand sliding higher on my thigh making me shiver.

"Normally I'd say the last thing he needs is to be spoiled. He is a brat, after all." He gave my thigh a squeeze and I almost whimpered, but managed to bite my tongue. "I think tonight I'll make an exception."

"What do you think, pet?" Sias trailed a thumb over my lips. "Can your two men cherish you tonight?"

I had to swallow a few times to get my voice back, I'd apparently lost it in the promise being bounced around.

"I'd like that," I managed, my body so wound up I felt like I was about to buckle into myself. "A lot. So much that I think my heart might stop beating."

"You'll live." The incubus smirked, squeezing my jaw a little with his fingers. "How adventurous are we feeling?"

"Whatever you want," I succumbed in a rush. "My brain is barely working right now. It's basically just horny goo leaking out of my nose."

Sias hummed thoughtfully, "Now, I like playing with my food a bit. How about you, Zane?"

"What did you have in mind?"

"A friendly wager." Sias lifted his eyes from me to Zane, his thumb still tracing my lip. "Who can make our sweet Dallas come the most in one night."

"Holy shit…" I exhaled, practically wiggling in my seat. Zane squeezed for me to hold still and I groaned.

"Stop flopping around or I'll kick you off the couch," he threatened coolly, before answering Sias. "You really think that's a fair bet, incubus?"

Sias's velvety laugh was not helping my wiggling situation.

"You don't think you can compete with me, vampire?"

Zane's hand trailed higher on my thigh, giving me a squeeze just before my hip.

"I think I'm giving you a run for your money after one night."

Sias's eyes took on a citrus hue around the floral pink centers, the challenge couldn't have been clearer if Zane had slapped him with a dueling glove.

I pivoted my head between them like I was watching the most intensely hot tennis match I'd ever witnessed, practically vibrating with the sexual tension between them that was likely going to result in me getting snapped in half in order for them to resolve it.

I was so goddamn happy.

"Is that so?" Sias quipped. "Do you accept the wager?"

"You still owe me from the pool game, demon. There's no way you're beating me tonight."

"A head start in order for it to be a fair challenge," Sias countered. "I'll let you have the first three orgasms, and I'll still beat you by a mile."

"Thank you. Thank you to whichever deity made this happen," I prayed. "Saint, Goddess, whoever. Thank you so much."

"Whoever has the most by the time he surrenders wins," Zane pitched, ignoring my prayer.

Sias reached across me and shook Zane's hand, sealing my fate.

"What qualifies as a 'surrender,' exactly?" I asked after the deal was struck. "Not that I plan on giving you two the satisfaction."

"Until you either physically can't come anymore, or you tell us to stop." Zane's broad palm squeezed between my legs, his lips close to mine as he whispered, "But before we wring you dry, hunter, I'm cashing in my winnings."

"Winnings?" I asked in a haze, lifting my hips to increase the contact. His proximity sank me into a fog of grave roses and rainwater, and I was helpless against it.

"The pool game." Zane's eyes watched me behind dark lashes. "I get to play with you first."

"I gotta start playing pool with you guys," I teased, groaning as Sias's fingers threaded through my hair to turn my lips his way.

"Do you want us to treat you like our pet tonight?"

My breath got stuck in my throat from the sting of his dominating pull combined with Zane sliding his palm over me, so I couldn't answer fast enough.

"Don't tell me we've already wound you too tight," Sias teased, nipping at my earlobe as Zane licked the other.

"I'm so happy right now," I said in a rush, my breath returning in a gasp.

"Answer us, hunter," Zane insisted, his grip making me lift off the couch with a gasp. "You're not getting fucked without verbal confirmation."

"Y-yeah. Yes." I had to answer before my heart leaped from my throat.

"Yes, what?" Sias probed, tugging at my hair again. "What do you want from us tonight?"

"All of it. The bet, the fucking, the whatever the hell you want —I'm in. I'm so in. But I'm adding a condition to this bet," I said, wetting my lips as I darted a look at each of them. "If I make you both come at the same time, I win."

"Same time?" Sias cracked a grin, both sets of his eyes turning to Zane. "I think a sex demon can outlast an undead vampire."

"I have a few decades of practice on you, demon. I can go all night." Zane gave me one last, blissful squeeze. "You're on, hunter."

The hold Zane had on my thighs slipped away as did Sias's grip on my hair, and I was left dizzy from the sudden loss of contact. Both men stood, my chin taken in Sias's fingers as Zane stepped in front of me.

"In the spirit of fairness, Zane gets to throat fuck you first,"

Sias explained, his thumb smoothing over my bottom lip. "I'll enjoy the show."

I don't know which was more erotic, watching Zane unsheathe his beautiful cock or how captivating it was to watch Sias's eyes flare into a lustful glow of neon pinks with flecks of black. It was the first time he'd seen Zane's skin, seen how blessed the undead creature was, and I could feel the beginning slithers of his newly darkened charm magic begin to stir.

"You've never experienced incubus charm magic, have you?" Sias asked Zane, his gaze sweeping up from his dick to his face. "I can show you, if you want."

"Show me," Zane confirmed, his fingers slipping into my hair as the velvet grip of Sias's void touched magic found us. The magic I was familiar with was still there, but it now had an edge of deadly chill as it settled over my skin. Instead of feeling my doubts and hesitations fall away like I was slipping from silk sheets, I felt them disappear into a fog rolling off my skin. It was as if they'd never been there in the first place.

My body floated in a state of aroused bliss, inhibitions banished to the void, and replaced by spider silk threads draping over my body in thousands of kisses.

Zane exhaled as his eyes hooded, his cock jerking as he pulled me closer. His fangs caught a flash of lightning as I lapped at the tip, shamelessly teasing him in a state of sex magic euphoria. The vampire's eyes sparkled with flecks of pink charm magic churning in the bloody pools, Sias's expert hold on us unlike anything else in the world.

The only magic that could wrap around a creature of the void like a cocoon and make him moan in pleasure.

"Can I touch you?" Sias whispered to Zane, only daring to put a hand on him after he was given a verbal agreement. Long, elegant fingers trailed over the thatch of hair below Zane's navel, snaking down to grasp the base of his cock, guiding it fully into my mouth.

Zane murmured a prayer to his Goddess as I swallowed him

down, and I was drunk on the bliss of how delicious his pleasure sounded.

"I told you his throat was like silk," Sias cooed, his fingers summoning a happy sob from Zane as he gave the vampire a cheeky squeeze when there was room.

"He has a free hand, you know," the vampire pointed out, stroking his fingers through my hair before giving me a teasing tug.

"That he does," Sias agreed, stepping in closer to flick his belt open before unlashing it from his waist. The leather strap was tossed over the arm of the couch, and my hand was taken from Zane's thigh to be repurposed for Sias's pleasure.

I slowed down to watch Zane admire Sias, the incubus more than equipped to make the immortal vampire swallow. Sias's eyes danced with color, resembling a rainforest of rich greens and vibrant pinks as he pulled out a couple of enchanted bottles I knew very well from his pocket. The small, palm sized containers seemed simple enough: two plastic, flat vessels with a thick, clear liquid perfect for any sexual occasion. One to lubricate, one to clean.

I had no idea the cost of a custom enchantment that never ran out of lube and a waterless cleaning element, but I had never seen Sias without them. The lube was self-explanatory, but the cleaning enchantment was damn impressive. The liquid inside was safe for all parts of the body (inside and out) and helped scrub anything unsavory from parts so you could enjoy all orifices interchangeably.

Kind of a sex demon staple.

It was always on his person just in case someone forgot to supply some, or he was caught in a spontaneous encounter.

Like fucking a necromancer and a vampire in an abandoned club.

A few drops were dribbled onto my palm before I wrapped my fingers around him, evoking a lovely groan from his throat.

An electric shiver rattled me as Zane's cock jerked in my throat upon hearing Sias's siren song.

The vampire watched Sias tilt his head back and sigh as I stroked him, longing painted across his handsome face. A storm of emotions lanced through me at seeing Zane pining for him, a bright flush on his pale cheeks as Sias moaned from my touch.

An unreasonable excitement threatened to rip me down the middle, the sting from the absurdity of my fantasy sneaking past Sias's charm to kick me in the ribs.

There was no way in hell I was actually seeing this. No way, in the name of all the deities, that Zane was actually watching Sias like he wanted to bend him over the couch and fuck his brains out.

Zane gripped my hair a little tighter at feeling my mind explode with sparks of dizzying daydreams, pushing his hips forward so I took more of him in. As I choked a bit and readjusted, I was held captive as Zane pulled Sias into a deep, languid kiss.

Sias hummed in appreciation at the vampire's skill, my fingers feeling the jolt of pleasure that Zane's tongue sent through his body.

In the heat of the moment, watching my wet dream play out in front of me in real time, I was viciously reminded that I was missing my right hand when I went to add myself into the pleasure train. My only free hand was wrapped around Sias, leaving me to be left unattended while the two hottest men on the planet made out in front of me.

I choked and coughed as I pulled free from Zane, slowing my grip on Sias but not releasing him.

"This went from being insanely hot to diabolical in a matter of minutes," I announced to them, drunk on charm magic and vampire dick. "You can't make out like that and leave me handless."

Sias chuckled as he nipped at Zane's lip, their kiss breaking so they could peer down at me.

"I told you he'd be bratty when we finally did this," Sias said to Zane. "Defiant, needy, wanting to be in the middle no matter what."

"He's nothing if not consistent," the vampire agreed.

"This was discussed?" I glanced between them, my soul ascending from my body. "This was all planned?"

"Why do you sound so shocked by this?" Zane demanded. "I told you I was in a harem before."

"And how often did I ask you to bring Zane along when you came over for dinner?" Sias tsked. "Really, pet. This has been a long time coming."

I blinked a few times to try and stabilize my vision, my racing pulse knocking my focus out of alignment.

"Neither one of you ever directly pitched a three-way. This is still on you. I probably would have gone for it if you'd gotten me drunk enough."

I was tugged to my feet by my men, both of them looking at me with that perfect blend of admiration and absolute annoyance.

"You're really frustrating," Zane told me, a loving scowl stuck on his face. "I don't know how you manage to make me want to punch you and kiss you at the same time."

"That's what I aim for: erotically aggravating." I grinned, wiping my chin clean with my wrist. "Now, I think you two mentioned a bet involving me getting fucked until I begged you to stop. Who's up first?"

Sias's eyes flashed a new shade of fiery flamingo I wasn't ready for, the color vicious with all the promises it held. His horns twisted, bending the gold around them, his new set of eyes flared with a bite of yellow fire and black ink. The vampire at his side let his fangs flash as he snarled, black vapor swirling up from his pale skin.

My two men peered down at me with lustful, loving hunger, like I was a sacrificial lamb tied to an altar, licking their lips as they prepared to consume me piece by piece.

I happily surrendered to my fate.

# CHAPTER
# EIGHTEEN

THE ENTIRE POINT of sex demon magic is to release a sense of sexual euphoria in order for the incubus or succubus to absorb the energy required for them to stay healthy. That beautiful bliss is different for everyone. Some people feel such a deep state of relaxation and confidence that they are free to explore the deepest, most private sexual desires to have the time of their life while the sex demon feeds on them. For others it's a surge of energy, like getting a shot of adrenaline in the ass.

Normally, I was in camp relaxation. Sias's magic would wrap me in silk, helping my toxic thoughts of shame or self-consciousness to fall away so I could be my most authentic self with him. I didn't have a lot of scruples when it came to exploring the expanse of my desires, so I was along for all the things a rich, powerful incubus could drum up for an evening dinner.

What had been a familiar touch of amber and tobacco silk draped over my skin as his magic touched me had changed to something terribly exciting and dangerous.

Sias's magic wasn't a warm blanket or a kick of unbridled debauchery. It was now a snake bite that punctured so deep into the marrow of your bones that you forgot the limitations of your fleshy prison.

Pain was irrelevant, it was like my body had forgotten how to produce the chemical associated with the sensation. My brain expelled any ideas of discomfort, ache, stiffness or hurt the moment his new void touched charm sank into my bones.

I bent in ways I couldn't before, held my breath longer than I should have been able to, felt a sharp blast of ecstasy when a thick leather strap cracked across my ass. The times when we would tread a little too far beyond what the charm magic could sedate in me, Sias looked to Zane to read my emotions when I wasn't able to speak and change course.

I usually had my mouth full. Or, I guess I should say my throat full.

There was something blooming in the heat of the seduction venom and bending the barriers of pleasure and pain, something coiling itself around my fragile heart and sealing the cracks within it.

Passing the reins over so completely hadn't ever been something I was willing to do in the past. But there, with them, the two people I trusted with my life, I gave myself over to adoration, worship, and work.

And Gods did they worship me. My skin felt electric with traces of their touch, their taste lingered like honey on my tongue. I was lost in the ecstasy of feeling Zane's grip on my hips, Sias's nails on my scalp, and their praising whispers floating in my mind.

*Pet.*

*Hunter.*

Their names for me had become a drug more powerful than anything I'd ever tried, and I craved to hear them growled into my ear over and over.

I felt adored, wanted, coveted like a treasure and desired like my body was the only pleasure they had ever known.

I lost count of how many times my body crackled with a bone melting orgasms, how many times I heard one of them whisper pet names while I felt my heart thundering in my chest. My sobs of pleasure were lost in the roar of the storm overhead, the crash of heavy rain drowning the rhythm of bodies enjoying each other.

Veins of white and silver flashed in the clouds, painting the room in snapshots of a dream I would never forget. Zane was more alive than I had ever seen him, his long hair stuck to his neck, red eyes fluttering as he pushed his hips into me. Sweat trailed down his jaw and fell across my chest, matching the smell of rain that clung to his skin.

Around him, tan arms crossed over his shoulders, nails leaving trails of lovely red lines as Sias ran his mark across him. His horns sent the lightning back into the sky, all of his eyes watching me like sharp daggers dipped in gemstone hues. When he slithered around to me, I was drowned in the bliss of tobacco and amber, shivering at the taste of grave roses on his tongue.

Zane slowed to watch us, lips pressed to my jaw, hands clutching my hips to keep me from trying to escape. His heart was pounding when I placed my hand across it, my phantom fingers tingling.

Through Sias's threads, he could feel my want, a string vibrating with a specific instruction. His eyes flared, sliding to me to make sure the order was correct. The vampire breathed in deep and met my gaze, and I nodded to him that I was sure.

"Do it," I confirmed. "I want it."

"It won't hurt," Sias whispered to me. "But you will be sore tomorrow."

"It'll be worth it," I said over my shoulder as he moved behind me, his fingers trailing down my sides to roam over the grip Zane had on my hips. "I have a bet to win, remember?"

The enchanted lube bottle was plucked from nearby, and my lips found sanctuary with Zane's as Sias made sure to get himself ready for what I had in mind.

"Breathe, pet," Sias ordered me, gathering my earlobe into his lips before giving it a love bite. "Zane, hold him open for me."

Zane's grip shifted, his eyes locked on Sias as I exhaled through the initial pinch of pressure. Sias steadied me with a hand on my lower back as he joined Zane inside of me, the burn muted by a new wave of snake bite charm magic. The discomfort or pain that I knew I should have been experiencing vanished like a breath into a winter night, lost in the bliss of his magic and my desire to feel them both at the same time.

My body hummed like an electric wire when they moved, the pressure within me a chokehold of intense pleasure. Hot, slick skin surrounded me on all sides, Sias's chest pressed to my back while Zane pinned me from the front, all while greedy hands gripped, and stroked, and pinched. The soft tickle of Sias's long hair trailed over my shoulders as I rolled my head back, my fingers lost in Zane's dark locks.

I pulled Zane closer to me, leaning my head against Sias's cheek to expose my neck. The threads between us vibrated like a strummed guitar, Zane's hunger flared like primal torches in his eyes. Across my back, Sias's heart hammered in anticipation as Zane's tongue trailed over his fangs.

"I don't want to hurt you, hunter," he whispered.

"You won't," I promised. "I put rose tattoos over my scars to cover up the bad memories. Tonight, I want to give them to you. Sias's threads will keep me grounded, keep the pain away, and let me heal."

"You're sure?" Zane met my eyes, holding them captive so he could peer into my soul. "I'll never forgive myself if I hurt you, Dallas."

"I trust you," I told him, leaning up to touch my forehead to his before turning to do the same to Sias. "I trust you both."

"I've got you, pet," Sias promised, hand sliding over my chest to rest at my heart. "I won't let you fall into the dark."

Zane leaned forward and kissed me, shifting his hips so I could feel how desperately he wanted to taste me again. I sighed into his kiss, my hand tightening in his hair as he trailed his lips down my jaw. Sias exhaled at Zane's cock sliding against his inside of me, his fingers pressing into my skin as his lips caught my temple and jaw.

Zane planted gentle, deliberate kisses from my lips to my throat, carefully placing each one to land in the center of roses etched across my scars. Feeling lips on my throat shook the threads around us though the raw scrape of panic drowned a quiet death as Sias tightened his hold around us.

My eyes stung with relief at feeling my fear quiet, giving me the strength to kick the door shut and stomp down on the lock. It wouldn't go away fully, not in one night. I knew it was going to be part of who I was for the rest of my life—that fear of a little boy being hunted in the dark, alone and afraid.

But this night, in the arms of the men I loved, I could at least starve those fears while I ran free for a little while. I could fall into a moment I never thought I'd ever be able to experience, knowing those fears couldn't reach me.

I shut my eyes and fell into that feeling of freedom, surrendering to them completely.

Zane's breath was hot on my skin, his fangs a shock of ice as they drove into my neck. The bite was fast and vicious, causing a thrum of ecstasy to pulse between us like a shared vein, shaking the threads tied around us. My lungs started to burn as I forgot to inhale, my heart squeezing as the edges of reality shook with shadows.

The void rippled out like a bloom, the fabric between realms danced with the sound of Zane's euphoric hum as he drank from me, wisps of black vapor pouring off his skin. In the seams between life and death, strings of amber draped over us like spider silk, tethering us and preventing us from floating away. The void moved like it always had, a dark expanse that neither ended nor began, radiating out forever in all directions between the cracks formed from the vampire's bite.

Standing still in the safety of the threads, riding on the magic bond between master and Thrall, I saw the network of pathways carved by the necromancers before me. Where the Thralls had been birthed was like polished obsidian, jewels extracted from bedrock as a gift from the Goddess. Tiny punctures of carefully sewn extensions left dots where lives had been stretched, given more time in this living world for a breath of time.

Others were scars left in the void by malicious, greedy claws, souls ripped and repurposed before being tossed back as rotten ghosts of what they once were. Not all dark magic was beautiful and kind. So much of it was taken, twisted and destroyed.

The void through the eyes of a necromancer was…beautiful. It was terrifying in its complexity, a network of fascinating and endless entropy that I could follow easily like a map. I saw the winding pathways, the scars, the windows left open and others nailed shut.

In the bliss of standing at the edge, my heart slowing from Zane's feeding while I held Sias's strings like a safety line, I saw the window we needed.

I peered through the eyes of a woman teetering on death's edge, the pull of the void like greedy hands at her back.

Around her was an incredibly tall crypt, a tower of skeletons loomed overhead watching with toothy grins and eyeless judgment. Her hands were too pale, blood slicked her palms. Flanked on either side of her like a swaying mob was an army of grunt vampires awaiting orders, their attention on their master. Their soulless eyes bled down their cheeks, fingers twitching and fangs ready.

She hated them.

Hated herself for being such a goddamn fool.

The flash of the crimson blade made her head tilt back, and she marveled at how beautiful the spray of blood was in the shine of the fae fire.

The soul that slipped into the void was stopped by the Goddess.

The threads in my grip yanked me backwards, my heart thundering as my body lit up like a fuse. I flew back into my reality as Zane lifted his head from my neck, teeth painted in my blood, a searing bolt of pleasure striking me the moment I felt him come undone. A vicious pluck of a harp string sang through us as we all shared the connection at the same time, losing ourselves completely.

I clung to them, sobbing as my body was hit with wave after wave of spearing pleasure, their bodies rolling against mine as they rode on the high of their releases. I was lost in the swirl of amber and roses, tobacco and rain-soaked novels. All I could feel was them, my fingers clutching black hair, my lips breathing into golden locks.

"I love you," I told them, my heart light and body heavy, dizzy, tired, and so fucking happy. "Goddamn I love you both so much. I will spend the rest of my life proving to you how much you mean to me."

I kissed them both, sweet lips and sharp metallic taste, and stayed lost in the bliss of feeling them fill me completely before they eased out gently.

My body throbbed with muted aches and exhaustion, Sias's energy starting to wane even after he'd feasted on us. His orgasm must have shaken him hard, spent him more than he had anticipated. I leaned back against him as Zane bit into his palm with his teeth, lifting my chin to drip a few wonderful, healing drops of vampire blood onto my tongue.

I felt myself start to slip into the void again, eyes rolling back into my head as I fell backwards into the darkness. A golden net caught me, but I saw the floating soul the Goddess had stopped hovering just below me, peering up like a lost koi.

I inhaled, all the aches and pains from the night washing away as my body healed from my Thrall's blood. While I wasn't going to be physically sore anymore from being wrung out from two sex starved deviants, I was emotionally and mentally tapped. My head swam from the dizzying heights of the night, feeling very much like an overworked locker room towel.

"The thought of having to find my clothes, walk downstairs, bathe and somehow make it to a bed sounds too fucking exhausting," I mumbled. "Who loves me enough to carry me?"

"If we have to walk, so you do," Zane said, sounding equally as spent as me. "I'll throw you over the balcony though if you want. Shorten the trip."

"Aw, there he is. That's the Zane I know."

"No throwing over balconies. I don't have the energy to set broken bones tonight and I desperately want a shower." Sias extracted himself from behind me and stood, stretching his body up to the heavens as the storm finished its tantrum. His lithe muscles caught the light of the moon peering through the thinning clouds, the sheen of his skin giving his body a razors edge.

Zane stood from the couch and cracked his neck, skin flushed and bright from the blood he'd drunk from me. Only his red eyes and the cooling black vapor betrayed him as something undead, otherwise he looked like a happy, blushing brute who just had the night of his life.

I marveled at the pair as they went through the routine of finding their discarded clothing before slipping them over their bodies, movements languid and relaxed. Sias's second set of eyes had closed, his horns reset in their natural curve. Zane licked his blood-stained teeth clean and passed Sias his slacks which had been tossed away almost over the railing.

In my dazed bliss, I took stock of the situation we had found ourselves in. The creak of the couch under me sounded worn and tired, the jade dance floor serene in the moonlight. We were sitting on the throne of Biodome, my enemy's club, a man who had somehow found a path around his hatred for me to allow us to stay.

The entire Demon and Human Alliance and Protection force was after us, Florence was off somewhere in the world with the Goddess's scythe, we had no money, little supplies, and shit for a plan. There was absolutely no reason for me to feel as hopeful and happy as I was staring at the two men slogging through the chore of getting dressed in front of me.

"You look rather pleased with yourself." Sias slid his belt back into its loops, tossing me a sly look. "I'm shocked you haven't been gloating about winning your bet this entire time."

"I did, didn't I?" I felt myself smile a bit more. "Damn, I should have put some stipulations on that outcome. Made you two do a stupid dance or something as a reward."

"There's another reason you're sitting there grinning like an idiot then?" Zane tugged his shirt over his head, raking his hair back with his fingers.

"I'm happy," I answered, surprised with the lack of stinging doubt at the response. "Ridiculously happy actually. All things considered, I think I should be a little more freaked out about our situation, but I can't seem to muster the give-a-fuck right now."

"We have tomorrow to wallow in our misfortune. We should enjoy tonight. With that said, I want to shower and crawl into bed, so." Sias waved his hand at my state of undress. "Unless you feel like parading around naked, get something on. I don't mind the view but I feel like your brother and our begrudging host might get testy."

Zane offered me a hand and hefted me to my feet, my legs wobbly from being twisted around all night. My jeans were passed over, and I slipped them over my hips before Sias tossed me my shirt. The three of us lumbered downstairs, tired and trying to pretend like the other inhabitants of the bar hadn't noticed our activities upstairs.

I wasn't optimistic that the thunderstorm outside cloaked all the noises we'd made. Sias never cared if anyone could hear his throaty groans when he was getting what he wanted, and Zane growled like a goddamn werewolf when he had someone wrapped around him.

The memory of their respective soundtracks had me shivering as we descended down to the basement, the thrill bouncing between the three of us. Zane gave my ass a squeeze when I got lost in the memory, and Sias trailed his fingers over my nape. If I'd had anything left to give them that night, I would have demanded another round before we made it into the little game room.

By some blessed miracle, both Marthas and Austin were

absent as we scurried past the dart board and empty beers. We had likely chased them off into one of the other wings of the club to try and escape our *activities*, which meant I was going to have to face them later. Barns had his door shut tight when we made our way down into the basement, another awkward encounter I wasn't looking forward to.

But that was tomorrow Dallas's problem. The only thing I needed to worry about in this moment was getting through the shower without passing out.

The tiny shower in the basement was a basic fixture held together with tape and a faded, flower covered shower curtain. Marthas had been right about the abysmal water pressure, but it had a large enough water tank to survive all three of us washing clean. We all ended up smelling like generic bar soap and hotel towels, which was arguably better than what we had started out with.

When I shambled out of the shower, last in line to bathe after Sias had entered the bathroom first like it was his right, and then losing to Zane in rock-paper-scissor for second place, I caught sight of the tail end of a mattress sliding into a bedroom. Wearing just a towel, I followed the curiosity into the room, wondering what the hell possessed the thing to move, only to find Zane setting up a second bed in the tiny room.

The beds Marthas had originally provided were maybe queen sized, impossible to fit more than two of us on there at a time. I had assumed Sias was going to claim a bedroom to himself, leaving me a bed and Zane a couch to lounge in to read the night away.

I hadn't been expecting a bed heist.

"What are you doing?" I asked, tired and dumbfounded as I watched them slide the beds together and stretch a sheet over, tossing pillows and blankets onto it lazily.

Zane unfurled a blanket over the right side and set his book on the edge. He punched a pillow into shape, propping it up against the wall for him to lean back on, then turned and motioned to the clothing I held in my hands. "I'm going to do some laundry while you sleep. Leave those by the door and I'll get to them."

Sias set his clothes where Zane had indicated, then slinked naked between the sheets like they were silk and not stiff, cotton monstrosities. He took up the left side and rolled over to tuck a lumpy pillow under his head. Malphie bullied past me so he could heave his massive body onto the mattress next to Sias, dropping his skeletal head onto his feet and sighing with absolute satisfaction. His claws snagged onto the blanket as he adjusted his big paws, butt wiggling as Sias called him a "good boy."

My mind was either too exhausted from the bombardment of mind splintering sex or the trip into the void I took to catch up with what was happening. I was in the middle of tossing my shirt near Sias's clothing when the scenario caught up with me.

"Wait." I got momentarily tangled in the garment as I flailed a bit, throwing it a little more forcefully than I should have. "We're all sleeping in here?"

Zane waved his book and I flipped him off with my missing hand.

"You don't like sharing a bed," I told Sias. "You're comfortable with us being in here?"

"I am." His eyes were emerald coated in moss, twinkling with shades that were an unnamed mix of both.

I felt a flutter in my chest, like a thread being stroked with the tip of a finger. My cheeks flushed as a thought came into mind, hilariously coy considering we had just spent the better part of the night exploring each other in truly personal and delicious ways.

Sias stretched his arm out and gave the space in the mattress between himself and Zane a pat.

"Come rest, pet."

I swallowed down the fist of emotions knocking against my chest, its fingers curled into my ribs and surging me forward. The last of my clothing and my towel was tossed away to join the pile Zane was going to wash, and I crawled into bed to sleep beside Sias for the first time ever.

"We've never done this." I knew I was smiling too much for something this simple, but it felt too amazing to stop. I had to angle my legs around the huge, undead lump taking up the foot of the bed, Malphie's eyes dimming as he tried to settle into whatever version of sleep void creatures could achieve.

"No, we haven't. I'm sorry for that." He ran his fingers over my cheek, lips and chin. "I haven't held someone since my spouses left me. It was too hard to imagine someone else in their place. I like sharing my body, I enjoy sex as the social and physical need it gives, but this is something I only wanted when, and if, I ever fell in love again."

I captured his hand and kissed his knuckles, my chest almost suffocating the words from existence before I had a chance to whisper them.

"I want to spend every single night in bed with you."

A sharp gleam of magenta shone over emeralds as his throat bobbed, and he leaned forward to kiss me. His lips were soft, careful, like the moment was fragile and precious.

The mattress behind me dipped as Zane crawled in, his arm draping over to stroke Sias's hair back over his horn. A warm hand landed on my shoulder, my vampire tugging me in his direction.

"Come here, hunter. I know you like to cuddle."

"You were supposed to keep that a secret." I looked over my shoulder at him. "The fuck, man?"

"Yeah, I wasn't ever going to do that." He pulled me close and settled into his pillow, scooping his book up with his free hand.

I rolled so that I could toss a leg over his, smiling as Sias curled up to be the big spoon in our interspecies sundae. Sias's arm wrapped around my chest, a long breath across my shoulder as Zane stroked his hair.

I placed my hand over Zane's heart to bring our hands together, and let the rhythm of his heartbeat against my palm, and the steady beat of Sias's at my back, soothe me into the abyss between consciousness.

I had almost drifted off, happier than I had ever been, calm and content, and reveling in the magic of being loved like I never thought I would, when the realization of where Florence was hit me with a brilliant backhand of clarity.

"Florence is at the Silence Steps," I blurted out, lifting my head from the drool already pooling on my pillow. Zane looked down at me as Sias kept snoring; Malphie kicked me a little for disturbing his sleep. I didn't have time to process the fact that the incredibly sexy incubus I had been longing to sleep next to for years was *snoring* when I tacked on a quick, "And I think she's dead."

# CHAPTER
# NINETEEN

I DIDN'T GET to finish my train of thought until the next morning.

According to Zane, I blurted critical information after snapping awake from a dead sleep, then proceeded to crash again like someone had yanked my batteries out. The dumbfounded Thrall had to wait in eager anticipation of whatever the hell I'd been talking about until I roused from a deep slumber. He'd had to mill around doing laundry all night wondering what the hell I had been talking about, which all things considered, was pretty funny.

"Why do you think she's dead?" Zane prodded as I filled my coffee cup, the warm vapor of roasted beans guiding me from a groggy haze.

"'Cause I saw it." I had to set my coffee down to rub at my eyes, then shuffled along to the secondhand table placed near the kitchenette. Three of the four chairs around the stained countertop matched, the replacement being a wicker back armchair with peeling armrests. Sias sat in it like he was the natural king of the round table, ankle crossed over his knee with the easy posture of born royalty. Malphie had his head resting on one of the frayed armrests, panting happily as Sias stroked the bone ridge at the top of his skull.

At his side was the court jester, working on his morning crosswords despite our clearly annoying banter. Funus was peering over the puzzle with the concentration of a person pretending to not be eavesdropping, but his glowing eyes swiveled in our direction more than once. He didn't want to raise the ire of the jester, who sighed loudly as I bumped the table with my knee.

"What did you see, hunter?" Zane pressed, taking the last available chair.

"It's hard to remember now," I said after swallowing down more coffee. "But I know for sure I saw the inside of the Silent Steps tomb where we found the council. I recognized the tall catacombs with the necromancer skeletons right before I saw an arc of blood."

"You dreamed this?" Sias asked, and I shook my head.

"No, it was during the uh…" I paused, glancing at our table mates who were trying to ignore us. "The very end of last night. When I drank Zane's blood."

"You saw this in the void?" Zane's question finally forced Funus to drop his facade. I nodded my answer and the skull's eyes flared in amazement.

"Tell me what you saw, acolyte," Funus insisted, giving Barnaby a sweet "thank you" as he was rotated to face me properly. "Tell me each step from beginning to end."

"Okay, well, it started with these two placing a bet—" I started and dodged Barnaby's pencil as it whipped past my head.

"Not that part, you dolt. Start with you going into the void." Barnaby brought out a replacement pencil, which was evidence he had planned on using at least one of them as a projectile this morning. The man had literally woken up choosing violence today.

Malphie, eager to help as well as play a part in the circus, was able to achieve the first step in the fetch process. The pencil was tragically destroyed by his big teeth, shattered into bits before it could be dropped at Barn's feet.

"I'm just following orders," I pointed out, nodding to the

skull, and got ready to see how many backup pencils Barnaby had stashed away.

"We can start with entering the void," Funus gently clarified. "You drank Zane's blood, yes?"

"Just a little bit to uh…you know. Keep me from being too sore today. My body had been through some heavy cardio, if you get my drift, and my ass needed some— HA!" I ducked the second attempt at lead assassination but was smacked in the back of the head by my bodyguard. The void hound repeated his pencil destruction with butt-wiggling enthusiasm. Sias laughed at me, which prompted Malphie to believe he was, in fact, doing a great job fetching.

Zane said his catch phrase, and I decided to focus.

"When I slipped into the void," I said, appeasing all the grumpy jerks at the table. "I was able to see more than usual. Normally, when I drink Zane's blood, I get lost. It's like falling through fog with no real direction. This time I had a safety net; Sias's threads kept me from dipping down too far. It was like watching the void out of an airplane window and seeing it from above the clouds."

"Above the clouds, you say," Funus marveled. "What did you see at that vantage point? How was it different?"

"It was beautiful," I admitted, unabashedly. "It's not endless nothingness, not really. There are pathways trailing all through it, connecting the plains together like veins. It has a rhythm of chaos and madness that can only exist between life and death." I shut my eyes to remember the vision, submerging myself in darkness to relive it more clearly. "I followed one of those pathways to Florence…and, I think I saw the moment she died. The blood arcing out came from her throat. And—shit."

"What?" Funus asked quickly. "What did you see?"

It made me wince to say, "Grunts. Lots of them. She was surrounded by vampires the moment she died."

"How many?" Zane pressed. "Manageable?"

"No." I rubbed at my eyes before I opened them, the exhaustion of hopelessness renewing an old headache. "Fuck no. We're never that lucky. It was a lot, Zane, if I'm remembering right. More than what I'm comfortable tackling with just the three of us."

"Four," Austin said as he meandered into the room, wearing just his jeans and Saint's Army dog tags. "If we're talking about killing vampires, I'm in."

"We're talking about Florence and her *army* of vampires bunkering down in the Silent Steps," I corrected. "Enough that we'd need a full team to crack through. These aren't just the wild, brain-dead grunts we're used to. These are controlled and have working bio magic."

"Fuck." Austin poured himself some coffee and leaned against the counter. "These are the tech ones DHAP was talking about?"

"Yeah. The scythe is with her, and she's in a fortress with a shit ton of walking death machines capable of overpowering us. They have death enhanced bio-magic. Even if we're able to gear up with some powerful magic blockers, which we do not have the money for, we're still outnumbered."

"I have a blocker and my tags." Austin touched his dog tags out of reflex. "I'm covered. You can't be turned, nor can the vampire. I'm assuming you're clear too." He looked to Sias, who lifted his coffee mug in an agreement. "That's one thing going for us."

"I'll need a blocker as well," Barnaby chimed in, and Funus's eyes grew pale.

"I dunno why you look scared, he almost killed me twice today," I told the skull, who didn't think I was funny at all. "Barns, you're not going to the murder tomb with us."

"If Funus is going, so am I." Barnaby crossed his arms and stared at his puzzle, now out of writing weaponry. "I will not argue this morning."

"Wow, in a mood today." I looked back to my brother. "How much equipment do you have?"

Austin looked a little guilty as he answered, "Enough for myself. I left in a hurry."

"That works," I told him. "One less body we need to arm and protect."

"I'm guessing you don't have a lot of favors you can call in for weapons, magic, charms, wards and gear, do you?" Austin sipped his coffee as I worked on massaging my headache into submission.

"Maybe after another cup of coffee I can work out a plan to break into Marthas's gun safe and leave an IOU. He usually has some good shit in there."

"Maybe don't do that," Austin pitched casually as Marthas showed up, looking very much like he heard me from the hallway. The gruff beard that had been growing on his cheeks had been shaved away, the bags under his eyes looked less bruised and exhausted than the previous night. With his hair combed and a change of clothes, Marthas was starting to resemble the ruthless leader of the Broken Horns, not a wraith haunting an abandoned club.

"I changed the lock from last time, Wilde, and put a thief ward in place that'll set you on fire from the inside out if you touch it. So please, take a crack at it. I'd love to start my day with a smile."

"You're welcome for helping you up your security." I shrugged when Zane cut me a look. "What? If I can get into it, it needs some guard rails. A safe that big shouldn't crack open with explosives."

"I take it you're trying to craft some idiotic plan to get to Florence if you're trying to break into my safe," Marthas said as he drifted over to the kitchen, starting another pot of coffee. As he grabbed the can of grounds from the cabinet, he passed Austin a shirt he had been carrying.

"Florence is at an old necromancy crypt called the Silent Steps with a horde of magic tech enhanced vampires," I explained. "So, breaking into your gun safe was a start, but it's not going to be enough to bring us home. We're going to need not only some serious firepower, but also protection, magic and a shit ton of luck."

"Why not just tell DHAP where she is and let them manage it?" Marthas shrugged one big shoulder. "They have all the things you're lacking."

"We can't let the scythe get into their hands," Austin said, tugging on the shirt that Marthas had passed to him. "I'm not convinced they'll destroy it if they know its potential."

"He's right," I agreed. "We can't take the chance that someone will get greedy and hold on to it. We need to make sure it's destroyed, not locked up, not studied, not stuck in a museum— *destroyed*. It's too dangerous and…whose shirt is that?"

Austin looked down at his shirt and scrunched his face in confusion.

"It's my shirt."

I narrowed my eyes at him, slicing my gaze into Marthas.

"Why did he have it?"

Austin rubbed at his face and exhaled through his nose as Marthas answered coolly, "He left it in my room last night."

Barnaby yelled at me as I shot up from the table, knocking over his coffee and getting Funus's jaw wet. Zane saved his cup before it toppled and Sias lifted his eyebrows up like he was enjoying the show.

I was frozen in place, pointing at the pair of harlots with my one remaining hand.

"EW!"

"Damnit," Austin groaned.

"The hell you mean 'ew'?" Marthas straightened a bit. "Your brother's a good-lookin' dude."

"The 'ew' was for you!" I stormed toward Marthas, who regarded me like I was an annoying, foul-mouthed gnat. "You're 'ew!' Austin, you can do so much better. I have so many hot friends."

"No, you don't," Marthas cut back in. "Because no one likes you."

"Ugh, my poor sensibilities," I complained through my urge to heave.

"Will you relax?" Austin groaned. "It's not that big of a deal. We had a good night. It was fun."

Marthas's grin made Austin's cheeks warm.

"Yeah, we did," the big imp added, in his best attempt at sounding seductive. "It was *very* fun."

He sounded like a drugged elephant trying to flirt, which apparently was Austin's cup of tea, because the man blushed like he was being wooed by Prince Charming.

This time I gagged and Austin punched me in the arm.

"You're not allowed to give me a single ounce of shit, Dallas," Austin snapped. "You and your entire entourage had an orgy on the roof last night. Glass houses, asshole."

"For it to be an orgy it has to have at least six people," Sias said, adding nothing to the conversation.

"Wasn't the roof," Zane mumbled into his coffee, also notedly unhelpful.

"So glad you two are here to help with this situation," I told them. "Love that we're a united front right now."

"Can we get back to planning how to tackle this Florence situation?" Austin offered. "And move on from this incredibly uncomfortable topic?"

"This incredibly uncomfortable topic is less fucked than the situation we're currently in," I admitted. "Unless we can summon an army or some amazing magic, I don't know how we can storm the crypt without getting murdered."

"We have another issue, acolyte," Funus swooped in with more bad news. "I believe Florence bringing the scythe back to the crypt, and her subsequent sacrifice therein, might be a prelude to something much more nefarious than we previously thought."

"Sorry, did you say sacrifice?" Austin's eyebrows tried to high-five his hairline. "She's dead?"

"Pretty sure she is, yeah." I slid my finger across my throat. "Had a vision last night. I won't get into the details because I don't think Barns has anymore pencils, but I saw Florence getting her throat slashed at the crypt."

"Who killed her?" Marthas asked.

"I dunno. I didn't see who was wielding the blade. Whoever it was has somehow gotten through her big, badass bodyguard too."

"One of your guys?" Marthas asked Austin. "You guys were chasing her too, right?"

"The blade can't be handled by the living," I said. "They have to be a necromancer or undead. Saint's Army wouldn't have been able to hold it, especially with as much life magic shit they have on them at any one time."

"Rival necromancer?" Marthas pitched. "You're not the only insane human out there playing with dead bodies, you know."

"I'm fully aware. It's my job to take those freaks out. As for a rival, I can't think of anyone who'd be able to go toe-to-toe with her and her goons. Do you?" I asked Austin, who shook his head. I turned my attention to Zane, getting the same answer.

"Everyone I knew who would be powerful enough is dead." Zane shifted the attention back to Funus. "What do you believe is happening at the crypt?"

Funus's skeletal face was grim, yellow orbs flaring around the edges as his voice grew deadly serious.

"The Silence Steps aren't just a resting place for the Goddess's chosen. At its very core, it is a doorway. This morning when you spoke of pathways, Dallas, you phrased it better than you could have known. Each time a soul enters the void, it leaves a small trail of energy in its wake as it transitions from living to dead. Most of those pathways seal permanently. Necromancers have the ability to rip deep trenches through the void to summon their Thralls, or dimple the fabric by holding a soul between life and death. The Goddess doesn't only make pathways and trenches, my dear boy, she can make doors."

My chest grew cold enough to freeze my throat for a second, but I was able to chip my words free one at a time.

"The crypt is a door. The scythe is a key." I held the worried skull's gaze as I asked, "Where does the door lead to?"

"To her," he confessed, sounding a little afraid. "Meant for her disciple, her chosen. I'm afraid in a horrible oversight only a Goddess could manage, she failed to realize that it could also be used by someone who wants to knock her off her throne."

"Please tell me that's fucking impossible," I pleaded, knowing in my gut it was pointless. "Please tell me a Goddess cannot be ousted by a mortal idiot."

"The blade of the scythe is made of her blood, Dallas. It was meant to grant power, but it is a weapon. It can be used against her, and can grant godhood to a mortal."

"What does that mean, exactly?" Sias asked what we were all thinking. "What happens if someone dethrones the Goddess of Death?"

"I don't know," Funus answered, fear crystal clear in his shaking voice. "The Goddess gave her scythe to us to bestow on her champion, to keep the doorway safe from any who would mean to disrupt the balance between life and death. To shepherd souls and guide her necromancy teachings."

"Why the fuck would she even bring that into the living realm if it can have such catastrophic consequences?!" I demanded, panic kickstarting my fury. "She has to know we're a bunch of angry apes trying to kill everything all the time! That's like handing a loaded gun to a pissed off gorilla with an agenda!"

"The Gods of our world play by rules we can't understand, acolyte," Funus preached quietly. "Trying to make sense of them would be like asking that very same ape to explain the weight of a living being's soul. It's simply beyond us."

"Well, that's just fucking great."

Barnaby raised his hand. "What did Florence getting sacrificed have to do with anything?"

"Good point, Barnaby," Funus said, brightening a bit by getting asked a studious question. "In order to knock upon her door, it requires a sacrifice and a display of necromantic power worthy of her attention. Whoever holds the scythe borrows a bit of her power, but that doesn't necessarily mean that the ability has been honed to knock properly. Our only hope is that whoever has this scythe isn't trained, or at the very least, is having a hard time wielding the scythe's potential."

"So, the only thing keeping us from falling into some sort of necromantic apocalypse is someone being terrible at magic?" I asked incredulously, and Funus hummed in agreement.

"That's my assumption, yes."

"Ancestor's ass," Marthas exhaled. "That's fucking bleak."

"Yeah," I agreed, trying to smooth the prickling sense of dread trailing down the back of my neck. "And I'm about to make it bleaker."

"What do you mean?" Barnaby asked, glancing at Zane as the vampire felt the rock of responsibility press down on my chest. My vampire met my gaze, a lifetime of sorrow and joy tumbled through his eyes as he tossed me a knowing, bittersweet smile. Sias's eyes were a heartbreaking shade of teal, a blend of sorrow and love that I was never going to name. Malphie whined beside him as his master placed a hand on his head.

"We can't do nothing," I explained. "We go, we hit them with everything we have, and we stop the door from opening."

"We've just established that you don't have the equipment to make this successful," Barnaby reminded me.

"Yeah, well. My thinking is that it might be a one-way trip."

"A suicide mission?" Barnaby balked. "Heaven and Hell, Dallas Wilde, you cannot seriously be pitching something that stupid."

"It's not stupid," Austin countered softly. "It's what we're supposed to do when the fate of everyone and everything is at stake."

"I'm with the fussy one on this, Wilde," Marthas added wearily. "Not that I'm not thrilled to hear you're going to get yourself killed, but for the sake of playing devil's advocate, we don't need to rush into martyrdom just yet."

"Unless something profoundly tide turning is hiding in that gun safe of yours, Marthas, I think we don't have a choice," I said. "Optimally, we will somehow make it out alive, but we need to make peace with the fact that we're probably not going to. We're going to have to go through a hellbent necromancer armed with both the Goddess's scythe and an army of tech vampires."

Marthas scrubbed a wide hand over his face, pulling his phone from his pocket to check a notification. The device was shoved back into his pocket, and he turned to leave the room, tossing over his shoulder on his way out, "Don't rush off to die before I get back."

Austin set his coffee cup aside and pushed off the counter. "I'll go grab my supplies and see what I can spare. If we leave right now, we can try and make it there by tomorrow morning if we don't stop."

"Funus, talk some sense into them!" Barns was growing more frantic as we all stood from the table. "This is stupid! There are other ways to handle this besides rushing to your graves."

"We don't have time," I told him as gently as I could, but I knew it was a tall ask for him to willingly let us leave. "We need to get there and stop the damn world from ending."

Barnaby knocked his chair back as he shot from his seat, stomping around to jab a finger into my chest, his inky eyes glassy.

"Now you listen to me, Dallas Wilde. You sit your butt down right now and come up with a better plan besides 'wing it and die trying.' That is unacceptable, and frankly pretty stupid, even for you."

"It's actually pretty on brand," I argued, hoping my smile would coax one out of him. It just made his eyes well up more. "Barns, I gotta try. I can't let everything go to shit because of me."

"This isn't on you," he pleaded. "This isn't your fault."

"Yeah, it is. She got the scythe because of me. I kicked the hornet's nest, so I gotta be the one that gets stung."

Abandoning me as an unsound mind, Barnaby turned to his

fellow incubus. "Surely you're not about to stroll into this idiotic plan, Sias. You have a knack for wrangling in Dallas when he's being insane, I'll help you tie him down."

"As much as I'd enjoy tying Dallas down, I'm afraid he's right, Barnaby. The plan isn't to rush to our deaths, I have an empire to reestablish and a fortune to reclaim, but I won't have anything to return to if this maniac kicks open the Goddess's throne room and causes mayhem." Sias gave me a bittersweet smile. "I have to make sure I'm there to protect him."

"Zane," Barnaby turned to him as the last bastion of reason. "Please tell me you're not on board with this. Tell Dallas he's an idiot, force him to think of something better!"

"I swear to you that I will do everything in my power to bring Dallas back in one piece," Zane promised quietly. "But there's no avoiding this responsibility. There's no one else who can stop them."

Barnaby blinked up at the ceiling and tried to take a steadying breath. "I can't believe I'm the only sane one here right now."

He flinched when I put my hand on his shoulder and pulled him into a hug, his body wooden and vibrating with anger.

"I'm really sorry I never paid rent on time, and that I forgot to bring you intimacy crystals a lot. It wasn't because I didn't like you, I just was in my own, fucked-up orbit and couldn't see beyond myself a lot of the time. If I could do it over, I would have tried a little harder to be a friend to you."

Some of the stiffness relaxed in his arms, his breath coming out in one long exhale that helped ease the shaking rage.

"You weren't that bad," he admitted after a beat, tossing his arms around my neck to hold tight. "You were never unkind, just sort of an ass."

"That's probably the best compliment I've ever gotten from a landlord," I said around a laugh, not bothering to banish the tear that fell at Barnaby's stellar review.

"That was my friendship review. As a tenant, you were horrible." He laughed when I did, his arms tightening a bit. "But I suppose I'll admit that you've been something of an annoying sibling these past months. I'm so glad I got to see you navigate your way to happiness. I'm proud of you."

"Likewise," I forced through the swell of painful happiness that ballooned in my chest. It pressed against the awful feelings of crushing low self-worth I'd let metastasize over the years, grinding against the painful truth that this was our last goodbye.

It hurt as much as it made me feel brave, important and loved. I wasn't going to let anything happen to this fussy, loving, strange man, even if I had to throw myself into the void and never come back again.

Barnaby deserved a good life. It was going to be my final gift to make sure he did.

The sound of bone scraping against wood shattered the moment, both of us turning toward the sound as it cracked into the room. Ushen was trying to maneuver their antlers through the doorway but was failing, the tips taking a chunk of doorframe with it by the time they wedged themself into the basement. I hadn't seen the wendigo chef since I'd gone bearing questionably obtained human meat in exchange for valuable intel, and I had missed their adorable, deer skull face and casual destruction of property. In their long arms were various bags they held carefully, avoiding their long claws so as to not snag the plastic. Ushen's eyeless face turned to us as they placed the bags on the table, the incredible smell of food permeating the air around them.

Malphie had gotten to his feet, a bone splintering growl rumbling from between his teeth. The orbs in his skull flared a bright, putrid color of rage, ready to attack the large thing stumbling upon our little nest. Ushen regarded Malphie with a tilt of their head, then reached into a bag at their side and extracted a large bone of suspicious origin, still wet and sporting tender bits of meat around the joints.

"May I?" Ushen asked Sias, who was staring in confused befuddlement at their sudden appearance. Sias blinked and granted permission with a flick of his wrist, and Ushen handed the bone to Malphie. The void hound leaned forward to sniff through his nose hole, a vacuum sound coming in short, questioning bursts. The horrible color of his eyes melted into a friendly shade, and the bone was snagged between black, razer teeth. Ushen gave the fellow skeletal headed beast a pat with the flat of his hand and Malphie's whole body wiggled in delight.

Ushen snagged one of the little booties that had fallen from their antler while taking out a piece of door and tucked it back in place.

"Good morning, Dallas Wilde."

"Hey, Ushen," I said in a mild stupor, scrubbing some tears off my cheeks. "What...are you doing here?"

The wendigo pulled a container from one of the many plastic bags, back hunched over the table so their little booties weren't knocked off again. With a flick of their long, black claw, one of the containers was popped open to reveal scrambled eggs, some various meats, grilled veggies and tortillas.

"I brought breakfast," the chef explained, helpfully adding, "No human meat. Only animal products."

I stared at the food, my stomach growling even with the dizzying emotional whiplash I was experiencing.

"I'm grateful, but I don't understand."

"Wow, you guys look depressed," Dex announced as she followed Ushen's trail of destruction, kicking a piece of wood out of the way with the side of her foot. Her much more likable jinn counterpart, Kimi, strolled in after her, scanning the surroundings with a look of judgmental wonder.

"I mean...this place is kind of depressing," Kimi lamented. "Some decorations would keep it from looking like a hostage den."

"I don't believe I asked you to critique my basement, nose ring," Marthas drawled as he brought up the rear of the parade, pausing to assess the damage to his door. The big imp growled as he probed the gash with his fingers, but moved past it to join the circus. "Ushen, I've seen you duck before."

"I was too excited," Ushen said, their voice not changing in inflection or tone to match the statement.

"What the hell is going on?" I finally blurted, feeling a little like I was losing my mind. "Barns and I were having a sweet moment and growing as people and then the what-the-fuck crew rolled in."

Marthas motioned to the gaggle before me, Dex popping a bubble while Kimi started making a breakfast burrito.

"You tell me, Wilde. This is your what-the-fuck crew, not mine. The only reason I let them in is because Ushen has food."

"I have key information that may help in your fight against Florence Pierce." Ushen spread their claws to display the spread of food on the table. "But first, we eat."

# CHAPTER
# TWENTY

"THEY SHOWED UP LOOKING FOR YOU," Ushen explained as we all dined on their heavenly breakfast foods. The eggs were fluffy, bacon crispy, vegetables charred just enough to give them a roasted flavor, and the tortillas were like warm clouds hugging them all in place. I was riding the bliss of stuffing my face as the wendigo spoke.

"I didn't trust them," Ushen continued. "They were the DHAP officers you brought to me once, long ago. They said to me, "Dallas is in danger, this computer file contains Florence Pierce's magic tech details." I told them I would not bring them to you, but I would relay the information."

"That's when they showed up at our place," Dex explained around a bite of food. It was the first time I saw her chewing on something besides gum. "They knew I worked for Sias making goodies somehow."

"I know things," Ushen said, like it was universally understood. "I brought the tech to Dex to help you. I knew you were staying here with Marthas, so I brought her to you when breakfast was ready."

"You knew about this?" I quizzed Marthas who was finishing his eighth burrito.

"I knew about it when they showed up on my security camera." He gave his pocket a pat where his phone was. "I'm learning about all of this in real time with you, Wilde, and figuring out how you're going to repay me for my doorframe."

"How is that on me?" I began to argue, but then waved it away like a fly. "Fuck it. Never mind, you're bulldozing this place anyway. Dex, what were you able to get from Florence's intel?"

"Remember when you brought me that fine piece of technology you found lodged in a vampire's head a few months ago and I said I was too homegrown to recreate it? Well, our friendly neighborhood wendigo here just handed me the blueprint of how it all works in some encrypted files from DHAP," Dex explained as she finished her last bite.

"They must have found it when they raided her offices," Sias mused. "What can you do with that information, Dex?"

"Well." She wiped her mouth with a napkin and leaned back in her chair, placing one hand on her full stomach. "I guess that depends on what exactly you have planned. It's all over the news that Pierce is MIA, and there's allegations she had something to do with the "unexplained, necromancy-related phenomena" happening throughout the city. I'm guessing since that one's involved, you're going to go headfirst into something stupid." Dex tilted her head my way as she spoke with Sias.

"I'd say it's more brave and heroic," I said at the same time Sias agreed with her and Zane nodded. "Hey, I have two boyfriends you can have. Free to a good home. Zane's almost potty trained but watch for Sias. He's a humper."

"The plan is to go after Florence," Zane told her, ignoring me. "We know where she is, but she's got more of those tech vampires with her."

"A lot of them," I cut back in, deciding to be serious for the sake of timing. "More than we can handle with just the four of us."

"Five," Funus spoke up for the first time in Barnaby's lap. "But I suppose I won't be lending a hand to the fighting."

Dex stared for a long time as she processed the talking skull, taking out a pack of gum and extracting a stick without saying a word.

"Okay," Kimi finally broke the silence, poised like she was waiting to catch whoever was going to faint from shock first. "Did anyone else see that skull talking or am I just really high?"

Dex shoved gum into her cheek and peeled her eyes off Funus to look to Kimi.

"What skull?"

The intoxicated jinn's eyes widened and she began panic giggling.

"The skull? In...wait." She turned and pointed to Malphie, who had parked his large body halfway lodged under Sias's chair. "You see that too, right? The big skeleton dog with the bone?"

Dex lifted her shoulders and said nothing, igniting a peeling shriek of laughter from her friend.

"Told you not to eat edibles before leaving."

"You are *cold*," I told Dex through my laugh.

"Can someone handle the poor, intoxicated girl so we can get back to business, please?" Sias rubbed at his temple.

"Maybe have some coffee," Funus offered, trying his best to be helpful, but it caused Kimi to cackle in terror. I let out a snort of amusement, not missing how Zane covered his mouth to hide his smirk. Sias rolled his eyes and looked to Dex to fix the problem, but the oni just shrugged like she had no idea what the issue was.

"You all need therapy, church, or both," my brother told us as he went to the jinn's rescue, taking Kimi gently by the elbow. "C'mon, I'll get you some water."

"This edible is insane," she was telling him, following like a high puppy. "Oh, can you bring me more burritos too?"

"He's nice. How'd he end up here?" Dex mused as she watched Austin guide Kimi to the couch. "Should we kick him out?"

I glanced around at the table and considered it.

"This is kind of a club of assholes, isn't it?"

"Goddess help me! *Focus*, hunter," Zane barked and looked to Sias. "Can you charm him so he stays on track?"

"No, no!" I sat up straighter in my chair and got back into character. Dex, Marthas and Austin did not need to see me drunk on Sias magic, because that Dallas got really loose with the truth and I didn't need to give them more ammo to tease me. "I'm good. Focused. We are back on track now."

"Great," Sias's purr sounded more like the low, threatening growl. "As we were saying, Dex, we are planning on taking the fight to Florence but we're concerned about the swarm of vampires she has with her."

Dex crossed her arms over her chest and tilted her chair back, rocking it on its back legs.

"How did the blockers work last time?"

"Not great," I admitted, wincing as the memory of Zane getting shot crawled over me like acidic spiders. "Their magic doesn't behave the same way as regular magic, so it just dampened it. With the amount of vampires I think there are, even substantial blockers aren't going to keep us from getting overwhelmed."

Dex stretched her gum out over her tongue and blew it into a huge, purple bubble before popping it with her tusk. Gathering the chewy substance back in her mouth, she chomped it a few times as she mulled over some ideas.

"You need a kill switch."

"That sounds promising," I said. "Something to disarm the vampires?"

Dex pulled her phone free and started typing, nodding along to a string of thoughts she kept hidden behind her chewing.

"You ever use something that emits an electromagnetic pulse to cut off power?" She turned her eyes to me but her thumbs kept typing.

"I've used a magical equivalent, yeah. Set up some wards to shut down security magic or disrupt spells."

"I can't get you something that will kill a horde of vampires, but I can get you something that will fry the chips Florence stuffed in their skulls." She finished typing and cracked her knuckles. "In theory, we can shut down whatever is causing them to retain their bio-magic abilities after death. Maybe even the playing field a bit."

I slapped the table. "That's what I'm talking about, Dex. That. We need a vampire muting switch."

"If we can get their bio magic turned off, that's a huge step forward," Zane agreed. "Is that something you can make quickly?"

"Normally no, but with these blueprints I can whip up something within a day."

"We don't have a day, love," Sias said. "We need it now."

"How now is 'now'?" Dex lifted her eyebrow.

"If we can't carve our way through these vampires before sunset, we might not have another. We need it immediately."

"Shit." Dex picked her phone back up and started typing again. "Okay, hold on. Let me brainstorm."

"Not to pile on," Zane said, piling on, "But say we get this kill switch, and it works as intended, it doesn't change the fact that they still outnumber us."

"They're also in a closed location with one entry point," Austin came back into the conversation, having planted Kimi on the couch with a blanket and more food to keep her calm. "We'll be tunneled into a meat grinder."

"There is more than one way inside." Funus lifted his bright eyes to him. "I know of a secret entrance that we can use that might give us an advantage."

"That helps, but we'll still be overrun quickly," Zane cut the celebration down before it could grow legs. "We need something to thin the numbers after we deploy Dex's kill switch."

I looked to Austin, hopeful he was going to bring it all home with a grand weapon he had secretly kept stashed away.

"This is when you say you stole a life magic bomb from the armory before you left Magnus, right? It's been tucked away in your bag and you were going to keep it to yourself until the moment was just right for a grand reveal?"

"What is it like in your head?" Austin asked me, sounding not at all like he was about to whip out a surprise bomb and go "taa-daa!" "Seriously, I know you got hit on the head a lot when we were training, but Saint's light, man."

"So, no bomb then?" I tried deploying the puppy dog eyes. "Not even a little one?"

"Is he serious?" Austin looked to my vampire and incubus.

"It would be nice if you had stolen something useful," Sias admitted.

"At least some extra life bullets or something," the vampire mumbled. "We're desperate for some good news right now."

I scrubbed away my wasted puppy dog eyes and stared down at the destroyed to-go boxes of breakfast foods Ushen had brought us. My mind was beginning to sound a lot like angry white noise as I tried to craft a plan that had us coming out ahead, but as it stood, we had something of a halfway successful, but still suicidal, mission. We *might* be able to get in and cut through some vampires before getting wiped out, but the odds weren't fantastic. Even if one of us managed to get to this unnamed asshole who murdered Florence and was armed with the scythe, how would we take them out? How would we kill them, destroy the scythe and keep the damn door to the Goddess sealed before we were ripped to pieces?

As I contemplated how hilariously screwed we were, and debated about eating away my misery with another burrito, the scraps of breakfast food left over were pulled off the table to make way for the good news we needed. A metal case added a few more scars to the old table as Marthas slid it across the surface, throwing the top open once it was in the center. Inside the foam and charm lined case was a cache of powerful enchanted weapons, brimming with all sorts of illegal magic to help us punch a hole through some undead fuckery.

Immolation bullets, true silence attachments for guns, endless sight scopes, concussion wards, paralytic grenades, acidic projectiles—enough magically infused illegal shit that would have put Marthas away for a good twenty years had DHAP ever discovered it.

I slipped on a pair of knuckle knives that popped with electricity as I curled my fist and cackled like a cartoon villain.

"I'm keeping an itemized list," Marthas growled as we started picking out weapons like kids at a deadly candy store. "Don't think you dying is going to get you out of paying me."

Austin was marveling at the grenades as he asked, "Do you have any life magic? Healing kits or anything?"

Marthas opened up a flap on the inside of the case and extracted three vials of concentrated life magic capped with wax sealed enchantments from exclusive covens.

"This will heal a hole in the head if you do it right," Marthas told us.

Zane sucked in through his teeth as I touched the side of one, testing to see if it would burn me. The glass was warm like sunlight over a window, but I came away with my remaining hand still intact.

"If you make me buy you two artificial limbs, I'm going to be pissed," Sias scolded me.

"These cost me a million each, Wilde. You get one," Marthas warned as I experimented with not burning my hand off.

"We'll take all of them," I argued. "Add it to my tab. We need all the firepower we can get."

"Your 'tab' is already substantial, and I don't like you," Marthas reminded me. "One. And if you argue with me once more, I'll shove it up your ass."

"Did you forget that this might lead to the Death Goddess getting kicked off her throne and unleashing some unknown horror upon the world?" I gestured to the treasure trove of goodies. "This is a hell of a start, and it gives us a real chance to make it work, but we *need* life magic to slice through the undead. You can kick my ass and make me work for you until I die, Marthas, but I need that life magic."

Marthas barked a laugh and slammed the case shut as I reached for the life vials. His hulking frame leaned over the case as I glared at him, his dark eyes simmering coals.

"And if you fail, I need to make sure I can keep myself and my crew safe. You're not the only asshole with people depending on you."

"If you don't give me supplies, we *will* fail," I hissed. "You want your crew safe? Their families safe? We're going to do that. I know you hate me, man, and I don't blame you. I've been an outrageous dick to you since we met, but I'm trying to do right here. Please."

Marthas ground my words between his molars, the muscle next to his nose twitching as he suppressed a snarl. He opened the case up and pulled one of the vials free, pushing it into his pocket, then left the rest for me.

I would have loved all three, but I wasn't going to push my luck. Two concentrated life essence vials would have to work.

"Okay, here's the plan." I went to rub my hands together and floundered, then opted to settle on an inspiring, leadership thumbs up. "Dex, head back to your place and work on the kill switch. Once that's ready, we'll get on the road to the Silent Steps. If we pack some spare gas containers, we can cut down travel time. We'll need to get there as fast as humanly possible."

"And when we get there?" Austin asked. "What's the plan?"

"My favorite, we go in hard and fast from behind," I said. "Hit them with the kill switch, mow down the grunts, and get to the door. Austin, let Zane lead since vampires won't notice him as quickly. Sias and I will follow, and we'll fan out with you following up behind. Barns," I turned to him as he straightened his spine, guarding Funus with his hands resting on the top of his skull.

"I'm going with you," he said before I could utter a single word otherwise. "I'm part of this now, and I'm not going to stay behind while everyone else runs off to play hero. I'm putting my foot down, Dallas Wilde." He stomped his foot for maximum effect. "I will not hear anything to the contrary."

"I need you to seal the entrance behind us," I continued. "Do not follow us inside, do you understand? Seal the door and plant the concussion wards around the crypt."

"Yes. I-I can do that." Barnaby nodded quickly. "Sorry. I assumed we were going to fight about this."

I tossed him a smile, which frazzled him into mirroring it. "I wouldn't dare do this without you, Barns."

"Good," he whispered after a beat, giving Funus's head a sweet pat. "I'm glad that's settled then."

"This is the part you're going to be mad," I cautioned. "We need to take Funus inside with us. He's the only one who can tell us where the door is."

Barnaby crumpled his face like he was trying to hold in an explosive sneeze, but nodded once he fought down the urge to argue.

"That seems reasonable."

"We'll take care of him," I promised. "I won't let anything happen to your skull—whoa. Funus, you okay?"

Funus's eyes were flickering like a dying bulb, the yellow in his eyes paling almost white. Malphie made a whining noise from under Sias's chair, his eyes doing a similar pulse with his teeth still resting on the massive leg bone Ushen had brought him.

Sias kneeled and stroked the skull of the hellhound, lifting its massive head to try and soothe him.

"It's alright, Malphaslanexus. I'm here."

"Funus?" Barnaby lifted the skull up, worry creasing his brow as Funus's jaw hung slack. "Darling? What's wrong?"

I felt a chilling and unwelcome sensation knock against the back of my mind. It lingered long enough to feel like dread or fear, its roots extending out into my chest to tangle itself around my ribs. The icy claws shook my lungs as I inhaled, wincing through the sting as another knock rattled my consciousness.

Funus clattered his jaw like he was freezing, his eyes swelling in a bright rush as he snapped back to consciousness. Malphie crawled forward into Sias's lap, forcing him to sit on the floor to hold the big, scared beast.

"Do you feel that?" Funus whispered quickly, turning his eyes to me.

I had started rubbing at my chest, the chill shaking me like I was sitting in a frozen lake.

"What's going on?"

"The door," he exhaled, terror lacing through his words like an electric wire. "It's been activated."

The fear that had lingered where the knocking started solidified into a knot that gripped the base of my skull, choking all thought from my mind. My body shook as I felt the ripples in the void, breath fogging like the room had fallen twenty degrees.

"We're too late?" Barnaby asked, holding Funus to his chest like he was trying to warm him up. "It's over before we even begun?"

"This can't be how it ends." Sias curled his arms around Malphie, stroking his fur with darkening fingers. The void hound was trying to comfort him, but was weak from the shake of the void. His big body shook, a sad whine escaping as Sias did his best to soothe his discomfort. Sias's second set of eyes were cracking open, mirroring the main set, a swirl of angry yellow and sorrow blue.

Zane had fallen back into a chair to lean his head into his hands, murmuring to his Goddess. I don't know what plea he was giving her, but it broke my heart to hear him sound so desperate.

"Can you stop it?" Austin swung his attention between me and Funus. "Slow it down somehow?"

"Funus, you said the door was activated." I curled my fists to keep from trembling and focused my efforts on keeping my voice level. "Does that mean it hasn't been truly opened yet?"

"The ritual has begun," he confirmed, stilling his clattering jaw. "But the door is still shut. We don't have much time now."

"It takes over a day to get to the Silent Steps by car," Austin said. "Do we have other options? A plane? Fucking teleport? Anything?"

"I don't have access to my plane now." Sias adjusted Malphie's head in his lap and scratched where his ear should have been. It made the undead hound kick his back leg a little. "Marthas, you didn't happen to spring for a custom teleport when buying all of these illegal goods, did you?"

"Have you priced those lately?" the frugal gang leader shot back. "Fuck no."

Another ripple of the void buckled my knees, and I caught myself against the table, causing Zane to surge to his feet. He caught me by the upper arm as I swayed, my eyesight going crossed for a heartbeat.

"I got him," Zane told Sias as he tried to wiggle his way out from under the void hound. "Stay with Malphie."

"Oh, Funus..." Barnaby was trying to keep Funus's lower jaw from falling off, his eyes flickering and dimming before brightening again.

"I'm alright," the skull said, sounding very tired. "I'm alright, darling."

I lost the battle with gravity and let Zane guide me into a chair, my head swimming with each knock at the door. Zane's skin was growing ashy as he smoothed my hair back, the flush from last night fading with the disruption to the void. The bright crimson of his eyes dulled like drying blood, his palm cold on my cheek.

Sias's eyes had started leaking black tears, horns curling in and discoloring the gold. He held Malphie to his chest and rocked him, the big beast growing suspiciously quiet as its eyes dimmed.

My heart was suspended in ice as it cracked, the weight of failure stabbing at me from all sides. The void was thrashing, churning from the disturbance at the door, and all of us suckers caught within its power were going for the same ride. My connection to the endless was weakening, and I didn't know what that meant for the two souls attached to me.

My world was starting to spin in a slow circle, the sensation not dulling as I squeezed my eyes shut and leaned my brow against Zane's.

"Stay awake," he whispered.

"I'm sorry. I'm sorry—" I tried, his head moving in a slow shake.

"Focus, hunter. Now is not the time for self-pity. This isn't over yet. Drink this and get some energy back."

I felt something against my lips, followed by the metallic taste of blood stabbing my senses. I licked my lip out of instinct, thinking I had somehow bit myself when I had been shivering. My tongue touched the line of vampire blood Zane had traced over my lips, and I felt my connection to the void sharpen like a blade.

My chest tightened, the ice of the void a weight that sank me down into the seam between life and death with just that tiny drop. I dipped through the veil, peeking to the other side like I was slipping into a dream. It was just a flash, just a moment, but it stretched long enough to turn everything upside down.

The void was in chaos.

The calm nothingness that stretched forever was now a roiling storm of cracked obsidian, shattered pieces frozen in a sea of broken ripples. The carved pathways from last night were crooked and bent, the souls that should be swimming in peaceful oblivion wild and furious. I tried to claw my way back to the surface to escape, to rush back to the other side before the nightmare could swallow me. The golden threads were fragile and weak, snapping the moment I grabbed hold. The shadow with red eyes that had guided me before was lost in the storm, dispersed and gone like smoke.

I was sinking.

Falling.

Doomed to shatter and break apart, turn into jagged pieces that would never find their way back again.

I tried to grab something, tried to scream for help, tried to kick my way back toward the seam of the realms but I was nothing. I had no body, no essence, nothing to keep me tethered to the reality I had fallen from.

All I had was panic, fear, and the soul deep realization that myself and everyone back in Marthas's basement was going to end up exactly the same.

Dead.

Broken.

And lost.

In my despair, in my helpless struggle raging against the inevitable, I saw a tiny bubble.

A perfect little pearl of iridescent splendor floated to me like a life raft amongst the madness. I watched it float by, followed it as it was partnered with another, and then another.

Within the shattered darkness, a wisp trailed past me with the swimming elegance of a koi. The trail behind it was smooth, like a stroke of paint on canvas, leaving behind a line of art that seemed to never end. It curled around something I couldn't see, or rather, something that refused to be seen.

I felt her there, resting outside my peripherals.

The Goddess of the broken domain had found me again.

The painted pathway from the pseudo-koi cracked open like a bolt of lightning, streaking through the madness before ending at a vision of the Silent Steps. The sun slid over the open mausoleum, the iron gate swinging open and crashing to the side from an unnatural gust of wind.

The image went black as she slid a bony hand over my vision, her presence swallowing me into a silence so deafening, so horrible, unbearable and suffocating, that I felt my soul scream for mercy. Fear like I had never experienced splintered me into fragments, each one falling into dust like old bones thrown against stone.

My lips felt the comforting, sweet kiss of death, of the Goddess.

Then—

Calmness.
Peace.
Nothingness.
Except one.
Tiny.
Bubble.
With the flick of a fin, I was sent back to life with a plan.

# TWENTY-ONE

I SURGED AWAKE WITH A GASP, the fog that had been weighing me down evaporating like steam.

"I know what to do!" I almost fell out of the chair, my knee clipping the table and hand connecting with the heavy case. I took a moment to cuss and blame Marthas for all my injuries, then pushed myself to my feet. "We travel the void! We use the pathways!"

"What?" Zane had gotten to his feet when I did, his skin flushed and alive again. His red eyes were bright and strong, his touch warm when he placed a steadying hand on my shoulder. "Dallas, what happened just now?"

"I feel...much better," Funus was saying, the flickering light show gone from his eyes. "Stronger. Honestly, the best I've felt in years."

Malphie was wiggling so furiously that he had knocked Sias completely over and was trying to give him his chewed up bone as thanks. The incubus had to muscle him to the side and command him to sit in order to escape, and I moved to help get him to his feet.

"I met the Goddess again," I told the dumbstruck vampire and skull as I dusted Sias off. "I think she…oh, actually, I think she kissed me."

"She…kissed you?" Sias asked, sounding dubious. "The Goddess of Death *kissed* you?"

"Yeah. I think so." I mulled it over and shrugged.

Sias repeated my shrug mockingly. "You *think* you were kissed by a deity?"

"Hunter," Zane stormed into the conversation. "Don't joke or fuck around right now. What *happened*?"

"The void is fucked," I explained. "It's out of order and completely trashed, but I saw a clear, open pathway to the Silent Steps. The Goddess showed me, then we kissed—platonically." I aimed the last word at Sias. "I think she gave us a boost so we can get there."

"This is incredible," Funus said from Barnaby's arms. "She has given you a blessing, acolyte, a rare gift. We have our strength back, but we mustn't squander it. We have to act fast."

"You said she showed you a path?" Zane asked, and I nodded. "You're sure?"

"Yeah, I'm sure."

"What do you mean a 'path'? Like a faster route?" Austin asked, jumping into the conversation.

"A path through the void," I said. "A straight shot to the crypt."

"Okay," Austin snorted. "How the hell does that help us? We can't travel the void—or at least, nothing *living* can."

"Do you know how to even open the void?" Barnaby asked. "I'm not an expert, but that seems rather difficult to do."

"Funus?" I turned to the skull, who flicked his eyes in a wince.

"Ah, no. I cannot. Not in a way that could allow bodies to travel through it."

"Open the void like those fucking tears?" Marthas asked, weary. "You're not doing that shit here, are you?"

"The tears! Marthas, you big, handsome genius. That's exactly what we need to do."

"Fuck no, you're not. Not here." He pointed at the stairs. "I lived through that once, remember? I don't need more therapy bills, Wilde."

"*How* do we even do that?" Austin inserted himself again. "Florence was using a laser to rip open holes with the scythe. We don't have either of those things."

"Hi." Dex raised her hand in the commotion. "The void crystal you brought me from those tears had the ability to cut through and make holes. Kimi and I had one of those chips I put in your phone shatter and pop a hole in the lab."

"We threw a medicinal charm into it to fix it," Kimi chimed in, having just woken up from a nap. "It was freaky."

"Do you have one with you?" I asked quickly.

"No?" Dex shot me with a damning look. "I just said it shattered and carved a hole into the void. You think I just tote that shit around?"

"Did any of you hear me when I said you're not doing that creepy shit here?" Marthas raged from somewhere in the room, but I ignored him.

"What about the one in my phone? Could you use that one?" I tried to hand her my phone but she shoved it back my direction.

"It's unstable. Trying to extract it would cause problems. Maybe a hole, maybe something worse. Hell no. We need a fresh sample, one that I haven't tampered with."

"Shit." I rubbed at my hair and looked to Austin hopefully. "This is your time to come in with a secret stash of void crystals and save the day."

"You have to stop putting that on me," he answered, sounding tired. "I don't have secret weapons, Dallas."

"Didn't we see DHAP taking samples of the void tear?" Sias reached down to pat Malphie as he presented his bone. "Do you think Preston and Seyyid could help?"

I started pacing, hoping my movement would jog some better ideas to the surface.

"There's no guarantee that they'd be able to get into wherever they're keeping those crystals, especially if they know how volatile they are. What about Magnus? Did he take any?"

"No," Austin said definitively. "He didn't even want DHAP taking that shit. He wanted it completely destroyed."

It was Zane's turn to placate the void hound by patting his bony head, wrestling the gnawed limb from his mouth before tossing it for him to fetch.

"Would there be any left at old sites? Maybe even some in the wood upstairs?"

"I had everything scarred by the tear ripped out," Marthas growled. "Nothing is left. I made damn sure."

"The old sites were scrubbed," Ushen said, quietly cleaning up after breakfast. "I heard witches were trying to find void crystals to help contain dark magic, but they were not able to successfully source them."

"Another dead end," I groaned. "Damnit, we keep sprinting ahead and hitting walls. Funus, there has to be a work around. A spell, a ritual…something. What if I take some of Zane's blood and you walk me through opening a channel. Maybe with the Goddess's blessing, I can manifest something."

"It doesn't work that way, acolyte. The void has rules," he explained gently. "Trust me, if I knew of a way, I would share it."

"We haven't tried it before. It's worth a shot," Zane began arguing on my behalf as I ground my brain for another idea. I paced in a circle around the room, pulling memories of the void to the forefront of my mind. I had seen the pathway so clearly, knew exactly where she promised we could go. Why in the hell would a Goddess show me a way without letting me through? Why keep the void sealed up when she needed us to use it?

I was missing something. The answer was there but I couldn't pin it down.

"I thought you said you trained fish?" Kimi asked from the couch as I passed by, sipping on a coffee Ushen had brought her.

"I do train fish."

"Then what's with the weird dog?" She lifted her feet onto the couch as Malphie trailed after me, holding his bone. "I think he has some serious mange, my guy."

"He doesn't have mange," I defended, staggering a bit when his big body leaned against my leg. His skeletal head was warm when I gave it a pat, his crow black fur soft when I gave his neck a scratch. His butt wiggled half-heartedly from the affection, and I knew he was just waiting for me to throw his bone.

"I mean," Kimi squinted at Malphie. "I can see his skull. That's not healthy for a dog."

"He's not a dog, he's a void hound," I clarified. "And he's the best boy."

"So, he's like…from the void?" She sipped her coffee again.

"Yeah. He fell out and tried to kill us. Didn't you, Malphie? Yes, what a good boy." I kneeled to try and wrestle the bone from his jaws. "You just wanted to rip us apart with those big teeth—*holy shit.*"

I angled the femur up to look at Malphie's obsidian teeth as they cracked through the thick bone, the gleam of light from the kitchenette reflecting the deep red enamel. The hound's jaw was packed with void crystal teeth, razor sharp and completely pure.

"Malphie's teeth!" I announced to the room. "His teeth are void crystals!"

"Are you sure?" Austin asked, and I tried to get Malphie to walk back over to the group but he dug his claws into the floor to play tug of war.

"Yes! Yes, I'm sure! C'mon, boy, show them your teeth!" I put my body weight into pulling the bone, causing Malphie to growl his splintering, bone aching noise.

"Malphaslanexus." Sias snapped his fingers and pointed to the ground before him. "To me."

I fell backwards as Malphie dropped the bone, obeying his master without hesitation.

"Open," Sias commanded his hound, snapping his fingers to signal for Malphie to lift his massive head and open his jaws wide. His eyes flared bright as Sias gave him orders, the pull Sias had over him absolute and without fail. Malphie's scaled tongue coiled in his mouth like a viper, flecks of broken bone stuck between his deadly teeth.

"Goddess, they are void crystals," Zane confirmed, amazed.

"Funus, do you think you can keep the tear stable—" I began but Marthas slammed his fist down onto the table.

"Fuck that. No," he yelled. "You're not opening a void tear here, Wilde. I'm not going to be near another one of those things ever again."

The anger in his voice did little to cloak the fear simmering just below the surface. Marthas wasn't a man who got quieter the angrier he was, a rolling storm that moved in like a silent hurricane of might. Fear made him loud and it made him mean. I couldn't say I blamed him, not after what he had experienced.

"It won't be like the one that opened on your dance floor, Marthas." I kept my words calm and free of judgment, because I knew the guy was one push away from marching us all out by gun point. "That tear was unstable, a rip caused by the abuse of magic. Funus is a member of the necromancy council, one of the most gifted in the field. He can keep it stable, we did it before."

"I don't care," Marthas said through his teeth. "Go somewhere else. Not here."

"I've seen what they can do," Austin came to our defense, maneuvering around the table to speak to Marthas. "I wouldn't agree to this if I didn't think they could pull it off without it going out of control. Funus has mastery over this skill, and Dallas and his men can handle the magic within."

"You don't know what you're asking me, army boy," Marthas warned him, anger taking a back seat to weariness. "You didn't see what I saw that night. Those girls screamed like something out of a nightmare."

"I wouldn't ask you if we had another option." Austin met his eyes and held them, the military training slipping from his voice as he said, "You gotta trust me."

"I don't even know you," Marthas parried, but he was being worn down.

"Have I lied to you yet?" Austin cracked a small grin, a devastating strike against Marthas's armor. "Other than the dart game?"

Marthas shut his eyes like he knew the battle was lost, his big shoulders slumping in defeat.

"You're going to really travel through the void? You're going to do something that insanely stupid?"

"I have to," Austin agreed, regaining his persona again. "I have to help them stop this evil, no matter what."

Magnus nodded, rubbing his eyes with his fingers.

"You're dangerous, army boy," he whispered. "You're the type that gets men killed."

Austin opened his mouth to say something but seemed to hesitate, his mouth closing when Marthas turned his attention back to us.

"You're going to need something to keep the living safe if you're going through the void. Since you jerk-offs are already well acquainted with lady death, we'll let you go in raw." Marthas aimed the colorful remarks at me, my vampire and incubus. "But you two," he gestured to Austin and Barns. "You're going to need wards."

"I can whip up some life magic wards back at my shop," Dex said, getting to her feet. "I can put those together while I work on the kill switch."

"No time for a trip. You can use my setup."

Dex, who was known for her tech abilities and not her people skills, made a face like Marthas had just passed gas in her presence.

"No offense, Mr. Marthas, but my lab setup is extensive. If I'm going to have any shot to make functioning life wards that can withstand traveling through the void *and* a badass vampire kill switch, I'm going to need more than the tools used to cloak security cameras and smuggle drugs."

"I'm no expert, but I think we got a little bit more than that going on," Marthas countered, back to his arid sense of humor. "All those magic infused weapons on the table, including the life essence containers reinforced with shatter wards, were made in-house. The witches I employ are silicon coven."

Dex's eyes almost fell out of her head as she stared at Marthas, Kimi lifting off the couch to scamper over with the blanket still draped around her shoulders.

"Are you being for real?" Kimi whispered, hugging Dex's arm.

"They don't take independent contracts," Dex argued, but sounded extremely hopeful that she was wrong.

"Whatever you say." Marthas headed up the stairs. "But if you want to work out of the lab the non-sanctioned witches worked in, follow me."

Kimi and Dex scrambled after him, getting tangled up in each other as they both tried to enter the stairwell at the same time.

"Okay, we'll just work on the tooth situation!" I called after them, listening to them falling up the stairs after Marthas. "And they're gone."

"How exactly are we going to wiggle a tooth out of this dog's mouth?" Austin asked. "That thing just cracked a bone in half like it was nothing. I can't imagine any of its teeth are loose."

"I'm not excited about the idea of someone sticking their hand in there." I eyed Malphie's teeth as he waited for Sias's command, watching his master with big, glowing eyes. "I know he's docile now, but if we crack a tooth, is he going to snap out of reflex?"

"I have control over him." Sias rested his hand on Malphie's head. "He won't bite unless I say."

I turned to Austin and Zane, both were looking expectantly at me.

"What?"

"Go ahead." Zane nodded to Malphie. "Sias says he has it under control."

"I have one hand left!" I held up my remaining hand as

evidence for my argument. "I automatically qualify to sit this one out."

"Don't look at me, vampire," Austin was quick to count himself out. "You're the most qualified here."

"He's got a point, Zane," I said with a wince. "If he bites you, I can heal you with my fun, horny blood. Ow." I rubbed at my arm after Austin punched me. "I can't talk about fun, horny blood when you've been banging my mortal enemy?"

"Dallas, if I had to avoid all the men you've pissed off, I'd be celibate."

"Stop laughing. You're my boyfriends, you're supposed to be on my side," I told said boyfriends, who snickered at my expense. "And Marthas has tried to kill me more than once. He's pretty far up the ladder."

"Hunter, you need to stop being so judgmental." Zane kneeled in front of Malphie and peered into his maw, scanning over his options. "Austin is a grown man and can watch after himself."

"*Thank* you, Zane," Austin said. "Never thought I'd be in a situation where I was defending my love life to my brother while an undead guy has my back."

I crossed my arms, feeling a little ganged up on, and not in the fun, sexy way.

"That's not the point."

"What is the point then?" Sias tilted his head as he looked at me, the question sounding genuine. "What are you worried about?"

"I'm not worried—" I started but sighed when Sias cut through my bullshit with a lift of his brows. "I'm not worried about you, Austin. I'm worried Marthas is going to hurt you. Manipulate you to hurt me. We finally have something of a relationship again after a decade and I don't want a skeleton in my closet fucking that up."

Austin, who was as ill-equipped to deal with emotional honesty as I was, shifted on his feet from the anxiety of being handed a slice of vulnerability.

"I, uh," he faltered, serving his own cupcake of honesty. "I don't know what to say to that, other than I appreciate you telling me. But I can make my own mistakes, and I don't think Marthas is one of them. At the risk of you throwing up, I gotta say…I had a lot of fun last night."

"Yeah, okay." I covered one ear since that's all I could do. "That's fine. I don't need to hear the details. If it was literally anyone else I would have follow-up questions about dick size, but I officially don't care."

"I care," Sias tossed out, making Zane snort a laugh. "He's a bottom, isn't he?"

"He says he's a verse, but I think he's lying," Austin continued, giving a size range with his hands like he was measuring a fish he caught.

Not that I cared at all, but it was a substantial fish.

"He's lying," Zane added to the conversation as he began testing some of Malphie's teeth with probing fingers.

"Gross. You're gross," I told Austin, but since I didn't want to be left out of the gossip circle, I said, "Really, that big?"

"He's a big dude. You're surprised?"

"I mean." I shrugged. "He's *tall*. That doesn't mean anything."

I smiled as Austin laughed, and I felt a tug of nostalgia at the noise. The last time I had heard that snickering we'd been kids joking about something juvenile and pointless. God, I had missed laughing with him; I missed pointless conversations that weren't tied to death, the void and the possible destruction of all things.

"I'm sorry you got mixed up in this shit, Austin, but I'm really glad you're here."

"I found one that's loose," Zane broke into the dick-talk and glanced up at Sias. "You got him, right? I'm going to try and snap it off."

"I got him." Sias placed both hands on Malphie's head, the tips of his horns curling just slightly. "Be stone. You feel no pain."

Zane reached his hand back into Malphie's mouth, past the scaled tongue and rows of obsidian daggers and carefully pinched a molar between his fingers. The hound's eyes flared, the sound of his breathing escaping his nose hole like wind through a tunnel.

Zane took a breath and held it, jerking the tooth to the side and snapping it clean off from Malphie's jaw. Malphie flinched, hackles up, eyes turning orange, and I grabbed Zane's shirt and tried to pull him back.

"Easy," Sias soothed, stroking Malphie's head until the yellow in his eyes calmed. "There. We're fine now."

Zane turned and handed me the molar, which sat in my palm like a dry piece of ice. Touching a piece of the void made goose bumps rise up from my wrist through to my shoulder, and I shivered as Zane went in for one more tooth.

I displayed the tooth in my palm for Austin to inspect, the tiny fragment of the void rolling across my lifeline. Austin was careful when he reached out to tap the bone like it might reach out and bite him. Satisfied that the molar wasn't going to turn his flesh rotten or steal his soul, he let me place it in his palm for a closer look.

"It feels like a paradox," Austin explained as he pushed the thing around in his hand. "Like when you hear a noise that makes your teeth hurt. It's sitting outside of my body, but the marrow of my bones feels irritated by its presence."

"Kinda cool, right?" I grinned as he nodded.

"Yeah, a little bit. Is this what it feels like when you do necromancy?"

"Kinda. It's a lot more intense when I have my full abilities. It feels like an icy octopus trying to pull me into the void when I'm still trying to keep control."

Austin shivered at the thought, and kept hold of the tooth as Zane dove in for another to add to the collection.

This time the tooth was more toward the front, a sharp incisor that was knocked crooked, probably from when I had fought him during our first encounter. Zane waited until Sias gave him a nod to proceed, then carefully placed his fingers over the slanted tooth.

"Sorry, Malphie," Zane whispered before ripping it free. The snap of Malphie's jaws made us all jump, his teeth missing Zane's hand by inches.

"Easy. Easy!" Sias wrapped his arms around Malphie and held tight, pulling him away from me as I stepped in to be Zane's puppy shield. "Calm. You're safe. You're alright."

"He's pissed." Austin had his hand on one of the weapons in the case, ready to unleash something on the hound if Sias wasn't able to get him under control.

"No, he was afraid," Sias corrected, stroking Malphie's head and neck until the dog calmed down. "He was confused that Zane was hurting him. I could feel it through the threads."

Zane gave my hip a pat to move me out of the way, sitting up on his knees to face the wary hellhound.

"I'm sorry, boy. I didn't mean to hurt you." He handed Austin the broken tooth and to show Malphie that he wasn't trying to be his enemy, held out the offending hand for the hound to sniff. The beast leaned forward on his claws like he was worried Zane was going to try and snatch a tooth out of his mouth again, giving a long, vacuum inhale to sniff out any trickery.

Zane was blessed with a nose nudge and nothing more, their bridge mended but needing time to fully heal.

"Did he hurt you at all?" Sias asked Zane, moving to examine his hand.

"I'm fine." Zane let Sias take his hand, scan it for injuries, and then pull him to his feet. "Did controlling him drain you?"

"No." Sias felt his cheeks where his eyes would open, the skin smooth and sealed. "It gets easier each day. Plus, after the Goddess made out with Dallas, I'm feeling rejuvenated."

"It was platonic," I repeated with a sigh. "This is going to be a whole thing, isn't it?"

Austin cleared his throat and took a few retreating steps away from us.

"I'm going to let you deal with...this situation, and run these teeth to Dex. Good luck, man." He gave a little salute and left me to fend for myself.

"I need to go pack," Barnaby stood from the table and picked up Funus. "And I'd like to talk to you, Funus, if you have a moment."

"I believe I can pencil you in," the skull joked, his chuckle not lasting when Barnaby didn't even crack a smile. They left us alone in the basement with Ushen quietly cleaning around us and Malphie resting his sore jaw on his bone.

"It was a little peck," I continued, chasing down the fleeting levity. "A cheeky little kiss on the lips. You're sounding a little jealous for an incubus with an exorbitant body count."

"First, I've never kissed a deity, so of course I'm jealous, and two." Sias moved to take my chin and hold me still, his eyes emerald dipped in vivid topaz. "I don't plan on kissing anyone else without discussing it with you and Zane. I'll let this one slide since I have no way of reprimanding her for kissing you without asking you. It was not very God-like of her to steal something so precious."

"We're so exclusive now that even a God has to ask to kiss one of us?" I asked, trying to tease, but I knew I sounded excited. My heart radiated happiness, warming me so completely it banished the chill the void teeth had settled over me.

"I'd like us to be." Sias swiped his thumb over my lips. "If you and Zane want that too, of course."

Zane wrapped his arms around me from behind and kissed my temple, the gesture so loving and familiar that it almost made me emotional. The casual way they loved me was breathtaking and terrifying, yet so intoxicating that I couldn't go on living without it.

"I don't think we'll be able to police what my Goddess does or doesn't do, but I appreciate the sentiment," Zane said to Sias. "I have no desire to go outside this relationship. I'd like us to be exclusive, pending any 'dinner parties' you need to attend, Sias."

"I dictate which 'dinner parties' I go to or host, and I have a feeling they've lost their appeal. Dining with regular people sounds bland compared to a vampire and a necromancer."

My grin was hurting my cheeks, and I allowed myself to drop my guard a few more inches.

"I'm not going anywhere else." I put my hand over Zane's and kissed Sias's thumb as he gave me another pass. "You jerks are stuck with me."

"Eloquently said, love," Sias responded dryly,

Zane's huffed laugh tickled my jaw.

"Idiot."

Zane rubbed my chest as I churned over the bubbling excitement at what was being offered and what waited for us on the horizon.

The Goddess hadn't just stolen me away to give me a nice segue into how I was going to bring up exclusiveness to my boyfriends. She had to give us a blessing so we didn't die while some unknown force was trying to knock down the door to her throne.

We were about to face a true unknown.

Normally, that level of adventure would get my heart pounding and blood burning for a good fight, wanting to either limp away with a trophy in hand or go out with a glorious bang. The thrill of knowing I would be dancing on death's edge is what I lived for, what I based my entire personality around and how I got to be so good at being immune to the fear of death.

For the first time since I was a little kid, I was afraid of what was waiting for me in the dark.

I was terrified I'd fail Zane and Sias. That they would get hurt.

That I'd lose them again.

"I'm scared," I admitted, knowing that Zane could feel my turmoil through our bond, and Sias was no doubt feeling some thread rumbling. "I'm not used to feeling this way, and I kinda hate it."

"I would be worried if you weren't." Zane squeezed me a bit more. "We're up against a force we don't know and the stakes are high. You're going to need to trust us in order for this to work, hunter."

I felt a pang of hurt from that, my response a little sharper than I meant it to be.

"Of course I trust you."

"You need to trust us enough to not throw yourself to our defense," Sias added, Zane nodding. "You just got Zane back, so the wound is still healing. And I know you still hate that I made it to the ocean before you could pull me back."

"I failed you both once," I admitted, a dagger of shame splitting me down the middle. "I can't let that happen again. If something happens to either of you—"

"We will be at your side," Zane promised.

"Fighting with you," Sias added.

"You say that now." I forced myself to smile instead of begging them to stay behind where it was safe. "Let's see how you like me after this is all over."

They were my new drug, a high I could never escape. A sensation beyond anything I'd ever felt or would ever feel again.

Sure, having a Goddess bless me with her power was great, but have you ever been hugged by your vampire while your incubus peppered sweet kisses across your lips?

Nothing could beat that. Not a damn thing.

# TWENTY-TWO

"AND YOU'RE ABSOLUTELY sure this is going to work?" Barnaby examined the tiny piece of tech that was going to decide his fate. "This will last the entire trip through the void?"

Dex flexed her tongue through a veil of gum and blew a bubble, snapping it with her teeth before answering the fretting incubus. Her iconic, stoic, oni stare was back in place after she had gotten her silicon coven fan-girling out of her system.

"If my numbers are right."

"How often are your numbers correct?" Barnaby teetered his hand from side to side as if to weigh his odds of dying. "Do you have an average?"

"I have a lot of repeat customers," she answered. "Hard to have that if my tech is getting them killed."

Barnaby gave our necromancy altar a worried glance and swallowed.

"Could you definitively say your success rate is in the nineties? High eighties?"

Dex gathered up her gum and pulled a bit from one of her tusks.

"I used a coven enchanted life magic container and piggybacked off stolen tech from an insane multi-millionaire's facility while using secondhand, albeit high quality, tech in the basement of a black-market gang leader. I'd give your odds a *solid* fifty-fifty."

"Oh, Gods." Barnaby wrung his hands almost raw. "Gods, I knew I should have listened to my mother and gone into hospitality."

"Barns, she's fucking with you," I told him from where I was setting up. In order for us to set up a proper death altar, we'd had to relocate to a section of the club that still had some floor left we could write runes on. The main dance floor was too destroyed to use, so we had to make do with the beautiful jade mosaic tiles on the upper deck.

Marthas was *not* pleased.

"Plus, you'd be terrible at hospitality," I continued with Barns. "You called me a bloated tart for entering your store without knocking on three different occasions."

He summoned enough annoyance to overcome his fear.

"Well, it was rude, Dallas. Even barn animals knock."

"Uh-huh. Come hug your skull while we get the final pieces together. Dex, you got the kill switch ready?"

"You're damn right it's ready." She handed me her masterpiece, which looked like an electronic store had coughed up a hairball. Stripped wire coiled over a bundle of what looked like a hive of tiny batteries, all within a bundle of silver tape normally used to patch leaky pipes. In the center of said mess was a carefully constructed circuit board dotted with melted metal, the heart of which contained one of Malphie's teeth. Punched through the tape was a red flip switch capped with a solid piece of clear plastic.

"You'll have five seconds to throw it once you flip the switch," she explained as I looked over the mess of tech. "The radius should be ten feet, so try and funnel them together if you can."

"Ten feet?!"

"It's my guess," she defended. "It might go up to twenty, but I don't know without testing it, which we don't have the luxury of."

"What's the radius of the life wards you made for us?" Barnaby sassed, back to being stressed. "Does it only cover the top half of my body?"

Dex rolled her eyes, chomping her gum.

"It'll cover all of your body. It's a ward. That's how wards work."

"How long will it last in the void?" Austin took the device she held out for him, the repurposed flip phone case alive with the amber glow of life magic coursing through a contained system. The analog buttons were worn away from use, leaving faint ghosts of numbers over flickering rubber.

"My guess is five minutes, but I'm optimistic it's closer to seven."

Barnaby barked out a laughing noise that suspiciously sounded like hysteria.

"Five whole minutes? Well, thank God we're not strolling through somewhere *dangerous!* Dallas, should we stop for bloody ice cream on the way there?!"

"The pathway is open. It's a clear shot," I reminded him. "If we only have five minutes, I'll get us there in five minutes."

"You can stay behind, Barnaby." Austin pocketed his tech, refusing to be frazzled by the time constraint. "There's no reason for us both to risk the travel."

Barnaby straightened himself and inhaled his composure. His short, trimmed hair was smoothed back into place over his ram-style horns, and he fixed his bow tie that had gone crooked with his panic.

"No. I'll be joining you." He had the humility to look bashful. "Sorry for the theatrics. I was just...hoping for more allotted time for the ward, but I trust Dallas can get us there in time. I have no reason to doubt that he'll purposefully allow us to be swallowed by the infinite nothingness."

"Thanks for the vote of confidence, Barns." I couldn't have

been more sarcastic if I had tried, my eyes nearly rolling back into my brain when he just nodded along, missing it completely.

Zane placed my handy murder toy duffel beside me, freshly packed with all the weapons we could possibly want for our journey into hell. Sias had his stupid golden guns loaded with immolation bullets, while Austin had strapped all of his pilfered Saint's Army gear to himself.

"You don't have any swords?" I asked Marthas as he reappeared with a few sets of body armor, tossing a vest to each of us. I caught mine before it smacked me in the face.

"No," the big imp replied. "Because I live in reality and no one fights with swords."

Austin adjusted the sword strapped to his back, which further annoyed him.

"No one outside of insane, vampire hunting zealots fight with swords. Use a gun, like a normal person."

"But swords are way more badass," I said, like the amazing non-normal person I was.

"You'll live," Zane said as he helped Barnaby strap his body armor onto his chest. "Stop complaining. Plus, you have a sword in your bag."

"You're not the boss of me just because we're going steady now, butthole. I'll complain all I want, and I want two damn swords. Austin, I'll arm wrestle you for yours."

"Sure." He held up his right arm. "Look at that, I win by default."

"Gentlemen," Sias scolded coolly. "The clock is ticking and you're giving me a headache."

"You heard Daddy. Time to get rolling." I got my body armor on, looped my duffel over my shoulder. I picked up Funus from his place next to the altar and stuck him under my right arm. "Since Barns is going to be wrapped up in life magic for the ride, you gotta sit with me this time, Funus."

"I appreciate the lift. I'm a bit allergic to life magic. It gives me the terrible case of death." His eyes sparkled with the joke, quite proud of himself.

To make sure none of us spiraled away during the hopefully quick, and not at all deadly trip through the void, Austin attached a length of cord to each of our waists, threading it around our bodies and double knotting them for safe measure. Since I was the guide, the void train started with me and ended with Austin.

We were the worst looking parade you'd ever seen, and moved like a disjointed centipede that couldn't figure out which end was its ass.

(The ass end was Austin.)

"Barns, Austin. You ready?" I rotated to look over my two brothers, both unrelated by any biological tether but more blood than anyone I'd ever known. My army sibling had his soldier persona tightly in place, face placid and focused, weapons sprouting out from all angles. Beside him was my equally brave, but less capable of showing it, brother who was armed only with his ward and a look of solid nausea.

"I love you guys," I told them, which did nothing to change their expressions. "I can't imagine going into this without you."

Austin gave me a nod, touching his dog tags out of reflex. Barnaby burped a little from the turmoil in his gut.

I was incredibly proud of them both.

"Wilde," Marthas called as we stepped up to the altar. "You still owe me for all this shit. Come back alive or I'm going to take it up with your stupid fish."

"My fish will kick your ass, so be careful," I warned him. "But I'll make it back, Marthas. Thank you for everything."

"Fuck you, Wilde. This isn't charity. You're going to be working for me for a long time after this." He crossed his big arms and looked Austin's way. "Don't die, army boy. We got unfinished business too."

Austin didn't respond, but didn't argue against it either.

Dex and Kimi stayed near the stairs, curious enough to watch if the experiment was going to work but not sharing in the camaraderie enough to be part of the situation.

Ushen waved a goodbye from beside Marthas, holding the leftovers we'd had to politely decline to take with us.

"Good luck, Dallas Wilde. May luck follow you and keep your belly full."

Malphie came to Sias's side when he snapped, his fingers resting on the hound's big head.

He looked my way, eyes lilac with hues of silver. "Ready, pet?"

"I fucking hope so." I adjusted my duffel by shrugging my shoulder and held tight to Funus. Zane placed his hand on my shoulder, anchoring me into the moment.

"You're not alone," Zane said. "Don't get lost in your doubts. I'll guide you through the void like I've always done."

"Last time you 'guided' me through the void, I was thrown around like I was being knocked through a pinball machine."

"I got you there, didn't I?" the vampire snapped back. "Trust me, hunter."

"I do," I told him, holding back my smile so he knew I was being serious. "Completely."

"Good." Zane tugged my shoulder so he could steal a kiss. "'Cause I'll throw you in ass first if I need to."

"Promises, promises." I exhaled some nerves free through my nose and tossed a glance to Sias. "You got your threads all sorted, yeah? Keep us from sinking in case Zane's aim sucks?"

"I'm not going to let anything happen to either of you." Sias slipped his fingers into my hair at the base of my skull, and pulled me into a sweet, but quick kiss. "Now, stop arguing with us and listen to your vampire. We have a Goddess to save."

My heart fluttered like a nervous baby bird before it turned to stone, rattling around in my chest like a boulder tumbling down a mountain.

It was time to see if the Goddess was a deity who was trying to help, or if she was playing games mortals couldn't win. We were either going to open the void and fall to our deaths, or be thrown into a lair of nightmares.

You know.

Normal Wilde bullshit.

We had weapons, a kill switch, a basic plan that wasn't totally insane, and hopefully the blessing of a Goddess on our side. All that was left was to take the plunge.

And hopefully not die.

"Remember your mantra, acolyte," Funus said from my arm. "She's already opened the pathway for you. Now you just need to walk it."

I shut my eyes as Zane tightened his grip on my shoulder, Sias's fingers curling through my hair.

"Focus," Zane whispered, and I did what my vampire asked. I cleared my mind of the hive of doubt, the buzzing terror falling away as I followed my training. I repeated the mantra, searched for the crack into the void, and reached my hand out to take control of the magic.

The void waited like a boiling sea on the other side, crawling forward like a starving monster waiting to feed. Malphie's tooth sizzled as I felt the spider silk of magic trail over my fingertips, solidifying into heavy tendrils that wrapped themselves up the length of my arm. My fingers danced around the pull of the magic, tangling the strings around each knuckle before yanking them tight.

My eyes opened as a thunderous crack split from Malphie's tooth, ripping up like a tree sprouting from a seed. Funus's eyes flared as the tear splintered out in several directions, the branches of the tree reaching for the glass dome. The growing branches slowed and widened, folding back into the trunk so the tear could widen into a vertical split.

The magic wrapped around my arm pulled hard enough to make me jerk, my molars grinding as I fought against the surge of energy.

"Don't fight it," Zane whispered beside me. "Control it. You know the void, hunter. Remind it who's in charge."

That was a hell of a lot easier said than done, and I tossed out a few choice words about how I felt about the void, the Gods and especially Florence fucking Pierce for making us go through it. Icy tendrils tightened around my arm, squeezing until it was almost too painful to stand. My arm shook, sweat beading across my hairline, my jaw aching from how tight I was clenching my teeth.

Zane's fingers dug into my skin to anchor me further, and Sias's nails scraped down my scalp to remind me to breathe. In a breath, I had a bolt of clarity rip through me like a bullet.

The void was chaos. There was no such thing as bringing order to chaos. I would know, I'm also a chaotic, untamed asshole, and I only respond to the orders I want to. The void didn't want me to try and wrangle it into place like a controlling authority figure.

It needed to be treated as an equal. Treated with understanding and compassion.

It needed to be loved.

If the void needed someone to take care of it, I could be that guy.

I had some experience in what it was like to be taken care of.

My pulse calmed as I breathed, relaxing my grip to ease the burden and let the magic flow freely. The tendrils unwound themselves and slithered up over my shoulders, wrapping around my torso like a spider grabbing a fly. A chill shook me for just a moment, the pulse of the tear syncing with the calm rhythm of my heart.

When I opened my eyes, the tear had our pathway waiting.

"Well done, hunter," Zane whispered against my temple. "Well done."

"Stick close," I told my little parade. "I don't know how much the void is going to like what we do next, even if we do have an alliance right now."

"Saint bless me, keep me within your light..." Austin was

praying as we stepped forward. "Do not let us falter from your path, keep us from falling into madness."

"Madness is exactly where we're going." I cracked my neck. "On three," I warned my group, pulling Funus to my chest. "One…"

"Goddess welcome us into your arms, may darkness shield us…" Zane squeezed my shoulder.

"Say one for me too, Zane dear." Sias curled his fingers into my hair. "I'd like to meet this Goddess."

"Two…"

"Funus!" Barnaby called out. "I know we promised not to discuss what we were until after we survived this, but I must confess—"

"Three!"

I rushed the tear and dove inside, Barnaby's voice warping as he screamed, "I love you!"

The shock of falling into darkness nearly knocked my breath from my lungs, the pathway before us tilting like an unstable bridge with too much slack. My feet kicked like a cartoon trying to race back to a ledge, the chill of the void sinking into my bone like viper fangs.

Zane's grip on my shoulder vanished, sending a sharp stab of panic shooting up my spine. My amicable alliance with the void slipped from my fingers, little pieces of myself starting to peel away as death picked at me.

The pathway started to fall away, a sideways picture of hope fading as my legs began to slow down. It wasn't until a golden thread yanked tight around my ribs that I managed to get my feet back under me, a figure with twisted gold horns curling dark claws through the thread keeping me alive.

Floating like two amber eggs near me was Barnaby and Austin, pulling their way toward me using the cord connecting us. I motioned for them to stay back because I was sure that if they got too close, I'd be turned to dust, and then everyone would be extra fucked.

The beautiful horned creature—Sias—set me back on my feet, a tangle of thread pouring from my chest like he had sewn gold through my ribcage. It flowed like a tapestry between us, reflecting against the shattered void in all its dying splendor.

My heart vibrated against the threads as a set of glowing red eyes opened beside us, sparkles of gold disappearing through its smoky body. The shadow being, my dark guide with crimson eyes, placed his hand back on my shoulder.

Zane.

His grip wrung itself into my shirt and yanked me forward, pulling me down the pathway faster than I could comprehend. My feet pounded against the path that wasn't truly there, running as fast as I could as Zane fired us through the fractured void. The cord around my waist tugged, the glowing amber eggs behind me bouncing along like cans tied to the back of a car.

I was thrown forward like a football, flying out into a slap of humid air and the shrill sounds of cheerful songbird. Landing face first on the soggy soil of a cemetery was one of the best feelings of my damn life. I gasped through the mud in my mouth and stared up at the cloudy sky, amazed with how beautiful it looked when freshly arrived from the land of the dead.

Funus let out a cackle from my chest, grass stuck to his teeth.

"I'll admit, acolyte, I was getting a touch worried there!" the old skull admitted. "Goddess bless, I feel like my heart stopped beating—and I haven't had one of those in centuries!"

Barnaby and Austin had come flying out with me, landing with just enough grace to not end up with mud on their faces. Their life ward flickered like a dying light bulb and fizzled out with only seconds to spare.

"Five minutes my ASS!" Barnaby raged, standing to knock dirt from his knees. "Oh my days. I never want to do that again. I may have vomited in the void and I don't know if that means I'm cursed."

Austin was smiling like a fucking maniac, and we attempted a brotherly high five but missed because we were a little too dizzy from landing on our heads.

Malphie came bounding out of the tear after us, quickly sniffing around the cemetery for a good spot to mark his territory before the last remaining void creatures escaped the darkness.

Zane's body was still materializing into a solid mass as he stepped out of the void, glowing eyes of molten red finding me as he pushed his long hair back. Sias stepped through as the tear snapped shut, horns resetting and second set of eyes sealing shut as he smoothed down his vest with one, wide palm.

I knew that I needed to get into character and get ready for the fight of my damn life, but they had this whole "too cool to look back at the explosion" energy going on as the tear snapped shut, and I was so weak for that. Not to mention they were still a little scary looking from the void, and that was starting to be a real turn on for me.

I was swooning a little too hard and forgot to care that we needed to actually find the crypt and you know…save the world or whatever.

"This looks familiar," Zane said, ignoring my pining. "We came this way when we left the Silent Steps the first time."

"That's how we'll get in," Funus agreed. "Only the council knew about that exit. I doubt they would have gone in that way."

I pulled myself up straight and held Funus forward so he could give us directions, spitting more mud from my mouth as we walked.

"The last time I was here, I left this place with a killer headache and some extra trauma." I hopped over a gnarled root peeking out of the ground and made my way to Zane. "And we had our first kiss here."

"We did." He furrowed his brow at me when I wiggled mine at him. "You have mud in your teeth, hunter," Zane scolded. I sucked the mud free and spit to the side, and he wrinkled his nose.

"Better now?" I showed off my squeaky-clean smile, which should have absolutely worked but he was being a stingy jerk.

"Focus. Now's not the time."

"Uh, now is the perfect time. We're going into what could be our last battle together, at the same place we connected for the first time. This is exactly when we're supposed to have a glorious make out session to get the blood flowing for a fight."

"The blood flowing in the wrong direction." Sias didn't even look a little ashamed as I tossed him a sharp look. "Keep your head in the game, pet. I'd like to survive so we can pamper you properly later."

"Without so much mud." Zane motioned to his mouth.

"Buzzkill and prude," I pointed to Sias and Zane respectfully. "This is prime romance shit and you're passing it up. Just sayin'."

As we made the trek through the old cemetery, the clouds above us cloaked the sun and cast a dreary shadow over centuries' worth of tombstones losing their grueling battle with gravity. The trees growing among the peaceful dead refused to sprout leaves, ignoring the emerging spring just outside the gates. Soggy earth stuck to our shoes and the moisture hanging in the air stuck to our skin and frizzed Zane's pretty hair. This godforsaken place was unpleasant no matter the time of year, which had to be a miracle of nature that rivaled bringing the dead back to life.

The only one enjoying the horrible nature hike was Malphie, who was so delighted to run through the mud and chase squawking ravens that he was often just a black blur of manic fur zipping around graves.

He was a puppy trapped within the terrifying body of a void touched hellhound, and he reminded us of this fact multiple times.

Carved into the earth of a jagged cliffside, a hauntingly ancient mausoleum sat like a fossil exposed to the elements. The building was the color of smooth slate, flanked with teeth of banded rock that gnawed on the edges. Whatever prayers, blessings or warnings that had been carefully etched into the stone above the entrance were long gone, leaving behind only the vague notion that what lay within was not meant for the living.

A studded iron door barred the outside world from peeking inside, the simple looped handle held a spiderweb at the center.

"This is it," Funus announced as we arrived. "The passageway of the Thralls."

"Cheery name." I scanned the door, thrown off by its simplicity. "Is there a puzzle for this one like there was with the mural?"

"Of course," Funus said. "Only Thralls can open it."

"Ask a stupid question," I muttered to myself, feeling a little like a jackass for not navigating that one myself. I pulled my duffel from my shoulder and turned to Barnaby. "You remember the plan?"

Barnaby was very busy pulling at a strap on his body armor, face set in a mess of worried despair.

"Plan? Yes. Yes, set the concussion wards in case something tries to get out." He gave the side pocket his wards were in a pat, then shook some clarity back into his mind and asked, "What if you need to get back out this way? Isn't this the only way out?"

"I'll send Zane out first," I said, dodging him trying to swipe at me. "I'll knock three times on the iron door, then wait for you to deactivate the wards."

"Alright." Barnaby tugged at the strap like he was hoping it was going to pop out a prize. "Do you mind if I have a moment with Funus? Just a second. I swear."

"We don't really have time..." Austin started but passed Funus over.

"Say whatever you need to say, Barns. Then we have to go."

Barnaby took Funus with both hands, holding the skull up to face him eye-to-eye. No amount of squaring his shoulders seemed to help steel him enough to summon his words, and he swallowed so many times I thought maybe he had gulped down his tongue.

"Gods, I had this all prepared in my head," he exhaled, color blooming over his cheeks. "A grand speech, a well-crafted confession with immaculate prose and heartfelt exposition. I even wrote a poem, and I can't remember a single word of it."

*Thank God,* I thought, but I kept it to myself.

"I have no doubt it would have moved me to tears." Funus's eyes shone like polished topaz, voice as gentle and sweet as a springtime breeze. "May I speak, since you're still gathering your mental notes?"

Barnaby adjusted his shoulders again, readying himself.

"Please do."

"Barnaby Dractovon the Third, I am devastatingly in love with you," the skeletal head of the necromancy council said, without a hint of poetry or doubt. "And whilst I cannot promise what the future holds once we enter this crypt, I can vow that I will carry you with me until the Goddess sees fit to let me dissolve into obscurity within the void."

A wall of tears stacked in Barnaby's eyes, breaking past the levy and streaming down his cheeks once he found his breath again.

"Oh," he managed, sniffing back the threat of a sob. "That makes me so incredibly happy, and heartbroken that we're doing this in a muddy cemetery."

"We rarely get to pick the right moments to fall in love," Funus laughed. "But even in a muddy cemetery, I'm happy to say it again and again."

"I will demand you say it every day," Barnaby promised. "Every single day once you're back in my arms. I will wait right here for you, in this horrible place, destroying my nice shoes, until I see you again."

Funus's eyes danced like a shooting star streaking over the sky as Barnaby placed a gentle, chaste kiss on his forehead.

I took Funus back as Barnaby held him out for me, the pain in his eyes at feeling Funus leave his grasp almost too heartbreaking to see.

"I'll keep him safe, Barns," I promised. "I give you my word."

"Keep everyone safe, Dallas, yourself included." He dashed a tear from his cheek. "I'll set up the wards once you're inside."

"Once we're back, we're talking about how you never told me you're a 'third.' I have to tease the crap out of you for that," I tossed over my shoulder as we approached the door. "I can't imagine a whole linage of Barnabys."

"Feel free to leave that *charming* attitude behind on your way out," he called after us.

"He loves me," I told Austin, who rolled his eyes. "Sias? Ready to go?"

Sias snapped his fingers and summoned Malphie, the dog trotting over with manic puppy energy until his master signaled for him to calm. The happy, bright glow of his eyes dulled into a serious hue of smoky gray, and he was once again a beast of the void. Sias's cheeks grew two lines as his magic stirred, the same darkness cooling Malphie rising to the surface.

"Yes, pet." His eyes settled into hammered gold sizzling with red around the rims. "I'm at your service."

I was starting to develop a kink for seeing him ready to rip someone apart while dripping in black magic, and I made a mental note to ask about coming up with a void themed safe word if we made it back alive.

"If you tell me to 'focus' right now I'm going to kick you," I told Zane as he inhaled through his nose. "You *know* that he's hot right now."

"Whatever you're thinking right now, I agree. But we need to make it back alive to explore it," Zane said. "So...pay attention."

"Cheeky," I drawled, then rolled my shoulders and refocused back on the task at hand, pushing sexy Sias thoughts to simmer next to daydreams of kissing Zane in the cemetery. "Can you do the honors, Mr. Thrall?"

Zane moved to the door and grasped the handle, then hesitated.

"Hunter."

"Yeah?" I pushed around Austin to try and see what was causing the delay. "Is it stuck?"

In the doorway to death, standing under the forgotten prayers of long dead necromancers, my vampire kissed me. For just a few seconds, my world was grave flowers and rain dancing on the edges of a memory of when I held him close under a bright, full moon.

"Never say I'm not romantic again," he whispered against my lips.

I swallowed like a nervous Barnaby. "Got it."

Zane jerked the door open, the metal screaming in protest from being disturbed from its long slumber, and we descended into the unknown horrors waiting for us.

THE DOOR SEALING behind us resonated through the crypt like a dying heartbeat.

We were plunged into a darkness only a subterranean tomb could summon, and I fought down the primal urge to scream back at the emptiness before us.

"We don't have to go far," Zane told us, but I knew he was announcing it for my benefit. "I can guide us there."

Austin clicked on a small flashlight and aimed the beam across the walls, illuminating just enough to show us how far the narrow passage went. The light was swallowed up by depth which made my stomach curl in on itself a few more times.

"I fucking hate this cemetery." My shiver rattled Funus's teeth, and I secured him a little tighter against my ribs. "And I'm going to be vulnerable here and admit I'm not a huge fan of the dark."

Sias's hand came to rest on my back, a soft wave of calming charm magic kissing me just enough to keep me from holding my breath.

Zane reached out and took my hand, guiding it to his waistband for me to hold on to. "The exit connects directly to the council chambers, so we need to stay quiet."

Funus's eyes glowed against the rock as we moved, the

smooth surface polished like black mirrors. The chill of being inside the earth cut through the humid air lingering near the door, the smell of rain-soaked dirt and ancient dust sat in the back of my throat. Our symphony of careful, scuffled footsteps echoed through the darkness as my heart thundered in my ears, my grip on Zane's jeans nearly cutting into my palm. Austin's circle of light floated around as he scanned for dangers, letting it rest on the floor so we could see where to step next.

The Thrall's passageway descended like a drill of carved stone steps, the walls covered in murals of rituals and rights I didn't know. I got flashes of Thrall births from the void, the Goddess extending her hand out to rip the heart of her vampire from the darkness, only to place their ashes in urns at her throne. It was her army of Thralls, Funus had said, waiting for their Goddess to summon them again. That would have been pretty handy right about then. I remembered with explosive clarity how I had faired in trying to resurrect one of her ashen pets, only to have the phantom thing blow up and knock me ass over head in front of the council.

Fun times.

Austin's flashlight slid over the paintings in a passing interest, but he stayed vigilant to keep the glow on the steps so we didn't tumble down them.

"Funus?" I whispered, adjusting him in my arm. "The Goddess kept all the ashes of her Thralls, right? Did she keep the ashes of the council members too?"

"We were not cremated. Our heads were removed to serve on the altar, but our bodies were laid to rest in the lower rungs of the catacombs beside the urns of our Thralls."

"Hardcore," I admitted. "Where is the Goddess's door in regard to the main chamber where the council used to be?"

"The Goddess's door is a ritual that must be performed within the council's chambers," Funus responded softly. "They have started the ritual, but I have a feeling they haven't been able to 'turn the knob' as it were."

"Where will this passageway lead us in the council chambers?" Austin asked.

"Behind the council altar, behind a rune protected door." Funus swiveled his eyes up to us. "I know the incantation needed to open it."

"We can't all pile in at once, it runs the risk of someone spotting us," I told the group, keeping my white-knuckle grip on Zane. "I'll creep in, and assess the situation, then send a signal back on what's going on."

"How?" Austin flashed his light my way, likely to check for signs that I was messing with him. "You suddenly know telepathy?"

I squinted through the interrogation light.

"Kinda. Zane can read my emotions. If the room is full of grunts, I'll think about something sad, like when I thought Kevin had died. You'll know to hang back and wait. If it's clear, I'll think about something provocative and fun, like Zane in assless chaps." I cracked a grin at Sias's chuckle. "He gets it."

"You're an absolute idiot," the annoyed seeing-eye-vampire said. "But that's a solid plan."

"Is he being serious? You can read his emotions?" Austin let out a rush of air through his lips. "Tough break, man."

"You have no idea," Zane sighed. "How long do we wait if you see grunts?"

"Two minutes, or if you hear me scream, '"Oh shit.'"

"I'm not in love with this plan," Sias added, doubt weighing on his words. "That leaves you alone with an army of vampires."

"I have the kill switch," I reminded him. "My plan is to deploy it and have us rush in to finish them off once they're not as deadly. Facing them when they're brimming with bio-magic would be like rushing into a brick wall of teeth."

Sias pressed his palm against my back and slid it up to rest on my shoulder.

"I know you can handle yourself, pet, but don't be reckless. You often bite more than you can chew."

"Don't try and be a badass," Zane added. "You dying because you want to face a 'wall of teeth' alone will piss me off. I'll haunt you in the void."

"Aw. My boyfriends care about me," I practically sang.

"They both just called you irresponsible and dangerous," Austin pointed out, but I ignored him because I was too busy swooning.

It was only a few million more stairs before we reached the bottom, the open floor expanding out like a horseshoe of smooth stone around a statue of a kneeling Goddess. It was the first time I had seen her with both arms, one holding her scythe to her chest while the other cradled a heart in a skeletal hand.

Her face wasn't the stoic, soulless icon staring forward with apathy for the mortals desperate to learn her teachings. This was a deity of compassion and love, moved by the creation of her only true children.

This was the Goddess the way Thralls saw her, and it was transcendent.

"She doesn't look terrifying," Austin marveled in a reverent whisper. "Almost merciful."

"Death isn't terrifying or merciful," Zane corrected lovingly. "It simply is."

"This place is where the Thralls worshipped. It was only meant for them. We tread here respectfully, out of necessity only." Funus sounded like he was apologizing on our behalf to Zane. "The doorway is there, just beyond the statue."

Austin scanned the wall behind the statue at the curve of the horseshoe, his light bouncing back with the shine of the polished stone. There was no obvious door like the one leading into the crypt, which caused us to pause and second guess just where it was he was directing us.

"It's hidden," he assured us softly. "Magically sealed to keep outsiders away from this sacred place. Once I use the incantation, the wall will fall away and allow you access."

I let go of Zane's waistband and passed him Funus, adjusting the duffel on my shoulder.

"Remember, sad thoughts, stay back. Zane in assless chaps, all clear. We good?"

Austin pointed the light at each person so they could affirm, and so I could see Zane roll his eyes more clearly.

"Funus, do your thing."

Funus's eyes flared like the breaking dawn, his voice a haunting hush as it trailed over the black stone walls.

"*Pulvis et umbra sumus.*"

The stone before us dulled and cracked like peeling paint, falling away like the wall had been made of ash. It fell to the ground and vanished, leaving an angled doorway in its wake, like a coffin had been etched out of the stone.

The silvery glow from the fae fire died behind the empty council altar, the dust of the dead members still resting in neat piles. A pang of sadness bit at me when I remembered their deaths, remembered how they howled against Magnus's ignorance in their final moments.

I didn't miss that Austin looked away, no doubt feeling a similar, horrible feeling, only his involvement likely bit a little deeper.

The doorway was shielded by the tall altar, which meant I could sneak out without immediately getting spotted if I was careful. From where the door was, it was impossible to see past the alter, and only the glow of the fire flickered around the edges.

I glanced back at my boyfriends, brother and friendly skull, and motion for them to stay put before I crawled out of the coffin shaped doorway.

I crouched low, walking in a quick, hunched position as I pressed myself against the back of the dead council's altar. It was silent other than the heatless crackle of the fae flames lining the walls, the stone freezing as it touched my skin. The smell of rotting clothing and stale bone stuck to everything like mold.

I slid to the far end of the altar and peered around it slowly, sweat starting to drip from my temples even as the hairs on my arms lifted from the chill of the tomb. In the dancing shadows of the fae fire, I saw Florence Pierce sitting with her back to the altar, arms lifted and murmuring a prayer. Before her was a broad circle painted with blood, runes slashed all around in the same macabre ink. This was alarming for many reasons, but the main issue I had with the scene was that she was supposed to be very dead. Which meant either I had been absolutely flying on vampire blood and made up the whole vision, or something was sideways about the entire situation.

Above her, the resting bodies of dead necromancers stood in silent vigil in the catacombs, the tower stretching up into capped darkness.

Beside each body was a grunt vampire in an equally tranquil state, as if waiting for a silent instruction, staring forward with bleeding eyes of glowing malice. If I deployed the kill switch in the center of the tomb where Florence was, I'd have a shot of getting maybe the top row of grunts with the pulse. I'd need to get them to rush down to my level if this was going to work, but my mind was looping back to the same glaring detail missing from the entire scene.

The scythe.

The entire reason for us being there was gone, and that really threw a wrench in the whole damn operation.

I exhaled and sent back a pang of sadness to Zane, warning him to hang back. It also made me miss my fish, and his cute little face.

There would be time to dote over him later and I'd be feeding him all the bloodworms he could possibly handle, but for the time being, I had to get those damn vampires down to my level so I could nuke their stupid bio-magic. I clipped the kill switch to the front of my body armor and pulled my gun from its holster. Yes, a sword would have been much cooler, but I had to keep my distance if I was going to have a shot at surviving this. I was disappointed too.

I took a knee and pressed my shoulder to the altar, peeking

around a bit more so I could try and line up a shot. One good bang, and hopefully she'd get pissed enough to send her army after me so we could zap their tech and I could unleash my secret weapons. Once the grunts were handled and Florence was whining about how I ruined her expensive tank top, we'd be able to convince her to cough up the scythe.

I'm sure Sias would love to get back into "finger painting" again.

Florence swayed as she whispered her prayers, long hair dancing as she sang in hushed desperation. Her fingers moved like she was trying to tickle the wind, her voice haunting as it flittered about the silent tomb. I eased further from my hiding spot to line up my shot, staying low to the ground to try and stay hidden from the grunts. They stared forward in one direction, still as death, nothing but muted hunger behind their melting eyes.

I held my breath, and aimed for her shoulder.

My finger had just started to tighten on the trigger when I saw a flash of red and the barrel of my gun fell off and clattered to the ground.

My reality struggled against the shock of the moment, my body stuck in slow motion as I jerked back, a large body with glowing red eyes lifting from where they had been waiting for me.

Hei stood like a mountain, a fanged sneer slicing across her face as she twisted the scythe in her grip.

She spoke low and vicious, blood red eyes stabbing into me with deadly intent.

*"Pulvis et umbra sumus."*

I'm not proud of how quickly I tried to run away from the big, scary oni woman holding the Goddess's scythe, but I feel like it would be dishonest to downplay the level of *oh shit* I felt when seeing her. The first few steps of my attempted escape were more of a crawl, my hand having to catch me as I surged backward in a full panic. My feet slid on the ground from the lack of friction on the slick stone, making my rotation awkward and terribly slow. My duffel fell from my shoulder and was stuck in the crook of my bad arm, the weight of it tilting me a little off balance.

I tried to bolt back to safety, but it was too late.

I had just enough time to see the panicked horror in everyone's eyes as the door sealed shut in a snap.

My escape and backup were now locked behind a solid stone wall I didn't have the power to open, and I had a feeling neither could Funus.

I stumbled to a stop once I was staring at a slab of defeat, and spun back around on my heels to face the devil rounding the altar. She moved like a wraith, a striding confidence only an unnaturally evil and powerful thing could have. The blade of the scythe dripped with the silver of the fae fire, her fingers curled over the bone handle with the relaxed ease of a trained fighter.

I took a measured step backwards and tossed out my best fake laugh, juggling my duffel so I could try and get inside of it. Having two hands in this moment would have been fantastic, because it's hard as fuck to wrangle a duffel with a stump.

"This isn't the bathroom. You take one wrong turn in the damn place and end up totally lost."

"Dallas Wilde." She twisted the blade as she walked, one thick braid tossed over the splatter of blood that had dried like rust across her chest. "Thank you for being predictable enough to come here."

"I think you are the very first person to say I'm predictable," I told her. "I have been trying to grow more as a person, and they say routines help with that."

"I will chase you down if you make me," she warned placidly. "Otherwise, you can come willingly and with dignity."

"That highly depends on what you're about to pitch." I slashed my zipper open and started digging around. "Because I'm usually open to try new things, but I feel like you're going to say something batshit insane."

Hei twisted the blade in her fingers, the flames sliding across the curved belly of the blade.

"The Goddess needs your blood to answer my call. I will kill you quickly, and she will answer. Then I will take her place as Death."

My fingers wrapped around the hilt of my sword inside my duffel.

"Yeah, that's about as batshit as I was expecting." I pulled it from the duffel and adjusted my grip. "I'll pass."

Hei pulled the scythe to the side, stance widening as she planted herself like a boulder in front of me. The dancing flames behind her threw her into shadow, only her glowing Thrall eyes pierced through the darkness. Her oni magic made them seem like they were on fire, raging flames licking the top of her head while her tusks sharpened.

Hei was terrifying enough as the only non-human Thrall that had ever existed, she didn't need to punch it up. She was a brick wall of trained muscle and deadly ambition, the scythe fit her grip like it had been made for her.

She didn't give me time to be afraid or to come up with a plan on how I was going to try and get around her. Hei moved like a stampede, thunderous and overwhelming as she surged toward me.

I swung my blade as she neared, slashing to draw her backward and give me room to maneuver, but she simply rotated away like a parent avoiding the flailing of a wild toddler. The undead oni spun the Goddess's scythe and hit my blade with the long hilt, deflecting my blow with such force it nearly ripped my weapon from my grip.

My arm screamed from the reverberation of the deflection, shoulder burning as I brought my blade up to catch a brutal swing aimed for my head. My stance was knocked off balance, my feet desperate to keep ground but forced to stagger backward. Her wide, bare foot lifted and kicked me square in the chest, sending me crashing back into the sealed stone wall while my lungs shriveled up like raisins.

Hei descended on me, eyes burning and blade swung back

ready to cleave me in a sideways slash, my air deprived lungs burning as I tried to inhale. I lifted my duffel as she swung down, catching her wrist with the bulky belly of my bag of murder toys. She grunted in annoyance but it gave me a sliver of an opening to take my shot. I kicked out and connected with her hip, rotating her sideways to free up enough room for me to give her a fantastic slash across her belly and up to her shoulder.

The cut would have her guts attempting to burst from her belly unless she got some healing from Florence, which I hoped would be the upper hand I needed.

Blood bloomed across her tunic style vest, but her anger made her mouth fill with shark teeth as she bore them at me.

My duffel was ripped away from my arm and thrown, my second attempt at gutting her had my only good hand trapped in a vise grip of thick, strong fingers. Hei twisted her hand, sending a searing line of pain from my wrist up to my elbow until my sword went clattering to the ground.

I threw my free elbow at her face, tried to kick at her kneecaps to force her down or backward, but she took the blows in order to get close enough to slam her forehead into mine. The knock to my head had me flirting with unconsciousness, a blast of painful, dazzling stars erupting through my vision as my brain rattled around inside my skull. My knees buckled as she grabbed my throat, closing off my airway as she dragged me across the floor. I kicked at her feet and tried to pound my fist on her arm, my lungs still fighting to recover and my head swimming.

Blurry dots of silver danced around me as I was dragged to the center of the crypt, a vague outline of Florence swinging her arms around comically hovered just within sight. Only when I was dumped onto the floor was I allowed to pull in a choking inhale of breath, my hand holding where my head connected to the ground.

The smell of dust and old bone got caught in the back of my throat as I gasped for air, the familiar, metallic scent of blood piercing through as I blinked focus back into my eyes. Florence was sitting a few feet away, legs crossed over each other with her arms in the air. A fountain of dried blood stained a stripe down her body starting at her throat, which had been split all the way around. Her lifeless eyes stared forward like icy orbs, colorless lips murmuring nothing.

Hei had killed the being she was tethered to and somehow still lived. Knowing how intense and intimate the necromancer-vampire bond was, I couldn't fathom how Hei had managed to do something so undeniably vicious. Every ounce of Florence's pain, agony and fear would have lanced through her like a searing knife, but the oni vampire seemed immune to feeling much of anything.

I was not a fan of Florence Pierce and was happy she was a zombie, but the whole situation still made my skin crawl.

Forcing my eyes away from what used to be the badass CEO of ReNew, I scanned my surroundings for my duffel. It had been thrown not far from me, the contents peeking out from the open zipper.

Hei had dropped me in the middle of the circle surrounded by runes, her looming figure standing over me. The blade came to rest at my throat, and she kneeled down to pluck the kill switch off the front of my armor.

The device was examined before being thrown over her shoulder, the pieces of it shattering and flying in multiple directions.

"This is sad," she mocked dryly. "I wanted you to be more of a challenge."

"You're gonna be dumping your guts from that slash soon," I reminded her with a grin. "Judging from the blood covering your stupid tunic, you don't have much longer before you pass out, and your necromancer is kind of very dead. How the hell you're even still alive is a damn mystery to me, but maybe you're just too shitty to die."

"You speak as if you know what's going on. It's a flaw of humans. You really believe you are smarter than the rest of us."

She pushed to her feet and delivered a swift kick to my ribs that kept me from standing, forcing me to curl in to protect my torso and deflect any more attacks.

"God, you are such a prick," I groaned through my teeth.

She unfastened the belt that held her tunic vest shut and let it fall, pulling the clothing from her broad shoulders to hang at her waist. The slash I had given her was healing quickly, the muscles knitting together like a fastening cocoon of flesh and sinew. Within her chest, I saw a pulsing light that thumped along with her heartbeat, the glow a haunting shade of green and purple that made her ribs stand out against her skin.

"I am more than your pathetic human necromancy, Dallas Wilde. My heart beats with fragments of old and new magic, technology weaving together powers of a demigod."

"You have a fucking mechanical heart?" I winced up at her glowing ribcage and shuddered. "Is that why you killed her? What the hell did she do to you?"

"A heart sleeve, comprised of necromancers' ossified feldspars to give me the power of a Thrall, death opal to keep me healed and stabilize my body so the magic can't rip me apart, a few patented techniques involving magic feedback loops and enhancements." She set the scythe down and let the shine of the fae fire dance across the blade. "I'm everything a vampire Thrall is and everything an oni warrior could be. And I will be a Goddess."

"Why not do something more fun, like take over the world like a cartoon villain?" I pitched. "Being a Goddess sounds boring as hell."

My plan, albeit a shitty one, was to try and keep her talking while I attempted to make a mad dash for my duffel. I was running low on options at the moment, and knew that if I didn't try something desperate and stupid soon, Hei was going to dice me up and throw open the doors to the Goddess's realm.

"If being a Goddess sounds boring to you, Dallas Wilde, we truly have nothing to talk about."

"Nooo, no, we have tons to talk about. Tell me about Florence. She was a real piece of work, right? Did you two date long or...?"

Hei rubbed at her eyes like she was trying to massage the annoyance from them, a move I was used to seeing, so I took my shot and bolted. I rushed for my duffel to grab whatever I could get my hands on, hoping for the acid projectiles or maybe a left-over concussion ward I could throw in her face. I had grabbed the handle just as I was getting my feet under me when I felt an intense pressure slam into my kidney.

My movement stopped as I was jerked backward, the death grip I had on my duffel had the bag falling open to let a few more of my goodies escape. I tried to fight past whatever had grabbed me, when I noticed I hadn't been grabbed so much as impaled.

The curve of the Goddess's blade arced out from my belly and around my hip, nearly slicing me in two.

It didn't hurt. I think I was beyond anything like that hurting.

I had skipped the line from agony to complete shock, because there was no way in hell I was going to survive it.

"Crap," I muttered, hating that it was probably going to be the last thing I ever said. Hei had given me the worst belly button piercing ever, and had used it to throw me back into the center of her stupid ritual with my duffel still gripped in my hand.

The blade was ripped from my back, which gave my body permission to start bleeding out every ounce of blood I had in my body.

I hit the ground like a bag of wet defeat, my hearing starting to take on a watery, muffled warp as I started to slip into dying.

Hei said something, probably like how I bleed pathetically or something, so I used the last bit of my strength to lift my arm to flip her off. Except it was the arm with the missing hand, so she didn't see the phantom middle finger.

Goddamnit.

Something in me made me try and shake an item loose from my duffel, my last dying attempt to make the situation not completely suck.

But I was cut almost in half.

I was bleeding out at an alarming rate.

And anyone who could help me couldn't get to me.

I was pretty screwed, and not in the fun way. I was going to die, for good this time, taking Zane with me to the void and leaving Sias alone and heartbroken. I was going to kill one of the men I loved, and abandon the other. Barnaby would never forgive me. Austin would blame himself. Kevin would shit on my grave.

I would never get to tell them how much I loved them. How much they meant to me. How I was a better person because of them, how desperately I wanted to love them back with everything I had.

Something rolled out of the duffel as I shook it and bumped against my head. There was a crack along the side that was splintering into sharp lines up to the lid, the gray contents inside tumbling along as it rolled.

My poor dying brain had to spin to put the pieces together, and remember why I knew what that glass jar was.

It was Zane's ashes. I hadn't packed them. I hadn't been sure what to even do with them. For some reason they were there, rolling into my face in a breaking jar while I bled out on the crypt's floor.

I began to feel a thundering boom radiate through the room, my vision developing little black dots that swam around like hungry gnats. Hei's voice was bouncing off the walls as she commanded her entry into the void, pacing and raging, white knuckles wrapped around the bone handle of the scythe.

The tips of my fingers were numb as I touched the lid of the jar, picking at a piece of tape stuck to the top of it. There was something stuck under the clear strip, trapping it against the lid like a fossilized bug in amber.

Who would have stuck tape to Zane's lid? Kind of rude. The jar felt sacred to me still, even with the vampire walking around again. No one should be sticking crap to his ashes.

God, I would have killed for some water. I was so thirsty.

I got my fingernail under the tape and peeled it back, bringing the strip close to peer at what was stuck to the adhesive side. My tongue was stuck to the roof of my mouth, vision darkening as my body began to shut down. The chill of death was crawling over me like tendrils, and I felt safe.

It was a bloodworm. That's what was stuck to the tape on Zane's ashes. I tried to laugh but I couldn't seem to put air back into my lungs. A damn bloodworm.

Kevin.

It was Kevin who'd put Zane's ashes into my bag, that cheeky little fish. Why the hell would he do that? What could I possibly do with a jar of dead vampire ashes? Throw them in Hei's face as a distraction? That might have worked when I wasn't bleeding to death, but it certainly wasn't going to do me much good now.

My eyelids were so heavy it was hard to keep focus on the jar. The darkness tunneling my vision had grown so solid it felt like I was peering into the void out of my peripherals. I thought I saw them ripple.

I thought I saw the Goddess beside me, thought I heard Zane's voice whisper to me.

Thought I saw the flick of a fish's tail.

The tendrils pulling me into the void changed course, traveling from my chest to my arms as I slowly flexed my hand. Death magic flowed from the darkness in my vision, bleeding out to meet my command. The palm of my hand was heavy with ice, the wisps of spider silk tightening as I spoke to the ashes.

*You said you could always find me.*

My heart was slowing down. My limbs heavy. My hand held on to the slippery tendrils of magic.

*Find me now.*

*Find me now.*

*Find me —*

# TWENTY-FOUR

THE GLASS SHATTERED, ashes churning up into the air like they were propelled by an unseen flame. The tendrils in my hand squeezed, and I held on with the last ounce of strength I had left. The darkness surrounding me rippled out like I had thrown a stone across the surface. I felt the Goddess put a hand on my shoulder.

Zane's ashes moved like a living painting, swirling and crashing together before solidifying into one final brushstroke. A vapor began to pour from it, a black cloud exhaling from the ashes like smoke out of the maw of a dragon. It crawled across the floor and slithered like a snake, lifting up into the form of a man with glowing red eyes as it found its prey.

The shadow descended on Hei like a ghost, wrapping her in a headlock as its body found its physical form. Zane snarled, skin ashen and too pale, eyes fully red and starved since his necromancer was so close to dying.

Hei tried to scream a command but her throat was sealed from Zane's grip, her blade spinning to try and slash at his legs. The blade nicked him, and ichor fell from the cut.

He was dying. Fading quickly.

But we weren't dead yet.

Zane inhaled through his teeth, his colorless lips and gaunt features making him look like a ghoul that had just crawled from the grave. When he roared out his command, his voice was twisted and broken, but deadly firm in its conviction.

"Don't you dare die, hunter. We're not done yet." He set his jaw and turned toward the sealed stone door, unlatching the lock with a low, growling, *"Pulvis et umbra sumus."*

Hei slammed her elbow back into Zane forcing him to buckle, landing a solid blow to his temple with the hilt of the scythe. She swung the blade up to lop off his head when three very fantastic shots punched through her torso and shoulder, igniting into a series of tiny fires from the holes they made.

Sias cracked off a few more rounds as he rushed from the newly opened door, golden pistols exploding with rounds as he forced her backwards with his shots. Malphie lunged from the door, jumping off the altar to try and snap his jaws around her neck but caught the scythe's handle instead. She used it as a barrier between herself and his jaws, screaming as more immolation bullets tore into her skin.

Austin circled from the other side, rushing to aid me while Sias kept the insane Thrall busy. Horror crumpled his face when he saw me, the severity of my injuries freezing him in mid kneel.

"Dallas...Saint's Light..."

"Zane," I managed, heart struggling to beat. "Blood."

Austin rushed to Zane and got him up, looping his arm over his shoulders to help drag him to my side. Zane was shriveling before my eyes, his mass shrinking against bone like he was being mummified in real time. His palm rested on my brow as he sank his fangs into his wrist and tore, oily, black blood dripped in coagulated crystals from the wound.

"Drink," Zane coaxed. "Please, my love. Please hang on."

My vision had failed when he spoke, my heart giving one last, tired beat right as the thick blood slid across my tongue.

I started to fall into the void, dipping backwards into the darkness to see the cracked seal Hei had created. She hadn't been able to get the door to open by invitation, but that hadn't stopped her from trying to force her way in.

The door was broken. Barely hanging on. One more solid push from the unnatural Thrall wielding the Goddess's key would fling the door wide open.

I felt my heart surge back to life, felt my body light up as Zane's blood ripped me from the void's embrace. My first gasp after death burned my throat and made me gag, but it had nothing on the absolute nightmare that was feeling my cleaved body heal itself.

"What the hell is happening?" Austin demanded as he watched me flop around from the healing process. "Why the hell are you *laughing*?!"

"It tickles so bad!" I managed through my giggling agony. "Oh my God, just kill me again! I hate this!"

Malphie yelped as Hei sent him flying into some of the catacombs, his body bouncing off a stone crypt. She roared, eyes flaring in anger and terrifying oni magic, and turned her gaze up to her waiting horde of grunt vampires.

"Kill them! Leave the necromancer for me!"

The grunts snapped to life and began to move, a surge of magic starting to bombard against our magic blockers like an unnatural storm.

"Oh no!" I whined through my giggles. "Sh-she broke the kill switch!"

"Fuck," Austin hissed, taking a few shots at the grunts as they began to scramble down the sides of the catacombs. "Our blockers aren't going to hold long."

"This is so bad!" I laughed, scrubbing my eyes free of tears to find Zane. He wasn't a mummy anymore, didn't look like a ghoul that had crawled from a grave, but he did look pale and weak from how close to death we had gotten. I reached up and brushed his hair back, regaining enough control over my snickering to take a measured breath.

"Zane," I said, swallowing. "You look like shit."

"Likewise." He smiled weakly and pulled me upright. "I don't think I'm going to be much help, hunter. I don't think I can stand."

"It's okay. Stay down." I kissed his lips before standing, knees a little wobbly.

"Deploy the kill switch, Dallas!" Sias screamed as he shot down a few grunts, switching to another weapon when one of his golden pistols ran out.

"We don't have it!" I told him, snatching a gun off Austin and taking down two more. A push of heavy compulsion magic nearly had me turning my aim to Austin, and I had to shake my head to fight against it. Austin swung his gun to Sias before forcing his arm up to shoot at the ceiling, sweat beading on his brow.

"Dallas, my blocker is failing," Austin admitted, voice strained from the effort.

"Run, hunter. Maybe I can pull them to me..." Zane was saying, trying to get to his feet but was too weak to stand. "Please, run. Get Sias and run."

"No. *No.*" I took a few more shots, keeping myself between the horde and Zane. Austin flanked Zane's other side and reloaded, shaking his head as more magic pulled at him.

"Dallas, if I shoot you, know it's mostly because of the compulsion and charm magic, not because you're an asshole." Austin fired a few more shots, his aim getting worse. "But you are a bit of an asshole for dragging me into this."

"Love you too," I told him, my mind starting to swirl. "For what it's worth, I think you and Marthas would be good for each other. Sorry I was weird about it."

"Shut up," he said, sounding tired. "But thank you."

We turned at the same time, pointing our guns at each other's head, pulled to turn on each other by the overwhelming need to obey the magic surrounding us by the grunts. Our hands shook, faces twisted into a desperate resolve as we fought against the pull.

"I wish...you weren't...a good shot right now..." I hissed.

"Yeah." He ground his molars, hand flexing around the gun. "You're kind of fucked."

The magic gripping me slipped, surged back with the force of a sledgehammer, then fell away again like someone had cut the power completely. Austin and I both immediately pulled our guns away from each other and turned our attention back to the grunts.

They had stopped in their tracks, some still climbing down the walls while others staggered forward and fell to their sides. They twitched and hissed, eyes flickering like the wiring had gone bad.

"Sias," Zane breathed, pushing my hip. "Go. Get to him."

I moved as Hei realized at the same time what was happening. Sias had his hands out, the inky stains present when he used his dark magic had twisted his elegant hands into sharp claws that curved like hooks. His horns had twisted up and branched out like thorns, the gold melting into the cracks at the tips. Black ichor poured from his second set of eyes which were blown wide, rimmed in gold and white.

The hold he had over the grunts was powerful, his void touched charm magic twisting him as much as it controlled them. He fell to one knee, his hands starting to shake as he fought to keep control.

It was a temporary hold, and one I was terrified might change him for good. I had to make it fucking count.

"Austin, take them out while they're fish in a barrel!" I screamed as I rushed for Sias, trying to close the gap before Hei could get to him.

Hei charged him, scythe swung back to sever the problem getting in the way of her goals. I wasn't going to let this psycho hurt Sias, or get her damn hands on Zane. If she wanted a fight, she was going to have to go through me.

No one was going to hurt my boyfriends, especially not some backstabbing blowhard that used to sling overpriced supplements.

I was out of weapons, out of ideas, and had just a few minutes before everything went to shit. I was literally a one-armed man with the luck of a broke gambler, fueled by the overwhelming need to keep everyone I loved safe so I could get back to my fish.

And save the world, I guess.

Hei hit the ground as I tackled her like a raging bull, my shoulder connecting to her ribs and lifting her off the ground a few inches. I felt something pop, and it stung like I had just aggressively hugged a wall, but the grunt of pain she made was absolutely worth it. Her big fist landed on my back a few times, her knee crashing up like a tidal wave to knock my organs around as I scrambled to get the upper hand.

She nearly threw me off her more than once, her sheer might almost enough to use me like training weights as we grappled. I took two sharp blows to the ribs, another to the jaw that cracked a molar free, but I managed to use my knee to pin one tree-trunk arm to the ground so I could land a few good hits myself.

"That's for Zane! And for hurting Malphie! And for stealing my damn scythe! And for stabbing a one-armed man!"

Her face was made of something stronger than iron, my knuckles breaking skin but hardly knocking her senseless like I had hoped.

"Hunter!" Zane called out, snapping my attention to him. He was holding Sias on the ground as he convulsed, the grunts around us starting to snap back awake as Sias lost control.

"Dallas, do something!" Austin called out. "My blocker is fucking dead!"

"Get to them!" I begged Austin, pointing to Zane and Sias. "Please, keep the grunts off them as long as you can!"

Austin rushed to them, his feet trying to trip over themselves as the bio-magic from the grunts started leaking out from Sias's hold. Zane shut his eyes and whispered a prayer I couldn't hear as he tried to keep Sias from knocking his head into the floor.

Hei laughed as I panted, desperate to get to Sias and Zane to keep them safe, horrified that Austin was losing the battle. My momentary distraction was all she needed to regain her strength, my hold on her failing as she wrenched an arm free to slam a row of sharp knuckles into my jaw. My surroundings spiraled clockwise as I pitched to the side, too dizzy to immediately jump to my feet again.

Hei rose like a mountain, unfolding her shoulders, blade spinning in her grip as she moved like a landslide to the ritual circle. The floor cracked from the middle of the blood painted circle, spreading out like a web dancing in the light of the far fire. The door was shattered, bits falling away as the veil between realms began to thin.

Hei had done it.

She had won.

The Goddess's throne was just ahead, and I had no cards left to play.

"They're going to die because of you." She grinned, teeth stained in blood. "You were never meant to have this scythe, you damn fool. You aren't her chosen, her *champion*. You were just a stepping stone to my ascension, and I will make sure all of your souls are ripped into pieces when I have control of the void."

The scythe caught the light as she gripped it, the blade throwing back the glow of the fae fire. It reminded me of the moon gleaming off its surface the night I kissed Zane, the night I realized the damn thing had been in my chest the whole time. It had been part of me for so long, waiting to be unleashed when the time was right.

When I was ready to be a necromancer worthy of wielding it.

That scythe was *mine*.

My chest warmed with the memory of the moonlight, the kiss, the release of doubt and fear of allowing myself to be something more than the scared kid running from his past. I was never afraid of death, but I sure as hell had been afraid of living.

Not anymore.

There was a knock against my sternum as the handle of the scythe began to turn, the sections twisting and aligning despite Hei's grip. Her face pinched, confusion furrowed her brows as the scythe jumped in her grasp.

"What the hell is happening?" she hissed through her fangs, her glowing heart starting to hammer against her chest. It pulsed in the undeniable beat of fear, each thump blinking faster than the last.

I grinned as the handle clicked into place.

"I'm taking my scythe back."

The reunion between myself and the Goddess's key was a dramatic one, as to be expected. Hei's fingers lost control of the wild weapon as it flung itself into me, knocking me back across the floor as it slammed into my chest. It was a lovely, familiar sight to see the handle sticking out from my chest again, and the soundtrack of Hei screaming as the cracked door sealed shut again made it all the sweeter.

I didn't have time to savor the moment, nor whine too much about it kicking my ass in front of everyone, because there was still the pesky matter of the swarm of grunts trying to kill us and a Thrall who wanted me dead.

I rose to my feet and grabbed the handle, yanking the scythe free of my chest and spinning the blade in my grip. The connection I had to the blade was instant, the surge of power from the Goddess healing all my fractures and easing the bruises left behind from our fight.

I rolled my shoulders and popped my neck, smiling at Hei.

"Ha," I teased. "Mommy likes me best."

Hei being the sore loser she was, stormed toward me with her head down, fists balled and ready to clobber me into the dirt.

"You piece of *trash*. You interloper! I'll crush your bones under my heel!"

Zane gave a sharp whistle to get her attention before he delivered a brutal haymaker to her temple, sending her crashing to the ground in a dizzy mess. My vampire was back to full strength, body no longer withered from the drain of my death or his blood loss, eyes fiery and fangs bright, bared and ready for a fight.

"On your feet," Zane spat at the woman. "I'll show you how a true Thrall fights."

Hei may not have been a true Thrall, but she was bloodthirsty enough to be feared. She barreled into Zane with everything she had, her blows punctuated with the roars of crushed dreams. Her oni magic made her appear to be flaming with white hot fire pouring from her mouth, a fire breathing dragon clashing against the renewed Thrall.

Zane blocked her attacks and knocked her back with a few of his own, their strength warring storms raging among the audience of the dead.

Austin's gunfire slowed as he retreated back to me, exhausted and slick with sweat and vampire blood. The grunts that had been staggering toward us had regained their fluid movement again, moving with unnatural grace and poise as they swarmed the lower level of the catacombs. My grip on the scythe eased when I noticed their eyes had turned a placid gold instead of melting molten red.

They descended upon their old master, grabbing her arms and legs as she tried to keep swinging at Zane. She tore through a few of them, knocking them down with a few swings as they latched on, but her waning strength was eventually toppled at the sheer number of bodies pinning her down.

Sias came to my side, horns back to their normal, dark spiral with his fingers dipped in ink, no longer hooked claws. His main set of eyes were pastel purple and calm, the second set glittering gold.

"They're mine now," he purred. "I won't keep them like I did Malphaslanexus, of course. Not in the market of keeping more than one vampire."

Said void hound returned to his master's side, limping a little from the fight but otherwise unharmed. His butt wagged as Sias placed a hand on his big, skeletal head.

"I heard that," Zane called over the dogpiled Hei. "I'm not *kept*, Sias."

"Not yet." Sias tossed him a wink with one of his lower eyes.

It was hot. I was into it on a spiritual level with full plans on demanding Sias expand on that statement and also wink at me with his cool void eyes.

For the time being, because it was the responsible thing to do (scary, right?) I moved to stand before the power-hungry monster that had tried to kill us and upend the balance between life and death.

Hei was on her knees, the grunts holding her arms to the side with enough pressure on her shoulders to force her into a deep bow.

"You little bastard…" Hei was hissing from the ground, blood dripping from her lips. "You ruined decades of planning, of ass kissing that horrible woman. You ruined my ascension to godhood."

"Yeah, I'm not sorry about that," I said. "You're kind of an asshole."

"You're short-sighted," she spat, tired and downtrodden. "You could have been a God. Instead, you're just her lap dog, her pet."

"No, I'm his pet," I pointed to Sias with my blade, then motioned to Zane. "And I'm his hunter. I know what I am and who I belong to, and I'm going to go home to the people that I love, and my cute as hell fish. But before I do that, I'm going to send you to explain yourself to the Goddess. I think she'll be very happy to see you."

Hei lifted her chin, her magic falling away so I could see the soul deep exhaustion behind the false vampire magic.

"I'm ready to face her. Make it swift and don't miss."

I owed Hei nothing, not a goddamn thing after the pain and anguish she put me through, but I did as she asked. My blade sang through the air as I freed her head from her neck in one slice, the Goddess's key ending her reign as a false Thrall. Her body fell into ash so fine it disappeared into smoke, leaving nothing behind for a proper burial. The Goddess would not allow even her physical form to stay behind.

Left in the wake of her disintegration was the device used to create her, a silicone band housing the brilliant magic that had given her a false vampire life. Where Florence had been was a matching contraption, binding them together in death.

There was nothing left of Florence Pierce either. Gone forever with her cruel, horrible Thrall.

I relaxed my grip on the scythe, inhaling as the weapon found its home back in my chest again. It wasn't as painful and dramatic as the reunion, but it did rock me back on my heels a bit when it wormed its way back into its resting place against my heart.

I fell into Zane's arms as he moved to my side, resting my head on his shoulder as Sias curled himself around me and squeezed. Zane held us both, pulling us tight so he could savor the victory. The chill of the tomb was replaced by the warmth of my men, their hearts beating in time with my own for a few, blissful moments. My world was amber and tobacco, grave roses and rain, all traces of death and dust forgotten.

"That really sucked," I said into Zane's shoulder, making him laugh.

"Understatement, but yeah."

"We need a proper vacation, gentlemen. Something with goddamn sunshine. Maybe a beach, and definitely alcohol. So much alcohol," Sias exhaled, chin on my shoulder.

"Amen," I agreed, burrowing deeper into Zane's arms for a few more seconds before forcing myself to peel away. I grabbed Austin by the arm and pulled him into a tight hug, surprised that he didn't shove me away. I got a full three seconds of brotherly bonding before he released me and gave my chest a solid pat.

"That's super fucked by the way." Austin nodded to my chest. "I could have gone a lifetime without seeing a scythe absorb into your chest. I'm going to have more nightmares, so thanks for that."

"Oh, you're so welcome. If you want some extra trauma, I can make out with Zane and make it pop out again. Where are you going? Austin, did you want to see it come out?" I cackled as he flipped me off over his shoulder, walking toward the stone door we came in through.

I turned my attention back to the grunt vampires lingering by where Hei had died.

"What do we do with the grunts?" I asked as I grabbed the devices left behind from the two evil bastards.

Sias hummed in thought. "I think I'll have them walk out into the sun, what do you think?"

"Solid plan." I smiled at him. "Make them do something funny first, like a coordinated dance."

The grunts lifted to their feet with Sias's silent command, shuffling in a single file line by the stone door like people milling in front of a shop waiting for it to open. I gave Sias my best puppy dog eyes and he rolled his, making the entire army of vicious vampire grunts give a polite bow.

I snorted a laugh. "Nice."

Funus was waiting for us through the stone door, having been set aside to stay safe from the battle beyond the Thrall's sanctuary. His eyes flared the color of sunshine when he saw us, his voice a sobbing mess of emotion.

"Oh, thank the Goddess! I felt the door cracking, felt everything shake and I thought everything was lost. I thought you were gone."

I scooped him up and hugged him to my chest, squeezing him for my benefit since he couldn't feel it.

"I'm glad to see you too, Funus. Let's go home, yeah? Barns is going to be very happy to see you."

"See *us*, acolyte—or, should I say, *champion*. You have the Goddess's key again; I can feel it within you. Well done, child." His eyes somehow warmed, flickering in the way that let me know he was smiling.

I couldn't help but be a little proud at that, like the way kids are proud when their grandpa tells them their drawing looks nice. It meant the world to me that the old skull thought I did a good job, and I hoped that I would be able to pay him back for everything he had done for me. And for Barns.

We made our way back up the insane stairs, and even though I had just defeated a badass Thrall hell bent on becoming a death deity, my fear of the dark hadn't diminished. It was a little embarrassing to have kicked that much ass and still need to hold my boyfriend's hand because it was scary.

Kind of dulled the moment, not gonna lie. I made them promise not to bring up that I kinda wimped out at the home stretch.

None of them agreed.

I loved them so much.

When we arrived at the iron door at the very end of our harrowing journey, I knocked three times like I'd promised to warn Barnaby not to set off the wards. Zane cracked the door and I peeked out, worried about Barnaby's natural tendency to overreact in the face of danger.

"Barns?" I called out, yelping as I dodged a rock clanking off the side of the door. "What the hell?!"

"Show yourself!" Barns called from an impossible distance. "I am armed! I-I have weapons! Many weapons!"

"It's me! It's Dallas!" I waved my good hand out the door and cussed as he nailed my palm with a rock. "Stop throwing fucking rocks!"

"I said show yourself!" the shrill idiot demanded.

"I can't if you're *throwing rocks,* you idiot!"

"I'll give you until the count of five! One!" Another rock pinged off the side of the door. "Two!"

"He's going to set off the wards," Austin warned. "And probably cause a rockslide and trap us in here."

"If I die in here because of that little shit, I'm going to haunt him so hard," I growled, shifting Funus around in my arms. "Sorry, Funus, this is going to get a little invasive."

"What do you—oh. Well," Funus sputtered as I looped my fingers into the massive cranial hole at the base of his skull. It was awkward for both of us, and I reminded him it was his stupid boyfriend's fault.

Barnaby had made me stick my fingers into my proud grandpa's head hole and I'd never forgive him for that.

I held Funus out of the door for Barnaby to see, hoping that would be the white flag needed to free us from the tomb.

"Funus!" Barnaby cried. "Dallas, is that you?"

I shoved the door open to cuss him out properly, having to yell across the damn cemetery as he raced over a hill.

"Why rocks!?" I yelled even as he hugged me.

"I broke the trigger for the wards when I was running away," he confessed, holding me tight and pulling Funus to his chest as well. "I tripped and it fell in mud so I had to go with plan B."

"Plan B was *rocks*?!" I hugged him tight. "You're an idiot and I love you so much."

"I know. I love you too." Barnaby exhaled, kissing Funus on the head before letting me go. "Please can we leave? I want to— OOH MY GOD." He pulled some rocks from his pocket and craned his arm back to release them on the grunts leaving the tomb, only stopping when I grabbed his arm.

"It's fine! Sias is controlling them."

"They cannot come with us!" Barnaby shrieked at Sias, even as the grunts were bursting into flames from the late afternoon sun. The cloudy skies had parted just enough to allow the lesser vampires to combust, their ashes drifting off with the humid air. It was a beautiful sight to watch.

I hoped it would be the last thing I remembered about the Silent Steps, because nothing was going to make me come back to this place again. Hei was gone, the door was sealed, the key was back in my possession and I planned on keeping it that way.

At least until the next ambitious jerk decided to test the barriers between life and death, or make a play for the Goddess's throne again.

Hopefully that wouldn't be for another lifetime or two, because I had other plans.

# EPILOGUE

"IS THIS GOING TO WORK?"

Dex popped a bubble at me for asking the question, and kept at her task.

"It's either going to work and I'll be a literal genius in the realm of magic tech, or it'll fail miserably and explode."

"Are those the only two options?" Funus swung his eyes between us, worry tugging at his kind voice. "It's either success or violent death?"

"She's just teasing," I reassured him. "Right, Dex?"

Dex popped another bubble. "Sure."

"Maybe we should rethink this." Barnaby wrung his hands for the millionth time. "I'm starting to get second thoughts."

"It'll work. Dex knows her shit." I gave Barnaby's shoulder a squeeze. "It'll be okay."

"I trust you. I just…I worry." Barnaby turned his big, doe eyes to Dex. "If you have any doubts, please tell me now. If something happened to him…"

Dex sighed, her apathy slipping in a rare show of emotion.

"I can't guarantee it'll work, but it won't explode. Maybe a tiny fire but…he's bone. He'll be fine."

Barnaby gave a nod, continuing to wring his hands like a fretting old woman.

Dex finished attaching the device to the base of Funus's skull, the magic within it pulsing and churning respectfully. It had been a hell of thing figuring out how to chip off some of the Goddess's blade without causing mayhem, but Dex and Kimi had created an enchantment that kept the chaos from spiraling out of control as we broke off pieces for testing. Between Kimi's witch prowess and Dex's knack for tech, the duo was able to do what Florence and her billions couldn't—control the blade's raw power.

It didn't hurt that they had the Goddess's favorite boy and Funus to help quell the tears when they did pop open.

Dex used the devices we snagged after we turned Hei and Florence into dipshit dust to craft something new, breaking apart the base components inside and repurposing them for something much better than making false Thralls.

Black opals had the power to heal, but they also had the power to rebuild even the oldest bodies. Pair that with the raw power of the Goddess's scythe?

Well.

That's a really powerful reanimation device.

"Once I turn it on, it should kick off the spell Kimi programmed," Dex explained to Funus. "I don't know how long it will take for the black opal to respond to it, or if the scythe's blade fragment will keep it stable, but if it starts smoking, I'll shut it down. Are you ready?"

"Yes." Funus turned his eyes to Barnaby. "I'm ready."

"I hope you know that no matter what happens, it doesn't change anything for us." Barnaby smiled at his skull boyfriend. "I will still be at your side. We can still travel and do all the things we planned."

"Of course, darling." Funus's sparkling eyes let us know he was smiling, but it was weak. "I just hope I can give you more."

"You give me everything," Barnaby said in a rush, eyes shining from hopeful tears.

"As do you." Funus's eyes brightened a bit more at that.

Barnaby released his hands so he could grip mine as Dex started the device, the iridescent greens, purples and pinks beginning to churn with flecks of crimson.

"I might throw up," he confessed softly.

"That's okay," I told him, squeezing his hand. "I'll only make fun of you a little bit if you do."

Dex chewed her gum like she was trying to dissolve it into dust, fingers tapping on her tusk as the magic device she had crafted flashed with the activated magic.

Black veins began crawling out from where the device was attached to Funus, moving like thick, onyx slugs over his cheekbones and jaw. Funus's eyes swiveled and tried to follow them as they slithered up over his forehead and into his nose, curling over his teeth and into his sockets.

Barnaby covered his mouth and got very still, holding his breath and probably his barf.

"How we doin', buddy?" I called to Funus. "You okay? Feeling some tingling?"

"I...I don't know..." the skull said nervously.

"Is this what you expected to happen?" I asked Dex but she shushed me.

The black veins thickened as they started to connect to each other, colliding and overlapping into tangles. Funus's bright eyes slowly dulled as the dark matter smothered his entire face, the pace of the slugs mutating into frantic worms that started to seep out onto the table.

Barnaby covered his face and turned away, holding my hand so tight I was worried he was going to break it. I winced but didn't dare pull away.

The black goop worming its way out of Funus started to take an angled shape, long lines expanding out and ending with flared digits. A thicker mass solidified at the center, branching out like an unfolding flower as it took a dome shape. A ribcage bloomed from its mass, the lines fanning from it thickening into bones before being coated in nerves, muscle, and skin.

Funus's skull sprouted features, a nose extending out to cover the hole at its center, just above a set of lips covering his teeth. Cheekbones were covered next, followed by a nice brow and sharp jaw, ears popping out just a bit too far in a charming way. The wormy substance began to slow as skin took on a rich brown, a mop of chestnut curls falling from his scalp.

The worms fell away once the last of his toes took shape, his body still and quiet on the table. My heart started to thunder from the breath I was holding, only exhaling when Funus's eyes slowly flickered open.

They were the yellow of honey, sweet and bright, looking for Barnaby the moment they opened.

"Holy shit," I finally exhaled. "Grandpa is *hot*."

Barnaby inhaled a sob as he finally forced himself to look, tears pouring from silently expecting the worst. His big, dark eyes widened at seeing Funus in the flesh, lanky and beautiful, with a sheepish smile creeping over his face.

"Hello, my love," he whispered, voice the same but now with a living weight to it. "I was hoping the rebuilding would lessen the extent my ears stuck out, but I see it was extremely thorough."

Barnaby moved to touch him and paused, always the gentlemen.

"Would you mind terribly if I feel your skin?"

Funus took Barnaby's hands in his and kissed his knuckles before pulling him into a hug that had Barnaby sobbing. Funus beamed as Barnaby took his face in his hands and kissed his cheeks, running his fingers through his hair and marveling at every part of his handsome face.

"You are perfect. You're *perfect*, Funus. I cannot wait to show you every single place I promised to take you. We'll eat so much wonderful food, see so many beautiful things."

"I will go wherever you are, my Barnaby." Funus kissed his palm, eyes shining with a true, flesh and blood smile. "We have our whole lives for adventure, and I plan on being at your side for whatever life throws at us."

Funus turned to me and stood, testing out his legs for the first time in centuries. He wobbled a bit, laughing as he had to sit back on the table, Barnaby holding him steady by the elbow.

"Ah, well, I'll have to get used to how these work. I'm a bit rusty." He grinned. "Dallas, it's lovely to meet you again for the first time. I meant to come give you a hug but I think I'm a little wobbly."

"You can hug me when you're not naked," I teased the no-longer-old man. "Plus, I think Barns gets to hog you for a bit. I'll get in some extra hugs when I get back."

"I'll take that deal." Funus laced his fingers with Barnaby's, sighing at the feeling.

"I'm a fucking genius," Dex whispered to herself, the magic of love not penetrating her marvelous mind.

I retreated to leave the lovebirds to their swooning, and made my way out into the foyer, where I caught Austin trying to quietly leave.

"Hey," I called out accusingly. "Are you for real?"

He sighed, shutting the door and turning my way.

"Yeah, alright. I was bailing before you made me hug you," he said as I hugged him, making a noise of disgust as I kissed his cheek. "You're an asshole."

"You don't have to leave, you know." I released him once he forced me backwards. "Sias said you can have a room here until you figure out what you want to do."

Austin ran a hand over his buzzed hair, eyeing the big chandelier hanging above the stairs.

"I'll make my own way. This place is huge, but I think I'll feel a little crowded here."

"You staying in the city?" I asked. "Preston and Seyyid said they're hiring on new recruits to DHAP after all this shit went down. Said they tossed Magnus out after his bullshit accusations against innocent people like Sias."

"Sias wasn't innocent." Austin lifted his brows. "He was aiding you and you were a person of interest tied to the destruction of the city."

"See? You already sound like a cop. You'd fit in great there. Plus, Sias was able to threaten the city with a fat lawsuit after it was proved that Magnus's accusations about me being in league with Florence were bullshit."

"Having a rich boyfriend must be nice," Austin said dryly.

"Oh, it fucking rules, man. I highly recommend it."

He rolled his eyes and asked, "I thought Preston and Seyyid would have lost their jobs after telling you to run out of the city."

"I'm no snitch," I snorted. "I'll take that shit to the grave. Or until I need to blackmail them for a favor later. They're still officers, so they're useful."

"Good to know. Maybe I'll look into working with DHAP." He shrugged. "Or maybe I'll go freelance. You could use some friendly rivalry."

"Yeah, I don't think so." I grinned as he chuckled. "You know where to find me. Let's not go another ten years without seeing each other. I'd like for you to be in my life, Austin."

"I'll think about it," he said, which was a hell of a lot better than "no." I decided that was good enough.

Austin slipped out the door as the sound of Twig screaming announced Zane's entrance, his arms full with suitcases I knew weren't his.

"Is he serious?" I asked as the vampire huffed the luggage next to the rest of Sias's mountain, stretching his back before scooping up his kitten.

"He assured me he needs all of it." Zane parked his bundle of fur into the crook of his arm, appeasing Her Majesty as she demanded chin scratches. "But I think his plane is going to drag on the runway with this much shit in cargo."

"My plane can handle twice that, I'll have you know." Sias appeared, descending the staircase like a prince ready for vacation. Malphie barreled ahead and ran over to sniff at Twig who peered down at him from her Zane throne. The big void hound was madly in love with the tiny queen, and she decided he was tolerated for the most part.

"We're going to be gone a month," Zane reminded the prince as he meandered over. "If you say you have more up there, you're going to throw my back out."

"Oh, my sweet vampire, I'll be doing that later." Sias grinned, planting a scandalous kiss on Zane's lips.

"Uh-huh. No more luggage, Sias."

Sias hummed like he was absolutely not done dragging more shit downstairs. He turned his emerald gaze my way and tapped his expensive watch.

"We leave in ten, pet. I want to be at the resort for dinner."

"Food dinner or incubus dinner?" I asked, smiling against his lips as he kissed me.

"Both," he purred, thumb stroking my chin before releasing it, adding lovingly, "If you're not by the car in ten minutes, I will leave without you."

"Love you too," I called after him as he went back upstairs, Zane groaning as he rubbed at his lower back.

"He's going to kill me," the big vampire complained.

"Yeah, you like it. You get to show off the muscles."

"Sure," he placated, leaning into the kiss I pulled him into. "If you're about to ask me to carry something for you, I will throw you out of the fucking window."

"Aw, you and your pillow talk." I kissed his smirk, because it was sexy and I was weak for it.

"Hunter," Zane said softly. "He will leave you if you're not ready."

"Yeah, okay. I got it. Steal his keys because I'm not going to be ready in time." I ran away before he could yell at me, rushing to my room to grab whatever I could before my boyfriends left me behind from our mutual vacation.

Kevin watched me with his signature Supreme Judgment Stare, spurned from having to wait on me for more bloodworms he clearly deserved. Naturally because of this, my packing was delayed further so I could marvel at how adorable my sweet, darling, perfect betta fish was.

"I still owe you. Not just for babysitting Twig while I was away, but for everything else."

I sprinkled some blood worms into Kevin's tank and smiled at my grumpy little savior. "You know, you could have given me a heads up about the whole 'connection to the void' thing."

He swallowed a worm down and side-eyed me. The explanation I got was one little bubble that floated to the surface of the water and lingered before it popped. I wondered if this was a sign, a message from a fish that might not be as mortal as I had thought. Was the bubble our shared connection to a plane of existence that few living beings had ever seen? Had we been soul bound since the day I had pulled him back from the void, too heartbroken to live a life without him?

Or maybe we had been bound long before that. Maybe Kevin had been expecting me to find him in the pet store that day. Maybe that one, important bubble was meant to represent something much more divinely engineered than I could have ever fathomed. Perhaps there was much more to my little fish than I would ever know.

Or maybe it was just indigestion from swallowing down high-grade bloodworms, because he shit immediately after that.

He was literally the best creature on the planet, and he kinda liked me.

I was the luckiest man alive.


*The End*

# ABOUT THE AUTHOR

Maz Maddox has always wanted to be an author.

Well, almost always.

At first she wanted to be a dinosaur, but that turned out to be extremely difficult. Giving up on her dreams to be a towering Allosaurus, she discovered her love for amazing stories and started writing her own.

Maybe one day she'll try the dinosaur thing again.

*Follow Maz:*

www.mazmaddox.com
Newsletter signup: subscribepage.com/subtomaz
Reader group: facebook.com/groups/maddoxsaloon
mazmaddox@gmail.com

facebook.com/AuthorMazMaddox
x.com/mazmaddox
instagram.com/mazmaddox
bookbub.com/authors/maz-maddox

## ALSO BY MAZ MADDOX

### STALLION RIDGE SERIES

Heartache & Hoofbeats

Claw Marks & Card Games

Suspects & Scales

Rocks & Railways

Mimics & Mayhem

Runes, Ruin & Redemption

Fate & Fortune

### RELIC SERIES

Smash & Grab

Sink or Swim

King & Queen

Lost in Amber

Gardens & Ghosts

### WILDE CONTRACTS

Find the Jinn

Steal the Key

Save the Vampire

### STANDALONE

Ethan & Jag Destroy the World

# THE ELITE (MULTI-AUTHOR SERIES)

Bullets & Butterflies